"Kate Carlisle dazzles and delights readers."
—Fresh Fiction

"Engaging and entertaining, sure to please both long-time fans of the series and readers new to the Bibliophile Mystery series." —Open Book Society

THE PAPER CAPER

A Bibliophile Mystery

Kate Carlisle

BERKLEY PRIME CRIME
New York

BERKLEY PRIME CRIME
Published by Berkley
An imprint of Penguin Random House LLC
penguinrandomhouse.com

Copyright © 2022 by Kathleen Beaver
Excerpt from *The Twelve Books of Christmas* by Kate Carlisle
copyright © 2023 by Kathleen Beaver

BERKLEY and the BERKLEY & B colophon are registered trademarks
and BERKLEY PRIME CRIME is a trademark of Penguin Random House LLC.

ISBN: 9780593201480

Berkley Prime Crime hardcover edition / May 2023
Berkley Prime Crime mass-market edition / September 2023

Printed in the United States of America
3   5   7   9   10   8   6   4   2

This book is dedicated to another great newspaperman, my brother, Jim Beaver.

Chapter 1

"San Francisco is a city of startling events. Happy is the man whose destiny it is to gather them up and record them in a daily newspaper!"
—Mark Twain's letter to the *Territorial Enterprise*,
December 23, 1865

Joseph Cabot was a multibillionaire, an entrepreneur, a technological genius, and a social media superstar. He had his creative fingers in dozens of the most lucrative pots, as well as a few that weren't so lucrative—but they made him happy so he didn't care. Real estate development, aeronautics, restaurants, manufacturing, and computer design, you name the industry and Joseph's name was invariably connected to all the top performers.

He was a gregarious man who loved people. He was a sportsman, too, and enjoyed everything from basketball to fly-fishing.

When something intrigued him, he would immerse himself in the subject. His latest obsession was windmills.

And he was a voracious reader. He loved books. He had amassed an impressive library of hundreds of rare antiquarian volumes as well as thousands of bestsellers in every genre known to man. It was Joseph's love of books that made him a superstar in my book.

But more than anything else he'd accomplished, Joseph considered himself a newspaperman. It was an old-fashioned term, but that was why it appealed to him. He loved being the owner and publisher of the *San Francisco Clarion Press*, along with its affiliated nationwide network of television and radio stations that specialized in the basics: news, weather, and sports. He loved the idea of keeping people informed.

The ladies of San Francisco high society adored Joseph, for obvious reasons. He was in his late forties, tall and strong and video-star handsome, with thick, graying hair and a twinkle in his bright blue eyes.

And he just happened to be one of my husband Derek's best friends.

The two men had met fifteen years ago when Derek and his Stone Security team carried out a daring operation to rescue Joseph from a group of militant kidnappers who had stormed an elegant conference room in Mindanao and forced him at gunpoint off the stage and into a van. They had transported him blindfolded to their lair in the middle of some jungle, where they threw him into a cage and then began the negotiations for his release.

Joseph refused to allow his company to pay a ransom to these hooligans, deciding instead to take his chances on escaping on his own. He had spent seven years in the military as an Army Ranger and was pretty sure he could outsmart his captors. But Joseph's business partners had balked at this plan and instead contacted Derek Stone to aid in liberating the stubborn man.

With negotiations falling through and the militants threatening to kill Joseph, Derek decided that their only choice was to overwhelm the captors, storm the lair, and rescue the prisoner themselves. And that was what he did. He led the raid himself and the operation was successful.

Once Joseph was back home and safe, he contacted Derek to say thanks. The two men began a friendship that has lasted to the present day.

Soon after Derek and I started dating, he insisted on introducing me to his friend Joseph. The three of us met for dinner and I found the older man to be smart and kind, with a good sense of humor. I liked him. When I learned that he was a booklover, as well as a major contributor to the Covington Library, I liked him even more. I knew we would be great friends for life.

My name is Brooklyn Wainwright and I'm a bookbinder specializing in rare book restoration. Anyone who loved books as much as I did was destined to be my new best friend.

"Almost ready, Brooklyn darling? We don't want to keep Joseph and the Covington crew waiting."

I jolted at the sound of his voice. Glancing up, I saw Derek leaning against the doorway of my workshop, smiling at me. I couldn't help but smile back. We'd been married almost a year now, and every day spent with him was even better than the day before.

"You're home," I said lamely.

"Yes. And you're still working."

"This book is so badly damaged," I began to explain, then stopped. "But I'm finished for the day. I'll have it cleaned up in no time." As I organized my work space, I wondered if my heart would always give a little jolt when I heard Derek's voice. His tone was deep and masculine with a whisper of the Oxfordshire country-side, along with a twinge of wry humor that always brought me instant pleasure. Added to that were his ruggedly handsome face and rock-hard body. The man had bewitched me from the first moment we met, de-spite the fact that he had used that first tender moment to accuse me of murder.

Ah, those were good times.

Derek studied the bedraggled pieces of book that I'd placed on top of a white cloth. "This is the book that Lisa Chung found?"

"Yes. She found it in the gutter. Can you believe it?"

Lisa and Henry Chung lived down the hall with their three adorable young children. I had been repairing the children's books ever since they moved into the build-ing a few years back.

"In the gutter." Derek frowned. "No wonder it's such a mess."

"I wish I knew how it happened." I sighed. How could one of the biggest bestsellers of the year have ended up splayed and torn in the gutter along Brannan Street? The book was the latest by Michael Connelly and I might've given up on rescuing it, except that he was one of Derek's favorite authors—and one of mine, too. I simply didn't have it in me to throw it away.

"I just need another minute," I said. "Then I'll change my shoes and we can go."

He glanced down at my feet and I watched his eye-brow quirk, but he said nothing.

"Unless," I began, "you're thinking my Birkenstocks would be the perfect party shoes?"

"They would . . . make a statement," Derek declared

after pondering for a moment. "They're really quite fetching, but . . ."

I had to laugh. His British accent, along with his choice of words, tickled me sometimes. "Fetching? Really?" My friends and family members were always giving me grief about my personal choice of work shoes, but what could I say? They were ridiculously comfortable. However, I would've never called them *fetching*—unless maybe I were a cave woman. The thick, clunky sandals definitely gave off a "Fred Flintstone" vibe.

"Don't worry," I assured Derek. "I plan to wear a pair of glittery yet painful stilettos for the occasion."

"That's my brave girl," he said with a smirk.

I snorted politely, then watched Charlie the cat slink out from under my worktable and saunter over to weave around Derek's ankles as her way of welcoming him home.

"And here's our Charlie." Derek leaned down and scooped her up, much to the cat's delight. As Charlie purred in his arms, I had to wonder if there was anything in the world more appealing than a big strong man cuddling a sweet little cat. I didn't think so.

Dragging myself back to my task, I finished arranging the pieces of the Connelly book on the white cloth. When my neighbor first brought it to me, the book had been dirty and wet from its time spent in the gutter. It was dry now, but there were skid marks on the cover, plenty of torn and creased pages, and the spine was dragging badly. Despite its haggard condition, I was determined to bring it back to its former luster, because that's what I did. I'm a bookbinder and I fix books.

I spread a second protective white cloth over everything, then pushed my chair back from the table.

Still clutching Charlie in one arm, Derek wrapped his other arm around my shoulders and kissed me warmly. Together we walked out of my workshop and into the living room.

"Give me two minutes," I said, "and I'll be ready to go."

Despite Friday night traffic, we made it across town in plenty of time. At the top of Pacific Heights we were able to snag a space in the parking lot of the magnificent Covington Library, which stood in all its elegantly Italianate glory overlooking the Golden Gate Bridge and the dark blue water of the Bay. At the front entrance, I stopped and took a deep breath of anticipation. The outside of the building was impressive, but walking inside was like stepping into another world. The foyer itself was dramatic with its gorgeous Tiffany chandeliers, black-and-white checkerboard pattern on the marble floor, and wide, sweeping stairways that led up to the second and third floors.

But then you stepped into the massive main hall and simply had to stare. I can still picture my little eight-year-old apprentice-bookbinder self, walking into this space for the first time. I had been mesmerized by the walls that were covered from floor to ceiling in gorgeous leather-bound books. At intervals across the room, glass display cases were filled with gorgeous antiquarian books and historically significant ephemera: a letter from Walt Whitman; symphony notes from Mozart; a baseball card signed by Babe Ruth.

Looking up, I was impressed as always by the coffered

ceiling three floors above me. The top two floors of the library opened onto the main hall and decorative wrought-iron railings lined the narrow aisles.

On occasions like tonight, there would be musicians playing up on the third floor. Guests could gaze up at the players and be treated to the performance itself as well as the amazing acoustics of the room. Usually it was a string quartet or trio playing a classical concerto or sonata, but tonight, because of the nature of this all-American event, there was a fiddler and a ragtime piano player. The tunes were what I would call old-fashioned, down-home Americana.

Standing behind the musicians tonight were four men in matching striped jackets and handlebar mustaches. I smiled at the thought that a barbershop quartet would be singing the most popular songs of the 1860s and '70s. It wasn't the usual type of musical offering, but the crowd seemed ready for it. It would set the tone for the gala opening night of the first annual Mark Twain Festival.

Underwriting this entire five-day event was none other than our good friend Joseph Cabot, whose literary hero was another American newspaperman, Mark Twain.

To organize the five-day event, Joseph had called upon the *Clarion*'s own very talented events coordinator, Ashley Sharp. The young woman had gone into overdrive planning the numerous Twain-centered activities that would take place at the Covington and various sites all over the city, starting today. It was shaping up to be one of the most ambitious, wide-ranging festivals the Covington had ever presented.

Just reading the schedule of events had sent shivers

up and down my arms. If I attended every activity, I wouldn't have a free minute to call my own until the day the festival ended. But that was okay, right? It would be fun. And it was only for five days. I mentally waved away my concerns because it promised to be a total blast. Or utter chaos. Either way, it would be memorable. And I would play a role in it.

A month ago, Ian McCullough had called and asked me to come by his office. Ian was president and head curator for the Covington Library and one of my oldest and dearest friends. He wanted to talk about the two workshops he hoped I would conduct as part of the festival activities. Naturally, one of the workshops was all about bookbinding. The other was connected to my fledgling interest in paper arts. I was to give a workshop in the Children's Museum on newspaper art. I agreed to that one immediately. It sounded like pure fun, especially since kids were involved.

"Your bookbinding workshop will be more complicated, as you'd expect," he said, then told me that I was to refurbish, rebind, and regild a vintage edition of *The Prince and the Pauper*, one of Mark Twain's many great novels.

Then he had handed me the book. It was a mess, to say the least. "I can barely read the title. The gilding is gone. These pages aren't bad, but the whole thing is catawampus." I held it up and we watched the entire book tilt dangerously. "And you're only giving me four days to finish it?"

"Come on, you can do it in your sleep," Ian had enthused. "First of all, the bones of the book are fabulous, and the rest of it will be, too, when you're finished with it. And here's the best part. We're going to set you up in the main hall with a live audience. You'll be holding court while you turn a *pauper* of a book into a *prince*."

I had to admit it was kind of a clever play on words.

"You're going to be on public display," Ian had continued. "You won't mind, will you? It's going to be a very popular event. We're setting up a few rows of bleacher seats for people to watch you work."

"Good thing I'm not shy," I had muttered. But seriously? Bleacher seats? In the main hall? This would be a first.

"You're talking to yourself," Derek murmured as we wound our way through the opening night crowd to find one of the three cocktail bars before the lines grew too long. "It's a sure sign you're nervous. What is bothering you?"

I frowned, a little annoyed to realize that I had an obvious "tell," while I couldn't read him at all. "You need to stop being so perceptive."

"I beg your pardon, love." He laughed, but quickly sobered. "Come now, darling. Are you nervous about this evening or about your bookbinding work this week?"

"Nervous? Me?" I thought about it. "Yes, I am. But it's not about either of those things. And I'm too embarrassed to talk about it."

He stopped me, holding my arms so he could study my expression. "Surely you can tell me."

He was right again. I could tell him anything, even if it was humiliating. "Okay, fine. There's a couple of things. First, I was thinking about the bookbinding job

I've been assigned to for the festival. It's not exactly glamorous."

"Glamorous?" Puzzled, he frowned at me. "But it's what you do, darling. Your work is fascinating. And despite your choice of footwear, you do it better than anyone else in the world."

I smiled and squeezed his arm. "Thank you."

"You're welcome, but it's simply the truth." He gave me a quick glance. "So what are you really bothered about?"

My shoulders sagged. It was useless to try and hide my feelings from him. "Okay, here's the deal. You know I really like Joseph and I'm totally psyched that I'm going to be working the festival with him. Even if I'm not doing anything very glamorous."

Derek ordered our wine and after leaving a nice tip, he handed me my wineglass. "Now, spill. Not the wine. Tell me what's bothering you."

I smiled again at that. "It's just that, well, lately, wherever Joseph is, there's Ella." Which only made sense since Ella was Joseph Cabot's wife. I winced. "I know that was a dumb thing to say."

The couple had only been married for six months so, yes, they were always together. I was being ridiculous, but really, did the woman have to be six feet tall and blond and gorgeous? Did she have to speak with that sexy Swedish accent? And her wardrobe was to die for, seriously. Anytime I'd ever seen Ella, she'd been dressed in some dazzling designer outfit that could light up a room. I, on the other hand, while always presentable, was much more comfortable and happy in my blue jeans and Birkenstocks.

But that wasn't the point.

Finally I admitted, "It's demoralizing, but I can't help it. I'm completely intimidated by her."

He glanced at me sideways and nodded sagely. "So am I."

"Oh, please." I rolled my eyes. "I appreciate you trying to make me feel better, but come on. You're tall, dark, and dangerous. The original international man of mystery. You carry a gun. Nobody intimidates you."

He laughed. "She does."

I stared at him for a long moment, realized he wasn't kidding, and shook my head. "What is it about her? It's almost indefinable. I mean, besides the looks and the hair and the attitude and . . . everything else. What is it?"

"First of all, darling, you are the most beautiful woman I have ever known."

I almost choked on my cabernet, and that would've been a real waste because the wine was really good. He eased my glass away from me while I took a minute to catch my breath.

"And you're fun and you're funny and smart, and simply adorable," Derek said. "I love being with you."

He had said lovely things like this to me before and they never failed to both thrill me and leave me tongue-tied. "Um, likewise," I murmured, embarrassed now.

He chuckled at my words, but then glowered. "Ella is not fun."

That stopped me. "What are you talking about?"

"The woman has no sense of humor."

I stared at him until realization dawned. He was right. "Why do you think that is?"

"Among other things, there's a language barrier."

"But she speaks perfect English," I said. "With a Swedish accent, of course, but still perfect."

"Yes, she speaks our language and even understands it," he continued, "but she doesn't always comprehend the feelings and the meanings behind the words. She doesn't understand nuance, so our humor goes over her head and confuses her. That's why she comes across as so serious."

"I've never thought about it that way." I frowned. "What must Joseph think? He has a great sense of humor."

He pressed his lips together. "Yes, he does."

"But she wouldn't think so because she doesn't get his humor." I crooked my neck, looking up at him as I thought about it. "Wow. Now that you've said it, I'm trying to remember if she's ever laughed at anything we've said."

Derek glanced over his shoulder to make sure nobody was listening in on our conversation. "Joseph and I have actually had this conversation."

"Really?"

"Yes. He says he didn't marry her for her sense of humor."

I grinned. "Okay, I can guess what he *did* marry her for." But then I winced. "I shouldn't have said that. It's not fair. I know she has many lovely qualities. She's beautiful and smart and she's always nice to me." So why was I so intimidated by her? I had to wonder.

Derek handed my wineglass back to me. "I agree she's smart. And Joseph has made it clear that she does, in fact, have many other attributes that he finds appealing."

I shook my head in amazement. "So you guys really have had this conversation?"

"Just so we're clear," Derek said, holding up his hand, "Joseph brought up the topic."

I nodded. "I wouldn't think you'd bring it up."

"Absolutely not." He sipped his wine. "We met for a drink about a week before he married her. I had been to his home a number of times and had met Ella, of course, because she worked in Joseph's house. It was truly a shock to learn that they were engaged. That night Joseph told me he was going to marry her and asked for my opinion. But before I could say anything, he forged ahead and gave me all the reasons why it was a good idea and why she was perfect for him. What could I do but agree?"

"Of course you had to agree." I took a sip of the cabernet. "You're a good friend."

"Perhaps a better friend would've told him what I really thought. But then we wouldn't be friends anymore."

"And that would be a shame."

He looked over his shoulder. "We should change the subject before we're caught out."

"Good idea." I held up my hand. "But before we do, I want to say again, that I think she is a really nice person at heart. She always has something kind to say."

"That is true," Derek murmured.

"If she were a witch, I would feel a lot better about my own feelings," I said, frowning.

He laughed. "I actually understand that. And now, seriously, let's switch topics."

"Yes, please."

We both glanced around the room, watching people

enter the main hall and mingle with others. Everyone was looking glittery tonight, which added to the overall good feeling about this unusual festival.

A few years ago, many members of San Francisco's book-loving society would show up to these events wearing unrelieved black from head to toe. The women dressed like beatniks from the fifties with their skinny turtlenecks, black tights, and miniskirts. All that was missing was a jaunty beret. These days, though, there were delightful bursts of color throughout the crowd and they brightened up the whole room.

Derek turned and gazed at me. "Tell me, what part of the evening are you most looking forward to?"

I smiled up at him. "The part where we go home."

He lifted my hand to his lips and kissed my wrist. "Coming home to you is always the best part of any day."

I leaned against him and laid my head on his shoulder.

"Darling," he murmured. "Have I mentioned lately how much I love you?"

I eased back, checked my wristwatch. "It's been a few minutes."

"Then it's well past time I told you again." He gave me a brief but meaningful kiss. "I love you."

"There you are," Ian said, rushing over to join us.

"Here we are," I said, welcoming the interruption by lifting my glass in a toast. "Good party, Ian."

"Thanks, kiddo." He glanced around anxiously.

"May I get you a glass of wine, Ian?" Derek asked. "You look like you could use one."

"I totally could, but I'd better stay alert."

"Why?" I wondered. "You've got everything wired

down to the last little detail. What could possibly go wrong?"

"Are you crazy?" he hissed, and slapped my arm lightly. "Don't jinx it."

"Sorry." I grinned, but as he continued to look around the room, I asked, "Who are you looking for?"

"The Swedish Bombshell."

Derek and I exchanged glances. "You must mean Ella."

"No," he whispered. "Her mother, Ingrid. Have you met her?"

"Not yet," Derek said.

"Well, apparently she's put herself in charge of to-night's agenda."

I gave him a quizzical look. "How did that happen?"

He glared at me. "How should I know? Maybe she used to be a party planner in Stockholm and wanted something to do."

I pondered the situation. "This festival is vitally im-portant to Joseph. It makes no sense that he would ever give her that sort of responsibility."

"Not Joseph," he muttered.

"Then who?"

He was still glaring. "Have you met Ella?"

"Ah." I exchanged a quick glance with Derek. Ap-parently Ella's ability to intimidate was far-reaching. "Joseph's wife is formidable, to say the least."

"You have no idea."

I stroked his arm. "Just breathe."

"What about Ashley Sharp?" Derek asked. "I was led to believe that Joseph had put her in charge of the festival events."

"Ashley is a complete wonder," Ian agreed, nervously glancing around the room. "She's excellent. Brilliant. But where is she?"

Derek pulled out his cell phone. "I haven't seen Joseph yet, but I'll be happy to call and ask him to straighten things out."

"Would you?" Ian sagged with relief. "Oh, thank you, Derek. You're my hero." But his attention was suddenly diverted by some scuffle going on near the entryway. "Oh God. I've got to go put out another fire." And he darted away.

I watched him scurry off, then turned to see that Derek was still talking on the phone to Joseph.

As soon as he ended the call, I asked, "What's going on? What did he say?"

"He very calmly said that Ashley Sharp is in charge of everything. Ella and her mother have nothing to do with any aspect of the festival."

"So why is Ian so upset?"

"I have no idea. And neither does Joseph."

I frowned. "I hate to say it, but it sounds like Ella and her mother might be gaslighting Ian."

"It's possible." He slipped his arm through mine and we began another stroll around the room. "Let's keep an eye on things, shall we?"

Chapter 2

"When I am king they shall not have bread and shelter
only, but also teachings out of books, for a full belly is
little worth where the mind is starved."
                            —Mark Twain, *The Prince and the Pauper*

Despite that one odd moment earlier when Ian threatened to have a nervous breakdown over the possibility
of Ingrid running the show, Derek and I managed to
enjoy ourselves. We had been to dozens of opening
night parties at the Covington over the years, for all
sorts of literary festivals and events. It was good to
meet new people and catch up with the old regulars.

These were book people, after all, and I loved them
all. But maybe that was the wine talking. I was on my
third glass.

I waved to an older couple who had just walked into
the hall, but we were all too far away from each other
to have any sort of conversation.

"There's Doris and Theodore," I said.

"They're looking quite spry, aren't they?"

I grinned. Doris and Theodore Bondurant were
both in their mid-eighties and were indeed looking

spry. They were Covington Library trustees and also
served on the boards of a number of other charitable
organizations. Together they were worth somewhere
north of a gazillion dollars, but you'd never know it
because they were completely down-to-earth, feisty,
and fun. The first time I met them was right here in
this room at an event very similar to this one. Doris
and I had hit it off immediately, and since that time,
she had hired me to work on a few dozen of her most
cherished antiquarian books. Best of all, she had also
recommended my services to many of her friends.

I waved to three women I knew from Bay Area Book
Arts, or BABA, where I taught classes in bookbinding, letterpress, and papermaking. Then I spied Gene-
vieve Taylor, who owned Taylor's Fine Books over on
Clement Street. She often called with a book for me
to refurbish and we had become good friends, especially after I solved a perplexing mystery for her a few
years ago.

"Ah, there you are."

We turned in time to see Joseph Cabot approach.
He wore an elegant tuxedo and was accompanied on
either side by his wife Ella and another lovely blond
woman. She was a slightly older version of Ella and I
assumed it was Ella's mother, although she looked
barely out of her thirties. With two beautiful fair-haired
women and the very handsome Joseph between them,
they could've easily been walking down a red carpet
somewhere in Hollywood or New York or Cannes.

We greeted Joseph effusively. I turned to his wife
and smiled. "Ella, it's good to see you."

"And you, Brooklyn," she said, beaming at me as she
took my hand. "You look so pretty tonight, as always."

With her soft Swedish accent, her speaking voice very nearly resembled a child's song. I couldn't quite describe it, but with her emphasis on certain letters and syllables in the words she spoke, it came across as charmingly old-fashioned.

"Thank you," I said. And this was why I couldn't hate her. She was just so nice and her smile was almost blinding. She seemed genuinely happy to see me and all I could do was smile back and return the compliment. "You look fabulous, as always. Your dress is stunning."

It was sapphire blue with silver threads running through the fabric, and it hugged her slim waist like a caress. But she waved my words away. "You're sweet."

I stared up at her, still feeling intimidated despite my conversation with Derek earlier. I mean, the woman towered over me! I wasn't exactly short at five foot eight, plus my heels added several more inches to my height. But Ella Cabot was at least six inches taller than me and her stilettos were even more stilt-like than mine. Five inches? Six? I couldn't tell, but it put her somewhere in the vicinity of around six foot four. She was slender and graceful with a peaches-and-cream complexion, big blue eyes, and all that lustrous blond hair. Tonight it was brushed back from her face and tucked into a sleek French roll and held in place with an elegant silver comb. Loose tendrils framed her face and lent her sophisticated up-do a sexy, flirty look that was almost too much for us mere mortals to take in.

And I really had to snap out of it. Ella *was*, in fact, a mere mortal, and it suddenly occurred to me that she probably could use a friend.

Ella turned and squeezed the hand of the older

woman on Joseph's other arm. "Mother, you remember Derek Stone."

"Of course I do," she said, giving him a brilliant smile as she shook his hand.

Ella continued. "Please allow me to introduce his wife, Brooklyn." She looked back at me. "This is my mother, Ingrid Norden."

"It's very nice to meet you, Ms. Norden," I said, shaking the woman's hand.

"So formal," she said. "Please call me Ingrid."

I nodded. "All right, Ingrid."

Seriously, these two women were blindingly beautiful on their own, but together they were a force of nature. Despite that, we all chatted easily for a few minutes. Then I happened to notice that Ian was stepping onto a small stage that had been set up at the other end of the large room.

Joseph noticed, too. He grinned and eased himself away from his wife and mother-in-law. "Now that we're all friends, I'm going to desert you. I have to go make a speech."

"Break a leg, sweetest," Ella whispered.

"Thank you, dearest." Joseph kissed his wife's cheek, then gave Derek a manly pat on the shoulder. "See you on the other side."

"Good luck," Derek said with a grin.

I watched Joseph stroll through the crowd, greeting people and giving the occasional handshake as he moved forward. Everyone seemed to like the man and I thought it had to be because of his admirable ability to make each person feel special in the few short seconds he spent with them.

I glanced at Ella in time to see her lean in close to

her mother, listening as the older woman murmured in her ear. Her mother didn't seem happy. The way she was whispering forcefully, it almost felt as if she was scolding Ella.

Ella, meanwhile, gazed casually around the room. Her mother continued her quietly intense rant, but Ella seemed to be ignoring her words.

As Ian took his place on the small stage, the crowd grew silent. "Good evening and welcome to day one of our first annual Mark Twain Festival!"

After a loud round of applause, Ian described a few of the highlights of the five-day festival. "Earlier today, surrounded by hundreds of San Franciscans, Joseph Cabot and several members of the Board of Supervisors proudly erected a beautiful statue of Mark Twain in Golden Gate Park."

Everyone applauded, and Ian continued. "Tomorrow night, at a special private event, we'll announce the winner of the first annual Mark Twain Festival Look-Alike Contest. The *Clarion*'s event coordinator will give more details about that in a few minutes."

Ian highlighted several festival events, including an evening of riverboat gambling for the grown-ups and, for the kids, a fence-painting event at the Covington's Children's Museum.

"Every day the festival will be giving away cash and prizes for all sorts of reasons," Ian said with a sly grin. "And finally, on the last day of the festival we'll hold our first annual Jumping Frog Contest adjacent to the shiny new Mark Twain statue near the polo field in Golden Gate Park. Because what would a Mark Twain Festival be without a Jumping Frog Contest?"

People laughed and Ian added quickly, "Based, of

course, on Mark Twain's classic, 'The Celebrated Jumping Frog of Calaveras County.'" After a short pause, he said, "Be sure and check the *Clarion* website daily for all the latest festival updates and the list of daily prize winners."

After some brief applause at the mention of prizes, Ian said, "And now I'd like to say a few words of introduction for a man who basically needs no introduction." He smirked at his little joke. "But I really do want to take a minute and share just a few of the qualities that make this man so important and special to the Covington Library and to San Francisco. If you want the full résumé, check his Wikipedia page, but I'll start with a little known background story that all of us at the Covington especially appreciate because we're all about books and reading. Many of you know about Joseph's 'Kids Read' project, but there are a few details you may not be aware of. In the beginning, Joseph's goal was to buy a book for every child in the city, because literacy is such an important component of one's self-esteem. And think about this: How can you sell newspapers if people don't read?

"But for Joseph, this wasn't about selling newspapers. This was personal. He admits that he wasn't much of a reader when he was young, except that he loved comic books. He especially loved to read about the superheroes and their constant fight for truth and justice."

Ian glanced at the faces in the crowd. "But there's something that Joseph never told anyone. He couldn't actually read until he was almost ten years old."

Some in the audience reacted with gasps of disbelief.

"It's true," Ian said. "The way he finally taught himself to read was through comic books. That's pretty amazing, isn't it?"

Along with the applause were a lot of admiring glances aimed at Joseph, who looked vaguely mortified by the flattering attention.

"Joseph's love of stories has grown and evolved," Ian said. "So much so that he recently told me that he reads at least one book a day." Ian glanced around the room. "I mean, I like to read, too, but that's ridiculous." He grinned and added, "And also commendable."

He paused again for the crowd's reaction, then said, "Now I do have a point to this story. My point is that there are a lot of kids out there who wouldn't think of picking up a book, but they'll definitely pick up a comic book. And that's how Joseph's reading program began. And within a few years it's become the biggest and most successful literacy program in the country."

The applause made Ian beam with pleasure. "Everyone in this city is familiar with the other highlights of Joseph's sterling résumé, so I'll just round it out by saying that while Joseph's media empire is vast, it all begins with his newspaper, the *Clarion*. Like his hero Mark Twain, Joseph is a newspaperman. He also happens to be a brilliant businessman and a social media superstar, but most of all, he's a wonderful friend and supporter of the Covington Library. Please join me in welcoming Joseph Cabot."

The cheers and hoots were so loud that my ears were buzzing, but I was happy for Joseph. He truly was a local superstar.

Joseph stepped onto the stage and shook hands with

Ian. Then Ian stepped down and Joseph moved to the podium. His speech was short, funny, and clever. He explained how his love for the works of Mark Twain first developed. "It all started with Tom Sawyer," he began, and proceeded to charm the crowd with a story about his ten-year-old self getting lost in the cave along with Tom and Becky.

He took a moment to reiterate the list of festival events, including the aforementioned Jumping Frog Contest in Golden Gate Park, the Riverboat Casino Night at the Embarcadero, and a special event for children, namely, a chance to paint a fence with Tom Sawyer. "Today is only the first day of the festival and while the 'Look-Alike' winner in our Mark Twain Festival Look-Alike Contest hasn't been announced yet, there are already tons of photos posted on social media by people who think they've seen him." He made a face, adding, "As you know, the winner is supposed to look like me. I've got to admit, some of those photos are more flattering than others."

The crowd laughed.

"Earlier today, we notified the actual winner of the contest." He had to pause again for the spontaneous applause. "Our team has thoroughly vetted him and right about now he's being measured for his new, princely wardrobe."

"Quite a twist," Derek murmured in my ear.

I gazed up at him. "Is the contest a little creepy or am I just being paranoid?"

"A bit of both, I believe."

Joseph moved on. "I hope I'll see some of you at the Jumping Frog Contest and the other events going on this week. They're all going to be a blast, and remember, there will be prizes."

The crowd cheered again, liking the thought of prizes.

"I'll wrap this up in a minute," Joseph said, "but I wanted to remind everyone that the festival committee has chosen a book to represent the festival and we're hoping San Franciscans have already downloaded it and are halfway through it by now. But just in case, all of our local bookstores are featuring the book at a nicely discounted price. Of course, that book is *The Prince and the Pauper*."

He had to wait for the applause to die down. This hall was filled with people who applauded for books. And prizes. You had to love it.

"Now you might think you know the basic story," Joseph continued, "but there's so much more to the book than you remember. So I encourage everyone in town to take the time to read it. And, shameless plug here, don't forget to read the *Clarion* every day to find out what's going on with the festival. 'Like' us on all your favorite social media sites using the hashtag *TwainFestival*."

He glanced out at the crowd and grinned. "And for those of you who think I've completely lost my moral compass, I'll remind you that everything we're doing this week is in support of the Covington Library. That's always our main goal."

Applause broke out again and he held up his hand. "Almost forgot. Anyone with kids will want to check out some special programs going on this week at the Covington. Our favorite bookbinder and papermaker, Brooklyn Wainwright, is restoring a book before our eyes this week and she'll also be working with the kids on newspaper crafts. Because we're all about newspapers, right?"

"Right," somebody shouted.

"So if you have a stack of *Clarion*s sitting in your recycling bin, bring them to the Covington, and Brooklyn will show your kids how to turn them into flowers and baskets and Christmas decorations and you-name-it. Her work is clever and fun." He waved in my direction. "Thanks, Brooklyn!"

I was totally caught off guard, but managed to give a shaky wave in response.

I leaned against Derek. "That was so nice of him."

He chuckled. "He's a newspaperman to the end."

"Okay," Joseph continued. "Thanks for listening to my long-winded speech, thank you for your participation, and as always, thank you for your generosity."

There was more hand clapping and then Joseph added, "Sorry, folks, but we've got one last announcement about the big contest the *Clarion* is sponsoring, and you won't believe the grand prize we're giving away. Here to give you a brief rundown is our events coordinator, Ashley Sharp. Please give her a warm welcome."

A young woman jumped up onstage and Joseph gave her a high five as he walked off, accompanied by enthusiastic applause.

Ashley was barely five feet tall, but her personality made up for it. She was in her twenties and very pretty, with long dark hair and big brown eyes that sparkled with humor. With the fervor of a high school cheerleader, she spoke quickly and excitedly about the look-alike contest.

"Unless you've been living in a cave for the last two months," she said into the microphone, "you'll have heard that we're holding an amazing contest based on *The Prince and the Pauper.* You all remember the story, right?"

She waited for people to chime in with "Right!" Then she responded, "Right! So that inspired us to have a look-alike contest. But"—she held up her finger to emphasize her next point—"with a twist! Instead of trying to find someone who looks like Mark Twain, we decided it would be more fun to find someone in town who looks like our very own Joseph Cabot!"

Even though many in the audience had just heard the story, they cheered loudly. After a moment Ashley continued. "The *Clarion* took a poll a few months ago, and believe it or not, Joseph Cabot is more popular than the mayor, the governor, and the manager of the Giants!"

There were more cheers and a couple of boos—the Giants were on a losing streak—followed by laughter.

"So, since everyone in town knows and loves Joseph, we thought San Francisco would enjoy the chance to find his doppelgänger."

Ashley continued at the same fast pace. "Now, Joseph already announced that we found our winner, but I want to add that we received several thousand entries and some of the people actually bear a slight resemblance to Joseph. These include six cats and two dogs, and I'll share a secret with you. One of the cats made it into the final round."

That brought on another gale of laughter and she quickly went on. "And I don't have to remind you that we're giving away hundreds of prizes every day. But the grand prize winner? The person who looks most like Joseph? That person will receive . . . one hundred thousand dollars."

"Wow," I said as the crowd erupted in more gasps. Everyone began to talk at once. The newspaper hadn't revealed the actual grand prize amount so this was the first we'd heard about it.

"That's enough money to kill over," I whispered.

Derek shook his head. "Bite your tongue."

I looked up at him. "Sorry. Couldn't help myself."

Joseph was standing near the edge of the stage and now he jumped up and rushed to the microphone. "What can I say?" he said cheerily, then pinched his cheeks. "Anyone with a face like mine deserves a break. Am I right?"

The crowd was eating it up, and when Joseph and Ashley waved and walked off the stage, they kept the applause going for another full minute.

Joseph grabbed Ashley's arm and pulled her through the crowd. Just as the audience began to engulf them both, I saw Joseph wrap his arm around Ashley's shoulders and hug her effusively.

Ooh boy, I thought. Hope Ella's not the jealous type.

"Good heavens," Ella said, her eyes wide. "He's going to be smothered by that crowd."

Ingrid gave her a pitying look and whispered, "Can you please stop being so stupid?"

My eyes widened and I looked at Derek. He had overheard the woman, too, but we did our best to pretend we didn't. I sneaked another peek at Ingrid. She hadn't bothered to conceal the scorn that accompanied her words. Ella didn't seem to notice, or else she was careful not to show she cared.

That was probably the best way to handle the situation, I realized. My next thought was, *I'm glad she's not my mom.* My mother would never have said something like that to any of us. Ingrid was the farthest thing from nurturing and I had no idea how to react.

That was because I had grown up with the world's best mother, and now I was lucky enough to have the world's best mother-in-law. When it came to parental love, I had it in barrels. But I understood what it was like to experience the opposite. My best friend Robin's mother had rarely come home to visit, let alone shown any affection or concern for her daughter. Robin had tried to be strong, but that kind of treatment always left a mark.

I shook myself out of those thoughts and considered Ella. She had everything going for her on a physical level, but if her mother treated her like this on a regular basis, her life was far from the perfect picture she painted. She acted as though she didn't care about her mother's sharp words, but I couldn't believe that.

I looked away from her in time to notice Joseph and Ashley approaching. They walked arm in arm in a way that I recognized as friendly and warm, but a quick look at Ella's mother assured me that she didn't agree. In fact, I was pretty sure there was smoke coming out of her ears. She was not happy to see this younger woman acting so cozy with her rich, handsome son-in-law.

Ella, on the other hand, didn't seem to notice or care. She dashed over to greet her husband and the event coordinator with a broad smile and she clapped her hands gaily. "You were both wonderful." She turned to Ashley. "You are such a good speaker, Ashley. You made everyone feel excited about the festival and the contest."

Ashley flushed with pleasure at the compliment. "Thank you, Ella. This is the best project I've ever worked on and I'm really grateful to Joseph for the opportunity."

Ella patted her arm. "We're equally grateful to you for your hard work and enthusiasm."

I caught Ingrid rolling her eyes. She obviously disapproved of Ella's effusiveness. Did she disapprove of everything her daughter did? Maybe she didn't like Ella being so nice to a young woman who could turn out to be a rival for her husband's affections. But she had to know that if Ella had reacted angrily and appeared jealous of Ashley, it would've been worse.

"Mother, dear," Ella said brightly. "Let me introduce you to Ashley. She's Joseph's event coordinator and she's doing such good work for the newspaper." She turned to Ashley. "This is my mother, Ingrid Norden."

Ashley inclined her head politely. "It's very nice to meet you, Mrs. Norden."

With her head held high, Ingrid nodded, queen to peasant. I found it impossibly rude, but Ashley took it in stride. In Ingrid's defense, she was so tall that she would likely look down her nose at almost anyone. Ashley nevertheless won some points for ignoring Ingrid's obvious ill will.

And again, Ella didn't seem to notice, but I did. And I thought, *Meow.* Watch out for those mama claws.

I gave Derek a quick look and he winked at me in a way that told me he'd seen the same thing I'd seen and we would talk later. How could I not love a guy who picked up on the same vibes that I did?

But when I took another quick glance at Ingrid Norden, she was clearly seething, even more than she'd been a minute ago. I made a mental note to remind myself that when Derek and I finally did talk later, I would point out that if anyone died tonight, that woman would be my number one suspect. Because, seriously, if looks could kill, Ella's mama would likely be arrested for murder.

Chapter 3

Be good and you will be lonesome.
—Frontispiece from first edition of Mark Twain's
Following the Equator

Extricating herself from her mother's eagle eye and her husband's whispered tête-à-tête with his events coordinator, Ella glided over and joined me. "Brooklyn, Ian tells me you have your own works on display here. I would love to see what you've done, but I'm not familiar with the library and don't know my way around. Would you mind giving me a short tour?"

"Not at all," I said, surprised and pleased by her request. "Anytime you'd like." I admit, I love showing off my work to anyone who asks. Still, I couldn't help that a smidgen of doubt trickled into my mind. Did she have an ulterior motive?

And could I be more suspicious? Lighten up, I told myself. Give the woman a chance. Besides, if her only motive was to get herself away from her witchy mama for a few minutes, I was here to offer my support.

"Shall we do it right now?" she suggested brightly.

"Oh." I gave Derek a quick look, then said, "Sure. Let's go."

"Wonderful." She slipped her arm through mine companionably—except she was so tall that my wrist ended up nestled against her elbow. I started to laugh but realized she hadn't even noticed. It was weird.

As we walked and chatted, I held on to the thought that she had been in a hurry to get away from her mother. I also figured she might've been rushing off to avoid watching young Ashley gaze dreamily at her handsome husband. It was hard to miss the fact that Ashley had a bit of a crush on Joseph.

But again, did Ella even care? Ashley was young and smart and exuberant and as cute as a button—a phrase that made no sense at all when I thought about it. I mean, really? Buttons were cute? But I digressed. My point was, Ella's mother obviously considered the younger woman a threat to her daughter's marriage, even if the daughter didn't.

As we strolled through the crowd, I stole a glance up at Ella and all those odd thoughts faded away. This woman was simply breathtaking. Even this close, I couldn't see a flaw. How could her own mother ever think that Joseph would stray from her? Not that looks were everything, I admitted to myself.

But even if her mother was focused on the possibility that Joseph was attracted to another woman, Ella didn't seem concerned about it. She looked positively serene.

Maybe there was some kind of cosmic law that prevented the beautiful Ella from suffering that sort of angst. Or maybe not. Maybe I was crazy, but boy, women like Ella seemed to have things all worked out. Whatever was going on with the woman, she appeared completely tranquil.

"You and Derek have been such good friends to Joseph," Ella said as we reached the far end of the main hall and turned right into another wide gallery hall. "I appreciate it so much."

"It's easy to be friends with Joseph," I said. "He's a wonderful person." I quickly added, "And it's been really nice getting to know you, too."

I was surprised to realize I meant it, despite the intimidation factor.

Ella glanced from side to side. "There are no books along this hallway, just artwork."

"Yes," I said. "Ian's intention with this area was to create a sort of oasis while passing from one book collection to the next."

"It is soothing," she said quietly.

"I think the lighting helps, as well as the choice of artwork." The lighting here was more subdued with pinpoint spotlights illuminating the wonderful works displayed on the walls. These paintings could've easily lined the walls of the Louvre or, more locally, the Palace of the Legion of Honor. The art represented every imaginable style and period, from Monet and Corot to Rembrandt and Franz Hals, to Boucher and Fragonard, to Picasso and all the way forward to Diebenkorn, Jasper Johns, and Frank Stella.

"I've never been in this part of the library," Ella said, stopping to study each painting. She chuckled lightly. "To be honest, I've only rarely been in *any* part of the library. This is all so lovely."

"Ian is an exceptional curator," I said.

"He is delightful, isn't he?" she asked.

"Yes, he is." And with that comment, Ella won my admiration.

I pointed to a wide doorway on the right. "Let's go in here."

"Oh, it's another exhibit hall. I had no idea this was here."

"There are actually six smaller galleries off this hall and they each feature various collections of books and ephemera."

"Such as what?" Ella asked.

"Well, in this first room they have a permanent collection of sports ephemera, including hundreds of baseball cards, tickets, programs, everything connected to baseball." I smiled, thinking of my father and the fact that he never failed to visit this room whenever he came to the Covington. "In the next room they have a fun exhibit of vintage cookbooks and early American shopping catalogs."

"I'm always interested in shopping catalogs."

I turned and noticed her biting back a smile, and I thought, *She actually does have a sense of humor. Color me surprised.*

We spent some time viewing the catalogs and had to laugh at the 1932 Sears catalog that sold everything from prefabricated houses to farm equipment to torpedo push-up bras.

I pointed to a third doorway. "Last year they brought in an extensive collection of Beatles memorabilia that was very popular. You wouldn't believe how many books and magazines have been written about the group.

And I have to admit I find those kinds of things fascinating."

"They are pieces of history," she murmured.

"Exactly," I said, pleased that she understood. I thought about sharing a story about my mother and her own personal Beatlemania collection, but decided against it. Despite the realization that she actually might have a sense of humor, I was still wary of revealing anything too personal to her. Frankly, I wasn't ready to accept that she had actually wanted to spend this time with me because it was pretty obvious that we had almost nothing in common with each other. I was sure her motive had little to do with me and everything to do with escaping from her mother for a few minutes. Was I being paranoid?

I was also amazed that she had bounced back so quickly from her mother's sharp tongue. Maybe she was so used to hearing her mother talk to her like that, that the comments just rolled off her back. But I didn't see how anyone could ever get used to that kind of abusive behavior.

Shaking off my thoughts, I walked into another room. "This exhibit features some of the books I've refurbished." It was a collection of books by English women authors that I had personally curated a few years ago. Ian thought the books—and what they represented— were important enough to keep as a permanent exhibit and I was grateful for it.

"Aren't these lovely?" Ella said. "You designed all of these book covers?"

"Many of them were in excellent condition so I left them alone for the most part. But some were really a mess, and in those cases, I used my own judgment to create something that I hoped people would enjoy."

"So you take a book apart and put it back together in a new and better way?"

I smiled at her words. "Something like that. When I find a book in bad condition, I want to make it shine again."

"You talk about these books as though they are your patients. As if you are a doctor."

I chuckled. "I guess I do. When I see a book that has been damaged, my only thought is, how can I fix it? I want to help it. Bring it back to life."

"You are lucky to have such a calling," she said. "Something that gives your own life meaning."

I blinked at her, then looked back at the books. "I've never really thought about it that way, but you're right. I *am* pretty lucky." I thought again of the way Ella's mother had rolled her eyes in disgust at Ella's words.

"There's one more exhibit that I want to show you," I said, pointing toward the doorway. "It's a fascinating look at the way poisons used to show up in paper and printing so that—"

I stopped speaking when I realized that Ella wasn't listening. Instead, she was focused on her wristwatch. "We should get back." She gave me a sorrowful look. "Forgive me, but I don't wish to leave my mother alone for too long."

"I understand." We headed back the way we came. I was bummed that I wouldn't be able to show her the Poisoned Papers exhibit. I had found the small display absorbing and read every bit of information the exhibit presented. It featured items from the world of paper and printing that had any connection to poisons. Many of the items on display had come from the Victorian age.

For instance, back in Queen Victoria's day, an enterprising newspaper printer had created a golden-hued powder that had been sprinkled onto paper and brushed with a tacky substance to hold the powder until it dried. Their intention was to sell thousands of copies of the newspaper for Queen Victoria's coronation.

Soon after that, a number of the workers died while others complained of seizures and stomach pain. Several of the workers claimed that their hair had turned green while others suffered severe vomiting.

A doctor investigating the workers' symptoms was not allowed to test the powder because its maker didn't want the formula to be stolen. But the Covington exhibit blithely suggested plenty of possible ingredients and configurations for duplicating the toxic powder.

The exhibit also featured stories of the many typesetters and printers who suffered ailments from the myriad fumes and particles produced in their work. Still others got sick because of their habit of holding the lead letter pieces in their mouths. A number of the inks used to produce the vivid colors found on various papers, including wallpaper, contained arsenic and other harmful ingredients.

I couldn't tell you why these stories were so enthralling to me. Maybe because I worked with paper and was always looking for new ways to add color and texture, but I was hooked. Every time I came to the Covington, I made a point of visiting the Poisoned Papers exhibit.

"This building is so beautiful," Ella said as we approached the main hall.

My mind had been so wrapped up in bizarre poison stories that I'd almost forgotten Ella's presence. I recovered quickly. "If you have a chance to come back this week, I would recommend visiting the Children's Museum. The displays there are a lot more whimsical than those in the main hall. If you come in the afternoon, I might have a chance to show you some things."

"I would like that." She gazed casually at the artwork as we passed by. "I was told that you'll be working here all week. Is that true?"

"Yes." I gave a short laugh. "Ian is putting me on display in the main hall. I'll be doing some bookbinding and gilding and leather work on an old copy of *The Prince and the Pauper*."

"That's what Joseph said. It sounds fascinating."

I smiled at her. "Since it's something I do every day, I shouldn't find it so fascinating, but I do. I love my work."

"That's wonderful. I'll look forward to seeing you in action."

As soon as we walked into the main hall, Derek and Joseph greeted us.

"You were gone awhile," Derek murmured.

"I know. Sorry." I squeezed his arm. "I was showing Ella some of my bookbinding work in the other gallery."

As we talked, I noticed that Ashley had moved away from Joseph and was now deep in conversation with Ian. Ingrid stood nearby and it took me a moment to realize that she was glaring at me with real hostility. Wow. If looks could kill, I thought again. Looking up at Derek, I whispered, "What's up with Big Mama?"

Before he could say anything, we watched Ingrid

grab Ella's elbow in a grip so tight, I worried that she would break her daughter's arm.

Through clenched teeth Ingrid whispered, "Where have you been?"

"Mother, please, you're hurting me." Ella whipped her arm away.

"I warned you," Ingrid hissed.

I shouldn't have been watching this, but how could I look away? For another few seconds I witnessed the older woman tormenting her daughter, then realized I really *could* look away. Ugh. I turned to Derek. "Maybe we ought to get another glass of wine."

"Excellent idea." Cool and calm as always—at least on the surface—Derek steered me away from the psychodrama. We strolled toward the bar and I leaned into him. "Derek. She's awful."

"She's been on quite a tirade since you left."

"I'm sorry I left you with her, but I'm pretty sure that's why Ella wanted to get away." I slipped my arm through his. "I was flattered at first but quickly grew suspicious. I mean, really, I couldn't imagine that she actually wanted to traipse through all those galleries looking at baseball cards and cookbooks. She had to have an ulterior motive."

"You're probably right, although I wouldn't poo-poo the appeal of a good set of baseball cards."

I laughed. "It's what every little Swedish girl dreams of."

We got to the bar and ordered two glasses of the cabernet.

The bartender approved of our choice. "It's remarkably complex, I think."

"I think so, too."

Then he showed us the bottle and I had to smile.

"It's from Dharma."

"Naturally," Derek said, swirling his wineglass and studying the color. "Ian wouldn't serve anything but the best."

Dharma was my hometown in the Sonoma Wine Country and the winery was owned and operated by several of my family members, as well as some other friends from the area.

"Their 2014 cabernet is one of my favorites," the bartender said.

I grinned at him. "Mine, too." And it made me happy to know that Ian had arranged to serve my family's wines at this event.

As we walked away, Derek said, "So you showed Ella the baseball cards and cookbooks. What else did you show her?"

"We spent most of the time looking at the books I'd redone for the English women writers exhibit."

"You did a lovely job on that one."

"Thank you." I smiled up at him. "You'll recall that some of the books were more of a challenge than others."

"I remember."

Ian had come up with the idea of a collection of great British female authors after I had put together a noir pulp fiction collection for him; another big success. Many of the pulpy paperbacks were Agatha Christie titles and that gave Ian the idea that it would be great to have a separate exhibit of English women writers. Along with the books themselves, Ian and his staff compiled a remarkable historical timeline with many details of the life and times of the authors, their families, and English society in general.

The exhibit was so popular that it stayed in the main hall for a full year before being moved to the smaller gallery where it remained a part of the permanent collection.

Many of the books used in that exhibit had come from the Covington's own extensive collection. Six of them were in such bad condition, though, that I was asked to resuscitate them.

"Ella seemed to enjoy it," I said, sipping my wine. "It was nice to talk with her. But after a few minutes she was anxious to get back to her mother, so I wasn't able to show her the Poisoned Papers exhibit."

"That's one of your favorites."

"Yes. But since she and Joseph come here pretty regularly, she might have a chance to see it on her own sometime." I shook my head. "I have no idea if it'll interest her. It's pretty gruesome."

"It's just as well that she didn't see the exhibit," Derek said. "We wouldn't want her getting any ideas."

I stared at him. "What do you mean?"

He leaned in closer. "Darling, you saw how Ingrid greeted Ella when you both returned. She can be quite malicious. I wouldn't blame the daughter for wanting to get back at her mother for her cruelty."

I stared at him. "By poisoning her? You're not serious."

He chuckled. "Of course not. But I must say, while you and Ella were gone, Ingrid threw quite a tantrum. She didn't shout or rant, but she very quietly insisted that Joseph track the two of you down and bring you back. She mentioned that it was rude of you not to include her in the tour with her daughter."

I opened my mouth to speak but no words came out. It took me a few seconds to recover. "Are you kidding?"

"No," he said flatly. "It didn't help that Joseph was completely wrapped up in a private conversation with Ashley."

"Ooh-boy," I said, grimacing. "That's what really annoyed her."

Derek nodded. "Exactly."

It wasn't like Derek to gossip—unless he was home alone with me. The fact that he was sharing this news made me realize how truly annoyed he was by Ingrid's attitude.

"Joseph did manage to calm Ingrid down," he said, "but I don't think you're her favorite person right now."

"That's so unfair," I insisted. "First of all, it was Ella's idea to take a walk. And second, well, Ingrid will have to get over it."

"I never said she was rational," he drawled.

I huffed out a breath. "She's not."

"And we'd better leave it at that."

I scowled. "For now."

"Yes." He stared into his wineglass. "I must say, though, that I was impressed by the way Joseph handled Ingrid."

"What did he do?"

"He told her that he completely agreed with her. That Ella is indeed easily influenced by outsiders."

"Seriously? He said that?"

"Yes." His lips twisted sardonically. "And he suggested to Ingrid that she attend every festival event this week for the express purpose of safeguarding her daughter."

I thought about it and began to smile. "That's pretty smart of him, and a little diabolical."

"Well yes, since Ingrid clearly has no interest in attending anything having to do with the festival."

"None at all, but now she's stuck." I took another quick sip of wine and thought for a few seconds. "Of course, now we're stuck with seeing her at all those events. But who knows? Maybe she'll actually enjoy herself."

"Do you think so?"

"No." I laughed. "It's too bad, though. Attending the events is another way of supporting the Covington."

"She wouldn't see it that way."

"Of course not."

"I suppose you'll be attending all the events?" he asked.

"I'm going to try."

"Good. I'll go with you."

"Really?" My mood brightened instantly. "I didn't realize you were such a Mark Twain fan."

"He's a brilliant writer," Derek said, then glanced around and lowered his voice. "But the truth is, while you and Ella were gone, Joseph asked me to assign a security team to each of the outside events."

I was immediately wary. "Is he worried about his safety during the festival? Did something happen to someone? Is Ella in danger?"

"Apparently they've received some odd phone calls. There were vague threats along with some hang-ups."

I clutched his arm. "Good grief, Derek. What were the threats?"

"So far they're connected to that look-alike contest."

I gaped at him. "You've got to be kidding."

"I wish I were."

Joseph would be announcing the winner of the contest tomorrow night at his home. It was a private, ticketed event and only a hundred people would be attending. Would the winner be in danger? Or would Joseph be the target?

"But . . . but it's just a contest. And it's all about *The Prince and the Pauper.* It's supposed to be lighthearted and fun."

"You know what they say, darling."

I frowned at him. "No. What?"

"It's all fun and games until somebody threatens your life."

"Words to live by." I gave his arm a light slap. "But this isn't funny."

"No, it's not." He wrapped his arm around my shoulder and pulled me close. "So we'll be extra careful this week."

I huffed out a breath. "This is happening because they're giving away so much money."

"I agree. I warned Joseph about the money, but he thought the amount would draw more attention to the Covington and to the festival itself. He wanted to make a statement."

"That's good of him, but the rest of it is troubling." With one hundred thousand dollars on the line, this contest had become serious business. And dangerous, apparently. I took a long sip of wine and thought for a moment. It wouldn't do any good to freak out about it, so for now I just sighed. "At least you and I will be able to spend more time together."

He grinned and kissed my cheek. "You always manage to look on the bright side."

I rolled my eyes. "That's me. Little Brooklyn Sunshine."

He chuckled. "I'll remind you of that when we're standing in a soggy field, watching frogs jump."

The thought gave me a little chill, but I was still looking on the bright side. "I'll wear my new boots."

Chapter 4

Love is not a product of reasonings and statistics. It just comes—none knows whence—and cannot explain itself.
—Mark Twain, "Eve's Diary"

On the drive home, Derek and I discussed more of the dangers inherent in Joseph's hundred-thousand-dollar giveaway. I was worried about tomorrow night's contest announcement, but at least that would occur at a private party inside his home. The rest of the festival events would be taking place all over town, mostly outside, and that made the risk even greater.

"You and your team have your work cut out for you," I said.

"It's really no different from any other assignment. We'll keep him and his family safe."

"I was thinking of Ingrid."

"I'm sure she'll be fine," he murmured. "Which reminds me, not to belabor my earlier point, but I still think it was a good thing that you didn't show Ella the Poisoned Papers exhibit."

"Why do you say that?"

"Think about it." He gave a light shrug. "Do we really want Ella studying the finer points of poisoning using parts of a printing press or concocting some brew out of ink and paper?"

"Do you really think she would try to poison her mother?"

"The thought did occur."

I had to smile. "Don't you think she'd be more inclined to use a knife or a gun, rather than go to all the trouble of studying the best ways to extract arsenic from wallpaper?"

"You're right, of course." He flashed a grin at me. "So I guess we can relax from now on."

"What?" I gaped at him. "You must be kidding."

"Of course I am," he said, deadly serious now. "We'll need to be watchful at all times this week."

The tone of his voice caused more of those shivers to dance across my shoulders and I was pretty sure I wouldn't be able to sleep at all tonight.

Despite the shivers, I actually did sleep easy and the next morning I awoke to the aroma of coffee and sourdough toast. This made me happy, even though it signaled that Derek was already awake and showered and dressed for work. I rushed to brush my teeth and throw on some clothes, anxious to spend a few minutes with him before he had to leave for his office. He didn't usually work on Saturdays, but he had called in his top agents for a strategy meeting today.

"Good morning, love," I said as I poured coffee into my cup. Derek sat at the dining room table, perusing the newspaper and finishing his breakfast of sourdough toast, a hardboiled egg, a slice of ham, and half an apple.

Under the table, Charlie was nibbling on some cat goodies.

"You should've awakened me," I said as I sat down with my coffee cup.

He leaned over and gave me a kiss. "But you looked so peaceful, I simply didn't have the heart to do it."

We talked about the latest headlines and chatted about our families. Our brand-new nephew Jamie was getting to be a great big boy, according to my mother, and Derek's parents were in Dharma this month. We made a plan to visit next weekend. Then Derek said, "We're due at Joseph's by six p.m. and unfortunately, I expect this strategy meeting to last most of the day. If I'm home by five thirty, will you be ready?"

"Yes. I'm working at the Covington from noon to four p.m., so I should be able to get home and be ready in plenty of time."

He raised an eyebrow. "Sounds like you've a leisurely morning ahead of you."

I gave him a wry smile. "It won't be all mani-pedis and seaweed wraps. I'm going to try and work on that damaged book before I take off for the Covington. We'll see how much I get done."

"Since I know you fairly well, I believe you'd rather be toiling over a torn book than luxuriating in a spa any day." He stood and took his dishes to the kitchen, where he loaded them into the dishwasher.

"You've got that right."

I joined him in the kitchen and poured myself another half cup of coffee.

"I've cut up the other half of the apple," he said, "and there's that lovely sliced ham. And eggs and toast if you feel like having a big breakfast."

"I'll start with the apple. Thanks."

He pulled me into his arms, kissed me until my brains went to mush, and then said, "Enjoy your day."

I cleared my throat. "My day is going really well so far."

He grinned. "Mine, too." He picked up his briefcase and keys, and was about to leave when I stopped him.

"I know you need to leave, but I'm really concerned about everyone's safety tonight."

He leaned against the doorjamb. "I was wondering if you'd mention it. I'm sorry I frightened you last night."

"It's just that, you know, we have a history with this . . . sort of stuff."

He walked back to me. "This . . . sort of . . . *murder* stuff, you mean?"

"Frankly, yes."

He ran his hands up and down my arms, trying to soothe me. "Darling, I'll have ten security agents at the party. Some will mingle with the guests and others will be part of the staff. Several will be posted outside. They will all be well armed and on guard the entire night."

I took a deep breath and let it out slowly. "Okay. Sounds like you've got things under control."

He kissed me again. "Yes, I do."

"Of course you do. Thank you."

He walked to the door and turned. "I love you."

"I love you, too."

He winked at me, then left the apartment.

Charlie had followed Derek to the door and now she sat and stared at me.

"Don't look at me that way. I didn't make him leave." I walked over and picked up the little cat. "It's just you and me, kiddo. Let's go to work." I cuddled her as I walked through the living room and into my workshop.

I had left the damaged Michael Connelly book on my worktable, covered by the white cloth. Removing the cloth, I took another look at the mess in front of me. Was this book really worth saving? I wondered. There were muddy tire tracks on some of the pages, which were bent and creased and folded in every direction. The entire book was catawampus from being run over by more than one car. I would have to rebuild the spine and realign the pages. I would probably have to soak each page in a light bleach solution to clean off the black marks left by the tires.

From a purely financial angle, it wasn't worth my time and energy to fix the poor book, unless you counted the altruistic glow I would get from simply doing the work.

I stared at the sad pages, and an idea came to mind. I could turn the work into an educational tool by filming it and uploading it to my burgeoning YouTube channel.

"Am I a marketing genius?" I said to Charlie. "Yes, I am."

She looked at me, unblinking, and I knew she was not impressed.

"You'll see," I muttered. A half hour later, the video app on my phone was turned on and my worktable had been transformed into a mini-studio.

Over the past few years I had been recording short videos about bookbinding and posting them online. I had links to the videos on my website and on all my social media pages. And while it was fun, I really didn't like to devote too much time to this kind of stuff because it was truly one of those things that could take over your life if you weren't careful. And even though I had developed an enthusiastic and growing following, mainly thanks to a short TED Talk on bookbinding that I was asked to do a few years ago, I wasn't interested in becoming a video star. I was perfectly happy being a bookbinder.

A few minutes into the video, I realized I would be stuck having to do a lot of editing later on. The fact was, I talked too much! I gave way too many details that would never matter to anyone but another bookbinder. Still, in the end I decided to keep everything I had taped and edit it later.

I would videotape the entire process of cleaning and rebinding the book. I would divide the finished product into segments: First, the initial description of the problem; next, a lot of quick shots of me taking the book apart; followed by shots of how I fixed each individual section; and finally, I would put it all back together.

When my alarm started screaming, I jumped up and shut it off. "Wow, three hours fly by when you're having fun."

I quickly straightened up the items on my worktable. I had been in another world for the last few hours—the world of bookbinding, one of my favorite places to be— and now I had just enough time to shower and dress and drive to the Covington to start on my new job.

Thank God you're here!" Ian cried out when I walked into the main hall.

I checked my wristwatch. "I'm twenty minutes early."

"But people have been waiting for the last hour."

I grabbed his hand and pulled him over to an alcove that led to the restrooms. We were all alone so I said, "Okay, what gives?"

"What are you talking about?"

"This festival has you spinning in circles."

He looked appalled. "You can tell?"

"Of course I can tell," I said. "Look, besides Derek, you are the coolest and calmest person I know. You never freak out. But yesterday and today, you've been a basket case. Is it all about Ella and Ingrid?"

He hung his head. "I'm ashamed to admit that they're a big part of it. They have me on edge."

"I've noticed. But Joseph told you that they are to have nothing to do with the festival."

"I know, and I'm still grateful to Derek for talking to Joseph about that." He took a deep breath and let it out. "But Ella called me a few minutes ago and said that her mother wants to visit the library and she would appreciate it if I would give her a private tour."

I frowned. "That's awfully pushy."

"She asked me very sweetly, not pushy at all."

I almost rolled my eyes. The woman knew how to get what she wanted. "But Ian, you're the president and head curator of this place. You don't have time for that sort of thing."

"Thank you!" He stood a little straighter. "But of course I said yes."

"Of course you did." I patted his arm. "That's because you're a good person."

He snorted. "And because Joseph Cabot contributes many thousands of dollars every year to the Library Foundation."

I grinned. "Well, yeah. There's that."

"I don't know why she makes me crazy. She's really a lovely woman who always says the nicest things."

"She does that to me, too," I said. "I get suspicious."

"I know, right? We're terrible!" He quickly waved his words away. "Don't worry about me. I'll make this work."

"Of course you will. You're charming and worldly and brilliant, and by the end of your private tour, Ingrid will be kissing your feet."

"That's a bit extreme."

I laughed. "Goofball."

We walked out of the alcove and I got my first look at the bleachers in the far corner of the vast room. "Oh my God. You actually set up bleachers."

"They're very nice bleachers," he said.

And they were. Three levels of tastefully designed bleachers covered in attractive cushions. And they were filled with people.

I turned around and took a few steps in the opposite direction. Ian followed me. "What's wrong?"

"First of all," I whispered, "I can't believe all these people are already here. You need to tell them to get a life."

"They're book people," he murmured. "This is their life. And it's mine, too."

I shrugged my agreement. "Okay, it's mine, too. So, do you think they're the type of book people who are going to want to kibitz about my work?"

He smiled. "Of course they are."

I had to grin. "I guess I'm okay with that."

He patted my cheek. "It'll be great."

"Thanks a lot."

He walked with me toward the bleachers. "I think I've got everything you asked for." He pulled a piece of note paper from his pocket and read the list. "Finishing press, sewing frame, wooden sewing cradle." He looked at me. "I had to ask one of the staff what that was."

"It's for punching holes in signature pages," I said. "After marking where the hole should go, you fit the fold into the open V of the cradle. Makes it easy to punch the needle into the hole. And then you sew the pages together."

He looked confused. "I'm sure all that made perfect sense to you."

I ignored the comment as I calculated how much work I would need to do on this book. "I won't know if I need the cradle until I've taken the book apart."

"I get that. Well, it's here if you need it." He glanced down at the list. "And if you need anything else, I'll send someone to the basement to borrow it from one of our staff."

The basement of the Covington Library was a rabbit warren of workshops available for use by visiting bookbinders. It was a wonderful space that hardly anyone knew about. It was also the spot where I found my first dead body, but I didn't need to dwell on that detail just now.

"Sounds good." I hefted a briefcase. "I've brought all the small tools I'll need."

Last week, Ian and I had gone over every aspect of the job and he'd given me the fragile copy of *The Prince and the Pauper* to examine. I could've taken it apart right then, but I wanted to wait until I had an audience who would appreciate all the finer details of refurbishing a book. I had bent the pages back as far as I dared in order to check out the strength of the threads. They were still holding strong and I hoped I wouldn't have to rethread the book, which might entail punching new holes and resewing the signatures.

I would replace the spine, which had almost disintegrated, and I would add new endpapers and a brand-new cloth cover with new gilding and embossing to restore the book to its original beauty.

We started to walk toward the bleachers, but I stopped abruptly. "Holy moly."

"What's wrong?" Ian asked.

"That's the biggest freaking cat I've ever seen," I said, staring at the creature skulking toward us.

He smiled. "It's a Maine coon cat. They get really big."

"It looks like a bear."

"It's not quite as big as a bear," Ian insisted.

"Well, maybe a small bear. And look at all that hair. It's really hairy."

"I prefer to call it fur, Brooklyn, although experts will accept either term."

"You know too much," I muttered. "Do you have any idea how much it weighs?"

"I do," he said. "Twenty-two pounds at his last weigh-in."

"Wow. My little Charlie only weighs seven pounds and I thought she might be putting on weight."

"Charlie's a petite little thing," Ian said. "She'll probably never weigh much more than that."

I knelt down to pet the humongous cat. Its eyes were a mesmerizing shade of amber and its fur—hair?—was really beautiful, a hundred different shades of brown and black and coral and blond, and so long and thick and soft, I'd bet its owner could easily fall asleep on it.

"You're a beauty, aren't you?" I murmured, then glanced up at Ian. "I never realized you knew so much about cats."

"It's Jake," he explained, kneeling down to tickle the cat's chin. "He grew up with cats, so when we moved in together, I became a cat person."

"That's so sweet." Then I frowned. "But this isn't Jake's cat, is it?"

"No, this is Lucinda's cat."

"Oh. That's really nice that you let your staff bring their pets to work."

"We don't, actually. But Lucinda's in charge of the big salvage job and it's keeping her here twenty-four/seven for the next few weeks." Lucinda was the chief conservationist for the Covington Library.

"Are you talking about the Mississippi disaster?" I asked. Last month the Mississippi River had overflowed its banks and caused flooding in a number of towns nearby. Several libraries were damaged and hundreds of rare and antiquarian books had been sent to the Covington Recovery Services Center.

"Yes," Ian said. "And since Lucinda doesn't have anyone at home to watch the cat, I told her she could bring her in."

"You're a good boss." I stroked the cat's luxuriously furry back. "What's her name?"

Ian gave me a somber look. "Pixie."

"Pixie." I smiled, than grinned, then began to laugh. "You are kidding."

"I am not."

"Pixie. Well, that's just perfect, isn't it?" I held my hand out for the cat to sniff. "Hi, Pixie. Hi, big girl."

Pixie butted my hand as a way of saying, *Don't even think you can stop petting me once you start.*

"Hey, she likes me," I said, scratching her ears.

"I hate to break it to you, but Pixie likes everyone. She's a friendly creature. Plus you're petting and scratching her just the way she likes."

"I've got that magic touch," I said. "Is she allowed to roam around freely?"

"No. She must've escaped. I'll take her back to the lab."

"Okay."

He picked up the behemoth creature and the cat stretched itself across his arms. "She's like a big fur coat."

"Isn't she great?" He grinned.

"She really is." But what was really great was the way Ian had taken so naturally to the role of cat person. It was sweet.

"Here you go, Pixie," Ian said, and headed for the EMPLOYEES ONLY door. "I'll check up on you later, Brooklyn."

"Thanks." I walked over to the worktable and the audience began to applaud. Surprised and pleased, I waved to them. "Thank you. I'm happy to see so many people here today. I'm usually all alone in my quiet workshop, so this is quite a departure for me."

"We'll be quiet," a lady in the first row said.

For some reason, everyone laughed and I eyed them all suspiciously. "I don't believe you."

There were more laughs and I shook my head. "I can see you're going to be a rowdy group."

"I promise we'll behave."

I pointed to the chatty woman. "I'll be watching you."

She grinned, loving the attention.

I lifted my briefcase onto the worktable. "I'm going to organize my tools and I'll explain the purpose of some of them as I do it. But first, I want to find out what you all hope to get out of this demonstration." I glanced around and took an educated chance. "How many of you are librarians?"

Out of the thirty people, twenty raised their hands.

"Wow. And how many of you librarians are here to mock me if I get something wrong?"

There were more laughs. One of the women raised her hand. "I'm sure you don't remember me, but I took your class at BABA three or four years ago. It was awesome."

"Of course I remember you," I said, and searched for her name in my memory banks. "You're Marianne, right?"

"Oh my God! Yes! You remembered."

"Of course. And your girlfriend was . . . wait. Don't tell me. Jennifer?"

"That's amazing." She was practically bouncing in her seat. "It's been, like, four years, right?"

"Something like that," I said. "I'm pretty good with names, but also, that was a very memorable class."

"God, yes!" Marianne cried and glanced around at the other faces. "OMG, you guys! There were a couple of murders while we were there!"

Some in the audience gasped, but others looked

excited—which was disconcerting. Were they expecting to see a murder here? I mentally rolled my eyes. That was absolutely not going to happen.

My smile faded. "Definitely memorable."

"Jennifer says hi," Marianne added. "But she couldn't make it. Her daughter's getting married this weekend."

"That's great," I said, my smile returning. "Tell her hello for me."

"Oh, I will!"

"Now who else do we have here today?"

A few hands shot up and I was glad, since I much preferred people raising hands rather than shouting things out.

I pointed to a man in the top row. "Yes, go ahead."

"I'm Stanley, a graphic artist. My girlfriend suggested that bookbinding might be a good way to expand my repertoire, so to speak."

"She's right. The bookbinders I know have started out as either librarians or graphic artists. So one might go into book restoration while someone else might go into book arts with papermaking, shadow boxes, accordion books, things like that. If you can imagine it, you can do it."

"I have a pretty good imagination," he said.

"That helps. There are a lot of creative examples of book art around the Covington, especially in the children's museum. I even have a few items on display myself, but I'm an amateur compared to some of the amazing book artists exhibited here."

"I'll check it out."

The ice had been broken and the rest of my audience clamored to speak up. I was okay with that since

I used the time to organize my tools and start brushing off the pages of the old book.

"I'll try to explain things as I go along," I said, "but I often get wrapped up in my work and will forget that you all are watching. If that happens and you have a question for me, please just ask it. Okay?"

"Okay," the group replied.

I explained a few of my tools and then things were quiet for the next five minutes. And that was nice since we were in a library, after all.

Finally I held up the faded green and gold book for everyone to see. "You've all probably heard that as part of the Mark Twain Festival, everyone in the city has been asked to read *The Prince and the Pauper*. I'm taking that one step further and actually restoring this copy for the Covington Library. I'm going to pass it around so everyone can see what kind of shape it's in."

I watched my group pass it from one person to the next with a lot more care than I'd expected. But then again, these were book people.

"This book is a first edition," I explained, "published in Boston in 1882. It has 441 pages and it's illustrated throughout with nearly two hundred wood engravings. In bookseller language, it's in moderately good condition. There's some light pulling and fraying of the cloth at the spine ends. The corners are lightly bruised with some mild rubbing, except for one corner that's abraded all the way through to the board. But the pages within are virtually unmarked, which is why, despite the somewhat poor state of the cover, the book is considered to be in good condition."

The book wound its way around the group until it was returned to me. "Thank you for treating the book with care. I can always tell when I'm in the presence of booklovers, and I appreciate it."

"Well, hell," Stanley said. "I figure the Covington gods would smite us if we ever dared to mishandle a book."

Everyone laughed, including me.

Now I sat down on the one high stool, pulled myself closer to the worktable, and held up the book. "You probably saw me brushing off the pages a few minutes ago and that's something I always do before taking an old book like this apart. Because, who knows where this book has been? How many different people have touched it? What sorts of strange microorganisms have invaded its pages?" I made a face and a few people laughed.

"I start with this stiff brush." I held up the thin, long-handled brush that resembled something an artist would use. "You'll notice that the bristle edge is flat and it really is stiff." I ran my thumb along the open edge, sometimes called the *toe*, to demonstrate its stiffness. "The stiffness helps the bristles get into the crevices of each page. A soft brush won't catch every little grain of dirt, but this one will."

I opened the book and demonstrated, running the brush briskly down the middle gutter as I pointed out how well the individual bristles could get in between the sewn pages. "This part of the demonstration might get a little boring or repetitive for you, because I'm going to brush down every single page. If you feel like leaving or taking a break, go right ahead."

I continued working, barely noticing when, every so often, someone would stand up and walk away. I didn't take it personally since that was how Ian and I had set up this demonstration.

I was only a little way into the book, but so far I was pleased to find very little foxing on the pages. I explained to the group that *foxing* referred to those patches of reddish brown smudges that often showed up on the pages of old books. They looked like specks of dirt, but they were actually produced by chemical reactions from microorganisms or oxidation.

That was the theory, anyway, and trust me, those tiny splotches were really hard to get rid of. I had tried everything from mild bleach solutions to Wonder Bread sponges.

That wasn't a joke. I had experimented years ago when white bread was rumored to contain something called "calcium peroxide." I figured that meant it could clean things and it might be able to soak up dirt, so I had folded a piece of white bread in half and rubbed it over some pages like a sponge. The bread actually did turn dark from the dirt collected on the pages, but it didn't bleach away any of the foxing. And it left my desk covered in dark chunks of dirty bread, which was weird.

As I brushed the pages of the old green book, I took a few photos with my phone. Even though the work I was doing right now was pretty mundane, I would still post the shots on social media as a way of introducing my followers to this special Covington assignment and the festival itself.

I always took photos of books as I worked on them. I measured and weighed the book and studied its shape and size, both for my own information and for the book's owners, too. Whenever I worked on a book, I took lots of notes in order to compare the before and the after. This book was nine inches tall by six inches wide by one inch thick.

I glanced up at the audience. "Has anyone read the book yet?"

"I read it just last week," Marianne said. "I remember reading it as a little girl, and it's such a different experience reading it as a grown-up. Lots of lessons to be learned, you know?"

"I know exactly what you mean," I said. "It's not exactly the Disney version, right?"

"Right!" she said. "I mean, parts of it are pretty rough, like when the prince is attacked by the other boys?"

"The original is not a story for children," another woman said.

I nodded. "There's a lot of commentary on the English government, politics, the treatment of their own people. And of course, the prince is suddenly seeing it all up close, through the eyes of a poor man. As the pauper, he quickly becomes a target of his own government's policies toward the poor."

"Mark Twain didn't spare our own government, either," the graphic artist said. "If you read *Huckleberry Finn* or *Tom Sawyer*, you'll see plenty of examples of our own policies toward the more unfortunate members of society."

"Indeed," another woman said.

I was able to continue working as the group carried on the conversation. I wouldn't think of putting an end to the discussion because not only did I enjoy it, but also this was exactly the sort of dialogue that the festival organizers wanted to encourage.

The afternoon passed by quickly and it was four o'clock before I realized it. I had finished brushing the pages and had begun to talk to the group about the work I would need to do on the cover and the spine. There were a number of questions that kept me talking for a while longer as I packed up my own tools in my briefcase. Then I picked up the book, slipped it into my tote bag, and wished everyone a good evening. On the way out of the hall, I stopped and spoke to one of the guards to let him know I was leaving for the day and that I had left a number of larger tools out on the work-table. He assured me that he would take care of it.

I quickly walked upstairs to Ian's office. It was al-ways a pleasure to visit his office and check out which fabulous pieces of art he had borrowed for himself. Now I felt a burst of nostalgia remembering how my bridal party and I had partied in his big beautiful of-fice, dressing and preparing for my wedding, which would take place in the garden. I chose to remember the day as being lovely and wonderful and hardly ever gave a thought to those bad people who'd been trying to kill me.

"Done for the day?" Ian asked.

"Yes. The guard downstairs said he'd keep an eye on the tools you brought me."

"We'll make sure everything is safe."

"Okay. If you don't mind, I'm going to take the book home with me. I can finish some preliminary work at home and then I'll be ready to take it apart when I'm back here tomorrow."

"Sounds good. Thanks, Brooklyn." He stood and joined me as I walked to the door. "So how did it go today?"

"Oh, it was great," I said. "The audience was really smart and appreciative."

"That's what I love to hear."

"Will we see you tonight at Joseph's?" I asked.

"Are you kidding?" he said. "Tonight's contest revelation will be the best part of the festival."

"I think so, too. I can't wait to see the look-alike winner."

He gave me an intense look. "Tell me the truth. It's just a little bizarre, don't you think?"

"I totally agree," I confessed with a small wince. "But hey, that's Joseph's decision."

"Yes, and since he's underwriting the entire festival, he gets to do whatever he wants."

I grinned. "I'll see you later."

"Oh, hey," he said. "Why don't you bring the book with you tonight so we can show some of the big money donors what you're working on. And bring a few of your tools along, too. You know, that bonefolder thingie and maybe one of those brushes you use. Whatever you think they might find interesting."

"Really?"

"Yeah," he said. "These are book people, remember? They'll dig it."

"I guess you're right."

"Plus the book is the one that everyone's reading, so I think they'll get a kick out of it."

I gave him a smart salute. "Whatever you say, boss."

With rush hour just getting ramped up, it took me twenty minutes longer than usual to get home. Still, I made it home before Derek, and I grabbed the opportunity to take a quick shower.

I blew my blond hair dry and styled it with my brush. Since it's basically stick straight, I tried to give it a little bit of a curl at the ends. I added blush, mascara, and lipstick, and checked myself out in the mirror.

"Well, you're no Ella Cabot," I murmured, "but you'll do."

I wore an outfit that I had found while shopping with my super-shopper friend Alex. The dress was a tea-length black chiffon that flowed beautifully when I moved. The fitted jacket was also black, but it was covered in black sequins with one diamond button at the waist. It could've worked for any semiformal occasion, but it was comfortable and I felt good wearing it.

My black shoes, on the other hand, were killer high heels that I knew would cause me pain. However, Alex assured me that the pain was worth it because they were the sexiest things she'd ever seen. "They're not Birkenstocks," she'd drawled.

By the time Derek arrived home, I was dressed and ready to go.

"Darling, you look . . . wonderful," he said when he saw me.

I smiled. "And so do you."

He wrapped his arms around me and kissed my neck. When he finally moved back, his grin was devilish. "I didn't want to ruin your lipstick."

I laughed. "Thank you. I wear it so rarely that it would be traumatic to have to reapply it."

He checked his watch. "I was hoping we could have a glass of wine before we left, but traffic held me up."

"We can have wine at the party."

"Of course we can. Are you ready to go?"

"Yes." I pulled my black coat off the back of the

dining room chair, grabbed my small evening bag and my black tote bag. "Ready."

"What's this you're bringing?"

I held up the tote bag. "Ian asked me to bring the book I'm working on and a few tools. He thinks some of the donors will be interested in seeing it up close."

"*The Prince and the Pauper*?" he asked.

"Yes."

He thought about it and nodded. "He knows his donors."

Little Charlie must've sensed that we were about to leave because she came bounding into the room to rub up against our ankles and purr. Derek reached down, picked her up, and looked her in the eye. "Your timing is impeccable."

The cat purred so loudly, I thought the neighbors might hear her. But I couldn't blame her when it came to Derek gazing into her eyes. "I think she needs a treat."

"I agree," he said. "She's a good girl."

I followed him into the kitchen, where he opened a cupboard and dropped something deliciously fishy into her bowl.

"What a lucky little lady," I murmured, petting her soft fur.

He put the treats back in the cupboard. "We'd better run while she's occupied."

I laughed and grabbed his hand. "Let's go."

Chapter 5

There is nothing comparable to the endurance of a
woman. In military life she would tire out an army of
men, either in camp or on the march.

—*Autobiography of Mark Twain*

Derek parked a half block away from the Cabot house.
We were close to the beach, where the air was cooler,
so I pulled my coat more tightly around me as I stepped
from the car. We walked the half block, then stopped
to stare at Joseph's imposing house on the other side of
the street. We were in Sea Cliff, an area of town I've
always loved, mainly because the air was clean, the
houses were big and lovely, and the view was seriously
one of the best in the world.

We stood and watched a series of limousines and
fancy cars drive into the wide car park in front of the
house and drop off their occupants. And it occurred to
me that the word *house* was completely inaccurate
when describing this place. It was a freaking mansion,
a Mediterranean castle, surrounded on all sides by gorgeous gardens and greenery, with thick terra-cotta
walls and numerous terraces on every level. Built on

the cliff overlooking China Beach with the Golden Gate Bridge standing sentinel in the distance, this place had to have one of the most exclusive and beautiful views in the world.

From where we stood, the house—er, mansion—appeared to be three stories high, but Derek pointed out that there was a lower floor that could only be seen from the water. That made this a four-story house. Wow.

"They've an elevator, as well," Derek murmured.

"Of course they do." Which indicated again that this was no simple little "house." More like a gorgeous walled fortress with one heck of a view.

"I'm officially impressed," I said as Derek took my arm.

"It is rather posh, isn't it?"

I smiled at his words. "Are we ready to face the formidable Ella?"

Derek leaned over and kissed my cheek. "You're not still intimidated by her."

"No, I'm not. Her mother, on the other hand . . ."

"Hmm, yes. Ingrid is quite a piece of work."

I frowned, thinking about it. "I've gotten over their intimidating personalities. But their looks, my God. Both of them are just stunning to look at. It's like if Marilyn Monroe and Sophia Loren were standing next to you, making small talk. You know, it can be nerve-wracking."

Derek was grinning at my examples, but said nothing.

"It makes me wonder," I continued, "what does that do to one's psyche? Spending your whole life being stared at and admired for nothing more than a shiny outer shell?" I shook my head, feeling silly. "Stop me anytime. I'm about to go into psychobabble talk and sound like my mother."

"Your mother always makes perfect sense," Derek said.

And that was one more reason why I loved him. "Thank you. And I'll stop talking about Ella and Ingrid."

He leaned down and kissed me.

"What was that for?" I whispered.

"For being perfect for me in every way."

Smiling, I gazed at him. "You're pretty perfect yourself."

"Thank you, darling." He thought for a moment, then said, "I've got to get something out of the car."

"Okay. I'll wait here."

He walked away quickly and I took the opportunity to admire his form.

After a few seconds I turned and watched more cars pull into the drive. Most of them were gorgeous and expensive, like Derek's car. There was a fancy foreign sports car in Day-Glo yellow that I couldn't begin to identify, followed by a huge tank of a car. That had to be a Rolls-Royce, I thought.

"Here we are," Derek said.

"That was fast."

"I couldn't leave you hanging here."

"Thank you," I said, delighted by the fact that he was so considerate. "But I was fine. Just watching the cars."

He glanced both ways. "Are you ready to walk?"

"Yes."

As we strolled across the street, I glanced around and noticed something unexpected.

"Hey." I nudged Derek. "Isn't that George Thompson sitting in the Mercedes across the street?"

George was one of Derek's best agents and a good friend of ours. For a tough guy who carried a gun, he was a sweetheart. Brave and hardworking, he had been with Derek's company for almost five years.

"Yes, it's George," Derek whispered. "But let's not blow his cover, shall we?"

"I'm not going to blow his cover," I muttered. Okay, maybe I'd been staring, but at least I wasn't waving and shouting like an idiot. Well, not yet anyway. And seeing George reminded me that Derek was on duty tonight. And that was why he'd gone back to the car. He needed his gun. Hmm. I took one last surreptitious glance at George before we stepped onto the sidewalk, crossed the driveway, and then passed through the open gates.

Here in this area were enough plants to supply a tropical rain forest. Hanging baskets had ferns and pothos cascading down in profusion. Massively large pots lined one long wall and held palm trees, fiddle leaf ferns, and rhododendrons. Bougainvilleas covered the outer walls, adding brilliant color. Bromeliads grew on driftwood mounted on the walls of the house by the front door. And every single plant looked healthy and perfect.

Joseph paid someone well to make sure the plants always looked that way. It was worth it, I thought.

"This is beautiful," I murmured, and stepped into the fortress.

And wow, the interior of the home did not disappoint. The foyer was as big as any normal living room and completely round, with a lovely crystal chandelier in the center of the ceiling. The walls were so white, it made me wonder if the room had just been painted. The hardwood floors were so highly polished that, again, I had to wonder if they had just been buffed.

A distinguished older gentleman wearing a suit with a burgundy vest approached. With a slight bow, he said, "May I take your coat, madam?"

"Yes, thank you," I said, and slipped out of it.

"Edith!" the man barked over his shoulder.

A petite young woman in a housemaid's uniform came rushing forward. She took my coat and said, "Thank you, madam."

"Thank you, Edith," I said, and wondered briefly why the man hadn't simply taken my coat himself since he was the one who had asked to take it. There was obviously a hierarchy here and it forbade the very important man from dealing with such trivial tasks as taking guests' coats. Oh, whatever. I had a tendency to dwell on those sorts of meaningless conundrums.

The well-dressed man said, "Have a lovely evening, madam."

"Thank you," I said. "What is your name?"

"I'm Hobson, madam. At your service." He nodded to Derek. "Commander." He spoke with a very proper English accent, even more proper than Derek's, if that was possible.

As I was turning, I happened to catch the way Edith was looking at Hobson. It was a look of pure contempt, but at least she was subtle about it. Her head was lowered enough that he couldn't see her, but I could. And for the third or fourth time in two days, I thought, *Boy, if looks could kill.*

There was a lot of that going around, I thought.

Maybe Hobson treated the housemaids badly. The

housemaid certainly thought so. It wouldn't be the first case of the head guy treating the little people with contempt.

"Thank you, Hobson," Derek murmured. Then taking my arm, he walked me through a wide archway and we stepped down into the football-field-sized living room. Maybe it wasn't quite the length of a football field, but it felt almost as massive, with an impressive cathedral ceiling and a magnificent stone fireplace and hearth that covered the entire wall at the far end. The western wall was made up entirely of floor-to-ceiling glass and the view was even better than I'd imagined it would be.

"I've got to get a better look at this," I said and led Derek over to the wall of glass to take in the view. From the rocky cliff and the wide, arched beach below the house, to the blue water of the Bay, to the Marin Headlands on the opposite shore, to the wide expanse of the Golden Gate Bridge turning a deep, warm bronze in the last light of the sunset. It was breathtaking.

I gazed at Derek. "This is just stunning. Imagine being able to look at this view every day."

"I believe I could get used to it," he said.

I glanced up at him. "Have you been here before?"

"Yes, of course."

"Oh, that's right. Your team had to come and prep for the security thing."

"Yes. And Joseph has invited me for lunch on occasion."

I frowned. "I knew that."

He smiled. "I've mentioned it a time or two, but you may have forgotten."

"I guess so. Sorry. Anyway, I didn't realize he had a butler."

"He has two butlers, actually. Hobson has worked for Joseph for years. In fact, he used to work for Joseph's father. So he's more than just a butler to Joseph; he's his right-hand man. Takes care of a lot of business for him."

"Is he from the same part of England as you are?"

Derek thought about it. "I have no idea where he's from. But he does speak the Queen's English quite precisely."

"That's what I thought."

He smiled. "And that's precisely why I don't know where he comes from."

I frowned. "I'm confused."

"Darling, keep in mind that anyone can be trained to speak that way. Just spend some time listening to the BBC. People strive to replicate the accent so often that they actually call it a BBC accent. Hobson has that, so who knows where he actually comes from. He could be from Louisiana."

I grimaced. "I hope not. Nothing against Louisiana, but I would hate to be so easily deceived."

He chuckled. "Don't worry, love. I doubt that Hobson is from Louisiana."

"I'm going to listen more carefully next time. See if I can catch him up."

"If anyone can, it'll be you."

We both looked back at the view for another long moment.

"That little housemaid doesn't like him," I murmured.

"I'm afraid Hobson has a supercilious streak that comes from being in charge for so many years. But he's actually very loyal to Joseph and quite protective."

"I'm glad," I said. After a moment I asked, "What does a second butler do?" I was suddenly curious about the whole setup.

He smiled at me. "He can be assigned to do whatever comes along. He may take on the duties of a valet. Or he might work with the kitchen, assuring that tables are set properly, meals are served in a timely fashion, and menus comply with individual dietary requirements. He may even be in charge of the laundry. Or the wine cellar, where he makes sure the bottles are stored properly and that inventory is regulated. He might take charge of the automobiles, or work with the mail and with deliveries, answering the door or the telephone. Or he might be asked to assist other members of the household. It varies, obviously."

"Wow, you really know a lot about butlers."

He smiled enigmatically. "I played the role more than once during my days at MI6."

My eyebrows lifted. "Really? I bet you looked really hot in your butler duds."

"Naturally," he said dryly, then smirked.

I gave a quick laugh, then glanced back at Hobson. "A butler's job covers a lot of ground, I guess. It's fascinating."

"We'll track down the under-butler later and grill him on his duties."

My eyes lit up. "Can we?"

"On second thought, Hobson might not want us to distract the man," he whispered.

I winced. "Good point. I would hate to get on Hobson's bad side." I thought again of that look from Edith the housemaid.

"He takes his role very seriously."

"I guess that's a good thing." I turned and took one last look at the view. "I wonder who cleans all these windows."

"We can ask," he said.

Joseph walked up just then. "Pretty cool view, isn't it?"

"There you are." I gave him a hug. "It's glorious. Your house is fabulous."

He shrugged. "It doesn't suck."

I had to laugh. "Well put."

He and Derek shook hands, then Joseph said, "I hope we'll have a chance to visit more tonight. Maybe I can give you a tour of the place."

"I would love that," I said.

"I'll make it happen." He glanced to his left and then to his right. "But just now I have to carry out my hosting duties."

"We'll talk later," Derek said.

As Joseph strolled away, a waiter walked by and Derek retrieved two glasses of champagne from him. I was reminded again that some of the guests and servers were members of Derek's security team and I took that moment to check out the waiter. Were those his real muscles or was he wearing a bulletproof vest? Could he have a gun hidden under his arm?

"Stop it," Derek murmured.

"What?"

"You're ogling the help."

I laughed. "I am not. Maybe just studying them a little. But hardly ogling."

Derek wore a frown as he scanned the room, which was quickly filling up with guests.

"What's wrong?"

"There are quite a few people here and it's still early."

"I heard there would be about a hundred here tonight."

"There are at least that many here already."

I followed his gaze and looked around the room at the dozens of beautifully dressed people who mingled and laughed and sipped their cocktails. "You're right. It looks like more than a hundred people to me. Good thing this room is so big."

"Yes," he murmured, not looking too happy about it. "The entire house can handle that many, but I'm afraid most of the guests will try to fit into this room. I'd better talk to my people. I want to make sure everyone is safe."

More servers walked through the crowd carrying silver platters of yummy-looking finger foods along with glasses of champagne and both red and white wines.

I checked out every one of them and tried really hard to look for any weapons they might've been carrying. Then I began to study the faces of the invited guests, looking for agent types. I was surprised to recognize the new mayor along with several members of the Board of Supervisors. They stood across the room looking very serious as they spoke to each other in hushed tones while they scarfed up the full tray of popcorn shrimp that a patient waiter held steady for them.

Nearby, the manager of a major league sports team

was deep in conversation with the hottest restaurateur of the moment and a hedge fund manager who had recently been indicted.

"Quite the cross section," I whispered.

Derek discreetly snorted a laugh. "Indeed."

"There you are!"

We both turned and saw Ian and his hunky husband Jake, heading straight for us.

Jake gave me a big hug. "Girl, you look absolutely fantastic."

"Thanks, Jake," I said, returning the hug. "I'm so glad you're here."

"What about me?" Ian said as he grabbed me in a hug.

I stifled a grin. "I just saw you two hours ago."

Ian sighed. "So the thrill is gone."

I laughed. "Never."

Ian checked out my elegant outfit. "Well, I must say, you certainly clean up well."

I smoothed my chiffon skirt. "Thank you."

"You really do look lovely," Jake said, gazing from me to Derek. "But then, you two are always the classiest duo in the room."

I hoped my smile conveyed my undying gratitude for that comment. Ian grabbed two glasses of champagne from another waiter and handed one to Jake. Ian took a sip, then scoped out the room. Leaning in, he asked, "So? What do we think?"

I pointed to the window. "I think this is the most wonderful house I've ever been in. Did you check out that view?"

"Oh, sweetie." Ian rolled his eyes. "Yes, there's the view, the house, the grounds, all beautiful, whatever, blah-blah-blah." He waved all that away. "Let's talk about these people. I mean, A-list, for sure. Right?"

"Oh, for sure," I agreed. "Especially now that you guys are here."

Jake threw his arm around my shoulders. "I love this girl."

"I saw her first," Ian said.

I glanced at Derek, who grinned amiably at their hijinks but then nudged Ian. "She's mine, mate. You can't have her."

"Ooh, territorial," Jake said. "I like that."

I felt like my smile might be permanently attached to my face. And why not? I was surrounded by three of the most gorgeous men in a room filled with VIPs. It was a pretty good situation to be in, I thought.

Naturally, at that moment, Ella and Ingrid walked in together—and the energy in the room, which was bright and lively to begin with, instantly sparked with some kind of zingy electrical charge that caused everyone to raise their party game. Conversations increased in volume and laughter grew raucous. Seriously. I exchanged a glance with Derek, who nodded. "Formidable."

Jake had his back to the doorway. "I'm catching a vibe," he whispered loudly. "What's going on? Is someone causing a scene? Can we watch?" He started to turn around.

"Don't turn around," Ian hissed, clutching his arm. "The Blond Bombshells just walked in."

"Oh! Your favorites."

Despite my own admitted obsession with Ella and Ingrid, I shook my head in reproach. "Honestly, Ian. You have to stop calling them that."

But Jake was shaking with excitement and paid no attention to me. "Ian told me all about those two gorgeous women. I simply have to meet them."

"You're in luck," I said drolly. "They're heading this way."

Ella and Ingrid had decided to wow the crowd by wearing identical slinky party dresses, except that Ingrid's dress was black and Ella's was white. They were low-cut in front and showed off loads of leg. The two women were definitely playing on the fact that they looked very much alike. They obviously knew the impact they were having on the assembled guests.

And they were eating it up.

"Brooklyn!" Ella cooed, and gave me an air kiss.

"Hello, Ella," I said. "You look wonderful and your home is beautiful."

"Thank you, my dear," she responded. "So glad you could come."

Ingrid, on the other hand, stared over my shoulder, ignoring me. I felt an unwelcome wave of hostility toward the snotty older woman and figured she was still mad at me for stealing Ella away the night before. Apparently she held a grudge.

I introduced both women to Jake and Ian, and before I could walk away, the two men had both women giggling.

Hearing those giggles caused shock waves to reverberate in my ears. But if introducing them to Ian and Jake had brought about that reaction, then my work here was done.

Derek walked off to have a private word with Joseph so I wandered through the crowd, sipping champagne and smiling at nobody in particular. Despite the afore-mentioned giggles, I was still trying to temper my negative reaction to Ingrid. I wasn't ready to make small talk with strangers so I ended up back at the wall of windows and watched the lights come on across the Bay.

"Brooklyn?"

I turned and saw Ashley Sharp standing nearby.

"Hi, Ashley." I reached out to shake her hand and was amazed to realize that she was even shorter in person, thanks to her smart choice of wearing ballet slippers rather than killer heels. Her facial features were almost delicate, like a beautiful little doll's. "Nice to see you."

"It's nice to see you, too."

She gazed out the window. "The view is awesome, isn't it?"

"It's overwhelming."

She hesitated, then said, "Well, I don't want to take you away from the party, but I wanted a chance to thank you for donating your time to the festival."

"I'm always willing to do my part," I said. "Especially if there's a book involved."

"Joseph has told me so much about you and your work," she said. "I'm just totally fascinated by what you do."

I smiled. "That's funny, because I happen to think your work is pretty interesting, too. You have a YouTube channel, right?" I was trying to be subtle, but I already knew the answer. The girl had two million followers and her audience was still growing.

"Yeah. It's doing pretty well." She grinned and I almost laughed at her downplaying her success. "My mother always says I've got a big mouth so she's happy I've put it to good use on the Internet."

"It takes more than a big mouth to do what you do. It takes hard work and real talent."

Her eyes widened. "Thank you. That's lovely of you to say so."

"Just speaking the truth," I said with a quick smile. Besides her huge YouTube following, Ashley made her living as an events coordinator and freelance marketing expert, which probably had helped to build up her YouTube numbers. She was currently working with Joseph and his newspaper to beef up interest in the Mark Twain Festival.

A waiter walked by and Ashley reached for two glasses of champagne. She passed one to me and said, "It's getting crowded in here so we should take every opportunity to grab the champagne while we can. Right?"

I grinned. "My philosophy exactly."

She took a sip, then frowned at something she saw. Her eyes narrowed and she took a deep breath. When she noticed me watching her, she tried to smile. She checked her watch, which was one of those big square things that was bigger than her wrist and monitored everything in her life—and also kept time, apparently. "Gotta go. Big night ahead."

"Okay." I held up my glass. "Thanks for the champagne."

This time, her smile was genuine. "You bet. See you later."

"Okay." But she was already gone.

I had to admit that I found Ashley Sharp fascinating

in a young, Gen-Z, happily-frenetic-livewire sort of way. With all those YouTube followers, she was considered a certified "influencer" in today's parlance. I wasn't even sure what that meant, but I could figure it out. She clearly had the uncanny ability to pimp whatever product a company chose to send her and for that they paid her lots of money. I imagined Ashley's marketing skills were her superpower.

Regardless of her skill set, Ashley Sharp was impressive. On a whim, I pulled out my cell phone and googled her name. She was indeed considered a proud member of Generation Z, which meant that she was in her early to mid-twenties. *So young,* I thought. I also read that her number of Internet followers had risen to 2.5 million. Sheesh.

Many of the Google entries referred to her simply as *The Magic Marketer.* Still others had turned her last name, *Sharp,* into various slogans, some cleverer than others: *Sharp as a knife; a real Sharp shooter; cutting edge Sharp.*

I stared out the window at the lights along the Marin headlands across the expanse of water. I thought again of the expression I'd seen on Ashley's face. She didn't look happy.

It had been more than fifteen minutes since I'd seen Derek and I wondered if he might be looking for me. I walked through the crowd toward the foyer and was immediately stopped by Ian, who grabbed my arm. "Some of the donors want to meet you."

"That's nice." I was always happy to meet book people. I took a quick look around but didn't see Derek in the crush of people. I would catch up with him eventually.

"They're waiting in the library."

Of course Joseph would have a library, I thought. The man was a fanatic about books, which I considered one of his best qualities.

Ian led me down a hall and into the library. I stopped in the doorway and had to take a breath. The room was big, no surprise, but it was also warm and cozy somehow. Rich mahogany bookshelves lined the walls and they were filled with hundreds and hundreds of books. I could smell the leather bindings and loved how the gilded spines twinkled in the subdued lighting. A long, velvety forest-green couch faced an antique library table with four chairs. A small Tiffany lamp sat on its surface.

Another chair, this one big and roomy and covered in soft burgundy velvet, was tucked in the corner. It looked so inviting, I was tempted to crawl into it and take a nap.

"It's beautiful," I said.

"Yeah," Ian said, grinning. "Pretty impressive."

"Coming from you, that's saying a lot since you practically live in the most gorgeous library in the world."

He grinned. "Let's meet the donors and you can browse afterwards."

"Okay."

A man and two women sat at the library table. Ian pulled the fourth chair out for me as he introduced me. The three Covington donors took a minute to gush about my work—which never got old. One of the donors, an older woman wearing a gold sequined top and a stunning diamond ring the size of my foot, finally pressed her hands together in a prayerful position. "May we please see the book?"

"Of course." I set my tote bag down and pulled out *The Prince and the Pauper.*

"It's sad and a bit shabby right now," I explained. "But it's going to be beautiful when I'm through with it."

"Oh, isn't it wonderful?" the man said, turning the book over in his hands. I smiled at him, recognizing a serious booklover when I saw one.

"Will it be put on display when you've completed your work?" the other woman asked.

"Yes," I said. "Ian tells me they're planning to exhibit it with several other copies of Mark Twain's works."

"How delightful," the man whispered.

"After the festival," Ian said, "we'll open a small permanent collection of books by Mark Twain and some of his contemporaries."

"I do hope you won't neglect the works of Bret Harte," the diamond ring lady said.

"Never," Ian declared. "He's one of the leading literary voices of the early American West."

"He was a Bohemian," the man said proudly.

The Bohemians were a group of young writers in the late 1800s who had a part in shaping the literary landscape of the West and San Francisco in particular.

"Are you going to regild the book?" the other woman asked.

"Oh yes." I reached into my tote bag. "You might enjoy looking at some of my tools."

These were real antiquarian book fans because they giggled with excitement over the gilding tools I'd brought with me. I showed them how the little grooved rolling tool would be used to produce the same lines and wavy patterns that were still barely visible on the cover of the original book.

It was twenty minutes of shop talk, but I enjoyed myself. After Ian shepherded the donors back to the party, I carefully wrapped up the book and slipped it back in my tote bag. Alone now, I glanced around the room. I decided to stow the tote bag underneath the couch so I wouldn't have to carry it around for another two hours. I wasn't sure how wise it was to leave the book hidden in here, but I checked and rechecked to make sure the bag couldn't be seen from anywhere in the room and finally felt sure of my decision.

I wanted more than anything to peruse the shelves of Joseph's library and take a closer look at some of the books. But I'd been gone quite a while and thought Derek might be wondering where I had disappeared to. I gazed around the beautiful room one more time and hoped I would have another chance to visit again someday. Then I hurried down the hall to find Derek.

Chapter 6

... being rich ain't what it's cracked up to be. It's just worry and worry, and sweat and sweat, and a-wishing you was dead all the time.

—Mark Twain, *The Adventures of Tom Sawyer*

I found Derek in the living room chatting with two of Joseph's business partners and their wives. He introduced me to all of them and we talked about the festival for a few minutes until we were joined by Joseph himself. After a minute of small talk, Joseph pulled Derek and me aside to suggest that he give me a tour of his home.

"Absolutely yes," I said eagerly.

"Would you like to start with the library?"

I smiled. "I just spent the last half hour in your library, showing the Mark Twain book to some donors. It's a beautiful space and someday I would love to spend more time looking through your collection."

"I'd like that, too," he said, grinning. "Someday. But for now, let's take the elevator and start at the top."

The ride in the adorable elevator made me very

happy. To be honest, it was the smallest, most claustro-
phobic space in the entire house, but that was okay because it reminded me of some of the lovely small hotels
I'd stayed in while in Paris. They all boasted elevators,
but good grief, they were tiny. Even if you could fit only
two people with luggage inside one of those minuscule
elevators, it was enough to qualify the hotel for four-
star status.

While Joseph's elevator was understandably small,
the three of us still managed to fit comfortably. For that
reason and so many others, his home was definitely
worth five stars and beyond.

The view from every room was the highlight, of
course, but the rooms themselves were a treat as well.
They were all so big yet so comfortable and in such
exquisitely good taste that I could've happily taken up
residence in any little corner of the house.

We made it down to the basement game room, where
we were completely distracted by a beautifully restored
foosball table and several antique pinball machines.

"Shall we play a game?" Joseph said.

I smiled. "Sure."

"Be careful, darling," Derek said. "Joseph spends
all his time down here."

Even this room had two luxurious couches covered
in silky pillows along with several chairs that faced the
windows to take advantage of the view.

"Did you do all the decorating yourself?" I asked.

Joseph hesitated, then took his turn at the pinball
machine. After racking up a few thousand points, he
said, "My first wife did most of it. She had a real eye for
putting fabrics and colors together."

"She sure did," I murmured. It was interesting to learn something new about Joseph. Mainly, that he had moved to this house with his first wife, Sandra. I knew that he had lived here for almost ten years and Derek had recently explained that Sandra had died of cancer five years ago.

"How did you and Ella meet?" I asked, curious to hear more details about Joseph.

Before he could answer, Ashley Sharp ran into the room. "Hello again," she said cheerily to me, then turned to Joseph. "It's eight thirty, boss. You said to track you down, so here I am. You ready to go?"

"We were just playing a little pinball," he said, shooting a look at Derek and me.

"I was almost winning," I said.

Joseph laughed. "No way."

"Come on," Ashley said, grabbing his elbow. "Let's go announce the big winner."

Joseph's smile to us was apologetic. "Time to morph back into businessman Joe."

"You wear both looks really well," I said, then added, "That was a compliment, by the way."

"Thank you, Brooklyn. I hope you enjoyed the tour."

"I loved it. Really, your home is so unique. Very special. Thank you."

"It was fun for me, too." He looked at Ashley. "Okay, Ashley. Lead the way."

We all followed Ashley, who bounced up the stairs with more energy than a happy six-year-old on a playground. Her energy level was impressive, especially after a long day and a few hours of partying. But then, she was young.

I almost groaned out loud! Hey, I thought, I was young, too! Barely thirty-five. I could bounce . . . if I wanted to.

Derek and I headed for the spacious living room while Joseph and Ashley continued up the stairs, where they would work out the final details of the announcement. I assumed the contest winner was somewhere up there, too.

Back in the living room, we noticed that everyone had started to migrate toward the fireplace at the far end. I saw a microphone set up and figured that was where Joseph would make the announcement.

Alone for the moment, Derek wrapped his arm around me and leaned in close. I felt him slip something into the tiny pocket on my sequined jacket and then he whispered in my ear, "If something happens, go directly to the car, lock the doors, and wait for me."

"What?" I didn't mean to shout.

"Calm down, darling," he murmured, stroking my back.

I tried to breathe and managed to mutter, "Easy for you to say."

What the hell? If something happens? What was supposed to happen?

Still trying to steady my breath, I casually felt inside my pocket and realized that he'd slipped a car key in there. I gazed around the room, trying to be nonchalant about it, and finally noticed that besides adding the microphone, Ashley had made other changes in preparation for the big announcement.

Several rows of folding chairs had been set up so that people could sit while others standing farther back could see over their heads. Along both sides of the room there were now a number of photographers lined up, plus a bunch of other people with notebooks opened and ready. I hadn't noticed so many of them earlier. I assumed they were news reporters and there were enough of them that they couldn't have all been from Joseph's newspaper alone. They had to have come from other outlets around town or around the state.

It made sense, because when it came to Joseph Cabot, everything was newsworthy.

Plenty of other partygoers had their cell phones ready to record the big event.

I noticed something else. A three-panel room divider screen had been set up directly in front of the doorway closest to the fireplace. The divider was arranged so that the audience couldn't see who was coming through the door. It was easy to guess that this was where the finalists would enter.

The excitement was palpable and now that I had a moment to take it all in, my mind zoomed back to what Derek had just said. What was he talking about? What was supposed to happen? Was he worried that someone would attack Joseph? Was anyone else a potential target?

We were standing against the wall nearest the foyer and the crowd was beginning to move closer to the microphone set up at the far end of the room. I touched my pocket and felt for the key. It was quickly becoming my security touchstone.

For the last hour or so I had been in party mode and had completely forgotten that the look-alike contest was the main purpose for the gathering tonight. But now the winner was about to be announced and I wouldn't be surprised if that person's life would be changed, possibly forever. One hundred thousand dollars could alter the trajectory of someone's life, especially if he didn't have a lot of money to start with.

Joseph's newspaper had been hawking the contest for weeks now so I should've been psyched up for the big reveal. But honestly, I had been so completely distracted by this house and that view that I had forgotten all about it. And even though I lived with a man whose business often involved rescuing people from dangerous situations, I normally didn't pay a lot of attention to possible dangers in my daily life.

But after hearing Derek's words of warning barely five minutes ago, I realized that it was time to pull myself back to reality. Anything could happen tonight. I just wished that Derek had given me a clue as to why he was suddenly on Red Alert.

I glanced around the room again and tried to figure out which of the guests and servers were undercover agents. I didn't recognize anyone from his office, but maybe that was a good thing. At least I wouldn't blow anyone's cover, I thought, smirking internally.

I continued to scan the crowd, examining faces and wondering if I could tell from someone's expression whether they were planning to endanger Joseph or anyone else here tonight. But all I could see were people enjoying themselves. Everyone was anticipating the big reveal in a few minutes. Nobody looked as if they were ready to cause havoc.

But how would I know? There had been those threatening phone calls, so someone had to be planning something. Maybe it wouldn't happen here, maybe not tonight, but they were out there waiting to hurt Joseph or his family. And the main person standing in their way was Derek.

And that realization was starting to freak me out.

I reached out to touch Derek's arm and immediately felt safer. I took a few deep breaths and tried to relax.

I saw Ashley step up to the microphone and take a moment to steal one last look at her notes.

Derek was still texting back and forth with his agents so I concentrated on Ashley. She seemed so comfortable standing there, but I thought again about the unhappy expression on her face a while ago.

I pushed that image away as Ashley began to speak.

"Thank you all for being here. I'm Ashley Sharp, events coordinator for the *Clarion*, and I'm thrilled to welcome you to the big reveal! In just a moment we'll announce the winner in the first annual Mark Twain Festival Look-Alike Contest.

"After receiving more than ten thousand entries . . ." She paused while everyone reacted to that impressive number. "Our fantastic judges have reached their final decision. And I know you're going to be blown away by the results."

There was light applause, which masked some of the sounds of movement coming from behind the three-paneled screen in front of the doorway closest to the fireplace. I imagined the machinations going on back there, getting everyone lined up to enter the "stage" area while trying to keep things quiet.

I'd had my doubts about Joseph making the big winner announcement here in his home. The newspaper had turned it into such a huge deal that I thought they might've taken advantage of the larger Covington Library venue for the big reveal.

But now that I was here, seeing all the photographers and reporters and other media representatives in attendance, plus knowing the security issues involved, it had probably been the best solution. Derek's team could keep a better watch on the attendees. And once the photos and news stories were published, it would have the same effect as a big splashy Covington event.

I rubbed my arms, amazed to realize I was nervous to hear who had won. There was that same sort of anticipatory "buzz" I'd felt earlier when Ella and Ingrid made their appearance. And speaking of those two, I glanced around to see if they were nearby, but I didn't see them in the room. They had to be here somewhere, though. They wouldn't miss this big moment. Would they?

For now, Ashley the Magic Marketer was enough of a draw for the photographers, who eagerly pointed their cameras in her direction. The various reporters had gathered around her and were rapidly writing down everything she said.

As she continued to speak, I suddenly heard the sounds of voices hissing in the foyer, just around the corner from where Derek and I were standing.

"How could you betray me?"

"I'm doing the right thing."

"You'll destroy everything!"

"Don't be so dramatic."

Derek and I both leaned closer to the archway and caught Ingrid standing nose to nose with Hobson the butler. She was shaking her finger at the man, then jabbing him in the chest, trying to make a point.

Hobson was growing angrier. He straightened up to his full height and glared at the woman. The look of fury on his face made me wonder whether he intended to squish her like a bug or just punch her in the face. He did neither, simply grabbed her jabbing hand tightly and shoved it away from himself.

"I could kill you for this."

"Calm down, Ingrid," he whispered.

"How can I calm down when you've ruined everything?"

"Me?" he said in a furious whisper. "You've already taken care of that."

"We had an arrangement."

He sniffed derisively. "And now we don't." He turned and stormed off, disappearing down the hallway.

That's when I noticed another man standing in the shadow of the doorway across from me, nervously chewing at his thumbnail. He was fair-haired and in his mid-thirties, I thought, and nice looking. He wore a tailored vest and necktie over a long-sleeved white shirt and black trousers. His outfit was similar enough to Hobson's that I speculated that he might be the under-butler.

There had to be a better term for that job, I thought.

Meanwhile, Ingrid looked mad enough to explode. She remained in the same spot for a few more seconds, literally shaking with anger. Judging from the look on her face, I imagined she would've loved nothing better than to track Hobson down and beat him senseless. And then she spied the under-butler in the doorway. "You!"

He shook visibly.

"Come here."

The man glanced around to make sure Ingrid was actually speaking to him. Then he shuffled from the doorway and walked toward her as though he were heading for the gallows. She grabbed his arm and pulled him in the opposite direction from Hobson.

"What was that all about?" I asked in a hushed tone. "Could you hear what Ingrid said?"

"Yes," Derek said quietly. "She told Hobson that he's ruined everything. I couldn't hear his response."

"And I'm pretty sure I heard him say, 'You've already taken care of that.'"

We stared at each other for a long moment.

"They had an 'arrangement'?" I said.

"None of it sounds good," Derek said.

"No. And did you see the way she was looking at him?"

"Yes, I did."

"I mean, if looks could kill, right?"

"Don't even whisper those words," he warned.

I winced. "They both scare me a little."

"I imagine they must've been arguing about Joseph," he said.

"Or Ella."

"Perhaps," he mused.

"But why was Ingrid so angry?"

I wondered where Ella had gone off to. Maybe she was working behind the scenes, helping the caterers arrange the dessert platters.

I almost snorted at that impossibility.

Derek turned to look in the direction of the fireplace. "Here's Joseph now."

I was glad I'd worn stilettos for the single reason that I could actually see over the heads of some of the crowd. Ashley stepped aside and Joseph moved up to the microphone.

Several men holding professional-looking video cameras moved a little closer and I decided they were from the local news stations.

"The time has come," Joseph said, his voice rich and mellow. "Are you nervous?"

There were titters and chuckles from the crowd.

"Me, too!" he said with a laugh. "And I already know who won!"

Someone shouted, "Put us out of our misery, Joe!"

Joseph laughed. "Okay, okay. I'll introduce our runners-up in a minute, but first, I'm very pleased to name our three distinguished judges for this contest. Please stand up as I introduce you." He quickly named three local celebrities who had been part of the judging committee. One was a chef at one of Derek's and my favorite restaurants. The second was a popular TV weatherman on San Francisco's top-rated news program. The third was a wealthy socialite who was basically famous for being famous and showed up at all the movie premieres and art shows.

The three were in different areas of the living room and they each stood, acknowledged the applause, then sat down.

And then Joseph announced the names of the runners-up. Two men walked around the panel divider and joined Joseph at the microphone. The crowd was relatively quiet as they stared at the two men and studied their features. Both of them actually looked a little like Joseph. It was mainly the hair, I thought.

"Pretty amazing, isn't it?" Joseph said, and grinned at the two men, who wore big smiles as well. And no wonder, I thought, since they were both going to receive a check for five thousand dollars for basically doing nothing.

"And now for the moment we've all been waiting for," Joseph said. "But first, let me remind you that the winner will receive a brand-new wardrobe, from hats and scarves to shoes and socks, courtesy of Brooks Brothers and Macy's Men's Store; grooming products and supplies provided by the Men's Salon at Neiman Marcus; and of course, a year's subscription to the *Clarion*." He chuckled, then took a deep breath. "And he'll also receive . . . One. Hundred. Thousand. Dollars."

I glanced at Derek, who was trying not to scowl. It was definitely a lot of money, which only promised to make his job harder.

At the mention of the money, the audience burst into wild applause, accompanied by screaming and shouting.

It was unreal, I thought, to be able to win all those prizes and money, simply because you looked a certain way. But it was Joseph's money. Well, it probably wasn't all *his* money. It had to have come from some business account and it would all be written off as a business expense.

"Okay, here we go." Joseph was grinning like a ten-year-old kid. "The winner of the first annual Mark Twain Festival Look-Alike Contest is . . . Tom Cantwell! Come on out here, Tom!"

I stood on tiptoe to get a look at the man but everyone else had the same idea, darn it, so once again I couldn't see a thing. Some people were even standing up on the chairs. The still photographers rushed up to get some good shots of both men. This was a major moment and would probably be the front-page story tomorrow.

I knew I would see the man eventually, so I bided my time and applauded along with everyone else.

And then it hit me. The name of the winner of the look-alike contest was . . . Tom Cantwell? I had been reading *The Prince and the Pauper* along with the rest of the city and knew that the name of the "pauper" in the book was Tom Canty. Wow, talk about a coincidence.

Joseph continued. "I want to tell you a little something about Tom. He was born and raised in the Bay Area and he still lives in the city. He's a voracious reader, which we can all relate to."

Since there were a lot of book people in the crowd, that line received a nice round of applause.

"Tom joined the Army when he was eighteen and stayed in for twelve years. He was awarded the Distinguished Service Cross, the Bronze Star, and the Purple Heart. Pretty amazing record, don't you think?"

This time the applause from all of us was thunderous.

I turned to Derek. "Can you see his face?"

But Derek had simply disappeared.

Chapter 7

Concerning the difference between man and the
jackass: some observers hold that there isn't any. But
this wrongs the jackass.

—Mark Twain's Notebook, 1898

I stared at the spot where Derek had been standing a
few seconds ago, then whipped my head around to
check out the room. He was nowhere to be seen.

Where had he gone? And why hadn't he said
something?

I strained to get on my tiptoes again to see over the
heads of the crowd. Had he gone up front to stand with
Joseph? That made the most sense since it had been
his main concern since he'd heard about the threatening phone calls.

But he wasn't there, either.

I took one step up into the foyer to try and get a
better look at the crowd, but I didn't see him anywhere.
Oh God.

No need to panic, I thought. He had to be here
somewhere.

Right?

If something happens, go directly to the car, lock the doors, and wait for me.

Why had he said that to me? Damn it! Now I was completely paranoid.

Seriously, where had he gone? Did something happen? Was this the moment he had been talking about? My heart began to race and I wondered if I should run out to the car as he'd said and lock the doors.

I decided to go the opposite route and chill out. At least for the next five minutes. If I couldn't find Derek after that, then I would panic.

Okay, time to chill. I relaxed my shoulders but noticed that I was wringing my hands.

"That's not chill," I whispered.

Okay, so I wasn't going to chill. And if Derek didn't show up in about ten seconds, I was going to burst into tears or scream. Maybe both. I anxiously felt for the key in my pocket. Yes, it was still there.

This was just stupid. Derek was somewhere in the house, doing something. I strained to see through the packed crowd, but couldn't spot my tall, dark, and dangerous guy standing anywhere in the room.

You're being silly, I told myself. *And now you're talking to yourself.* I took a breath and said, *Calm down. Just calm down.*

What was wrong with me? I was an independent person! Derek didn't have to report his every move to me! I took some more deep breaths. Everything was fine.

I was starting to get angry. Mostly at myself because it wasn't like me to be so freaked out by something like this.

But hey, I wouldn't be so freaked out right now if

Derek hadn't warned me to run to the car and lock all the doors earlier.

So this was all his fault.

That worked for me.

Maybe he had gone down the hall to use the bathroom. I had to admit that was a real possibility. So why hadn't he told me where he was going?

I shook my head in disgust. We weren't joined at the hip! Get over it. He was probably talking to one of his secret operatives in another room. Or maybe he was talking to Hobson.

I sighed. He would show up in a minute and I would feel like a fool for worrying so much. But again, I reminded myself that it was all Derek's fault for making me paranoid.

Maybe he had stepped outside to get some fresh air. No, he wouldn't do that. Maybe he was at the bar, getting another glass of champagne for me. That would be very sweet of him, but I doubted he was doing that, especially since I could see a couple of waiters walking through the crowd with trays of champagne-filled glasses.

So maybe . . . he had simply disappeared.

For the tenth time I checked that the car key was still in my pocket. Yes, it was. Rather than stand here and panic, I needed to move, so I walked quickly through the foyer—or as quickly as I could in these ridiculously strappy stiletto heels. Pushing open a swinging door, I found myself in a huge kitchen filled with caterers and helpers putting service trays together. The under-butler was quietly supervising the activities, going from counter to counter. He watched as two women placed small desserts on at least twelve fancy trays. At the sink, two men were washing dishes and loading the dishwasher with dirty plates. They were all too busy to pay any attention to the guest—me—who was wandering through the kitchen.

At the far end of the room was an open doorway that led to a fully stocked butler's pantry.

Wow, this was a nice space, I thought, then mentally smacked myself. *Focus!*

I zipped through the pantry and saw another door at the opposite end.

Too many darn doors in this place, I thought. But I pushed open the next door and found myself back in the living room. The fireplace was right here and it looked bigger and even more beautiful up close. The room divider was still standing and it blocked everyone's view of me. That was one small blessing.

Joseph himself stood right in front of me, still at the microphone, where he chatted with the winner, who, from the back, appeared to be someone who had fallen on hard times, if his wrinkled shirt and scuffed shoes were any indication.

So this was the guy the judges had chosen as Joseph's look-alike? From where I stood, I could only see his partial profile. I couldn't see any resemblance. Or maybe it was the week's worth of stubble on his face that was throwing me off.

Suddenly someone tapped me on the shoulder. I whirled around to find Derek smiling at me. "Hello, darling."

"You!" I cried.

"Where did you go?" he asked. "I was looking for you."

I wanted to curse him but threw my arms around

him instead. "I—I didn't know where you went." The words came out a little wobbly, but I didn't cry or sniffle or anything. Because, really, that would be insane.

He wrapped his arms around my waist. "I'm sorry, love," he whispered, "but as soon as Joseph announced Tom's name, I knew I had to move in closer. I alerted my operatives as well. I had hoped you would stay where you were and simply enjoy the show. I went back there to find you, but . . . well, here you are."

All the while he spoke to me, he was looking around, aware of everything happening nearby.

"What are you looking for?" I whispered. "Are you expecting trouble?"

"Always."

Later I would give him grief about leaving me in the dark, so to speak. And for making me feel like a fool. For now, I was just relieved that he was here.

Joseph was still talking to Tom at the microphone and the crowd appeared to be mesmerized. They were alternatively laughing and gasping and sighing, and all the while, I still hadn't seen the winner's face.

"Did you meet the winner?" I asked.

Derek nodded his head. "Yes."

"Are you concerned about him?"

"Not particularly."

"So you don't think he'll try to hurt Joseph?"

"No." He frowned. "He's a genial sort."

"But you're guarding him, too?"

He pulled me close and kissed the top of my head. "We'll talk later."

At that moment, Hobson the butler appeared in the doorway behind us. "If you'll pardon me, sir. We're removing the room divider panel."

Derek glanced at me and I knew he was considering whether or not to duck back into the kitchen.

"That's fine," he said with a nod to Hobson. Two men in waiters' uniforms folded the room divider and carried it out of the living room.

Derek and I moved closer to the wall near the fireplace. I realized we were on full display, which wouldn't have bothered me except for the fact that Derek seemed to be expecting danger at any minute.

"It's all been explained in the *Clarion*," Joseph was saying, "but I'll briefly repeat what's going to happen this week. Just like in *The Prince and the Pauper*, Tom and I will change places. Tom will move into my rooms upstairs and will take on many of the duties that I normally perform at home each week."

"Dude," someone in the audience called.

It was Tom's turn to chuckle. "I know, right?"

"Totally." The guy in the audience sounded like my dad, who was a diehard Grateful Dead fan. It sounded like Tom was, too, and it seemed that he'd thought to bring a friend along for moral support.

Joseph continued, "Tom lives in an SRO in the Tenderloin, otherwise known as a single room occupancy, so we've made the decision not to invade that space. Instead I will be moving to an unknown location, where I will perform janitorial services for the next four days."

The room exploded with laughter.

"No way!" a woman cried.

"You're going to be a janitor?" someone said. "Get real!" And they howled with laughter.

"It's not much of a hardship," Joseph insisted mildly,

"considering the kind of *real* work so many people do every day."

I glanced around at the people who had spoken out and had the strongest desire to smack them upside the head! There was nothing wrong with working as a janitor. In fact, we'd all be in a lot of trouble if the janitors of the world went on strike.

I suppose I was a little sensitive because years ago I'd spent several summers working as a housemaid in an exclusive Sonoma hotel. It was hard work, and to be honest, there were times when I really hated some of the snooty attitudes I encountered. But I made enough money to pay for my books for three semesters of college, and that was what mattered to me at the time.

Also, Derek and I knew that Joseph had spent a few years after college working with a charitable foundation to rebuild houses that had been devastated by storms. Would that be considered menial labor by these people?

I could feel myself getting more riled up by the snobbish reactions of the crowd and I had to talk myself down. *Deep breaths*, I thought. At that very moment, Derek slipped his arm through mine and I could've kissed him as I felt a wave of calm envelop me.

People did whatever they had to do to get by in life, I thought. And as if he had overheard my silent rant, Joseph held up his hand to quell the crowd. "As Bob Dylan might say, we're all 'gonna have to serve somebody.' So this will be my way of serving for the next few days."

"Bet you a thousand dollars you won't last that long," someone shouted.

Joseph grinned at the speaker. "All proceeds from side bets will go toward the Covington Library's Education Fund." He bowed. "We thank you for your generosity."

That was clever thinking on Joseph's part and the party guests loved it.

Someone else guffawed. "If you moved into that SRO, where would you hide your butler?"

"If you recall the story, it's Tom who receives the services of a butler."

Anyone who'd lived in San Francisco for any amount of time knew that there were dozens of SRO buildings all over the city, especially in the Tenderloin and Mission districts. Most of the buildings were large, fifteen to twenty stories tall, with dozens of single rooms on every floor. Many of the residents had to share a bathroom down the hall.

Some of the buildings acted as halfway houses for folks who had recently been released from jail and were required to check in with a manager every day. Others were simply low-rent housing for people down on their luck. SROs weren't exactly a happy place to live, but they were light-years better than sleeping on the streets.

Joseph ignored the rest of the comments and appeared ready to wrap up his speech. "Now, Tom and I will be going upstairs to my suite, where we'll get him all spruced up and ready for his first photo op. But I won't be leaving you alone down here. Ashley will be on hand to answer any questions while I'm gone."

"How about a quick photo op?" one of the newsmen asked.

Tom struck a silly pose and the audience laughed.

"At least he has a sense of humor," I murmured. He would need it with this crowd.

Derek nodded. "All I know is that Joseph likes him. That says a lot."

Then Joseph stepped away from the microphone and waved his hand at Tom. "Ready to go?"

"Sure," Tom said.

"I'll introduce you to some of these folks as we head for the elevator."

"Sounds good to me," Tom said gruffly. "I'm a people person."

Joseph returned to the microphone. "One more thing, folks. You're going to want to stick around for the big reveal, so we've laid out a nice spread in the dining room for everyone to enjoy. The cocktail bar is open, and you're welcome to wander downstairs to the game room or out to the terrace to enjoy the cool evening and view. That's how I like to spend my time when I'm able to."

With Tom close at hand, Joseph walked straight over to Derek and me.

And that's when I got my first real look at Tom Cantwell. He wore a scruffy pair of old Levi's and an ill-fitting sports jacket. His hair was long and wavy and unkempt, but he still managed to convey a sense of composure.

Joseph introduced Tom to me and I shook his hand. "It's good to meet you, Mr. Cantwell. Congratulations on winning the contest."

"Hey, thanks, Brooklyn. Cool name. And a great city." He grinned.

"My parents thought so," I said, smiling back at him. "I hope this week is good for you."

"I hope so, too." He gave me a curious look. "Joseph said you're a bookbinder. What does that mean?"

"Basically it means that I refurbish old books that have fallen on hard times."

His smile was mischievous. "Maybe you can help me out then. I could use some refurbishing."

I smiled back, delighted by his comment. "I usually work with paper and leather, but I'm always open to new experiences."

He patted my arm. "You're a good girl, Brooklyn. I like you."

I stared at him for a long moment. Despite his disheveled appearance, Tom carried himself with an odd sort of dignity that I found appealing. "I like you, too, Mr. Cantwell."

"It's Tom," he said. "Just Tom."

"All right." I nodded. "Take care, Tom."

"Words to live by," he murmured, and winked at me. Then Joseph led him toward the elevator, stopping to chat briefly with another group of people.

I could hear some of the guests commenting on how much Tom looked like Joseph. I hadn't seen it, but maybe I had concentrated too much on his clothing and his scruffy beard and shaggy hair.

I could hear the conversation Tom and Joseph were having with the other group. "Nah, I didn't enter the contest myself. A friend of mine sent in the application on my behalf."

"That was some friend," a woman said.

"Yeah, my buddy Wyatt," Tom said. "He thought I might have a chance. Guess I'll have to split the money with him."

"Woohoo!" a man hollered.

"Aw, rats, Wyatt must've heard me," Tom said, and everyone laughed.

Joseph stopped at the archway and checked his watch. "Okay, folks. We'll see you in an hour."

He walked into the den, where the elevator stood. Tom signaled to his buddy Wyatt to join him. Derek intended to stay close to Joseph and I intended to stay close to Derek, so we followed.

At that moment, Hobson walked from the foyer into the den.

"There you are, Hobson," Joseph said jovially. "Let me introduce you to Tom Cantwell."

Hobson's expression froze, then he scowled in a way that must've intimidated hundreds of housemaids. "I know who he is."

Joseph shrugged off his words and turned to Tom. "This is Hobson. He'll be your butler for the week."

"Nice to meet you, Hobson." Tom turned to Joseph. "But seriously, man. What am I supposed to do with a butler? No offense, Hobson."

I started to smile, but Hobson's intense expression stopped me.

"I take no offense from you, sir." Despite the words, Hobson managed to look down his nose at both Tom and Joseph. Maybe it was his natural expression, his "resting butler face," so to speak.

"But surely," Hobson continued, "if you hope to emulate Mr. Joseph for even a week, you would be wise to use the services of a butler. I am not available, but Mr. Leland can help you."

He sounded like a character out of a Regency drama, but since I liked Regency dramas, I couldn't complain. The butler took hold of Joseph's arm and pulled him a few feet away from Tom. I thought maybe he wanted to speak privately, but then he didn't bother to lower his voice. "I have no intention of leaving your side so I suggest that you instruct Leland to attend to Mr. Tom's needs."

Wyatt turned to Tom. "Hear that? You got needs, man."

Tom smiled at his friend, but shook his head. "No, I don't."

"Look," Joseph said easily. "Let's all just play by the rules. Tom will take my place until the festival ends, meaning that he will live here in this house and enjoy all of the privileges that that entails, including the use of my butler, my chef, and my driver, if necessary. I, on the other hand, will live a simpler life for the same amount of time. I'll do some manual labor each day, which won't kill me, and at the end of the festival, we'll compare notes and see what lessons we learned."

"Sounds fair enough," Tom said.

Hobson cleared his throat. "But I never agreed to abide by those rules." He leaned in close to Joseph. "I've told you that I won't work for anyone else." He waved his hand toward Tom. "And I told you why."

"And I told you to go to hell," Joseph replied through clenched teeth. "We both know too much about each other to continue this fight."

"I know enough to ruin you," Hobson snarled.

I had to admit I was shocked. Up until that moment Hobson had been as snooty as usual, but now he was actually threatening his employer. And Joseph sounded so angry. I'd never seen him lose his temper, but he was close to it right now. And I couldn't blame him.

The two men stared at each other heatedly, then Joseph's expression changed to puzzlement. "Why are you doing this?"

Hobson sniffed with resentment. "How many times must I continue to repeat myself?"

Joseph's lips were pressed together in an irritated line. Finally he cut off the conversation by turning to Tom. "Let's go."

Wyatt pulled Tom up close and whispered, "You don't need a butler, man. I'll help you put your pants on."

Tom snickered loudly enough to draw Hobson's attention. The butler glared at him and Wyatt maneuvered himself between Hobson and Tom. Shaking his finger at the butler, he said, "Watch yourself, Hobsie."

Then Wyatt pushed Tom into the elevator behind Joseph and he scurried to join his friend in the small space.

Joseph held the door open and watched Hobson brush his shirt and gather his wits. Then he straightened his shoulders, sniffed imperiously, and walked out of the room.

With Hobson gone, Joseph stared at Derek and me. "Well, now you know that my butler is a bigger snob than I am."

Derek merely raised an eyebrow. "Are you all right?"

"I'm fine," Joseph muttered. "Can you have one of your people keep an eye on Tom?"

"Already done," Derek said.

"Thank you." Joseph gave him a quick nod. "And maybe get someone else to keep an eye on Hobson. Lord knows what he plans to do next."

"I'll alert my men."

"Appreciate it. I'll have Leland take over Hobson's duties for now." The elevator door slid shut.

I looked up at Derek. "Aren't you going up there?"

"I've already got three men and a manicurist up there."

"Sounds like a movie title."

Derek chuckled, then sighed. "I just hope none of the reporters got wind of those threats."

"I hope not," I said. "It wouldn't be good for Joseph."

"No."

"I didn't realize that Hobson was so adamant about staying with Joseph. It made me feel bad for Tom."

"I believe Joseph did, too."

"Oh, for sure." I slipped my arm through Derek's. "The two men seem to have a few secrets between them."

And I had no doubt that if some savvy reporter had witnessed the scene that had just transpired, they would grab on to that juicy tidbit and start digging until they uncovered all of Joseph's secrets. For safety's sake, I checked the den door and found it was still securely closed.

"I told you that Hobson used to work for Joseph's father," Derek said.

"Yes."

"He was quite young when he started," he continued, "so I imagine he and Joseph got along well from the beginning."

"They go back a long way together."

"Yes."

"I've heard stories about Joseph's father," I said. "He was supposed to be a pretty bad guy."

"He was a criminal," Derek said under his breath. "Definitely a bad guy. And that may be another reason why Joseph bonded with Hobson. The man might've served as his protector."

"What did the father do?"

Derek sighed and I could tell he was disturbed by everything that had just happened. "Let's talk about this later. I'd like to make sure that things are going well with the rest of the guests."

"Okay." Was it wrong of me to want to hear some gossip about Joseph's father? Probably. So I would just have to be patient.

We walked back into the living room. Some of the guests were still gobbling down those amazing appetizers and others had moved on to the dessert platters. And there was still champagne.

We made our way through the crowd and over to the bay window. Derek ran his hands up and down my arms. "Are you all right?"

I thought about it and admitted, "I'm a little shaken. But I'll get over it. So I take it Leland is the under-butler."

"Yes," he said. "Leland Bingham. We ran a complete background check on him. He was trained at the International Butler Academy in the Netherlands. Highly qualified, apparently."

"Good to know." I gazed up at him. "Do you really have a manicurist on your payroll?"

He laughed. "Of course."

"I hope they're board certified."

He kissed my cheek. "Naturally."

"You think you're pretty smart, don't you?"

"I try."

"Okay. I'm glad." I let out a breath. "That was upsetting."

"Yes, it was." He snagged a glass of ice-cold champagne from a passing waiter and handed it to me. I readily accepted it and took a hearty swig in an attempt to quell my nerves.

The party chatter grew louder, which made sense now that the initial big reveal had occurred and everyone had seen Tom for the first time. Somehow I had thought that a lot of people would be gone by now, but why would they go when they could continue to quaff champagne, nibble on luscious goodies, and trade gossip with the other guests?

Many of the reporters were on their cell phones, texting updates to their newsrooms and anxiously awaiting the grand finale to the story. The makeover.

I personally couldn't wait to see Tom's makeover. But I was still disturbed by Hobson's odd remarks. Where had that attitude come from?

It made me wonder if Hobson's negative attitude was the real reason why Derek and his agents had been hired to keep an eye on Joseph. I couldn't imagine that the normally devoted butler would actually defy his employer. If he did, it would mean the end of his job. So what had happened to change his attitude?

I suddenly remembered the argument Hobson had had with Ingrid earlier. I tried to remember their words to each other.

"You'll ruin everything."

"I could kill you for this."

Was their argument somehow connected to the one between Hobson and Joseph? Would Ingrid complain to Joseph about the butler? That couldn't be good for

Hobson, could it? But then, maybe Hobson argued with everyone.

But how smart was it to argue with your employer? Joseph had seemed angry enough to throw Hobson out of the house and I had to wonder why the butler had continued to insist.

"I won't work for anyone else. And I told you why."

"And I told you to go to hell."

Why was Hobson so unwilling to work with Tom for four measly days? What was the big deal? None of it made sense.

More importantly, I thought with a sigh, it was none of my business. But Joseph had looked so hurt by Hobson's words, it made my heart ache. I wanted to know what that was all about.

I glanced up at Derek, saw the glint of resolve in his eyes. That's when I knew that he was just as determined as I was to find the reasons behind the arguments, knowing that angry words could easily escalate to disastrous actions.

Chapter 8

Against the assault of Laughter nothing can stand.
—Mark Twain, "The Chronicle of Young Satan,"
Mysterious Stranger Manuscripts

I checked my wristwatch. It was about nine o'clock.

"You know you can go home at any time," Derek said.

"Aren't you staying until the very end?"

"Of course. At this point I'm here to provide security for Joseph so essentially I'm on the job. But that shouldn't have to affect you."

"If you're staying, then so am I." *Even if I have to sneak into the library and take a nap*, I thought. And that would hardly be the worst thing in the world.

Derek held out his champagne glass and clicked it against mine in a mini-toast. "Thank you, darling."

I stretched up and kissed his cheek. "You're very welcome."

His lips twisted in a rueful smile. "I can tell you're worrying and I know why, so let's change the subject. Tell me what you thought of Tom."

I smiled. "I liked him. He comes across as a normal, salt-of-the-earth guy who somehow found himself down on his luck and is making the best of it. He's smart, and from the few things he said, he seems to have a fairly good handle on this contest situation. He's not taking it too seriously, which is probably a good thing."

"He does come across as sincere." He sipped his champagne. "Although we've been fooled before."

"I don't think he's trying to pull the wool over anyone's eyes. I'm concerned, though." I frowned. "I hope Joseph gives him some financial advice. One hundred thousand dollars is a nice little chunk of money and it won't last very long if you can't get a handle on it. I mean, what if he blew it on a two-week bender?"

He broke out in a grin. "You sound as if you speak from experience, and yet I would bet you've never been on a bender of any duration in your entire life. Admit it."

"Maybe not," I said defensively. "But I watch public television."

He laughed. "Did I mention that I love you?"

"I love you, too," I said, foolishly pleased to hear him laugh.

He glanced around at the crowd. "It's odd. There are a lot of people here, but we hardly know any of them."

"I haven't seen Ian or Jake in a while. They probably went down to the game room. Ella's probably down there, too. She seemed to be having a good time with them earlier."

"Do you want to join them?"

I thought for a moment. "Maybe in a while. I'm still trying to chill out after those two ugly scenes earlier."

"I believe we're both a bit on edge."

"It was unexpected," I said. "Plus you're basically on duty here and that always makes me a little nervous about your safety." I mentally shook myself. I shouldn't have mentioned it. It wasn't Derek's fault if I tended to freak out once in a while. But the thing was, I didn't tend to freak out! So tonight was special, I guessed. "Pay no attention to me. I'm actually having a pretty good time. I like Joseph, and Tom seems interesting. And this crowd is pretty stellar. But . . ."

"But we have little in common with most of them."

I smiled. "Well, some of them are book lovers."

He smiled. "That counts for something."

I took another big sip of champagne. "Okay, let's liven things up. Tell me a joke."

He grinned, but before he could say another word, Ian and Jake walked up.

"Perfect timing," I said.

Ian grinned. "You two party animals are just the people we've been looking for."

I exchanged a look with Derek, whose eyebrows were quirked in disbelief. I almost laughed. We were so *not* the party animals they were looking for, but I loved them anyway.

"We've been in the game room with Ingrid and Ella," Jake whispered theatrically.

Ian grinned. "So do you want to go outside and gossip?"

"I would love to," I said. "But it's awfully cold."

"They have heaters. And they put a bunch of blankets out on the chairs. You'll be warm enough." Ian pulled his phone out and checked the time. "We still have a good half hour before Joseph and Tom return."

I glanced at Derek. "Want to?"

"I know you do," Derek said amiably. "So let's go."

As we walked to the door, I noticed Derek texting someone. He glanced up. "Just letting my people know where I am."

"Good thinking."

Because it was cold, we had the terrace all to ourselves. I grabbed a blanket and wrapped it around my shoulders. A tray on the nearby coffee table held a full bottle of champagne and numerous glasses. Derek handed out glasses and poured the bubbly liquid into each of ours.

"Thanks, Derek," Ian said.

I took a sip, then the four of us sat down on the two couches that faced each other. "So tell us about your good time with Ella and Ingrid."

"We have to whisper," Ian said. "Don't want any eavesdroppers."

"Yes, please." I nodded vigorously. "We don't want to make any enemies."

"So," Ian said, patting his partner's leg. "Jake, you start."

"Okay. Well, Ella seems sweet," Jake said. "But Ingrid. Look out. She's nasty. And she doesn't take crap from anyone."

Ian frowned at Jake. "I totally agree about Ingrid. I hate to say it, but she's got a bit of a *vicious* streak. Especially when she's losing at pinball."

Jake nodded dramatically. "She really took it out on Ella, poor girl."

"She was doing the same thing at the Covington last night," I said. "She gets really mean."

"Oh, for sure." Ian gave me a meaningful look. "But

the scary thing is, Mama would peel the skin off your face if you came after her baby girl."

"I suppose that's typical," Jake said, then wrapped his arm around Ian. "Happily, that won't happen with us."

I smiled. "You guys aren't a threat to her equilibrium."

"Exactly," Ian said.

"But *you* are," he said, giving me a look.

I winced. "I really got the evil eye from her last night. And I didn't do anything!"

"It was her perception of the situation," Derek said.

"And she was wrong," I grumbled.

He winked at me. "Yes, she was."

Jake grinned. "But we had a good time playing pinball. They're fun to hang out with."

Ian sipped his champagne. "They were in party girl mode. Dishing on everybody here."

"I love them for that alone," Jake admitted. "Except for the aforementioned vicious streak."

I chuckled, then took a quick glance around to make sure we were still alone out here. I was also careful to check that the windows upstairs were all closed, knowing how well sound traveled.

Ian scooted forward in his chair. "So what do we think of Tom?"

Derek's phone beeped just then. He gave me a meaningful look and whispered, "I'll be in the kitchen."

"Okay," I said. "Be careful."

He moved quickly to the door and disappeared inside. I knew he would be happier hanging out with his undercover waiters than listening to Ian and Jake and me dishing the dirt. I had to admit, though, that I wasn't in the mood to hear more about Ingrid and Ella. Still, it was always entertaining to talk to Jake and Ian.

"So," Ian began. "Do we know who was hired to do the fluff-and-fold job on Mr. Tom?"

Jake patted Ian on the knee. "We're in the home of gazillionaire genius Joseph Cabot so you know that he's hired a complete spa staff for Mr. Tom. They'll hose him down and soap him up and shave and coif and wax and buff him to the max. I wouldn't be surprised to find out Tom's having a mani-pedi as we speak."

"He is," I said, and smiled. I knew for a fact that the man was getting a manicure because Derek had an agent assigned to do the job.

"Is it wrong to be jealous?" Ian wondered.

"Not at all," Jake said. "It would be a total gas to be part of the fluffing squad."

"Or to be the one getting fluffed," Ian said.

"They must have a dozen fashion consultants from Brooks Brothers standing by, ready to dress him up to the nines. He'll walk out looking like a million bucks."

"Do you think Joseph is up there supervising?" I asked.

Ian didn't have to think about it. "Absolutely. He won't be able to help himself."

"I wonder if they're videotaping some of it."

"I hope not," I said. "I can't imagine Tom would be happy about that. And I don't think Joseph would be, either."

"No, you're right," Ian said soberly.

"But don't forget," Jake added, "Ashley has her You-Tube channel. She'd probably love to get some snippets of the makeover to share with her followers."

The two men chuckled, then Ian grimaced. "If the bombshells thought they could get away with it, poor Ashley would be dead by morning."

I shivered involuntarily. "I'm going to pretend I didn't hear that one."

"Sorry, sweetie," Ian said, and slapped Jake's arm. "We're behaving very badly."

Jake looked contrite. "I blame the champagne."

"We both need a spanking," Ian said.

I held up my hand. "Stop making me laugh."

"We're sorry," Ian said, and looked at Jake. "Ready to go inside?"

Chilled, he rubbed his arms. "More than ready. You coming, Brooklyn?"

I gazed up at the starry night sky. "I think I'll stay out here for a few more minutes."

Ian checked his watch. "Joseph should be coming down in about ten minutes."

"I'll be there." I watched them walk to the door. "Hey, if you see Derek, tell him I'm still outside enjoying the view."

Ian gave me a thumbs-up. "You got it, sweetie."

Once they were gone, I pulled the blanket tighter. Even though there was a serious chill in the air, it felt good to be out here rather than inside. I sidled up to one of the tall heat lamps and felt the radiant warmth. But the shivers didn't go away. I knew why. Ian's comment about Ashley ending up dead had hit me right in the solar plexus.

I knew the guys were just joking around. And honestly, they were always so funny! It was my own fault for taking it too seriously. But having been around violent death too many times to count, I had a hard time finding jokes about murder funny. And coupled with Derek's dire warning earlier, I had to figure that Joseph had actually been expecting some sort of attack tonight.

The thought made me nervous, but I wasn't about to leave the party. I didn't want to miss seeing Tom's makeover, and Derek and his security team wouldn't be leaving until every guest had gone home and Joseph and his family were safe.

And naturally I wasn't going to leave without Derek.

Which meant that I would be here another hour or two. I told myself that nothing was going to happen here tonight. Derek was in charge and all would be well.

I felt calmer when I gazed up at the sky and a few zillion stars twinkled back at me. Starry skies were a rare sight in a city known for its famous rolling fog banks. The fog here was so prevalent that for several years it even had its own Twitter account. "Karl the Fog" had over three hundred thousand followers, last time I checked.

So to look up and see such a clear sky was as rare a sight as it was beautiful. Still, it was getting colder so I folded up the blanket and headed for the side door. As soon as I walked back into the house, the instant warmth enveloped me.

And once again, the party elves had been busy, most importantly in the foyer, where a large round table had been set up. It was covered with dozens of tasty-looking miniature desserts. Eclairs, Napoleons, fruit pies, cream pies, seven-layer chocolate cake, crème brûlée, delicate fruit tarts, pots de crème, tarte Tatin, an assortment of cookies, and more. An industrial-sized coffee and tea service had been set up, along with fancy porcelain cups and saucers.

I wished they'd had a contest to name every dessert on the table because I was pretty sure I would win.

Minutes after I returned to the living room with a tiny éclair and two delicate Madeleines, Ashley walked in holding a small video camera. It was disconcerting, given the conversation I'd just had with Ian and Jake about videotaping some snippets of the makeover. But she was probably getting ready to tape the moment when Tom was revealed.

The microphone was still set up at the far end of the room and more chairs had been added. I grabbed a chair in the last row while most of the other guests were migrating to the chairs closest to the microphone.

Ashley waited at the far end, wearing an excited grin. "You're all going to want to see the transformation. You won't believe your eyes."

Waiters continued to make their rounds, still carrying champagne flutes and wineglasses, along with small plates of chocolates.

Derek sat down next to me and we both waited with the rest of the crowd until Joseph walked back into the living room. He went straight to the microphone, but didn't say a word, just waited for everyone to stop talking. Some in the crowd were giggling and snickering, so Joseph continued to wait.

Staring at Joseph, I was reminded that he was a very good-looking man. He continued to say nothing so I whispered to Derek, "What's going on?"

"They're about to introduce the new, improved Tom," he said.

"Okay." I watched Joseph, but he didn't speak. After another long moment, Tom walked up and stood next to . . . Joseph? Or was it Tom?

Finally the second man spoke. "Friends, let me reintroduce you to Tom Cantwell."

The man who had walked out first grinned and waved to us. "I'm Tom."

I gasped.

I wasn't alone. A combination of astonishment, delight, disbelief, and confusion showed on everyone's faces. And then everyone began to talk at once.

"Are you kidding me?" one guy asked.

A woman kept repeating, "No way. No way."

"This is impossible."

"You just blew my mind."

"Oh my," a middle-aged woman with surgically enhanced lips whispered. "He's so beautiful."

"Of course he is," another woman declared. "He's the spitting image of our own beautiful Joseph."

Joseph heard their comments. "Priscilla, Madge," he said with a groan. "Get a grip."

One of the women seemed flustered that Joseph had overheard her. "Well, it's true. I mean, well, you're a fine-looking man, Joseph. But Tom. He's . . . well, look at him. I mean, he looks just like you."

The way she said it might've seemed inane, but she spoke the truth. Tom Cantwell was incredibly handsome now. He wore a black silk shirt tucked into elegant black wool slacks. His belt was black, of course, with a tasteful silver buckle, and he wore black socks and black leather loafers that looked as soft as butter.

Unlike an hour ago, Tom was now smooth-shaven.

I was surprised at what a difference it made. His salt-and-pepper hair had been cut and styled and was brushed back off his face. He looked as handsome as any movie star—which was exactly what I'd always said about Joseph.

Even from halfway across the room I could see that his fingernails had been cleaned and buffed. Derek's agent had done a really good job with the manicure.

"Holy moly," another woman said, sounding befuddled. "You guys could be twins."

Another man in the back shouted, "You need ancestry.com, Joe. I think you've found your long-lost brother."

Joseph just laughed. "That would be great if I'd ever had a brother. But I've got to admit that Tom comes pretty close as far as looks are concerned."

"It's uncanny," someone said.

"You've got a doppelgänger."

Ashley handed her camcorder to an assistant, who continued to record as Ashley stepped to the microphone. "Okay, folks. We've come to the end of tonight's festivities. Here's a quick rundown of the Mark Twain Festival events over the next few days. Tomorrow on the Embarcadero it's casino night on a riverboat! Tuesday in Golden Gate Park is our Jumping Frog Contest. It's going to be wild—and there will be prizes."

"Bring your own frog?" somebody shouted.

She laughed. "No, we'll have frogs for everyone."

There was some applause, then she continued. "Monday at the Covington Children's Museum, we'll be borrowing from Tom Sawyer and painting the fence."

"What happens to Joseph and Tom after tonight?"

"Thank you for caring," Joseph drawled, and we all laughed. "Tonight after everyone leaves, I will be driven to an undisclosed location where I'll stay for the next . . ." He checked his wristwatch. "Four days."

"With or without your driver?"

Joseph made a face. "I'm playing the pauper, so no driver. I'll have to find another means of transportation." He looked at Tom. "How do you normally get around the city?"

Tom glanced back at Joseph. "I usually walk, but every so often I'll spring for a bus ride."

Joseph grinned and patted his stomach. "I can use the exercise."

"Oh, come on," one of the women said. "You could be going to the Ritz-Carlton. How would we know?"

Before Joseph could comment, Ashley piped up. "Oh, you'll know. We've invited all the people of San Francisco to take part in the contest by trying to find Joseph. If you spy him somewhere, you're welcome to e-mail us a photo and tell us where you saw him. You could win a thousand dollars."

"I'm just going to follow your car," someone said.

Joseph laughed. "Good luck with that."

"And thanks to Tom," Ashley added, "we'll be writing up a daily column featuring the best walking routes around the city."

Joseph smiled and said, "That's our promo queen."

Ashley beamed.

"So what about the prince?" someone asked.

"Glad you asked," Joseph said. "Starting tonight, Tom will officially reside in my home. He'll sleep in my bed. Eat in my kitchen, watch my television. He can even read my mail. And of course, he'll have the services of my butler, Leland." He looked across the room at the foyer. "Isn't that right, Hobson?"

Derek and I glanced over at the foyer, where Hobson stood watching. He grimaced severely and said, "Harrumph."

"Hobson has officially registered his approval," Joseph said cheerfully.

Everyone laughed and applauded, but Derek was already out of his chair and running into the foyer. And when I looked back at Joseph, I couldn't see any laughter reaching his eyes.

I jumped up and followed Derek, who clutched Hobson's arm. The butler now wore a look of complete innocence. But for the first time I noticed that he was holding a baseball bat.

"He's got a bat!" I cried.

Three of Derek's men dashed into the room at that very moment. All of them had their weapons drawn.

"It's all right," Derek said, but he still had a firm grip on Hobson's arm.

One of the men grabbed the bat from Hobson. "You won't be needing that."

"I haven't done anything," Hobson protested. "You're overreacting."

Derek said, "That's what happens when you come in carrying a baseball bat after threatening your employer."

Then he turned to his agents and said, "Thank you." He nodded at them to back off.

It was clear that Derek and his people had expected Hobson to react badly to Joseph's announcement after hearing him yell at Joseph earlier. Even though he'd brought a bat with him, this time the butler hadn't done a thing but make a face. So far. But what would happen when Joseph tried to leave the house and Hobson was forced to stay behind?

I guessed we would have to wait and see what Hobson intended to do. Would he endanger Joseph? Or would he take out his frustrations on Tom?

Obviously, Derek wouldn't let anything bad happen to either man.

I had been daydreaming about finding a quiet spot to take a little nap until Derek was ready to go home, but there was no way I could take a nap now. Things were just starting to get interesting.

Chapter 9

Everyone is a moon, and has a dark side which he never shows to anybody.

—Mark Twain, *Following the Equator*

Once the excitement in the foyer had ended, Joseph finished his speech at the microphone by bringing it all back to *The Prince and the Pauper*. "This look-alike contest is all about that book. So read the book, folks. You'll be glad you did."

Ashley popped up to the microphone. "And be sure to check the festival schedule in the *Clarion* every day for events and happenings. We hope to see you out there."

The guests applauded and then stood and began to walk toward the foyer. Several housemaids waited along the wall with guests' coats slung over their arms.

It took about a half hour before the crowd was thinned down to essential staff and a few others, like me and Derek. I was surprised to see Ella and her mother lounging on the couch, drinking champagne. I'd barely seen them during the party, but they seemed ready to party now. I couldn't figure them out.

While I dutifully approached them, Derek left to track down Joseph.

Ella smiled at me. "Brooklyn, I've barely seen you all evening. I hope you've had a nice time."

"I did. It was a lovely party. Thank you, Ella."

Ella nodded. "You're welcome, dear."

Ingrid stared at me, scowling as if I'd kicked her puppy. I just couldn't figure her out, unless she was still steamed about me taking a walk with Ella at the Covington Library the night before. If that was the case, then the lady had serious mental issues. I didn't know how Joseph could stand to have her staying in the same house with him.

But in-laws. What could you do?

While Ella and I traded superficial compliments and chatted about tomorrow's festival activities, I allowed my mind to drift to other thoughts. It was ironic to think that Tom Cantwell was the only halfway normal person who would be sleeping in this house tonight. I hoped that Derek planned to have one of his agents staying in Tom's suite with him and a few more scattered around the house. With Ingrid and Hobson around, I was worried about the look-alike's safety.

And now I wondered if Ella or Ingrid had overheard the confrontation between Joseph and Hobson earlier. Were they aware of Hobson's strong opposition to Joseph's participation in the look-alike contest?

Of course they were! Having overheard Ingrid's argument with Hobson shortly before he lashed out at Joseph, I had to believe that the two women knew how Hobson felt about being forced to leave Joseph's side.

The butler was a pain in the neck. He was a high-handed stickler for propriety and it was becoming crystal clear that he ruled this house and the family in a much stricter fashion than Joseph ever would've. Of course, I had to admit that Joseph was partly to blame since he seemed to put up with his butler's domineering attitude. Maybe it was just easier to let the man have his way than to constantly argue with him.

Derek had said that Hobson used to work with Joseph's father. I wondered if maybe that had something to do with Joseph allowing Hobson so much latitude.

Did Hobson really know something that could destroy Joseph? What in the world was that all about? And why was Hobson so freaked out about working with Tom for a few days? Why was he so adamant that Joseph couldn't go without him for a few nights? How could a butler become so angry over something as trivial as a look-alike contest based on a book by Mark Twain? The contest promised to introduce more people and money to the Covington Library, so how could anyone argue with that?

Derek walked back into the living room. "Hello, ladies."

Ella and Ingrid both sat up and batted their eyelashes. They said a few words to him and finally I grabbed his hand. "If you'll excuse us, I wanted to show Derek something."

We strolled away and he chuckled. "That was subtle."

"Sorry. I've hit my limit for gracious banter."

We stepped inside the deserted library and I turned to him. "You talked to Hobson. What did he tell you?"

Derek shook his head. We sat down on the sofa and he spoke quietly. "Apparently they've had this argument before. Hobson is insisting on staying with Joseph because he says he's so devoted to him."

"That's it? I don't believe it."

"I don't, either." Frustrated, Derek ran his hand through his hair. "They were clearly fighting over something much more serious than whether or not Hobson would act as butler to Tom this week."

"It sounded like an old argument they'd had before."

"Frankly, I thought Hobson had a point when he suggested that Leland Bingham take care of Tom this week."

"That makes sense," I said. "And that's what they're going to do. But Hobson is still very angry. He doesn't even want to be in the same house with Tom." And that annoyed me. Was it because Tom didn't have a lot of money? If so, that was a clear indication that Hobson was prejudiced. I thought about that for another moment. "I don't get it. Remember that argument Hobson was having with Ingrid?"

"Yes." Derek thought about it. "They were very angry with each other, but it didn't seem to have anything to do with Tom."

"No. Their disagreement must've had more to do with Joseph or Ella."

Derek sighed and leaned back against the cushion. "There are too many factions fighting in this house."

"I agree. But I still don't believe that Hobson's only issue is that he wishes to be the one to take care of Joseph." I scowled. "He's a butler. He doesn't get everything his way."

Derek smiled. "Darling, you're obviously unfamiliar with the hierarchy of the British butler system."

I shook my head. "Obviously. Seriously, though, Hobson should do whatever Joseph tells him to do."

"I happen to agree," he said. "And I explained to

Hobson that on a more practical level, Joseph is playing the role of Pauper. He can't be seen to have a butler waiting on him. There are going to be reporters sniffing all over town to catch Joseph in the act of *not* being a pauper."

"What did Hobson say to that?"

"Hobson thinks the whole prince and pauper thing is a bunch of nonsense." Derek glanced at me. "He didn't use that word."

"No, I wouldn't think so."

"A few days ago when they realized that Tom was going to be the winner, Joseph agreed that he would stay in the SRO." Derek shook his head. "Tom was the one who balked because he said the place was a hellhole and nobody should have to stay there who didn't have to."

"But isn't that the whole point of the exercise? You know, the prince should experience the hardships that other people deal with every day."

"Yes. But in this case Tom was adamant, and I see his point. The change would involve a lot of government red tape just to get Joseph into the place, even for a few days. That's when Joseph decided he would stay at the Covington and put more emphasis on the fact that he was carrying out the various janitorial chores rather than where he was sleeping."

"I'm excited that he'll be at the Covington! I can visit him when I'm there for my bookbinding sessions."

"But even when Joseph was going to stay at the SRO, Hobson was insisting on staying there with him."

I blinked. "Isn't that taking the whole manservant thing a little too far?"

"Indeed it is. And not only are the rooms too small for both men, but my people wouldn't have been able to provide any security for him."

"And Joseph's security is your main objective."

"And it should've been Hobson's as well," he said.

I frowned. "Hobson is a little bent, isn't he?"

"He takes his job very seriously."

"That's being generous."

He raised an eyebrow. "I suppose it is."

I decided to change the subject. "So what were you all talking about just now?"

"I wanted to tell Joseph what we overheard. He reminded me that the contest is very important to the newspaper and to the citizens of San Francisco. I honestly didn't realize how much the whole city is wrapped up in the contest."

"I see it mentioned all over the Internet and social media."

"And apparently the rules are iron-clad," Derek said. "Joseph is honor-bound to abide by every one of them. And he's okay with allowing people to track him down and submit photos and commentary on what they see. It's an integral part of the look-alike contest. And so are the prizes."

"I know," I said. "The whole thing is based in social media. That's Ashley's handiwork."

"I'm getting that." He paused. "It's not that he would be sued or lose his business, but it's possible that if anyone catches Hobson helping Joseph, he could get reamed in the press so badly that his reputation would suffer. He was even wondering if the newspaper would survive."

"Oh, come on," I said. "It wouldn't go that far."

"Maybe not. But they have those silly hashtags on every page and everyone seems to be getting into it."

"I'm aware," I said. "Hashtag *TwainFestival*. Hashtag *PrinceandPauper*."

"That's the world we're living in."

"I know." I yawned. "Sorry."

"We can leave, darling."

"Are you sure?"

"Yes. I'm tired as well."

"But what about Joseph?"

"I'm sending three men to drive him and stay with him. And I'm leaving five men here at the house. They'll keep an eye on Hobson and the family and they'll make sure Tom is safe."

"So we can go?"

He smiled. "We can go."

"I hope they're not followed."

"It's taken care of."

I looked up at him and smiled. Of course he'd taken care of all the contingencies.

He helped me up and we walked into the foyer, where I was surprised to see the housemaid standing there with my coat. "I hope you haven't been waiting here this whole time," I said with a smile.

"I don't mind, ma'am. Have a good evening."

"Thank you, Edith. You, too." I felt like a jerk for making her wait.

But you had to figure that handing out coats was probably an easier task than washing dishes or cleaning the bathrooms.

"I'm so ready to go to sleep." As we walked through

the crisp night air to the car, I had the niggling sensation that I had forgotten something important. But I was too tired, and my feet were too sore, to give it much thought.

"It's been a long evening."

Once we were in the car, though, I turned to him. "I know Hobson was trying to convince you that their argument was all about the contest, but we heard him threatening Joseph. And I caught his murderous expression a few times."

"Joseph isn't taking any of their arguments very seriously by the way," Derek said. "He said he forgives and forgets."

"Maybe he's used to it," I said. "Maybe Hobson is always arguing with him. And with Ingrid, too," I added. "But I'm not used to it so I'm not going to forgive him so quickly. And I'm certainly not going to forget it."

"Darling," Derek murmured, the sound of his voice like dark silk. "I never forget."

I slept badly and woke up alone Sunday morning. I hurried to get dressed and then jogged out to the kitchen, where Derek was pouring a cup of coffee. "Oh, thank goodness you're still here."

"And good morning to you, too." He handed me the coffee mug and kissed me. I melted a little, especially when I realized there were warm croissants sitting in a small basket on the counter.

"Oh my God, croissants?" I whispered. "I love you, Derek."

He gazed at me for a long moment. "You love baked goods."

I smiled. "You're right. I do. Thank you."

He leaned against the kitchen counter, watching me. "You didn't sleep well."

I took a first bracing sip of coffee. "I realized in the middle of the night that I completely forgot my tote bag at Joseph's house. I'll need it for my bookbinding session at noon."

"So you've got to pick it up this morning." He set down his coffee cup. "I'll go with you."

I was hoping he would offer. "If you're too busy . . ."

"It's Sunday and I'm free to spend the morning with you. I'd also like to go by and check in with my men. They were keeping a watch on Hobson. He was quite out of sorts last night."

"I know. I want to make sure Tom is okay."

"I believe Tom is more resourceful than we think," he said, "but we should check on him, as well."

"Are your agents still in the house?"

"Three of them left this morning."

I blinked. "They left?"

"Yes. But there are still two agents staying there. And the other three will be back for the evening shift."

"Okay." I let out a breath. "And everyone made it through the night?"

"Yes."

"Good." I stared at my half-eaten croissant and sighed. "I can be ready to leave in two seconds."

He laughed and picked up his coffee cup. "I'll give you ten minutes."

I breathed more easily. "Thanks."

"Darling, are you sure you're ready to go out again tonight? It's the Riverboat Casino event."

"Oh wow. I completely forgot." I brushed my hair away from my face, trying not to feel too beaten down.

"Don't worry. I'm still a little sleepy, but I'll rally. All I need is, you know, this croissant and another cup of coffee. Then I'll be fine."

He laughed. "That's my girl."

We each drove our own cars to Sea Cliff since I would have to leave for my bookbinding class while Derek met with his two agents stationed at the house. We both found parking within a block of Joseph's home.

There was a marine layer this morning so the air was cool. Instead of a jacket, I had worn a puffy vest over a turtleneck.

Even in a thick parka and blue jeans, Derek still managed to look dangerous and drool-worthy. But maybe that was just me.

I rang the bell, and we waited at the front door for a full minute before Hobson opened the door, looking rather dapper in black trousers with a matching vest over a pin-striped shirt and a paisley tie. "Commander," he said. "Good morning."

"Good morning, Hobson," Derek said.

Hobson inclined his head toward me. "Ms. Wainwright. Won't you please come in?"

"Thank you," I said, and we followed him into the house.

The first thing we noticed in the foyer was a ladder and a toolbox.

Hobson sighed. "I beg your pardon for this inconvenience. Stipley was just changing a lightbulb."

"It's no problem," I said, and stared up at the handyman. He looked about thirty years old, tall and thin with straight hair that was long enough to flop over his eyes. His faded jeans had some rips across the knees and his flannel shirt was torn at the elbows. His work boots, on the other hand, were brand new and expensive. He looked as though he were going for the shabby chic handyman look. It worked for him.

"For God's sake, Stipley," Hobson needled. "What is taking you so long?"

"Now look, Hobs," the thin man said. "This chandelier is ancient and these lightbulbs are fragile. They don't always fit so perfectly."

"Well, hurry it up," Hobson muttered.

"Yeah, yeah." Stipley dropped the bulb into the socket and began to twist it slowly. He made a grunting sound with the effort. "I've gotta finesse this sucker . . . hold on . . . crap. It broke."

Hobson's face turned red with seething fury. "Stipley, you are a disgrace! Take your ladder and get out of here. You can try to fix the lightbulb later when we don't have guests."

"If you say so, man."

"I do say so! And if you don't like it, you can quit."

Stipley shook his head as he climbed down off the ladder. Instead of skulking off to sulk, he walked right up to Hobson and stared him in the face. "I *don't* like it. And I don't like you. But I don't quit on Mr. Cabot." Then he picked up his toolbox and walked out of the foyer.

"Stipley!" Hobson shouted, glaring at the ladder. "Get this thing out of here!"

The handyman walked back into the foyer. "Jeez, Hobson, take a chill pill. I was just coming back for the ladder." He quickly folded up the ladder and carried it out of the room.

There was complete silence until Derek finally said,

"I trust the household has recovered from last night's festivities."

Hobson took a deep breath and exhaled slowly. "We're all doing quite well this morning, sir."

Apparently some of us were doing better than others, I thought. Hobson seemed completely out of his mind with rage. Stepping forward, I said, "I'm afraid I left my tote bag here last night and I'll need it for work today."

Hobson frowned. "I didn't see anything like that, but I can look around."

"You don't have to trouble yourself. I left it tucked away in the library."

He swept his arm out. "Then please go right ahead."

I smiled at Derek. "I'll be right back." I took the doorway that led down the hall to the library, where I'd met with the Covington donors the night before. The room was just as impressive with light pouring through the windows. I knew I shouldn't take the time to peruse, but I couldn't resist. I scanned the nearest shelf and saw that there was a complete set of Jane Austen's books, gorgeously bound in navy blue morocco leather. I carefully pulled out *Sense and Sensibility* and saw a miniature portrait of Jane Austen encased in glass and embedded in the leather. It was like looking at a tiny work of art.

I couldn't just walk away. I had to take the time and look at each of the covers to see what the bookbinder had done. Sure enough, each book cover held a tiny piece of artwork just like the first one.

Oh God, I coveted them all.

"Better get out of here before you do something unlawful," I muttered. "Like steal the whole set."

Laughing at myself, I walked over to the couch, knelt down, and felt around underneath. I wasn't sure why I'd worried that the bag would be gone, but it was right where I'd left it. I pulled it out and checked that the book was in the same state I'd left it in. Of course it was. I pushed myself up from the floor and stood, slipped the book back into the tote and secured the bag over my shoulder, then returned to the foyer.

"You found it?" Derek asked.

"Yes." I patted the leather bag. "Right where I left it."

"Excellent," he said, and winked at me.

His wink made me wonder what I had missed in the few short minutes I'd been gone. Or maybe the wink meant that he was relieved that I'd found the bag. Had he been worried? Were we both starting to expect trouble wherever we turned?

I shook those thoughts away. Apparently my active imagination was taking over my brain.

"Have you seen your people yet?" I asked quietly.

"Yes. I just had a quick word with George and Roley and everything appears to be copacetic this morning. Tom's on his way downstairs and I told both men they can take a break while I'm here."

Roley, otherwise known as Roland Mitchell, was a relatively new hire for Derek. He had worked at the FBI for ten years and come highly recommended by people Derek trusted.

"We like copacetic," I said.

"Indeed, we do."

I turned when I heard footsteps coming down the stairs. Glancing up, I smiled. "Good morning, Tom."

"Good morning, Brooklyn." He wore a beautiful thick cocoa-brown sweater over a white T-shirt with plaid Bermuda shorts and expensive sneakers. His clothes were obviously brand-new and very expensive, but he didn't look self-conscious about them. He looked handsome and relaxed.

Tom saw Derek and gave him a snappy salute. "Top of the morning to you, sir."

"Hello, Tom," Derek said, and shook the man's hand. "I hope your first night in the royal chamber was comfortable."

He chuckled. "It was . . . different. But yes, it was comfortable as could be." He saw Hobson then and smiled genially. "And good morning to you, Hobson."

The look Hobson gave Tom might've frozen a lesser man's blood, but Tom faced the butler head-on. "You have something to say?"

I couldn't blame him for deliberately drawing fire. It would be impossible to live in this house if he simply let Hobson maintain his status quo of insults and negativity.

"You." Hobson sniffed to show his disgust. "How dare you show your face in this home? You have disgraced our entire household."

"And how'd I do that?" Tom asked, then glanced over his shoulder at me and Derek. "Can you dig this guy?"

"I've received a full report," Hobson charged, "that you were seen skulking through this neighborhood with several of your slovenly ne'er-do-well friends, rummaging through trash cans to collect cans and bottles. This behavior won't be tolerated."

Tom leaned into Hobson. "Then maybe you should tell your neighbors to stop throwing away perfectly good bottles and cans. The money I make redeeming their trash could feed a family of four for a month."

Hobson snorted a laugh. "And what do I care about that?"

"You should care," Tom said patiently, "because that family of four deserves to live in dignity just as you do."

"Not if they didn't work for it."

Tom cocked his head. "I'll wager that spending the day collecting bottles and cans is harder work than you've ever done in your life."

"Don't make me laugh."

Tom looked at the older man. "Gosh, Hobson. You don't seem to be learning the lessons of *The Prince and the Pauper.*"

"I don't give a fig about that stupid book or your stupid contest."

Tom chuckled. "Whether you give a fig or not, I'll be spending the next few mornings skulking around your neighborhood, so maybe you should warn your neighbors not to be so cavalier with their recyclables."

"I'll do no such thing! And maybe you should—"

"That's enough," Derek said, taking one step closer to the two men.

Hobson looked startled, as though he had only just realized there were others witnessing his rant. He turned up his nose and started to walk away. But before he could get halfway across the foyer, the doorbell rang. Hobson's spine stiffened and he turned and walked back to the door.

"Hey, I'll get it," Tom said jovially.

"No, you will not," Hobson snapped. "Move away from the door this instant."

Tom held up both hands in surrender. "It's all yours, pal."

Hobson was practically shaking now. His lips were pressed together in anger, but he refrained from saying another word to Tom. It made me wonder if Joseph might've given the butler another ultimatum to behave himself. If so, it hadn't helped. He was just as surly this morning as he'd been last night.

Hobson pulled the front door open and, in his stiffest butler tone, said, "May I help you?"

I could see a man standing on the front step wearing a familiar delivery service uniform of camp shirt, Bermuda shorts, and work boots. He held out a manila envelope. "Delivery for Joseph Cabot. But he has to sign for it."

"Hey, I can sign for it," Tom said cheerfully.

Blocking Tom's access to the doorway, Hobson glared at him. "What part of 'not in this lifetime' do you not understand?"

Tom turned away and looked ready to laugh out loud. Luckily he controlled himself; otherwise, I worried that we'd have another battle on our hands.

The deliveryman handed Hobson a clipboard and a pen. "Here you go."

Hobson quickly scribbled his signature, then handed back the clipboard and took the envelope. "Thank you, my good man," he said, and closed the door.

"Hey, Hobs," Tom said. "If that's for Joseph, you should give it to me. I'm supposed to read his mail, remember?"

"Not while I have one breath left in my body," Hobson muttered angrily. "And my name is Hobson. Not Hobs. Not Hobsie. Hobson."

"Gotcha, buddy."

Hobson's teeth clenched together. "And. Not. Buddy."

Tom's mouth was curved in a big, silly smile. He didn't appear to be insulted at all, despite Hobson's best efforts. This was all just a crazy game to Tom.

And frankly, I could appreciate his attitude, given that the contest itself had put him in ridiculous circumstances. And then there was Hobson, who was completely inflexible. His fury wouldn't allow him to budge one millimeter, so if Tom could maintain that attitude for a while longer, he might just survive living in the same house with Hobson.

Ella walked into the foyer at that moment, her high heels click-clacking against the wood and marble floors. She looked almost reserved this morning in a black pencil skirt and a purple cashmere sweater. "Hobson, did I hear the doorbell?"

"A delivery for Mr. Cabot, madam," Hobson said.

"Oh." She frowned, then glanced around and noticed Derek and me. Her expression changed from bored to semi-interested. Then she saw Tom and wrinkled her nose. "What are you doing here?"

He laughed. "I live here, duchess. Remember?"

"How could I forget?"

I was taken aback by her rudeness, but I probably shouldn't have been. After all, her mother was Ingrid, a truly world-class snob, and as they say, the apple doesn't fall far from the tree. Amazing how both women fit in perfectly with Hobson.

After a moment of struggle, Ella fixed a smile on her face, turned to Derek and me—well, mainly to Derek—and said, "How nice to see you both this morning. Would you care to join me for coffee on the terrace?

I'm looking forward to enjoying the cool morning air. It reminds me of my childhood in Stockholm."

"You're very kind to ask," Derek said. "But Brooklyn and I can only stay for a few minutes. I needed to have a word with my men, and Brooklyn had to retrieve something she left here last night."

"Oh, what a shame you can't stay," she said, trying to sound sincere.

"It was a lovely party last night," I said. "You're a wonderful hostess." Even though I'd barely seen her at all. I was pretty sure that she and her mother had been hiding out in the game room all evening, per Ian and Jake.

She smiled. "Thank you. It's always such fun to have friends visit."

Hobson stood by a side table on which a lovely silver platter had been placed.

"You need any help, bud?" Tom said, hovering close by and clearly goading the supercilious butler.

I could see Hobson's back going up and had to admire Tom's ability to keep the guy on his toes. Obviously, I was Team Tom.

"I told you," Hobson said, nudging him away. "It is my job to deal with Mr. Cabot's mail. I open each envelope to review its contents." He made a show of pulling open a small drawer and removing an ornate knife. He used it to slit open the envelope and then returned the knife to the drawer. He peered inside the envelope and pulled out two pieces of heavy parchment paper.

"After I've reviewed the mail," Hobson continued, "I set it on this silver tray for Mr. Cabot's perusal. Nowhere in the description of my responsibilities does it say, 'Show the mail to some rapscallion.'"

"Watch it, dude," Tom said. "I happen to know what that means."

"It's Sunday," Ella said, puzzled. "Who would send something on a Sunday?"

"It's from the Covington Library, madam." Hobson held the document close to his face and squinted to read it. "I'll need my glasses to read the small print, but it appears to be a proclamation, recognizing Mr. Cabot's contributions to the City of San Francisco and to the Covington Library, et cetera, et cetera."

"How boring," Ella said lightly.

Hobson actually chuckled, then quickly covered it up with a sarcastic sniff.

He did a lot of sniffing, I thought.

Ella left the room and Hobson turned his attention back to the document, studying the second page carefully.

"Oh, bollocks," he said under his breath. "This one is for Mr. Cantwell."

Tom was leaning against the wall closest to Hobson but now he straightened and tried to look over Hobson's shoulder. "Something for me? Cool. Let me see it."

"Stay away from Mr. Cabot's mail," Hobson shouted, but then had to take in a deep breath and let it out slowly. He sniffed again, as if it would help him gain strength. It didn't, and he bowed his head as though the mere act of shouting had taken all his energy.

"But you said that one of them is for me," Tom said reasonably.

"Stay away!" He pressed his hand to his forehead as if Tom was giving him a headache.

"Jeez, man, cool your thrusters," Tom said. "I'm not

going to steal the mail. I just want to see who sent me something."

But Hobson blocked the way so Tom moved a few feet back. And now the butler was hunched over and clutching the edge of the side table as though he were protecting the crown jewels.

Tom glanced at Derek and me and shook his head. "Is it just me, or is this guy some kind of control freak?"

Derek and I said nothing, but I had to agree. Hobson was taking the notion of job security to a new level while also acting directly against his employer's strict instructions. It was strange.

"Hobson," Ella said, striding back into the foyer. "Have you seen my mother?"

"N-no, m-madam," Hobson whispered. He hadn't moved away from the side table, but now he was swaying back and forth. His head drooped, but he quickly straightened. Then his head sagged again and he began to shuffle from side to side. He was now wobbling so badly that he bumped into the wall.

"Hobson?" I said.

Tom frowned and backed up a few more feet.

I glanced up at Derek, who met my gaze with his own look of concern.

"Hobson," Derek said briskly. "Are you all right?"

The butler mumbled something incoherent.

Tom took a step closer, but Derek held up his hand to stop him.

"Hobson!" Ella cried. "What's wrong with you?"

At that moment, Hobson began to sink to the floor. Derek grabbed hold of him around the waist and eased him down.

Derek turned and shot me a look. I ran over and

stared at the proclamations. They were beautifully designed with fancy hand lettering. I was about to pick them up and take a closer look, but noticed the warm golden glow of the paper.

"Oh no." I glanced at the envelope and saw that the return address was the Covington Library. But something was very wrong. "Don't anyone touch these items."

"Damn it, Hobson, snap out of it," Ella demanded.

I touched Derek's shoulder. "I'll call the paramedics."

Tom looked at Derek. "Is he drunk?"

Derek knelt down beside Hobson and pressed his fingers to the man's throat. "No. He's dead."

Chapter 10

We find not much in ourselves to admire, we are always privately wanting to be like somebody else. If everybody was satisfied with himself there would be no heroes.

—*Autobiography of Mark Twain*

"Dead?" Tom shouted, and quickly scrambled back.

Ella began to scream like a banshee. I had no idea what a banshee sounded like, but if they sounded anything like Ella right now, I prayed I would never have to hear the real deal.

"I'm calling the police," I said.

Derek nodded. "Excellent. Thanks."

I pulled out my phone, then walked out of the foyer and into the living room. I could still hear Ella's hysterical shrieks, but they weren't as loud in here and probably wouldn't cause my nose to bleed.

I pressed Inspector Janice Lee's name to make the phone call, but she didn't answer. I left a brief message and was hopeful that she would return my call quickly since I'd mentioned the fact that I was staring at a dead body lying in front of me. Again. I hoped she would be able to hear Ella in the background, too. That would give extra impetus to my message.

I stepped back into the foyer just as the brisk staccato tapping of high heels on the hardwood floor announced the arrival of Ingrid. "Ella, stop your caterwauling! They can hear you all the way across the Bay in San Leandro." I wasn't sure Ingrid even knew where San Leandro was, but I appreciated her sarcasm.

The older woman glanced around, frowning, and suddenly noticed Hobson. With a brisk clap of her hands, she declared, "Hobson, get off the floor right this minute. You're setting a bad example for the servants."

"Mummy," Ella cried. "Hobson is dead!"

"Quiet!" I shouted, and the instantaneous silence felt really good. I turned and looked at everyone in the foyer. The looks I got back from Ingrid and Ella were both resentful and confused. Apparently they didn't understand why I would dare to yell at them. I pointed to the side table. "Something on this table poisoned Hobson. He's dead. It happened almost immediately, so I'm warning you all, don't come near this area. Don't touch anything. And don't touch Hobson, either. Do you all understand?"

"I'm cordoning off this room," Derek said, sounding like the Commander he had once been. "This is a crime scene and the police will be here any minute. Brooklyn is correct. Everyone needs to stay clear of this area."

He briefly texted George and Roley, and the two agents came running toward the foyer in seconds. George came from the kitchen and Roley had been upstairs.

Roley's eyes were wide. "What's going on?"

"How can we help, boss?" George asked.

"Just guard the body, would you please?" He pointed to Hobson, then indicated the side table. "Something on that table poisoned him within seconds of him touching or breathing it. You're not to touch anything. And get the rest of these people out of here."

"Roger that," Roley said with a firm nod.

George gave me a searching look. "Are you both all right?"

I smiled at his concern. "Yes, thank you, George."

"We'll need to treat this area as a hazmat scene," Derek said.

"Will we need masks?" Roley asked. "Respirators?"

"For now, I believe we're safe if we just keep the foyer clear," Derek said. "We'll wait for the police, then we'll determine how the substance was ingested. But other than Hobson, nobody else in the room has been affected and we want to keep it that way. Everyone needs to vacate this space."

Roley gave another nod. "You got it, boss."

The two agents were already nudging Ella and Ingrid and Tom out of the area. At that moment, Stipley walked into the foyer and I saw George meet him and talk for a moment. The handyman spun on his heel and headed out of the house.

Leaving the competent agents in charge for a moment, Derek and I walked outside to take a minute to breathe in the clean air.

"I'm going to call Joseph," Derek said. "We need to make sure he's safe."

The contest rules prohibited Joseph from using his sophisticated smartphone, but for emergency purposes, he'd been given an inexpensive flip phone, a so-called burner phone, to use during the week while he was playing the role of the Pauper.

"Joseph, it's Derek. Are you all right?"

Derek hadn't put him on speaker, but it was easy enough to hear Joseph's words, especially when I pressed my ear up next to Derek's. "Of course. I'm fine."

"I'm afraid I'm calling with very bad news."

"What is it?"

Derek broke the news of Hobson's death to him. At first the man didn't say a word. Then I heard him say, "You've got to be kidding. That can't be true."

"I'm sorry," Derek said. "But it's very true, and there's more."

"Tell me everything, damn it. Fast."

"Hobson was murdered. The police are on their way."

"What?" he shouted.

"We can talk about the details later," Derek said. "Right now, you've got to get over here. I'm going to call for a car to pick you up."

"But the contest . . ." Joseph hesitated, then said, "Never mind. That's not important. I need to be there."

"I'll contact the three agents staying there with you. They'll get you home."

Derek looked exhausted as he ended the call. I understood the feeling.

I walked over to the terrace wall and stared out at the Marin Headlands.

Derek joined me and we were both quiet for a few minutes.

"It's beautiful," he said.

"Yes," I whispered. "The cool morning air reminds me of Stockholm."

He tried to suppress a laugh. "That's very rude of you."

"I know. I'm sorry. But it begged to be said."

"Yes. Sadly it did."

"My only defense is that rudeness seems to run rampant in this house."

"It does get to be a bit much." In most cases, that would've been as close as Derek would get to criticizing anyone. But I knew that this group had driven him to the brink.

My phone rang and I stared at the screen. "Inspector Lee." I answered, gave her our location, and was told she'd be here within a half hour.

I slipped my phone into my pocket, grabbed Derek's hand, and held it tightly. "So." I gave him a sideways glance. "Hobson. I did not see that coming."

"Nor did I." His jaw was clenched in a way that told me he was already mulling over different possibilities and scenarios. Gazing at me, he asked, "How did you know not to get close to the parchment?"

"I didn't," I admitted. "Not at first. From where I was standing in the foyer, I couldn't see the proclamation paper at all. Hobson was busy being rude to Tom, blocking him from getting hold of the proclamation that was meant for him. He was blocking it from me, too."

"The ultimate irony," Derek said slowly, "is that Hobson probably saved Tom's life by withholding the document."

"How strange is that?" I said. "Anyway, I couldn't see the paper until he dropped it onto the side table.

And then it was too late. When I walked over and got a look at that distinctive golden glow, I knew almost certainly that it was the murder weapon. I just don't know how they managed to duplicate the formula."

"It was just as you described it in the Poisoned Papers exhibit."

"Exactly," I said, and gave Derek a contemplative look. "We can probably assume that Hobson never saw the exhibit. Otherwise he might've known to avoid touching it."

"That's a semireasonable assumption," he said.

I sighed. "But who in this group did see the exhibit? Who saw it and thought, hey, that's a perfect way to murder someone?"

"Problem is, it's actually a terrible way to murder someone."

"I agree." I explained to Derek in more detail the process of concocting the poison and then adding it to an adhesive.

"Would that be difficult to do?"

"Well, I'd consider it difficult. And I'd assume that whoever it was had to have seen that exhibit and read all the literature that the Covington handed out."

"There's literature attached to the exhibit?" Derek asked.

"Yes. They have printed index cards that you can take."

"And these cards tell you how they applied poison to the paper?"

"Well, not specifically," I admitted. "In the original case, they didn't do it on purpose. It was an accident. The card simply explains that it was done, but doesn't go into *how* it was done. But a smart, devious killer could extrapolate from there."

"I would guess that it just takes one query on Google," Derek said wryly, "and you've got yourself a formula for poison. And by extension, murder."

"The exhibit makes it pretty clear without actually spelling it out. I found it all fascinating, but then I'm a book and paper geek."

He smiled at me. "I fully appreciate your geekiness."

"Thank you."

But now he frowned. "It would've been far simpler to slip some cyanide in his morning coffee and be done with it."

"I agree, but where's the creativity in that?" My mind wandered back to the scene in the foyer. "Did you see how Hobson was holding the paper up to his face? I think he was literally breathing in the poison."

"He didn't have his glasses with him," Derek remembered. "Said he couldn't read the small print."

"And he kept sniffing the whole time," I said. "He was always doing that. With his nose in the air. It was his way of showing his contempt."

"Unfortunately you're right. This morning his contempt was aimed at Stipley and Tom, but I've seen him behave that way with others." Derek scowled. "And it killed him."

"A cautionary tale?" I wondered. "Killed by his own contempt?"

Derek gave me a long, level look. "Who hated Hobson this much?"

I matched his look with my own. "Who didn't? We saw him fighting with Ingrid last night. And Joseph.

And Tom, of course. And just this morning there was Stipley. And remember the little housemaid, Edith? The one who took my coat when we first arrived last night?"

"Yes, of course."

"He was so condescending to her." I shook my head in disgust. "I hate to keep mentioning about that sniffing thing he does, but he was doing it to her, too. I guess she wasn't holding the guests' coats in a way that pleased him." I rolled my eyes. "Such a snob. I saw Edith give him a few dirty looks right there in the foyer."

"Hmm. I'll talk to her," he said. "Or rather, I'll suggest to the police that they talk to her."

"I doubt she had anything to do with Hobson's death, but she's one more name on the list of people who might've held a grudge against him."

Derek turned to me. "I don't know why we're assuming that Hobson was the intended victim. The two proclamations were addressed to Joseph and Tom."

"That's right." I patted his shoulder. "And the deliveryman specifically announced that the envelope was for Joseph Cabot."

"Yes, he did. We all heard it."

"But since I like both Joseph and Tom, I would rather not think of them as potential victims."

"I feel the same way," Derek said, "but it appears that they were both targeted. Which means I've got to call in more agents to protect them."

"It would really make things easier for all of us if Hobson were the intended victim. He was a pretty awful guy. Always picking fights with people."

"Yes. He was quite vocal in his aversion to Tom."

"That's putting it mildly," I said. "And don't forget that Hobson threatened to reveal some deep dark secret of Joseph's. They had that horrible fight just last night and I'll bet that wasn't the first time they fought."

"And yet Joseph trusted Hobson with his life," Derek said. "We talked about it briefly last night, but Joseph once told me that his butler was the best friend he ever had."

With friends like that, I reflected, but didn't complete the thought. "Maybe Joseph came to realize that he was trusting Hobson with too many secrets. Maybe he worried that Hobson was about to betray him."

Derek stared out at the gray sky. "So Joseph could have arranged for the poisoned parchment to be delivered, knowing that Hobson would insist on opening the envelope." He looked to me. "I believe we need to visit that Covington exhibit again. And maybe even do our own experimenting with the process."

"I love that idea in theory, but it sounds pretty dangerous." I made a mental note to stop by the Poisoned Papers exhibit later today to revisit the highlights. "Okay, so we were talking about Joseph."

"Yes," Derek said. "Don't you think it's rather convenient that the envelope arrived while Joseph was away from the house?"

"Both convenient and suspicious," I said, leaning my elbow against the railing. "Oh, and I know you don't really suspect Joseph of this crime, but I'll play along."

"No, of course I don't."

We both considered the Joseph scenario for a minute. Then Derek said, "Tell me why you think Joseph might've arranged to poison Hobson."

"Well, I don't, actually, but we're playing along, right? Last night when they were arguing, Hobson threatened to reveal some deep dark secret that could ruin Joseph. And thinking back on that moment, I wonder if he was angry enough to have killed him. I mean, how could he trust Hobson after that? And we saw him when he was angry. He practically turned purple. How could Joseph trust someone who's so volatile?"

"He did seem to have lost control of his emotions."

"To be honest," I admitted, "Joseph wasn't doing much better. I mean, he was really fuming. They were both furious with each other."

Derek shook his head and muttered, "Over this stupid contest."

"At first I thought Joseph was simply angry on Tom's behalf because Hobson was being so demeaning toward Tom."

"I had that thought as well," Derek said. "Hobson was nearly apoplectic that Joseph expected him to be Tom's manservant for a few days. But there was a lot more going on beneath the surface than just the contest."

"Exactly. And I think that Joseph was much more annoyed that Hobson was threatening to reveal a dark secret than he was about the butler's bad attitude toward Tom."

"That make sense," Derek reasoned. "It's much more personal."

I smiled at Derek. "We could always simply ask Joseph."

Derek smiled back. "We could indeed."

I stared out at the view. A quarter of a mile away, over to the right, the bottom half of the Golden Gate

Bridge was revealed while the top half was still shrouded by the marine layer. I gazed up at Derek. "You know, Hobson could've planned this whole thing as a way to kill either Joseph or Tom. He's so fussy and demanding. I bet he had the brains and the perseverance to figure out the formula for blending the golden powder with the adhesive."

"I agree with everything you've said about Hobson, except that if he'd planned to kill Joseph with this gold powder, he wouldn't have opened the envelope."

"No. He would've handed it to Tom and watched him die. Or he would've waited until Joseph showed up, given him the envelope, and watched *him* die."

"Which means that Hobson can't be our killer."

"Well, no," I admitted. "Unless he intended to commit suicide."

Derek raised an eyebrow. "Which isn't likely."

I stared out at the water and frowned. "This is beginning to sound like a scene from *The Princess Bride*."

He laughed. "Nevertheless, I'm inclined to believe that the poison that killed Hobson was actually meant to kill Joseph."

"Not Tom?" I asked.

"No, not Tom," Derek said. "Because before last night, nobody knew Tom."

"And Tom really isn't much of a threat to anyone."

"Well, except that he'll get a hundred thousand dollars of Joseph's money."

I chuckled. "If that were the motivation, then Ella would be our number one suspect."

"True," Derek said. "But I can't see the money being the motivation. It's literally a drop in the bucket of Joseph's bank account." He shook his head. "The money would never come out of Joseph's bank account. It's a corporate expense. A corporate write-off."

"Of course," I said. "So, I'm going with Joseph as the intended victim."

"A good guess," Derek agreed.

"Do you have a guess?"

"I'm not ready to write off Hobson as the intended victim."

I gave him a speculative look. "That's bold."

"That's me in a nutshell."

I chuckled.

Derek took my hand. "Let's walk."

"Okay." We left the terrace and strolled out to the front of the house, where a wide patio featured two sets of tables with umbrellas attached and plenty of chairs. The sun was starting to break through the clouds so we sat in the shade and Derek texted George and Roley to check up on things inside the house. They both responded that everything was quiet.

I supposed we could've simply walked back into the house to find out how it was going, but neither of us wanted to be inside just now. It might've had something to do with the dead body lying in there and some poisoned materials that were responsible for the death of Hobson.

We'd both seen our share of dead bodies in the few years that we'd been together. Right now, I was just happy to appreciate the clean air of Sea Cliff and the clearing sky. It was so much nicer than studying murder.

Derek asked, "Why do you think Hobson was always so rude and insensitive to people?"

"I have no idea where his anger and sociopathic

behavior come from, but he was that way with every-one. It was just his thing."

"His . . . thing," he repeated slowly.

I smiled. "His raison d'être. His purpose in life. You know, I'm a jerk, therefore I am."

"So his life's purpose was to make people miserable."

"Maybe. I mean, he was kind of a jackass."

"We haven't talked about Ella or Ingrid," Derek said. "They both seemed to like him. Until that awful argument happened between him and Ingrid."

I gazed at him for a minute and finally said, "Ingrid is surely capable of murder, but I'm not as certain about Ella. What do you think?"

Derek considered the question. "I believe both of them could hold a grudge, and they're obviously jeal-ous of other women."

"I haven't seen Ella get jealous of anyone. Even when Joseph was hugging Ashley, Ella showed almost no reaction at all. Of course, Ingrid was beside herself. So maybe Ella lets her mother fight her battles for her."

"Maybe."

"But more importantly," I said, "I just don't know if either of them would be able to work the poisoned parchment angle."

He rubbed his jaw thoughtfully. "What about Ashley?"

I blinked a few times. "Ashley. Wow. I never even considered her as a suspect."

"She's very close to Joseph."

"True. But why would she care about Hobson?"

"Maybe Joseph confided in her." Derek pushed his chair back from the table. "Maybe he told her that

Hobson was making threats. If she cares about him, she might turn on anyone who threatened him."

I thought about it. "She definitely has brains and ambition. If anyone could formulate the gold powder and adhesive into a poison, it would be Ashley. She's a wizard."

"She is quite talented and personable." He nodded. "But I can't see her concocting some poisonous powder on paper to kill her boss's butler."

"Concocting poisonous powder on paper is much more my style," I said lightly.

"Shhh," he said, pressing his finger against my lips. "We ought not mention that to Inspector Lee."

As if on cue, the gate was pushed open and Inspector Janice Lee walked onto the front patio. She was putting her phone in her purse when she glanced up and smiled. "You guys. Of all the gin joints . . ."

I grinned from ear to ear. "Inspector Lee. I'm so glad to see you."

Derek stood. "Hello, Inspector."

"Commander," she said. "Brooklyn."

I beamed at her, and after a second or two of indecision, I grabbed her in a hug.

"Easy there, girl," she said, and laughed as she lightly slapped my back.

"It's just so good to see you," I said. "What's new in your life?"

"Oh, not much." She shrugged. "They're trying to match me up with a new partner."

"Really?"

When we first met Inspector Lee, she'd been partnered with Nathan Jaglow, a wonderfully patient man in his fifties with curly gray hair and a sad, sweet smile. He had been the good cop to her bad cop, but he had retired a couple of years ago to hang out with his grandkids. From all indications, Inspector Jaglow was loving the life he was living.

Ever since then, Inspector Lee had been flying solo. A new partner would be an adjustment for her. And for me, too, I thought. Although it wasn't about me, I reminded myself.

"I hope they find someone fantastic," I said. "You deserve the very best."

"That's sweet of you," she said.

"I mean it. You're the best and that's what you deserve in a partner."

"I completely concur," Derek said.

I rolled my eyes. "Sorry to gush."

"Hey, gush away. I like it." She sat down on one of the chairs and leaned back. "We'll see how it goes. Anyway, it's been a while. Guess you haven't been causing much trouble lately."

"I've missed you so much that I arranged this little bit of trouble just for you."

She patted her heart. "You shouldn't have."

I shrugged. "I know, but I couldn't help myself."

"Darling," Derek said in a loud whisper. "Let me remind you, this woman has the power to throw you into a jail cell."

"And don't forget it," Inspector Lee said lightly.

I grimaced. "You're right, and I shouldn't make a joke of it. There's a dead body inside the house and it's got a really weird story to go along with it."

She reached into the pocket of her trench coat and

pulled out a small black leather notebook. "So why don't you two give me a few quick and dirty details about the story and the victim and the players before I go inside and do my thing."

"Okay," I said, ready to start talking. But she was staring at the terra-cotta walls that extended up for three floors and her gaze seemed to rest on the fourth-floor terrace with its full-sized telescope aimed at the heavens. The terrace afforded a view in every direction, including "up."

"Wow. Nice place."

"Oh, it's nice all right," I said. But meanwhile, I was still staring at the notebook, which had a nifty black pen attached to the inner cover. I'd seen it once before and had admired it. I also admired her gorgeous trench coat, which was buttery soft and beautiful and matched her incredibly beautiful boots. Oh, what the heck? I coveted her entire wardrobe.

Inspector Janice Lee was first-generation Chinese American. She had been born and raised in the Chinatown area of San Francisco, where her mother still lived above a fabulous dim sum restaurant on a side street off Grant Avenue. Janice had recently trimmed her straight black hair so that it brushed her shoulders in a thick blunt style.

She was ridiculously chic and I was one of her biggest fans, even when she was giving me grief about finding another dead body.

"The victim is the butler," I began.

She stopped writing. "Is this a joke?"

"Unfortunately, no," Derek said, and proceeded to explain, in simple terms, the circumstances as far as we knew them, including the possibility that the idea to concoct the poisonous substance may have originated from a Covington Library exhibit.

She looked at me. "What's this exhibit all about?"

"It's called Poisoned Papers," I began, "and it's comprised of all sorts of paper and equipment used by the old printing presses back in the 1800s. They have samples of wallpaper that contained arsenic and various books whose inks were derived from poisonous substances. And they feature a lot of lead pieces that came from old letterpress machines. But the highlight, as far as I'm concerned, is a copy of an actual newspaper published for Queen Victoria's coronation that was dyed gold for the occasion. Except that the gold powder, when mixed with an adhesive and applied to the parchment paper, was poisonous."

"They actually showed the real stuff at the Covington? Isn't that kind of dangerous?"

"Yes. But each item in the exhibit is encased in thick Plexiglas for security purposes."

She shook her head. "That's something, I guess."

"The exhibit is still there. It's in one of the smaller galleries off the main hall."

"Interesting." She paged through her notes. "So the butler is dead and you think he was poisoned by some powder he touched or inhaled that allegedly came from the Covington Library. And that exhibit is still running."

"That's the gist of it," I said.

She flipped a page in her notebook and read. "And so far, the suspects include the billionaire newspaperman, his wife, her mother, the event coordinator, the cook who's also the housekeeper, the under-butler, the housemaid, the handyman. Anyone else?"

"There are probably others. This guy was an equal-opportunity meanie," I explained. "Nobody seemed to like him."

"He antagonized a lot of people," Derek added. "But the problem comes in finding someone who has a motive to kill him as well as a knowledge of poisons and how they can be applied to parchment paper."

"That's quite a Venn diagram," Inspector Lee said.

"Yes, isn't it?" Derek said.

"It seems like a lot of work," she said. "Your killer could've accomplished the same result with a box of rat poisoning."

"Exactly," Derek said. "They went to quite a bit of trouble and expense, first designing these false proclamations, then coating the parchment paper itself, and finally sending the envelope by messenger to Joseph Cabot, hoping the intended victim would open the envelope. So even though Hobson the butler opened the mail, it could've been intended for Joseph, or Tom, since one of the proclamations was meant for him."

"Complicated," she murmured.

I frowned at Derek. "I just realized . . ."

"What is it?"

"I'm pretty familiar with the Covington exhibit. Do you think someone was trying to frame me?"

"No, darling. You had no motive to kill Hobson."

I didn't like the man, but I'd be keeping that little secret to myself. I slipped my arm through Derek's. "I'm going to hold on to that."

Derek smiled at Inspector Lee. "Brooklyn is not a suspect."

"That's too bad," she said, biting back a smile.

"Oh," I said, remembering another detail. "The return label on the envelope indicated it was sent from the Covington Library. But it's not the Covington stationery. The killer faked it."

Derek continued, "Of course, Hobson the butler wouldn't have known that. He probably just saw the Covington name on the label and assumed it was legitimate."

Inspector Lee wrote down a few more notes, then closed her notebook. "Time for me to meet the players."

She took a step toward the front door, but Derek stopped her. "This door opens onto the foyer," he explained. "I've already had that room cordoned off to keep everyone away from the body and from the poisonous contents of the envelope. Let's go around to the entrance off the terrace."

"Good idea. By the way, Brooklyn." Lee turned to look at me. "Will you have a few minutes this afternoon to show me that poison exhibit at the Covington?"

"Sure." I checked my watch and calculated my timing. "I'm supposed to give a workshop there starting at noon." I had debated canceling the workshop, but now Inspector Lee had just given me another reason to be there. "I'll be in the main hall of the Covington all afternoon. Whenever you're ready to look at the exhibit, I'll take a break from the workshop."

She gave my arm a light, friendly punch that would probably leave a bruise. "Appreciate it."

Chapter 11

> A detective don't like to be told things—he likes to find them out.
>
> —Mark Twain, "Simon Wheeler, Detective"

Derek led the way to the terrace and Inspector Lee slipped her notebook into the pocket of her trench coat. Then she stopped, turned, and took in the view. "That is spectacular."

"Isn't it great?" I said.

"Yeah, it really is." She leaned over the thick railing and got a good look at the Golden Gate Bridge. "This was worth that hideous drive across town. Thanks."

"You're so welcome," I said with a laugh, as though I'd invited her to a special party instead of a murder investigation.

"Seriously awesome." She took one last look at the Bay, then turned and faced the door. "Guess I'd better get to work."

Derek reached for the door handle and held it open for Inspector Lee, who said, "Thanks, Commander."

I followed Derek and Inspector Lee into the living

room. She stopped and glanced around. With a nod, she said, "Nice room. Big. Classy."

"Everything is big and beautiful around here," I said.

She said, "Huh," and followed Derek over to the archway that led to the foyer.

We all took one step up, stood under the arch, and stared down at the body of Hobson.

"That's him," I said helpfully.

She looked at me. "Thanks for pointing that out, Brooklyn."

I shrugged. "I have a knack for this stuff."

She fingered the duct tape and looked at Derek. "I'd like to get rid of this."

"Of course," Derek said. "It was a temporary way of keeping people out of the foyer."

"I appreciate that. My team will replace it with crime scene tape."

"Good." Derek signaled to George and Roley, who jumped into action. "We'll take care of it."

They carefully peeled back the tape from the archway entrance and from the other doorways leading into the foyer. George crumpled it up and walked into the kitchen to throw it all away.

As soon as the tape was removed, Inspector Lee approached the body.

"Wait," I said. "Please."

Inspector Lee turned.

"You need to wear a mask and gloves if you're going to get anywhere near the body."

She nodded. "I wasn't going to get too close, but you're right. Thanks." She turned and moved within about six feet from Hobson's body and simply took in the whole scene. After a minute she glanced up at

Derek. "The coroner will determine time and cause of death, but just for my information, do you have a ball-park estimate of what time he died?"

"It happened at eight twenty-two," he said, and glanced at his watch. "Almost an hour ago."

"Okay." She nodded, and wrote it down. "That's precise."

"I happened to look at my watch as it was happening."

"Good man," she murmured.

He certainly was, I thought, feeling very proud that Derek had noted the time of death, especially because it hadn't even occurred to me. The only thing I'd noted was that the parchment paper Hobson was holding had a golden glow. So I guess we each had our own special areas of interest and expertise.

Inspector Lee glanced over at George and Roley. "I'm Detective Inspector Lee. Who are you guys?"

"They work for me, Inspector," Derek explained.

"Good to know."

"I'm George Thompson," he said, and gave her a snappy nod of his head.

"You look familiar," she said.

"He's worked on several other cases for us," Derek supplied.

She nodded. "Yeah, I thought so. Good to see you, George."

George's cheeks turned red, beyond pleased that she remembered him. "Good to see you, too, Inspector."

Roley stepped forward. "I'm Roland Mitchell. Everyone calls me Roley."

"Roley?" she said.

"Yeah. It's sort of, you know, a nickname."

"Good enough." She jotted down their names. "Can you tell me where the residents of the house are?"

"I have their locations written down," Roley said, opening his own notepad. "Mrs. Cabot and Mrs. Norden have retreated to their bedroom suites. Stipley the handyman is in his workshop off the garage. Leland Bingham is working in the kitchen. And Tom just got back from a walk."

She glanced at Derek for clarification.

"Tom is the winner of the look-alike contest," he said. "He's staying here for several more days while Joseph stays elsewhere."

"And he's back from his walk?"

"Yes," Derek assured her. "He has a habit of going out to collect cans and bottles."

"Sounds neighborly," she said.

"It's how he makes money," I explained.

"Got it." She checked her notepad. "And . . . Leland?"

"Leland Bingham is Mr. Hobson's assistant," I said. "They call him an under-butler."

She raised an eyebrow but didn't comment. "And what about Joseph?"

Derek answered. "I called him to let him know what had happened and then sent a driver to pick him up. He's en route and I don't know when he'll arrive. But I can find out."

"That would be good. Thanks."

"I don't know if you're interested," I began, "but this Mark Twain Festival goes on for a few more days. Tonight they're having a Riverboat Casino Night in the Embarcadero. I know you'll be interviewing everyone here, but if you wanted to see some of the players in action, you're welcome to stop by. It could be interesting."

"Hmm. Let me see how far I get with the interviews today and then I'll decide about tonight."

"Okay."

She closed her notepad and slipped it back into her pocket. "My crime scene guys should be here anytime now. They'll cordon off this area officially and then I'll begin interviewing the residents."

"Would you like us to find a room you can use for the interviews?" Roley asked.

"Might be a good idea," she said. "Nobody appreciates a curious police detective wandering in and out of their bedrooms."

George grinned. "No ma'am."

She glanced at me and winked. "Of course, if anyone was to complain about my curiosity, they'd just make themselves look guilty."

"That's right," I said.

Inspector Lee retrieved her notebook again and perused it for another moment.

Derek ended the call he'd made. "Joseph should be here within the next thirty minutes or so. Heavy traffic out there."

"Tell me about it," she said with a nod. "If for some reason I don't see him come in, can you let me know when he gets here?"

"Of course."

She craned her neck to get a look at the items on the side table. She was a safe distance away from the powdery poison, but it was still disconcerting to watch her. She turned and looked at me. "Run through it for me. This is what was delivered earlier?"

"Yes."

"And the butler opened the envelope?"

"Yes. He touched it, opened it, and he also sniffed it. It's an affectation of his."

"What do you mean?"

I sniffed. "He sniffs, like that. It's his way to convey that you are beneath contempt." I demonstrated by lifting my nose and sniffing again.

"That's . . . friendly," she said flippantly.

"I know, right?" The sniffing had bothered me, but now that Hobson was dead, I didn't want to go on a tirade about it. The butler hadn't been very friendly, but he must've had some good qualities or Joseph wouldn't have cared for him as much as he did. Shaking off the negative thoughts, I pointed to everything on the side table. "All this stuff constitutes your basic murder weapon."

Ten minutes later, Inspector Lee was in the kitchen interviewing the cook/housekeeper. She had wanted to wait until Joseph got home before starting her interviews, but he was still held up in traffic.

Derek and I had suggested that Joseph might be the key to the puzzle of Hobson's death since the envelope had contained a proclamation intended for Joseph. We had pointed out that Tom received a proclamation as well, but we couldn't really see him as a suspect. Of course, that would be for Inspector Lee to determine.

We had also told her about Joseph's big fight with Hobson the night before. Knowing about the fight wouldn't sway her one way or the other because Inspector Lee invariably arrived at her own conclusions after interviewing everyone else involved.

Derek had received an e-mail from one of his operatives working on an unrelated assignment in a Central European country. The two were texting back and forth and Derek was studying other information while he waited for Joseph to arrive. After another few minutes, he turned to me. "Just received a text from Joseph. He'll be another fifteen minutes. There's a traffic accident that seems to have affected half the city."

"Rats." I was antsy. I could just go home, but I didn't want to. Not yet. Finally I stood. "I'm going to walk upstairs and take a look around."

Derek glanced up at me. "Do you have a valid reason to go up there?"

"Of course." I smiled. "I want to eavesdrop and check out who's sleeping where."

"In other words, you're snooping."

I shrugged. "*Snooping* is such a tawdry word."

He tapped my nose playfully, but his words were somber. "Be careful, darling."

"I will." I flexed my muscles and stretched my arms. "No worries."

"Even if Ingrid doesn't give you grief, Inspector Lee might if she finds out you're sticking your lovely nose where it doesn't belong."

I frowned at him. "You're trying to make me feel paranoid."

He grinned as though that had been his prime objective. "Just something to think about."

"Hmm. Well, I just need to move around for a few minutes. Plus I'm dying to see more of the house."

Derek chuckled. "Joseph gave us a tour of the house just last night."

"But we didn't see any of the bedrooms."

"That's because they're private."

"I'm not going to pilfer the family jewels. I'm just going to take a little stroll. If anyone up there asks me what I'm doing, I'll just say I'm looking for the bathroom."

"There's a bathroom right around the corner." He pointed to one of the doorways.

I shrugged. "Maybe it's occupied."

"It's not, but that's a good comeback."

"Thank you."

"You know I appreciate your devious mind," he said. "It's one of the things I love most about you."

I kissed him. "Likewise."

"Just be careful." He checked his watch. "I'll give you ten minutes and then I'm coming after you."

"I'm counting on it."

To avoid the foyer—and the body of the poisoned butler—I took the long way around, crossing the length of the living room and using the door that led into the kitchen. I walked through the massive open-concept space, gave a quick nod to Inspector Lee, who was still interviewing the cook, and moved into the family room. After crossing to the hallway, I took the stairs to the second floor.

Joseph hadn't included this area on our tour, calling it the "private family quarters." But he had explained that there were four bedroom suites on the floor, each consisting of two bedrooms and a sitting room, plus a large bathroom and at least one spacious walk-in closet. In between each suite were several smaller single bedrooms. I had a feeling that these smaller rooms had been designed to accommodate one's maid or valet. It all sounded very Regency-esque.

Did Hobson have a suite of his own up here? Given his dual role as Joseph's valet, maybe his bedroom was directly connected to Joseph's walk-in closet. But then, the guy ran the entire household; I had to imagine he had his own separate quarters and I pictured something large and impressive.

I didn't want to venture into Hobson's space for fear that I would inadvertently leave some evidence of my "snooping" for Inspector Lee to discover. That wouldn't be a problem, I reasoned, since I had no idea which room was his.

I wondered if Ella had her own suite or if she shared a suite with Joseph? While that may have been the situation, I was absolutely certain she wasn't sharing the suite with Tom Cantwell. Maybe she and her mother were bunking together for the week. I almost laughed at the picture of those two women sharing the same living space even for one day. It was even money on which one of them would survive.

The stairway opened up into a wide hall that ran the length of the house. I followed it until it turned a corner, then I saw that it continued down the entire width of the house. I quickly realized that the hallway formed one huge square. I retraced my steps, recalling that halfway down the first length of hall, I had passed an open door and I wanted to take a peek inside.

I ventured into the room, curious to see everything. There were no personal items anywhere, so I assumed this suite was currently unoccupied. The main room was a good-sized sitting area with a door on each side.

Each door led to a large bedroom, bathroom, and walk-in closet. Nice.

"Hello?"

I nearly jumped out of my skin at the sound of the voice. Pressing a hand to my chest, I turned and saw Tom Cantwell standing in the doorway. At least, I thought it was Tom. He looked too much like Joseph for me to be sure.

"Tom?" I said.

"Hi, Brooklyn. Didn't mean to startle you."

"That's okay." I blew out a calming breath. "How are you?"

"Good." He stepped into the room and glanced around. "Pretty nice digs, huh?"

"Yes. I was just giving myself a little self-guided tour."

"I did some of that last night," he admitted, gazing out a window to check the view. "It's always interesting to see how the other half lives."

"It sure is," I said a little lamely.

"It makes me a little antsy," he said, heading back to the door. "I need to get out for another walk."

"The police are here and they're interviewing everyone. They might want you to hang around."

He frowned. "That's a bummer. Maybe I'll just go out to the patio for some fresh air."

"I imagine that's okay. Just let them know."

"Got it." He walked to the end of the hall and disappeared down the stairs.

Darn. I should've kept him talking, but I was still feeling the aftereffects of the shock of hearing his voice. I hadn't noticed last night, but the tone of his voice was very similar to Joseph's. I knew the two men weren't related. How could they be? But to look so much like each other and then to sound so much alike? It was . . . disturbing.

I was still a little shaky from being found by Tom and I took that as a sure sign of my own guilty conscience. I wondered how well Tom had slept in one of these ridiculously grand rooms. Was it an odd feeling to be sleeping in someone else's space? Or was he loving it? I had a few hundred other questions, but they would have to wait.

Despite the beautiful furnishings, the amazing views, and the sheer grandeur of the family quarters, it felt lonely up here. I realized that with Joseph spending his time somewhere else, there was no spark in the air. No anticipation. Joseph was a bigger-than-life character, a true leader, and as far as I was concerned, a fascinating man. Without his presence, it felt like everything in the house was on hold.

Maybe I was the only one who felt that way, but I hated the thought that he might be the true target of a killer.

And with that thought, I decided I'd seen enough. It was time to head back downstairs. But as I walked down the hallway toward the stairs, I heard Ingrid's voice. And then Ella's. One of them mentioned Hobson. I kept walking until I was certain they were both inside the room closest to the stairway, discussing Hobson's death, among other topics.

I pressed myself against the wall as close to the open door as I could get without being seen. From there, I could hear everything they said.

"Things have changed, *sötnos*," Ingrid said in a mildly lecturing tone and using a term I wasn't familiar with. I assumed it was Swedish.

Ella didn't seem all that familiar with the word, either—or maybe she just wanted to give her mother grief, because she said, "Oh mother, speak English."

"Fine," she said. "Just pay attention to what I'm saying and start showing more support for my decisions."

Ella sighed heavily. "But, Mummy."

"Don't argue, *älskling*," Ingrid said. "Now that Hobson is gone, we are on our own. And that is a very dangerous place to be."

"I'm not on my own," Ella insisted. "I have Joseph. He is my husband, in case you've forgotten."

Ingrid laughed, but it wasn't a particularly pleasant sound. "You'd be smart to make sure your husband doesn't start sticking his nose in our business."

"But, Mother, our business is *his* business. So how would we stop him? Joseph owns the house. He has the money. He is my husband. He makes the rules."

She sneered. "*Löjlig.* Don't be an idiot. Perhaps he does make the rules, but you have power, too. Need I remind you?"

"No, Mummy."

"What if he decides to get rid of you?"

Ella gasped. "He would never do that! Look at me. I am beautiful. I am the perfect wife. He loves me."

Ingrid grunted contemptuously. "You are a silly, naïve woman."

"And you are an old woman who takes pleasure in belittling me. I'm tired of it."

"Don't be rude, dear. I don't belittle you. I *teach* you. You're still young and you have a lot to learn."

Ella made a *tsk*-ing sound that only emphasized how young she really was. "You're right about one thing," she said. "I do have power, and I've earned it on my own. And you would be wise to remember that."

Ingrid laughed again, and the sound gave me a chill. She lowered her voice. "Do you not see the way Joseph looks at that young woman, Ashley? The way they spend all their time huddled together in earnest conversations?"

"That means nothing," Ella insisted. "They work together."

"That is how it starts," Ingrid said. "Soon they'll find ways to spend weekends together, then travel together. All under the guise of 'work.' And soon, you are brushed aside."

Ella laughed. "You're being silly, Mama. Look at me. Now look at her. She is a little waif with no shape to her."

Ingrid huffed out a breath of annoyance. "I didn't raise you to be such a fool."

Neither woman said anything for a moment, then it sounded like Ella was munching on something. "These chocolates are so good. Are you sure you don't want one?"

"Yes, I'm sure," Ingrid said firmly. "I don't wish to turn into a *Sockergris*."

"A sugar pig! Mother!" But her protests were weakened by the fact that I could hear her continuing to chew. "I'm just hungry. It seems I'm always hungry."

Ingrid gasped, then said, "*Lilla gumman*. Are you pregnant?"

Lilla gumman? I repeated the phrase to myself. Was that another endearment of some kind? I would have to remember to look it up, along with all the other words I couldn't translate. Not that I would remember them. Ingrid seemed to toss them into the conversation at random moments.

Ella hadn't responded right away, but finally she answered—and I detected a sort of twisted amusement in her tone. "Should I be?"

Ingrid laughed. "Oh, *dotter*. You have charmingly evil instincts even if you're not very bright."

"Humph," Ella grumbled. "I'm sure there's a compliment in there somewhere."

No there wasn't, I thought. But then, these two had a strange, almost adversarial relationship.

"Mama." Now Ella's voice was simpering. "What are you going to do without Hobson?"

Ingrid sighed. "I am not the only one who will suffer without Hobson. Don't discount the fact that Hobson was a key player in convincing Joseph to marry you."

"I would've convinced him on my own."

Her mother snorted a laugh. "You go ahead and believe that."

"Mother!"

"Never mind, sweetie. From now on, you will have to be very careful. The first thing we'll need is to get Leland on our side."

"I already have him on my side," Ella said coyly.

"Because you flirt with him."

"Whatever works, Mother." Her tone had turned hard.

Ingrid didn't seem to notice as she began to pace. "Joseph is a decent man and that's part of the problem. Hobson and I made plans." She stopped to stare out the window. "And there's no reason why we can't continue with those plans. But I don't want Joseph interfering. He's very smart and he keeps tight control on everything."

"I can keep Joseph in line," Ella claimed. "But Hobson ran everything around here. Do you really think Joseph wants to deal with the daily running of the house with all its problems?"

"He won't have a choice. Leland isn't capable. Yet."

"I can plant some ideas in Joseph's head," Ella said. "We can suggest that he give me control of things, at least around the house. And I can train Leland."

"Not while I'm still breathing," Ingrid muttered.

I could hear Ella's heels tapping against the hardwood floor. Was she pacing now? "Hobson was mean and sometimes so are you. Joseph is never mean."

"Hobson got things done," Ingrid said roughly. "Sometimes one has to be pushy to get things done."

"He wasn't just pushy," Ella murmured. "He was a ruthless bastard."

The sound of a slap reverberated and I jolted.

"Ow!" Ella cried. "Mother, stop that!"

That vicious slap was a shock. I had to admit it rattled me a little and I hoped they hadn't heard me gasp.

"You know nothing," Ingrid said angrily. "Hobson was our protector."

"But didn't you tell me that he betrayed you?"

Ingrid huffed. "He didn't actually betray me. We simply had a small disagreement. We would've ironed things out if he hadn't . . . oh God." She took a moment and seemed to shake off the pain. "But he was always protective of me and that wouldn't have changed."

"Maybe, maybe not," Ella countered. "Joseph is my protector."

"Don't be a goose," Ingrid snapped. "The man isn't right in the head. He is insisting we go watch frogs hop tomorrow."

"Oh, Mother, relax," Ella cried. "It's a silly Jumping Frog Contest. From one of the books he loves so much. And you promised you'd go with me."

"Oh, I'll be there," Ingrid said, adding under her breath, "but I don't have to like it." She paced back and forth and I wondered if she would say anything else. Finally she moaned, "Why did Hobson have to die?"

"I don't know," Ella said, but she didn't sound very sympathetic.

Ingrid lowered her voice and I had to strain to hear her words. "I believe that the poison that killed him was intended for someone else."

Ella gasped. "What do you mean? Do you mean Joseph?" There was another gasp as understanding dawned. "Do you mean me?"

"I can't be sure. But I suggest you keep your eyes and ears open for the next few days. Especially while that vagabond, that *luffare*, is living in our house."

"Tom? He's not a tramp," Ella insisted. "Well, not exactly. I mean, he's poor, so that's a problem. But he's very handsome and he was nice to me. He looks a lot like Joseph. A bit thinner, but I'll bet his thigh muscles are strong from all that walking."

Ingrid made a guttural sound, obviously disgusted by her daughter's words.

I was a little disgusted myself. I was ready to sneak away, but Ingrid spoke again. And her voice was bitter enough to curdle a grown man's blood. "Listen carefully to my words, *dotter*."

"All right, all right."

"Pay attention," Ingrid said. "Be careful. Anyone can see that this man Tom is related to your husband in some way or other. And it would be just like Joseph to sentimentally sign away half of his worldly goods to that man. The half that should lawfully come to you. We can't let that happen."

"We won't," Ella said, and for the first time I heard the steel in her voice.

I rubbed my arms to quell the chills. These women were awful!

I tiptoed away from the door before the two of them could catch me eavesdropping. As I headed for the stairs, I heard a scuffling sound at the end of the hall and turned to see Leland Bingham disappear around the corner.

Oh God! Had he been listening in on the women's conversation, also?

More importantly, had he been watching me the whole time I'd been eavesdropping?

Another sound came from the end of the hall and I watched Edith, the young housemaid, come around the same corner where Leland had disappeared a moment ago. She carried a stack of linens and was giggling as she pushed open another bedroom door and walked inside. Had Leland said something to cause her to giggle? It didn't matter, I thought. What mattered was that she hadn't seemed to even notice me, which I considered a good thing.

At the top of the stairs I finally began to breathe easier. Then I hurried down the steps and dashed out of the house.

Chapter 12

Pity is for the living, envy is for the dead.
                    —Mark Twain, *Following the Equator*

After ten minutes of staring at the tiny tufts of white waves skimming the dark surface of the Bay, I felt cleansed enough to move on. Those two women were toxic!

Replaying the creepy conversation between Ella and Ingrid, I seriously wanted to hurl. They were so corrosive and I was very worried about their intentions toward Joseph. And Tom, too. And I had to wonder about Leland.

I took another minute to breathe in the sea air and channel my own kooky mother, who would've instructed me to align my chakras, be in the moment, and absorb the sights and sounds and scents around me.

The marine layer had burned off and the sun was beginning to warm the air. The sky was crystal clear and the Golden Gate gleamed gloriously in the sunshine. The briny mist was refreshing. Life was good.

I stepped back inside the living room and saw Derek sitting at the far end, talking on the phone.

Inspector Lee stood near the open door to the kitchen, talking quietly to George and Roley. She lifted her chin to acknowledge me, but continued her conversation with the two agents.

From here I could see one edge of the crime scene tape that stretched across the archway.

I walked over to Derek, who still sat in the occasional chair facing the couch and the wall of windows. He spoke quietly to someone on the phone, but as soon as he saw me, he ended the call.

He stood and wrapped his arms around me. "You look as if you've seen a ghost," he murmured in my ear.

"Something like that," I muttered, and held on to him for a few more moments.

"We'll talk about it later."

"Oh, you bet we will," I said, nodding. "But first, I need to tell you that I think Leland saw me listening in on the conversation between Ella and Ingrid."

"Did he say anything to you?"

"No, but he might say something to those two women. Oh, and Edith the housemaid may have seen me up there, but I think she's harmless."

"Careful, darling." He gazed at me, not smiling. "Those could be famous last words."

I cringed. "I hope not."

At that very moment, the front door opened and Joseph stepped inside.

Derek stood and pointed to the body still lying on the floor. "Be careful."

"Oh Jesus," Joseph whispered. "Oh my God."

Kneeling next to the body were two crime scene

guys dressed from head to toe in hazmat uniforms, complete with hoods and booties.

Inspector Lee stepped to the door of the kitchen. "Mr. Cabot?"

"Yes." He froze. "You're the police."

"Yes sir. Be careful here." She pointed to the narrow walkway next to the wall. "Stay behind the yellow tape."

One of the CSI guys stood and held the crime scene tape out a few inches. He pointed to the living room. "It's okay, sir. There's enough room for you to walk through here."

"Yeah, okay. Thanks."

Derek moved quickly to the edge of the foyer and reached out to guide Joseph into the living room. "Come this way."

I saw Inspector Lee give Derek a quick nod of approval and then move back into the kitchen to complete the interview she was conducting there.

"Sit down, Joseph," Derek said.

"Okay," he whispered. His face was almost gray with shock. "Good Lord." With his elbows resting on his knees, he bent forward and buried his head in his hands.

"I'll get some water." I jogged to the other end of the living room and walked into the kitchen. I filled three glasses with cold water and returned to set one glass on the coffee table in front of Joseph. Then I handed Derek a glass and kept one for myself.

Joseph remained with his head buried for nearly five minutes.

I noticed that the medical examiner was on the scene now. He, too, was dressed in hazmat gear and was probing and testing Hobson's body for time and cause of death. He checked the dead man's skin and his mouth and nose for discoloration, irritation, and discrepancies.

I knew that once he got the body back to the morgue, he would conduct more comprehensive testing. For now, though, he and the assistant began to zip Hobson into one of those horrible black bags. And pretty soon the dead man would be carried out to the medical examiner's van.

One of the techs stood at the side table, carefully slipping each of the golden-hued proclamations and the manila envelope into their own individual evidence bags. The tech was also dressed from head to toe in a white hazmat suit with a ventilator covering his face.

Once everything was bagged, he began to sweep any excess powder from the side table into a separate bag using a short, stiff brush, similar to the brush I liked to use for sweeping out the gutters of my books.

The tech put all the evidence bags into a steel briefcase that held the tools and gear he regularly used for his job.

Once everything had been removed from the side table, he began to dust the surface for fingerprints.

Earlier, Inspector Lee had explained that the techs would also dust for any fingerprints on the proclamations and envelope, but not until they returned to the lab and could control things more carefully. After all, we still weren't sure exactly how the poison had been transmitted.

I had told her that, according to the poison exhibit at the Covington, it was the gold powder that killed the workers at the printing press back in the 1800s. But here, we couldn't really say whether it was the powder

or the adhesive material—or something else entirely—
that had caused Hobson's almost instant death.

"There's water for you, Joseph," I said, pointing to
the glass on the nearby table. I felt incapable of doing
anything else to help the man.

After another minute, he lifted his head. "Thanks,
Brooklyn." But he didn't reach for the glass. Instead he
looked at Derek. "Is this really happening?"

"Yes. I'm sorry."

He sighed. "I've known him longer than I've known
my wife. Longer than I've known you."

Derek pulled a chair over and sat down facing Joseph. "You and I have known each other for about fifteen years now."

Joseph shook his head. "Can you believe it's been
that long?"

"Back then, we were willing to take ridiculous
chances with our lives."

"I'm still taking chances," Joseph said with a cyni-
cal eye roll. "Have you met my second wife?"

His joke shocked me, but Derek just chuckled. "Yes,
and she's lovely."

It was the perfect reply to the other man's bizarre
comment. Of course, having overheard Ella and her
mother talking, I wondered if there would be some
even more bizarre comments. But I was absolutely
sure that Joseph had no idea that the two women were
plotting. Exactly *what* they were plotting, I couldn't
say. But Joseph needed to know. Unfortunately, it
wasn't my place to tell him. And more importantly, I
didn't think he would believe me.

Joseph chuckled dryly in return. "Yeah, Ella's a
knockout. And I have no idea what I'm doing with her."

"Joseph, you love her."

He slanted a look at Derek. "Do I?"

"You know you do, mate. You married her."

I sat on the arm of Derek's chair and pretended to be invisible. The last thing I wanted was to interrupt their conversation, but I was clinging to every word. It wasn't that I was nosy or anything, but . . . okay, yeah. I was nosy. And I was okay with that.

Joseph grunted. "Want to hear the truth? I married her because Hobson convinced me that I should."

Hobson? My eyes widened. *So what Ingrid had told Ella was the truth.*

"He wouldn't have given you that advice," Derek insisted, "if he didn't recognize that you loved her."

Joseph sighed. "I don't know anymore."

My mind was reeling. After overhearing the psycho chitchat between Ella and Ingrid, Joseph's words were really starting to make me wonder. Had Hobson truly controlled everything that Joseph did? Had he actually played the role of grand puppet master around here?

I shook my head at the idea. It was just too unreal. Joseph was a powerful man. He didn't need anyone else to control things around here. Or did he?

"You know you love her," Derek was saying. "But you've just lost someone very close to you and it's making you question everything else in your life."

"You've got that right," Joseph said. "Still, it really was Hobson's idea. He said she would take good care of me."

I almost laughed out loud. *Seriously?* That woman had no interest in taking care of anyone else but herself.

But Derek continued in his upbeat way, trying to

keep Joseph calm. "Now, why would Hobson say that if it wasn't true?"

"I don't know," Joseph said, and shook his head. His eyes glazed over and I thought he might be silently reminiscing. "Hobson and Ingrid worked together for years in the home of some high-powered wealthy minister in the House of Lords."

"I thought he used to work for your father," I said.

"He came to work for my father after leaving the House of Lords. And Ingrid followed him." Joseph shook his head. He still seemed to be in a daze, moving and shifting in his chair and staring into space, almost as though he were drunk. As though he'd consumed a bottle of wine with a six-pack beer chaser and no longer knew if he was coming or going. He blew out a breath. "So Hobson knew Ella all this time, since her mother was my father's housekeeper."

"I knew that Hobson worked for your father," Derek said slowly. "But I wasn't aware that Ingrid did, also."

"Yes, those two have known each other forever. I guess that means that I've known them forever, too. Ingrid used to run this place. Well, let's be honest. Hobson ran this place, but Ingrid took care of the staff and the upkeep of the kitchen and the bedrooms. You know, all the regular duties. And after Ella finished college, she moved in to help her mother."

"I didn't know that," Derek said.

"Then a few years ago, Ingrid began to complain about arthritis in her knees and Ella took over the job of head housekeeper."

"That's quite an amazing story," Derek said.

"Yeah." Joseph gave a short laugh. "And a year or

so after Sandra died, Hobson began suggesting that I date Ella. She was a nurturer, he said. She had a natural ability to encourage the staff to work hard for the good of the group. Hobson said that, as a housekeeper, Ella demonstrated the same sort of nurturing talent that she would show a husband."

I almost spit out my water. *Nurturing? Ella?* Was he living on the same planet as the rest of us?

So Ella and Ingrid had both known Joseph's first wife, Sandra. This was getting more bizarre by the minute, but one thing was very clear. Hobson had surely manipulated Joseph into marrying Ella!

And that was just sad. Joseph was a lovely man, a self-made billionaire who ran huge corporations. But I was starting to question his ability to run his own life.

"Hobson told me she was exactly what I needed in a wife. He said she would be good for me. It certainly didn't hurt that she's a beautiful woman."

"She is indeed," Derek murmured.

"Still, it took me another year to get over Sandra's death." Joseph sighed. "To be honest, I'm not over it yet."

"Of course not. You don't get over something like that."

"No." But he chuckled dryly. "It was odd to watch Hobson suddenly turn into some kind of matchmaker. He thought I should get married again. It would solve all my problems, he said." Joseph sighed. "Despite Hobson's less than subtle urgings, it took me four years before I was ready to date Ella." He gazed at Derek and then glanced up at me. "I still miss my Sandra."

Looking back at him, my eyes threatened to tear up. I had to get a grip and face facts. This was how Hobson had manipulated Joseph. By playing on his loneliness and grief.

I suddenly wondered whether Ingrid had played a part in the marriage manipulation. No, I really didn't wonder at all. After overhearing her words earlier, I was certain that she had been right in there, manipulating from the sidelines.

As if he were reading my mind, Joseph said, "You know, Ingrid was a gem of a housekeeper. Tough as nails on the staff, but she got things done around here."

"I can believe that," I said.

He chuckled. "Yeah. So when Ella was hired to be my new housekeeper, I was happy that Ingrid was willing to continue living here."

"That was generous of you," Derek said.

Joseph shrugged. "Well, look at this place. We have so much room, and she's Ella's mother, after all. It would've felt wrong to throw her out on the street." He chuckled lightly. "So she just stayed. And it's actually been a good thing to have her here because she was able to take all the time necessary to train Ella for the job. Ingrid was able to show Ella all the specifics of taking care of this house." He smiled sheepishly. "And me."

Derek nodded, but said nothing.

"It's actually nice to have Ingrid here," Joseph repeated, as though he were trying to convince himself. "Because I'm always working and often traveling. So Ella has her mother here to keep her company."

Was it wrong of me to think that might not be the healthiest arrangement I'd ever heard of? Obviously Joseph was a generous man, but it felt like these two women—and Hobson—had been manipulating and milking him for all he was worth.

Joseph took another sip of water and his thoughts suddenly veered off into a new topic. "Hobson and I had a bad fight last night."

"Yes, I know," Derek said. "But you must not let that eat away at you."

"I can't help it. I said some things . . ."

"You and Hobson would've straightened everything out by now if he hadn't been killed."

Joseph sucked in a breath and let it whoosh out. "I swear to God I wanted to kill him." He gazed at Derek, looking miserable. "I was so angry."

"You didn't mean it, though, and that's what you have to remember."

"I was still angry this morning," he admitted. "But I was angry at myself because I knew he was right."

I wanted to ask him what he meant, but I didn't want to interrupt him. I would have to ask Derek later.

Joseph continued, "When you called and told me what happened, I couldn't believe it. All I could think was that I needed to tell him I was wrong. But it was too late and now he was dead. I wanted to kill him and now he was dead. It's . . . well, it's devastating."

"But you didn't kill him," Derek said sternly.

Joseph didn't seem to hear him. "On the drive over here I convinced myself that I could handle this. That I was okay. I was certain I was ready to look at his body and deal with this tragedy. I thought I was prepared." He shook his head and breathed heavily. "But I'm not. Oh God, I'm not."

And he buried his head once again.

Derek and I walked outside, leaving Joseph alone for a few minutes.

"Are you all right?" I asked.

"Yes. Though it's hard to hear some of what he's saying."

"Joseph isn't a passive man," Derek insisted, then thought for a minute. "But he was truly devastated by his wife's death."

"I know she died of cancer."

"Yes," he said. "She was in remission for a while, and then it suddenly returned with a vengeance."

"Oh God. That's tough."

"Yes. He buried himself in work for a few years. And then one day he called to tell me he was getting married. I must say, it was quite a shock."

"I guess so."

He wrapped his arms around me and simply held on for a long moment. I could feel the cool breeze mixing with the warm sun on my shoulders as well as the heavy weight of his strong arms across my back.

Finally he leaned back to meet my gaze. "We should go inside and see how he's doing."

"I guess we'd better."

We stepped into the living room and saw that Joseph was sitting in the same chair with his head still buried in his hands.

When we sat back down in the chairs next to him, Derek said his name. "Joseph."

He slowly lifted his head and stared at us through red eyes. Obviously, he had been crying, and I wondered if he was feeling the loss of his friend or if he was suffering the deep-seated guilt that came from the argument they'd had the night before.

"Joseph," Derek said again.

"Yes?"

"You should cancel the rest of the festival," Derek said flatly.

Joseph's eyes widened. "What did you say?"

"You don't need the added pressure," Derek said. "Hobson is dead. Nobody would blame you if you canceled the whole thing. Or at least postponed it for a few months."

"No."

"But—"

"Just . . . no." He shook his head, then spread his hands out. "It's . . . impossible. The entire city is involved. Our newspaper is running stories twice a day and we have events every afternoon and evening for the next four days. And there's Tom."

"Tom would be the first to agree with me," Derek said.

I looked back and forth and saw the determined look in both men's eyes.

"Tom isn't in charge," Joseph said stubbornly. "He might be playing the role of prince, but he's not actually in charge of anything."

"I'm aware of that." Derek thought for a moment. "Okay, then how about if you put Ashley in charge? You can have her attend the activities and give the speeches. She's good at it."

"I agree, she is. But then, what do I do?"

"You stay home."

"And do what?" Joseph demanded with a short laugh. "Believe me, I'm better off working. I appreciate what you're saying, but canceling the festival is out of the question."

Derek stood and stared down at the man. "So you're going to continue to spend the next few days doing janitorial work at the Covington Library and sleeping in an efficiency apartment in the basement while mourning the loss of one of your closest friends in the world?"

"Well, when you put it like that," he said with a note of sarcasm that I actually welcomed. It gave me some hope that his sense of humor was still lurking in there somewhere. Hopefully, that meant that he wouldn't be sinking into a dark hole of despair anytime soon.

Not that I would blame him for sinking. He had just lost someone near and dear to him, despite yesterday's ugly argument with Hobson.

And despite the fact that I hadn't cared for the butler. I had considered him a supercilious bully. But it was obvious that he and Joseph had been close.

Derek tried one more time to convince Joseph to cancel the festival. "You're going to be a constant target for gossip and innuendo. You'll be interviewed and photographed and judged all week," Derek continued. "And I hate to even mention this, but there will surely be speculation that you had something to do with Hobson's death."

"You know I didn't."

"Of course you didn't," Derek said quickly, "but you know how the media treats these sorts of stories. It's going to get ugly."

"I *am* the media," he muttered. "I can handle it."

"Of course you can. But the point is, for the next few days you'll be expected to spend all your time giving speeches and glad-handing people all over town. You'll have to be convivial and sharp and fired up at all times. And frankly, you're none of those things right now."

"I'm always convivial," he groused.

Derek bit back a smile. "Of course you are."

Joseph laughed, but there was little humor in it. "Don't worry, I'll get there."

"Now, you brushed over it a minute ago, but let me remind you again. You are a suspect in a murder investigation."

"Suspect?" He was incredulous. "I wasn't even here."

"You actually didn't have to be here to make it happen. It appears that everything was arranged in advance."

"What in the world does that mean?" he demanded.

I squeezed Derek's arm as a way of reminding him that Inspector Lee was nearby. I didn't want her to get the wrong idea if she heard Derek discussing the murder with Joseph.

"It means that you're a suspect," Derek said, his tone hushed but just as adamant. "I know you didn't do it, but the fact remains that you could've done it."

"This is ridiculous," Joseph said.

"If you think that's ridiculous," Derek said, "listen to this: You could also have been the intended victim. And since the killer failed to get you this time, he could try again. In other words, you could be next."

Joseph snorted. "Now that's absurd."

"Mr. Cabot?"

We all turned and saw Inspector Lee hovering in the archway. I wondered how long she'd been standing there. Had she heard any of what Derek had said to Joseph? Did it matter? I played the conversation back in my head and didn't think anything too damaging had been said or that Derek had acted inappropriately.

Besides, Inspector Lee had always admired Derek

and still called him Commander out of respect. She would never accuse him of such a thing.

The inspector took one step down into the living room and walked over to Joseph with her hand outstretched. "Mr. Cabot, I'm Detective Inspector Janice Lee. I'm very sorry for your loss."

Joseph took in another breath and exhaled. "Thank you." He shook her hand.

"I realize it's not a good time, but I would appreciate your help. Would you mind answering some questions for me?"

Joseph gave Derek a look that indicated that he was finally understanding Derek's concerns. "I'd like Derek to stay."

"Fine," the inspector said easily.

Unfortunately, that was my cue to leave. I stood. "Sorry to interrupt, but I'm going to take off now."

Derek checked his watch. "You need to get ready for work."

"Yes."

"All right." He looked at Inspector Lee. "Excuse me for just a moment?"

"Of course."

He glanced at Joseph. "I'll be right back."

I gave Joseph a quick hug and whispered, "I'm so sorry."

"Thank you, sweetheart," he said softly.

Derek and I walked into the foyer, staying behind the crime scene tape all the way to the front door. We stepped outside and he said, "I'm going to stay awhile longer."

"I know. Joseph needs you." I pulled my car keys out

of my purse and adjusted the tote bag on my shoulder. "But there's something I have to tell you before I go."

"What is it?"

"While I was listening to the two women upstairs, Ingrid basically said the same thing that Joseph did about Hobson convincing him to marry Ella."

"That's interesting," Derek said slowly. "What else did they say?"

"Ingrid thinks that Tom and Joseph are related. She's worried that Joseph will sign over half his estate to Tom and leave Ella with nothing."

"That would never happen," Derek insisted. "Joseph would never do that."

"Maybe not, but Ingrid sounded convinced. Which makes me even more concerned about their intentions when it comes to Joseph."

Derek clenched his jaw. "I won't allow any harm to come to him."

"I know you won't. I just wanted to let you know that they're awfully sneaky and we should watch them carefully."

"And by 'we,' you mean 'me and my agents.'"

I smiled. "Of course." I gripped my keys. "You'd better go back inside. I'll tell you the rest later."

"Yes." He skimmed his hands up and down my arms. "We'll talk more."

"I'll be at the Covington this afternoon from noon until four. Maybe longer, if Inspector Lee shows up."

"I'll call you."

I looked into his eyes and could see how troubled he was. I touched his cheek. "Please do."

He kissed me. "Be careful, my love."

"I will, and I hope you will, too."

He nodded. "Absolutely."

I started to walk away, then turned. "And please take notes. You know how I hate to leave just as we're about to get the whole scoop."

He smiled then. "I'll get it for you."

I blew him a kiss and headed for my car.

Chapter 13

There was never yet an uninteresting life. Such a thing
is an impossibility. Inside of the dullest exterior there is
a drama, a comedy, and a tragedy.
—Mark Twain, "The Refuge of the Derelicts," 1905

I hated leaving Derek at Joseph's house. I knew he was
a good friend of Joseph's and would be able to get him
through the police interview. And Derek was a professional. He dealt with these sorts of horrible things all
the time, but still, I felt bad leaving him. All the way
home, I mentally wrung my hands worrying about it,
and thinking that I could've called Ian and canceled
the bookbinding workshop. But I hadn't. I didn't want
to let Ian down.

So it looked like I would spend the rest of my day in
a state of supreme guilt. It wouldn't be the first time.

Once I got home, I barely had time to feed Charlie
and eat a quick sandwich before it was time to drive
to the Covington and start my workshop. As I pulled
into the parking lot, I realized that my guilt was beginning to recede. Which of course made me feel even
guiltier.

"Idiot," I muttered as I walked into the Covington. The first thing I noticed was the crowd of people sitting in the bleachers and standing around my worktable, checking out the bookbinding tools. Ian stood nearby guarding my tools, and when I walked up, he flashed me a silly grin.

I pulled him aside. "What's with all these people?"

"They're here to see you," he said, still grinning. "Turns out, you're a hot ticket. Word gets around."

"That's crazy." I loved hearing him say it, but I couldn't believe it, especially because the only work I had done yesterday was brushing off the pages to get rid of any tiny bits of dirt or microscopic bugs. Yes, I had meticulously brushed off all 441 pages of *The Prince and the Pauper* and everyone watched me do it. And now they were back to watch more?

"Need I remind you, these are book people?" Ian said. "Book people would be happy to watch you fold paper for three hours."

"It may come down to that," I muttered.

"I hope not." He chuckled. "Now get to work."

I glanced at the crowd, then back at Ian. "Can you please ask them to step back a few feet from the worktable?"

"Don't worry. I've got them all sitting in the bleachers."

"Thanks, pal." I gave his arm a light punch for good measure. "Oh, and we have to talk later. Joseph Cabot's butler, Hobson, was murdered this morning."

"What?"

"Shhh!"

He lowered his voice. "What happened?"

"That's what we have to talk about." I quickly explained in thirty words or less about the manila envelope that Hobson opened and how he died almost instantly.

"Brooklyn, that's terrible."

"And by the way," I continued, "the return address on the envelope was the Covington Library."

His eyes grew as big as saucers. "What the—"

"Shhh!" I grabbed his arm. "We'll talk later."

"You bet your boots we'll talk," he said through gritted teeth, and dashed off toward the stairs.

"Welcome, everyone!" I said to the crowd. "Thank you so much for being here."

I pulled out my copy of *The Prince and the Pauper* and held it out for everyone to see. "I'll pass this around for everyone to take a look." Because there were more people here today, I added, "And I know you'll all be careful with the book, but I still like to remind everyone that it's old and fragile, so please treat it with care."

I knew I wouldn't have to watch every single person handle the book to make sure they treated it respectfully. That's because my regulars in the crowd would do the job for me.

"I always begin by sweeping off the pages with my stiff brush. I started that job yesterday and I was able to finish all 441 pages before I got here today."

Someone in the audience said, "Yay!"

"Thank you." I laughed. "Who said that?"

A woman on the top row raised her hand. "Me."

"Marianne?" I frowned. "What are you doing here?"

"I can't stay away. This is so much fun."

"Well, thank you for being here." I gave her a grateful

smile, then raised an eyebrow. "But seriously, you're a glutton for punishment, girl."

There were some laughs and then I got down to work. "I explained yesterday that the pages of this book are in surprisingly good condition, so we're mainly going to concentrate on creating a new cover and adding end-papers and a new headband—the small, woven piece that sits protectively at the top of the spine. We'll add some gilding to the cover and we'll rebuild the inner spine so the book will be able to last another hundred and fifty years or more."

They applauded. It took me off guard. "Thank you, but you guys really don't have to applaud. I'm just glad you're interested in this kind of work."

"It's so fascinating," one woman said. "I appreciate that you can explain it to us in commonsense, down-to-earth language."

"Well, that's mostly how I speak all the time," I said with a grin. I opened my portable tool kit, took out my X-Acto knife, and held it up. "So let's get started."

At that very moment I felt the brush of soft fur around my ankles. If I didn't have a cat of my own, I would've freaked out, but instead, I just smiled. Looking down, I said, "Hello, Pixie. Are you here for more bookbinding lessons?"

She wound her long, thick tail around my left ankle and I bent down to stroke her back. "God, she's huge."

"And gorgeous," someone in the audience said.

"Yes," I agreed. I stood up straight and let Pixie ramble freely around the area.

The book was finally returned to me. "Did everyone get a chance to look at it?"

"Yes," a bunch of people said.

"Good." I held it up. "Because the cover and the endpapers are going to be replaced with shiny new ones, my work doesn't have to be too precise at this point. I just have to remove the entire cover from the textblock."

"What's a textblock?" someone asked.

"Basically, in layman's terms, it's the paper the book is printed on, sewn together in what's called signature pages."

I opened the book to the endpapers. "I'll use the knife to slice along the hinge, essentially separating the cover from the textblock and spine."

I demonstrated. It was quick work.

There were a few gasps and someone said, "Eek!"

"It's okay. Don't panic. I'm a professional."

That brought a few laughs and everyone seemed to settle down. I knew how they felt, though. Watching someone cut a book apart could be traumatic for a booklover.

"It's going to be beautiful again very soon."

Within a minute, I held up the heavy textblock in one hand. "This is the textblock."

Then I held up the book cover—consisting of the front, back, and spine—still all connected by the hinges.

And they applauded again.

Marianne shouted, "Yay!"

I wasn't sure I'd ever get used to such enthusiastic reactions to what was a low-key demonstration, but I was gratified that they were enjoying themselves.

Lucinda came running over and grabbed Pixie. "I'm sorry if she disturbed your lecture."

"She didn't," I assured her. "She's a welcome addition anytime."

Lucinda looked relieved. "Thanks, Brooklyn." Then she turned and walked quickly back to her office.

I smiled at the group. "Okay, the first thing I'll do at this point is check that the textblock is standing straight and not askew, which can happen to a book after a hundred and forty years. Then I'll check that the threads are still strong enough to last another century. Finally, I'll have to scrape off all the old glue from the spine. First, because with a book this old, it's probably animal glue, which tends to stiffen and shrink with age. And second, because it's clumpy and old and we want to make it new and smooth."

I walked around and showed them the stiff old clusters of glue stuck to the spine.

"We'll get rid of it by brushing on a solution of methylcellulose, which will soften and loosen the old glue so that, when it dries, I'll be able to easily scrape it off."

I help up a large wooden press. "This is called a finishing press and I'll use it to hold the textblock vertically so that I can work on the spine."

I released the screws and opened up the space enough to fit the book, spine side up, within the blocks, then I tightened the screws until the book was stable. "You can see how important this tool is when you're doing repairs on the old spine or when you're building the new spine."

I poured a small amount of methylcellulose into a glass jar and began the busywork of brushing it onto the spine, then waiting for it to dry. During the time it took for the solution to dry completely, I answered questions about this book and about my work in general.

When the methylcellulose was dry, I tested it by pulling a small corner of it away from the spine. It had taken on the consistency of rubber cement so I knew it was ready. I used a thin lifting knife with a sharp edge to peel away the methylcellulose along with much of the old glue and some of the tattered bits of thread.

"See how it picks up all the clumps?" I said. "Isn't that great?"

"It's like a miracle," someone said, with so much reverence that I almost laughed.

These book people were sweet.

I happened to check my watch and was shocked to see that three hours had passed by. I knew I'd taken a lot of time answering questions, but at this rate, I wouldn't be able to finish the book in the next three days.

But that was okay, I realized. Whenever I was able to finish the book, Ian would be happy to take it and add it to his new Mark Twain display.

"So that's it for today," I said to the group. "Thanks for being here."

There was more applause and then some people gathered around with additional questions for me. A couple of folks in the audience were anxious to take one of my classes at BABA and I happily handed out brochures from the Book Arts center along with my business card.

It helped to have my head cheerleader, Marianne, singing my praises. I promised her a cut of the proceeds and she laughed. But I would have to think of some way to thank her.

My audience had left and I was packing up my tools when someone spoke to me. "They told me I'd find you here."

I looked up and saw Tom Cantwell standing nearby.

"Tom. Hello." I couldn't hide my surprise. Not only because I hadn't expected to see him standing here, but mostly because it was still a shock to realize how much he resembled Joseph.

"After I talked to the detective, I had to get out of the house. So I was out for a walk and thought I'd check out this place."

"You walked all the way here?"

"I walk everywhere."

"But this week is kind of different," I said.

He shrugged. "Because of the contest, yeah."

"That," I said with a laugh, "and because I'll bet you have a car and driver at your disposal."

He chuckled. "I do. And to tell the truth, the driver did give me and my buddies a ride over to Fillmore Street. But then I made 'em all get out and walk up Pacific Avenue to the top of the hill. I don't want us to get too used to this temporary lush life."

"I've walked up that hill," I said. "And I know it's grueling."

The hill from Fillmore up to the Covington was long and very steep. I had walked it myself a few times, but if I'd had a driver standing by, I would've happily passed on the walk. Exercise was one thing, but these San Francisco hills were a whole different animal.

He brushed away my concerns. "We took a few breaks to pick up cans and bottles."

Now that he'd brought it up, I felt duty-bound to give

advice. "I hope you're careful out there. This city is filled with tourists who don't always pay attention to the traffic laws." And didn't I sound like my father? I mentally shook my head.

"Funny you should mention it," Tom said. "We're usually pretty good at avoiding the cars, but just a few minutes ago I almost got hit."

"What?" I asked, alarmed. "What happened?"

"Now, don't get all worried. My buddy Wyatt yanked me out of the way." He spread his arms out. "And look at me. I'm fine."

He did look fine. He was wearing another beautiful new sweater, this one navy blue. And he was wearing Bermuda shorts again, even though the air was cool. I had a feeling he liked to wear shorts because he was always out walking and carrying around cans and bottles. That had to work up a sweat.

"Did you report it to the police?"

He shrugged. "Nah. The cops don't want to hear from us."

"But things are different now," I said. "You should call the cops."

"Look, it happens. We try to be careful and stay out the way, but some people just like to make trouble."

"Some people are jerks," I muttered. "Were you standing out in the street?"

He frowned. "No. I was on the sidewalk. But this car was coming up too fast and must've lost control. Wyatt thought they might jump the curb and nail me." He chuckled. "He was exaggerating, but still, I was glad he got me out of the way."

Jump the curb? Was he kidding?

My nerves were jumping now. "Uh, I'm glad, too. Wyatt sounds like a good friend."

"He's got my back and I've got his."

"It's nice to have someone like that who'll watch out for you."

"Yeah. Especially in this town. It can get rough out there without your posse."

"Did Wyatt happen to notice what kind of car it was?" I tried to sound casual, but what Tom had described didn't sound normal at all. And since I lived with a security expert, I was used to being suspicious of everything.

"Doesn't matter," Tom said easily.

I tried to smile. "Humor me."

He shrugged. "I didn't see it myself, but Wyatt said it was a 911 Carrera Cabriolet. That's a Porsche, a nice one. And speedy, too. He said it was a real pretty midnight blue."

"Sounds deluxe," I managed to say.

"Yeah. Wyatt knows a lot more about cars than I do." He chuckled. "He was impressed that I almost got hit by such a cool car."

"Cool car or not," I said with a scowl, "people who drive those high-performance cars think they own the road."

And again, I was sounding like my father. I glanced down at my tool case and realized that I had packed it already. I let out a breath and tried to relax. "Well, you want a quickie tour of the library?"

"You don't have to bother, Brooklyn. I really like libraries, and this one is pretty fantastic. I'm happy to just wander around."

I smiled at him. "I don't mind taking a few minutes to point out some highlights."

Tom gave a slight bow of his head. "Then if you don't mind, I'd appreciate that."

So I did just that, showing him the most interesting exhibits—to me anyway—that the Covington had running. He enjoyed the giant Audubon book of birds and the different Shakespeare folios.

I caught him staring up at the walls and smiled. "Pretty impressive, isn't it?"

"That's a lot of books," he said.

"Are you much of a reader, Tom?"

"I'm a real fan of the library." He glanced around. "I mean, the regular library. I try to check out five books a week."

"That's a lot of reading."

"My life is pretty simple these days," he admitted. "But even in the past when things were looking dark, books always got me through the rough spots."

I walked with him down to the smaller galleries and we talked about reading. He liked experimenting with all sorts of genres and he read a lot of nonfiction, too.

In the hall leading to the small galleries, I explained what treasures each room held. At the last minute I decided not to show him the poison exhibit. Hobson had just been killed this morning and we still didn't know who the intended victim was. That exhibit might hit too close to home for now.

But I did point the way to the children's museum. "If you have a chance to visit, I think you'll enjoy it. The exhibits are much more whimsical and user-friendly. Some are even hands on."

"Sounds like a good time."

"It is. And that's where the kids will be painting the fence tomorrow. You know, the Tom Sawyer thing?"

"Oh yeah. I'm supposed to be there for that."

"I hear that you and Joseph are expected to be at all the events this week."

"That's right. I've got a pretty full schedule to follow."

"Well, you can check out the children's space right now and then you'll know where to go tomorrow."

"I'll do that," he said. "Thanks, Brooklyn. I appreciate it."

"Brooklyn!"

I turned and watched Inspector Lee jogging toward me from the main hall. "Hey, you made it."

She stopped short when she saw Tom standing next to me. "Hello, Mr. Cantwell."

"Hey there," Tom said with a curt nod.

"Of course, you two have met," I said. Tom mentioned that he'd been interviewed by the detective earlier at the house.

"Yeah, we're acquainted," Inspector Lee said. To Tom she said, "I didn't expect to see you here today."

"It was a spur-of-the-moment decision," Tom said. "I've got some of my buddies outside."

"Is your buddy Wyatt out there?" she asked.

Tom frowned, clearly not trusting the woman—a cop. "Maybe. Why do you want to know?"

"Because he was at Mr. Cabot's house with you last night and he was with you earlier today. He might be able to help with our investigation."

"He didn't see anything."

"Sometimes a person doesn't know what he saw until I ask him specific questions." She wasn't defensive and she didn't get in his face. She just spoke normally and I appreciated it. "He might've seen the messenger drop off that envelope. Or he could've seen a suspicious person near the house." She appealed to his good nature. "I'm hoping he'll be able to help me out."

I could tell that Tom was reluctant, but finally gave in. "Yeah, okay. But don't badger him. He's a sensitive guy."

Her lips twisted in a wry grin. "I rarely badger. I'm more of a pester-and-nag type of person."

Tom gave a hesitant smile. "Okay. But I'm about to hit the road and he'll be leaving with me."

"Okay, look." She checked her wristwatch. "I've got to take care of one thing here with Brooklyn. Would you mind hanging around for another fifteen or twenty minutes? No longer than that. I'd really appreciate it."

He had to think about it. Finally he said, "Yeah. Okay. I'll look around in here for a few more minutes, then we'll be waiting in that garden out there."

"Thanks, Mr. Cantwell."

"It's Tom."

She grinned. "Thanks, Tom."

"See you, Brooklyn," he said. "Thanks again."

"You're welcome, Tom."

As soon as Tom walked away, I pulled out my phone. "I need to call Derek and have him contact Tom's driver. I don't want Tom walking around, especially at night."

"Brooklyn, he walks all over town almost every day."

"Yeah, but someone tried to run him down this morning."

She gave me a look that defined incredulity. "Good to know. Call the driver. Then you and I will talk."

*   *   *

After I told her what had happened to Tom and how Wyatt had saved the day, Inspector Lee and I looked through the Poisoned Papers exhibit.

I led her past several examples where poisons were used to heighten the color of some Renaissance-era manuscripts.

Then I stopped in front of the golden-hued newspaper story. "Here's the scenario that was used to kill Hobson."

She read the descriptions and looked at the photographs. "It seems awfully complicated and dangerous," she admitted.

"It wouldn't be too hard if you know what you're doing," I said. "And as for being dangerous, that's true, but only after several steps are taken."

"Yeah, and when those steps are taken, you can kill someone."

"That's true. But the powder and the adhesive are inert until they're mixed together."

"Right," she said. "So do yourself a favor and don't mix them together."

"Well, yeah."

With a light snort, she read more details of the golden-hued newspaper poisoning. When she had finished reading, she turned to me. "So I'm right in thinking that this spells out the entire method used in the poisoning this morning."

"It doesn't give step-by-step instructions," I said. "But if you know anything about chemistry and poisons, you can figure it out."

"Fascinating," she murmured.

"I know, right?"

"Yeah. And I'm concerned that if someone was able to poison the butler this easily, I should probably shut this exhibit down."

"What?" I said. "No!"

She smirked. "Really, Brooklyn?"

I made a really sad face. "I know what you're saying, but do you really have to shut the whole thing down?"

"Look, I get the historical significance of all this, but it obviously gave someone a textbook plan to kill the butler. And if one person can figure that out, so can others."

"I know you're right. It's just that this exhibit is so cool." My shoulders slumped. "Don't you hate it when someone comes along and wrecks it for the rest of us?"

"That's why we can't have nice things," she said, patting my back.

"I really loved this exhibit."

"That's because you're a twisted girl, Brooklyn."

"I know, I know." I scowled at her. "But you're a killjoy."

"And proud of it."

My phone rang and I pulled it out of my pocket. "It's Derek."

"Answer it," she said.

"Hi, Derek," I said. "I'm here with Inspector Lee and she says hello."

Inspector Lee held up her hand. "I have to go."

"Derek, can you hold on? Inspector Lee is taking off."

"Of course," he said. "I'll wait."

"Thanks for the tour," she said. "I'm going to go talk to Wyatt and the rest of Tom's friends now. Maybe I'll see you at the next event."

"It's the Riverboat Casino tonight and then fence painting here tomorrow."

"I'll be in touch." She dashed off to meet Wyatt and I hoped the man was stable enough to be able to handle the police interview.

I brought the phone back to my ear. "Hi. Are you on your way home?"

"Yes," Derek said. "You're still at the Covington?"

"I'm walking out right now."

"Then I'll meet you at home," he said. "We have a lot to talk about."

Chapter 14

Right is right, and wrong is wrong, and a body ain't got
no business doing wrong when he ain't ignorant and
knows better.
— Mark Twain, *The Adventures of Huckleberry Finn*

Derek and I didn't get a chance to talk right away because he barely made it home before it was time to
leave for the riverboat. And on the drive over to the
Embarcadero, just as we were about to delve into our
individual stories of the day, Derek received an important phone call from his agent in Europe and had
to spend the next twenty minutes debriefing him.

"He made it to the embassy," Derek announced
when he ended the call.

"That sounds like good news."

"It is." But he gave me a look of regret. "I'm afraid
I can't tell you much more without breaching national
security."

"So if you told me, you'd have to kill me?"

He tried to hide his smile. "Exactly. So don't push
me, because I would miss you."

"That's so sweet," I said, pressing my hands to my

heart. But I didn't bug him to share the details. I figured he would tell me everything eventually, around the same time as the rest of the world heard about it.

I anticipated that the Riverboat Casino Night would be a fun event, but I was still feeling too nervous to enjoy it. After all, the day had started with Hobson's murder and ended with the news of a possible hit-and-run driver aimed at Tom. How could I get into a party vibe?

But as I stepped onto the deck of the boat, I reconsidered. First, because everyone seemed to be having a fabulous time. And second, because nobody appeared to be dead.

That was a win-win in anybody's book.

In addition to that, this authentic riverboat had been lovingly restored with every surface gleaming in the last rays of sunlight. There was a good crowd, the big band sounded fabulous, the casino games were always fun, and the prizes promised to be outstanding.

For me and others, the real highlight of the evening was the variety of costumes that the guests wore, particularly the women. Ella and Ingrid stood out, having outdone themselves by dressing as old-time dance hall girls. Their outfits were colorful if a little tacky, with their brightly colored ruffled skirts worn well above their knees and their very low-cut tops.

I was surprised that those two had gotten into the spirit of the moment, despite the reality of Hobson's murder earlier that day. It was a relief to see it. They flirted and laughed with the guests and even performed an impromptu can-can dance, sashaying around the deck, swinging their skirts up and shaking their booties, to the delight of everyone on board.

I had no idea if the riverboats of Mark Twain's time had employed dance hall girls, but nobody seemed to care whether historical accuracy was enforced or not. Everyone was having too much fun. And when Ella laughed, I could see what had originally appealed to Joseph. She really was charming and beautiful when she wanted to be.

I couldn't figure out what made Ella and Ingrid tick. I knew for a fact that Ingrid had nothing but contempt for events such as this one, and that went double for the upcoming Jumping Frog Contest. I didn't know Ella's opinion of the festival or the individual events, but I knew her mother had a big influence over her. Yet here they were, going above and beyond to make everyone think they were having the best time ever.

Tom and Joseph were both dressed as riverboat captains, complete with those fancy garters around their elbows to hold up their sleeves. As Joseph explained to the crowd, the garters were a practical fashion accessory for working men everywhere and they pulled off the look with flair. The crowd, after plenty of cheers and laughter, had to agree.

Joseph had the microphone and cheerfully announced every time someone won a big poker hand. I didn't know how he could maintain that jovial quality after he'd lost his close friend and butler only hours before. But he'd been through some bad times in his life and it looked as though sheer determination and will would get him through this one, too.

The casino tables had been placed across the main deck and there were several bars scattered about, as well. An elegant buffet was available on the next deck up, which some of the crew referred to as the "hurricane deck." There was every kind of food anyone could possibly want, including pasta with different sauces, tacos with all the trimmings, beautifully prepared steaks, and veggie kababs. This was San Francisco, after all, so there were choices for vegans, vegetarians, pescatarians, and meat lovers alike. And then there were the dessert platters. All I could say was, nobody would go hungry tonight.

Up on the very top deck, the big band musicians were playing the hits of that era. It wasn't exactly what Mark Twain would've been listening to, but this crowd was loving it. And dancing to it, too.

While Derek called his team together for a quick meeting, I glanced around and spied Ian and Jake at the roulette table. I crossed the deck to give them both hugs, then Ian said, "First, let's get you a cocktail."

Jake asked, "What will you have?"

"A vodka tonic," I said. "And I'm just having one."

"Are you driving?"

"No, but Derek is on duty tonight so I want to be halfway aware of things, just in case."

"On duty?" Ian asked. "As in secret agent duty?"

I glanced around, hoping nobody had overheard that. "He's got a few security guys here tonight. Just for good measure."

"Would this have anything to do with the murder this morning at Joseph's house?" Jake asked.

I winced. "You know I can't talk about it."

Ian winked at me. "That's okay, sweetie. We'll talk later."

"Let me put a bet down for you," Jake said, fiddling with a handful of poker chips. "It'll cheer you up. What's your lucky number?"

"Seventeen." I grabbed that number out of thin air, then remembered it was my mom's birthdate. Guess we'd see how lucky it was.

"Okay, here goes." He placed two poker chips on seventeen black, and the dealer began to spin the wheel.

It took almost a minute for the thing to slow down and for that little ball to bounce around and finally land. On number seventeen.

"Oh my God," I whispered.

"Girl!" Jake cried. "You won!"

"I can't believe it," I said.

"Believe it."

The dealer handed me a fistful of green tickets. "Here's your winnings, ma'am."

"These should be yours," I said, holding them out to Jake.

Jake held up both hands. "No way. Your number, your prize."

I stared at all the green tickets. "How come there are so many?"

"Because of the odds," Ian explained.

"The house pays thirty-five to one in roulette," Jake continued. "And since I put two chips down for you, you get seventy chips back."

"Which they pay in tickets." I held up all of my green tickets. "I get it."

"That's right, Greenie," Jake said, chuckling.

Ian grinned. "Looks like green is your new signature color."

"Looks good on you," Jake agreed.

I smiled. "Who knew?" I would have to remember to thank my mom for being born on that day in June.

Since this was a charity event, nobody would actually

win any real money tonight, but we would win gift cards and all sorts of great prizes that had been donated by dozens of companies and individuals who loved the Covington—or just loved a charitable deduction. Everyone attending had been given a certain number of poker chips to play with. When someone left a table, they'd trade each poker chip for a green ticket. At the end of the night we would bring our green tickets to the cashier and that was where we'd collect the gift cards and other prizes, depending on how many green tickets we amassed. The remainder of the proceeds would go to the Covington Library Foundation.

That was fine with me because it wasn't about the money; it was about having a good time. And contributing to the Covington. And of course, celebrating the life and works of Mark Twain. Joseph was very good to give us regular reminders of why we were here.

"Somebody's a big winner."

I turned and saw Ashley standing a few feet away.

Ian gave her a big hug. "Hi, beautiful."

"Ashley, pumpkin!" Jake said, and grabbed her in a quick hug. "You look gorgeous."

She beamed with pleasure, and I would bet that he was the only person on the planet allowed to call her "pumpkin." She wore the chic, modern equivalent of the dance hall girl look with a short, black sequined dress with fringe on the short sleeves and along the swingy hem. The fringe shimmied with every move she made.

"Hey," I said. "How are you, Ashley?"

"I'm doing really well, Brooklyn, but looks like you're doing even better. How did you win all that so quickly?"

"It's roulette," I said with a happy shrug. "There's no skill. It's all luck."

"Well, it looks like your luck is riding high."

"How are things going on your end with the festival?"

"Oh! You wouldn't believe how many people have tweeted and posted photos of men they think are Tom and Joseph. Thousands! And what's really incredible is that the *Clarion* subscription numbers have almost doubled in just the last few days. Joseph is totally psyched. It's a real phenomenon!"

"That's exciting," I said. But I couldn't help wondering if maybe one of those tweets had belonged to someone who, instead of taking a picture, had decided to plow into Tom with his car.

"I hate to even ask you this," I said, "but has the paper received any threatening e-mails or tweets?"

"Oh, we always get those," she said with a casual shrug. "We have a whole department that handles those kinds of nuisance e-mails."

I gave her a half-hearted smile. "People can get a little crazy when there's so much cash involved."

"Tell me about it." She stared across the boat and frowned. "Is that Ella?"

I glanced in the same direction. "Yes. She and her mother decided to come in costume. They're dance hall girls."

"Wow. I did not have that on my bingo card."

I gave a quick laugh.

"Well," she said with a sigh. "I guess I'd better go say hello."

"We'll be around if you want to play roulette," Ian said.

"I'll try to get back here," Ashley said. "You guys are the fun ones."

"You know it, girl," Jake said.

Ashley walked away toward Ella and Ingrid, stopping every few feet to greet someone in the crowd.

"She's a doll," Jake said.

Ian nodded. "And so smart."

Jake began to fiddle with his poker chips. "Do you want to play another round, Brooklyn?"

"I think I'd better quit while I'm ahead."

"If you change your mind, we'll be around."

I gave Jake a hug. "You're the only one I want placing my bets for me."

"Aw, sweet!"

Without warning, an earsplitting bang erupted.

I automatically ducked. Was that a gunshot?

"What the hell was that?" Ian asked.

Women screamed and people across the deck began to run for cover. Others ducked under the gambling tables.

Jake grabbed Ian's arm. "Let's get inside."

A tremendous cry came from directly across the deck, where Ella and Ingrid had been standing just seconds ago.

The drawn-out shriek was followed by a heavy splash.

"Oh my God!" a woman cried.

"Man overboard!" someone shouted.

Someone had fallen into the water!

Ingrid shrieked, "My baby!" She stared over the railing, waving her arms and screaming for her life.

Ella had fallen into the water? How? Why? Good grief, did someone shoot her?

Seconds later, Tom scrambled up onto the railing, steadied himself, and dived neatly into the Bay.

Derek came racing from the other side of the boat and I went running over to see if I could help. Three of Derek's agents joined him.

And following in their wake was Inspector Lee. She spoke into a two-way-radio device as she moved directly toward Derek.

Before she could say a word, Derek said, "Ella Cabot fell overboard and Tom Cantwell dove in after her."

All of us stared over the railing to see the woman flailing in the water a few feet out from the boat. Tom swam right over to help her, but she was all tangled up in the many ruffles and layers of her dress. Every time she tried to scream, she swallowed more water and choked. She tried to shout for help but all we heard were gurgling sounds.

I watched several people pull out their phones and video the whole scene. None of those people bothered to try and help Ella. They just kept recording. I thought it was horribly rude, but that was how things were these days. And when it came right down to it, what could anyone do for her? Her rescuer Tom was right there and I was certain he wouldn't let her drown. Not on his watch.

Despite Ella's attempts to fight him off, Tom was able to hold her head firmly above the surface of the water and he seemed to be talking to her, calming her down.

Ingrid's high-pitched screeching turned to sobs as we all watched Tom rescue Ella.

Joseph appeared and grabbed Derek's arm. "What

the hell happened? What's wrong with Ingrid? I was talking to the captain when I heard screaming."

"Try not to worry," Derek said quickly. "Ella fell overboard, but she's going to be fine. Can you please try to calm Ingrid down and keep everyone else from panicking?"

"Good God." Joseph sucked in air and nodded. "I'll try. Okay." But he continued to stare over the railing at his wife being held afloat by Tom.

"We've got a boat coming," Derek added.

At that moment a small lifeboat approached at high speed carrying two men. One man turned off the engine and steadied the boat while the other reached over the side and grabbed hold of Ella, yanking her into the boat.

It was a relief to see her sprawled inside the boat. I didn't see any blood so I hoped she hadn't been shot. She looked like the proverbial wet hen, unfortunately, and I could tell she was furious. She couldn't stop hacking and coughing and I wondered how much Bay water she'd swallowed. There were stories in the paper all the time about the pollution that was washed into the Bay from agricultural runoff.

But that wasn't the worst danger to her health, I thought. The worst danger was that there was someone on this boat who might've deliberately pushed her into the water. She could've been badly hurt. I scanned the crowd and wondered who could've done it.

I stared down at the lifeboat. Now that Ella was safe, the other agent reached a hand out for Tom, but he waved him away. The agent argued with him for a few seconds, but then handed him a sturdy life preserver

and motioned for him to swim to the ladder at the side
of the dock, about fifty feet away.

I turned back to Derek. "I thought I heard a gunshot. Did you hear a gunshot?"

"I heard something that could've been a gunshot,"
he said, "but there's a lot of traffic nearby so it could've
been a car backfiring." He glanced over my shoulder.
"Inspector Lee might know the answer."

"I haven't been able to verify that there were gun-
shots," she said to Derek. "I've got a couple of officers out
on the pier questioning witnesses and bystanders."

"Thank you," he said.

"Can you give me more details of what happened
here?" Inspector Lee asked. Derek's serious attitude
matched hers so I decided to shut up for now and ask
questions later.

Derek gave her the full story, ticking off each occur-
rence as though it were a bullet point on an itemized
list. "Mrs. Cabot fell into the water. We don't know if
she accidentally fell in or if she was pushed. Her
mother was nearby and might know the answer, so I'll
arrange for you to talk to her. You already know that
some of us heard what could've been a gunshot."

"We're looking into that," she said.

Derek nodded. "Tom Cantwell dived in after Mrs.
Cabot and helped save her. My men arrived quickly in
a lifeboat and brought her to the dock. Mr. Cantwell
refused help from the lifeboat crew and instead swam
over to the dock."

"Yeah, I've talked to Mr. Cantwell a few times." Inspector Lee studied her notes for a moment, then closed
the notebook and slipped it into her pocket. "I'm going

down to the dock to meet Mrs. Cabot and Mr. Cantwell. And I'll want to talk to your guys in the boat."

"I'll go with you," Derek said, and the two of them left the riverboat.

Joseph came running over. "Where's Derek?"

"He's with Inspector Lee," I said, pointing in the direction they'd gone. "They're just leaving the boat to find Ella and Tom and the guys in the lifeboat. They need to interview all of them."

"I'll catch up with them," he said. "I've got to make sure that Ella's all right."

"What can I do to help?" I asked.

He stared blankly at me, then snapped back. "Thanks. Can you ask the band to start playing again? The music might help calm people down."

"Sure."

"And would you mind making a quick announcement that we've got lots of great food and fun gambling and, oh, you know, blah blah blah."

Despite the serious moment, I chuckled. "Sure."

"Brooklyn, you're a gem."

"Joseph!" a woman cried. We both turned and saw Ingrid scurrying across the deck. "My Ella! My baby!"

I quickly stepped back a few feet to get out of her way. Her breath was coming in halting gasps and I was concerned that she might start hyperventilating. She flung herself at Joseph so dramatically that he had to struggle to stay upright.

"She's safe," Joseph said, and wrapped his arm around her shoulders. "Calm down now. We're going to go find her. You'll come with me."

"Oh, thank heavens! I thought she was going to die! I can't lose her, Joseph."

"We won't lose her, honey. She's fine. Just very wet and probably mad as hell. Let's go."

Very wet and mad as hell was a pretty good description of what they'd find when they tracked down Ella, I thought.

Joseph led Ingrid away and I admired his patience and kindness. Joseph hadn't seen what happened to Ella because he'd been involved with the donors and guests. But the last time I saw Ingrid, she had been standing right next to Ella. Had she walked away? Had someone noticed her leaving and taken advantage of the moment?

I reminded myself of my promise to Joseph and took off up the stairs to find the musicians.

"Brooklyn, wait."

I watched Ashley hurry up the stairs. "I've got to go talk to the band."

"What happened?" she asked. "Do you know where Joseph went?"

"Yeah. He and Ingrid went to meet Ella."

"Where did she go?"

I couldn't help but look puzzled. "I thought you were right there. You said you were going to say hello to her."

"Yeah." Her eyes widened. "But I didn't make it. I kept getting interrupted and then I stopped to get a glass of wine. And then . . ." She giggled. "I flaked. Sorry."

"Ah." She hadn't come across as a flake before, but everyone was entitled to a slip once in a while.

"Ella fell overboard," I said without easing into it.

"What?" she cried. "Overboard? Ella? Are you kidding?"

"Not kidding. They're investigating right now. Pretty sure she'll be fine, but I imagine she's pretty traumatized."

"Of course! How horrible!" She looked around, every which way. "Where's Joseph? What can I do?"

"I'm so glad you asked," I said. "I'm going upstairs to get the musicians to start playing again so the rest of the guests don't get cranky."

"Do you want me to do that?"

I smiled. "No, there's something else. Joseph wanted me to announce that the games are still going on and the buffet is fabulous and there's dancing on the top deck and . . . you know, all that good stuff. You could probably do that a lot better than I could. Do you mind?"

"Absolutely not. I'll take care of it."

"Thanks, Ashley."

She skipped downstairs and I continued my climb to the top deck, where I tracked down the musical conductor to give him Joseph's message. He wore a tuxedo and was younger and hipper than I'd expected, with a goatee and a neatly trimmed ponytail.

"I was just waiting for my cue," he said with a sly grin. "We'll get back to grooving right away."

"Thank you, maestro."

I started to head downstairs and that's when I looked out and noticed the view. The lights of the city sparkled all around us and the Bay Bridge was spectacular, all lit up and beautiful. It was all reflected in the water and the undulating waves that caused thousands of twinkling lights to drift and move with the tide. I took a slow breath and was finally able to relax for a quick minute.

And that's when I started wondering about Ashley.

*   *   *

It was more than an hour before Derek finally returned to the riverboat. In the meantime, left to my own devices, I was lured to a blackjack table and quickly developed an obsession with the game. I just kept winning. I couldn't tell you how or why. I wasn't a complete poker novice, but I also wasn't exactly a high roller. And I wasn't really paying close attention because my mind kept wondering what Ashley had been doing while everyone else was watching the drama of Ella falling off the boat into the water. Had she been telling the truth? That she just "flaked"? She didn't seem like the flaky type. But why would she lie?

Frankly, I couldn't picture her getting away with pushing Ella into the water. First of all, Ashley was a petite woman while Ella was positively statuesque. So I couldn't work out the logistics of that scenario.

So maybe Ashley was telling the truth. Maybe she just flaked. That still didn't work for me, either, but I couldn't come up with any other possibilities.

Ian and Jake stopped by my table several times to marvel at all those green tickets I was accumulating. My new nickname of "Greenie" seemed to have stuck.

Once Derek stepped onto the main deck, I cashed out, handed some poker chips to my dealer for whatever role he'd played in helping me win, and dashed over to join my husband.

"How's Ella doing?" I asked first thing.

"Let's walk." He slipped his arm around my waist and we strolled away from the crowd to the back of the boat, where very few people were congregating. "She's fine now. Shaken up, obviously, and traumatized.

Physically, though, she didn't suffer anything worse than some scrapes and scratches."

"Wow, that's lucky." We stopped and leaned against the railing. "I think I would've gone into shock before I hit the water."

"She did," he said. "It was a good thing Tom jumped in when he did because he truly saved her life. Our lifeboat arrived a minute later, but without Tom talking to her and calming her down, it might've been too late. Her mental state deteriorated rapidly, but thanks to Tom's quick action, she survived. And now she's almost back to normal."

"Did she tell you if someone pushed her?"

"Yes. She said that someone came up behind her and they didn't just push her. They scooped her up and tossed her overboard."

"Did she see who did it?"

"No," he said, and I could tell he was irritated by that.

"And nobody else saw anything?"

"Apparently not," he said through clenched teeth.

I couldn't blame him for being angry. There were plenty of people on the boat so how could someone be thrown overboard and not have one other person witness it?

I tried to picture the scene. "The person would have to be in good shape to lift her up like that and toss her into the water. She probably doesn't have much fat on her, but she's tall. It would be awkward."

"Awkward indeed," he murmured.

"I spoke to Ashley before everything happened and she told me she was going to go and talk to Ella. I asked her later if she had talked to her, and she basically said that she flaked. She claimed she kept getting interrupted and didn't make it across the boat."

"She couldn't have picked up Ella and thrown her in the water."

"No," I admitted. "But her story was still pretty weak." I shrugged. "Anyway, did Ella describe the guy who grabbed her? Short? Tall? Was he strong? Did he make any noise? You know, any grunting or groaning?"

Derek began to smile. "You should've been there, darling. You ask all the best questions." His smile faded. "I'd like to answer them, but unfortunately Ella was rather vague. I'm willing to chalk it up to nerves. But tomorrow Inspector Lee will take another go at her. She wasn't any happier than I was with Ella's non-answers."

I looked right at him to gauge his feelings. "Do you and Inspector Lee think Ella is lying?"

He stared right back at me. "Do you?"

I had to think for a minute. "I can't imagine why she would lie about this." I waved my hands to erase that thought. "Actually, I *can* imagine why she would lie, but the scenarios running through my head are too outlandish to even contemplate. I mean, if she jumped on her own, she was taking a pretty big chance. It's a long way down to the water. What if she'd hit her head on the side of the boat? She could've been killed."

"Exactly," he said flatly. "I'm having the same problem believing her story. I think it's because, over the years, we've met too many nice people who turned out to be sociopaths. I believe we're jaded."

I wanted to laugh, but the reality of his statement hit a little too close to home. "I think you're right."

"Please understand," he hastened to add. "I'm not calling Ella a sociopath."

I smiled. "Of course not. I know what you meant."

"We'll question her again tomorrow and I'm certain she'll be much more cohesive than she is tonight."

On the drive home, Derek reminded me that we hadn't even talked about all the events that had happened earlier that day.

I rubbed my neck, feeling exhausted. "This morning seems like a year ago."

"It does," he agreed. "But I'd still like to hear what happened at the Covington."

"And I really want to hear how Joseph got through his interview with Inspector Lee."

Derek nodded. "As you would expect, he was . . . upset."

"That's understandable," I said.

"The problem for Joseph is that he wasn't home when the envelope arrived."

"Oh, right," I said, suddenly realizing how Joseph might not understand everything that happened. "So he didn't have any perspective on what actually occurred."

"Exactly," he said. "I wasn't certain whether I would be of any use to him by staying, but as it turned out, it was a very good thing that I was there." He sighed. "Unfortunately I was able to lay out the entire ugly scene, both for him and for Inspector Lee."

"And how did he take it?"

"It was very upsetting for him."

And for Derek, too, I thought. "I'm so sorry."

"It's odd," he said. "Joseph is one of the strongest people I've ever known. But as I was describing what

happened, how the envelope arrived and how angry
Hobson was at Tom, and how he finally lost his ability
to maintain control, Joseph seemed to lose it as well."

"I imagine that was hard for Joseph to hear."

"It was. And then he broke down completely when
Inspector Lee questioned him about the fight he had
with Hobson."

"He seems very guilt-ridden about that argument."

"Oh, indeed." Derek was quiet for a moment as he
turned a corner. "I don't believe he's used to being
questioned about anything. He's the ruler of his empire and he insists that everything in his world should
run like clockwork. When something breaks down, he
just calls someone to fix it. But in the case of Hobson,
nobody can fix it for him."

"And he can't handle it," I said.

"That's right," Derek agreed. "He can't accept it."

I turned to look at him. "You've put your finger on
the problem."

"You think so?"

"I do."

When the light turned red, he slowed to a stop. "But
there's another bigger problem," he said. "Joseph won't
admit it, but Hobson was his best friend. If Ella left
him tomorrow, he wouldn't miss her as much as he's
missing Hobson."

"But their relationship was so toxic," I said.

"It looked that way from the outside, especially what
we witnessed last evening," Derek said. "But I've seen
their interactions in the past and they were very cor-
dial, very friendly. I'm not sure what the truth is."

"You certainly know them better than I do. But boy,
hearing that argument between Joseph and Hobson?

That was brutal. And then I had to overhear that wacko conversation between Ella and Ingrid earlier today."

"You only gave me a few of the highlights," he said. "What else did they say?"

I sat back in my seat. "Give me a minute to organize my thoughts because they said a lot." I took a moment to think back to the crazy conversation I'd overheard, then began to relate as much as I could recall to Derek.

When I was finished, he was quiet for a minute, then shook his head. "I'm so angry. Joseph doesn't deserve to be surrounded by this toxic group of people."

"It's pretty bad," I agreed.

He took a deep breath and exhaled slowly. "If nothing else, they certainly are an argumentative bunch," he said.

I laughed. "You have a way of understating things that is just so perfect."

"Thank you, darling." He made the right turn onto Harrison and drove a block in silence.

"I'm going to suggest something," I said, "and you let me know what you think."

"All right."

"I think everything changed when Joseph married Ella."

He glanced at me. "I'm certain that you're right."

"Really?"

"Yes."

"Okay." It felt good to be validated. "So with that in mind, who do you think killed Hobson?"

"That is the million-dollar question," he said. "And the only way we'll solve it is by determining who was capable of turning that gold powder into poison."

"Oh hell." I scowled. "You're right, and it's really annoying."

"Thank you." He chuckled, but then his eyes narrowed. "But I agree, it's terribly frustrating to know that Hobson's killer is hiding in plain sight and we can't figure it out."

"But we will," I insisted.

He reached over and gripped my hand in his. "Now you were going to tell me about your day."

I took a deep breath to calm down. "Thank you for switching away from that frustrating subject."

He chuckled. "Anytime."

"So I told you that Tom came by the Covington."

"Yes. Did he tell you what he was doing there?"

"He did. He mainly came by because he likes libraries, but also because Joseph had talked about how great the place is, so he was curious. And by the way, Tom is a big reader. He said he checks out five books a week from his local library."

"That's impressive."

"I think so, too. He has a lot of time on his hands and he likes to spend it reading. When he's not out collecting cans and bottles, that is."

"It wouldn't be the worst way to spend your day."

"It sounds really good to me." I twisted in my seat to face him. "But I haven't gotten to the most important part. Tom told me that he almost got hit by a car this afternoon."

"I beg your pardon?"

"You heard me right. He downplayed it, didn't even think it really mattered. But he admitted that Wyatt actually had to yank him out of the way of this speeding car."

"Well, thank goodness for Wyatt."

"Yes, but here's the thing. And you know I'm not into conspiracies, but I think it was deliberate."

"Why do you think so?"

"Because Tom was standing on the sidewalk. He wasn't out in the street."

"I see."

"And Wyatt likes cars, so when he heard the driver gunning the car's engine, he paid attention. He noticed that it was coming toward them really fast, and just as it looked as if it might jump the curb, he yanked Tom out of the way."

"Jumped the curb." Derek frowned. "As though he were aiming straight at him."

"Exactly."

He considered that new bit of information as we turned onto Brannan and finally pulled into our underground garage. He parked the car, then gazed at me. "Did Tom happen to notice what kind of car it was?"

"Tom didn't, but Wyatt did. He immediately identified it as a late-model 911 Carrera Cabriolet. Midnight blue."

Derek considered this. "I know a number of people who own that car. It's a very popular model."

"You would know."

He smirked. "I'm a bit of a car fanatic myself."

"I know," I said fondly. "So what do we do about it?"

"I'll ask Joseph if he knows anyone who drives that type of car." We both stepped out of the car and Derek reached for my hand. "Did you happen to mention this to Inspector Lee?"

"Funny you should ask," I said. "She was there at

the library, checking out the poison exhibit. When I left her, she was on her way to interview Wyatt and Tom about the car."

He nodded firmly. "Good."

"What I want to know is, why would anyone go after Tom?" I frowned, remembering Ingrid's words of warning to Ella. "Is it because someone thinks he's related to Joseph?"

Derek considered that. "Or do they think that the man collecting bottles actually *is* Joseph?"

The thought hit me like a ton of bricks. "Of course! Someone thinks that Joseph is out there playing the role of the pauper, collecting bottles and cans."

And just like that, chills ran down my spine.

We rode the elevator in silence, both of us wrapped up in our individual thoughts. The door opened on our floor, and I took two steps into the hall—and stopped and looked at Derek.

"It's a little annoying to know that you're always one step ahead of me."

He wrapped his arm around me. "Not always, darling. Oftentimes you're well ahead of me. But we always end up walking together."

I beamed up at him. "That was good. You're good."

He laughed and kissed me. "I love you."

We walked into our apartment and Charlie greeted us with head bumps and slinky moves around our ankles. "I dread the day we walk in and Charlie just sits on the back of the couch staring at us with contempt. Like a regular cat."

"That day will never come," Derek said with confidence, and picked up the cat. "She's much too friendly and loving."

I watched the two of them and felt my heart swell. This was my little family and I was so lucky to have them.

Derek was studying me. "Are you crying, love?"

I'm not crying, you're crying, I thought as I blinked away the tears. "Maybe just a little. Because you and Charlie make me so happy."

"Come here." Still clutching Charlie, he pulled me down on the couch and the three of us held on to each other for a long time. Any more talk of murder could wait until tomorrow.

Chapter 15

If you pick up a starving dog and make him prosperous,
he will not bite you. This is the principal difference
between a dog and a man.

—Mark Twain, *Pudd'nhead Wilson*

Monday morning I woke up early and made it to the
kitchen while Derek finished showering. I started the
coffee and began to cut up some fruit for breakfast.

"Isn't this a lovely surprise," Derek said when he
walked into the room.

"I've gotten so used to you fixing breakfast, I forgot
what it was like."

He glanced around. "You seem to have picked it up
again."

"I have," I said proudly. "There's sourdough toast in
the oven and I cut up some strawberries and an apple.
And coffee, of course."

"Coffee, too? I'm impressed."

"Very funny."

He grinned as he poured himself a cup, then pulled
out two pieces of toast and placed them on small plates.

I took butter and apricot preserves—made with love

by my mother—out of the fridge and set them on the kitchen bar. Derek reached for the bowl of fruit and spooned some onto both of our plates.

Instead of the more formal dining room, we sat down across from each other at the kitchen island.

"If you feel like talking about it," Derek began, "I have a few more questions regarding Tom's potential hit-and-run driver."

"Sure." I buttered a chunk of toast. "Ask away."

"You said last night that you told Inspector Lee about it."

"I did, and she was planning to meet up with Tom and Wyatt in the rose garden after I left. Unfortunately, with all the excitement last night, I forgot to ask her what Wyatt told her." I frowned. "Not sure she would've told me anyway. But she would've told you."

"Where did the incident happen?"

"It was in Pacific Heights. Tom and his buddies were walking to the Covington from Fillmore Street. They were pretty close to Fillmore, though, so it wasn't too steep a climb yet."

He nodded. "I'll give the inspector a call and ask about traffic cameras."

"But it's all residential," I said. "I doubt there will be any traffic cameras."

"The homes up there are very expensive," he reasoned after taking another sip of coffee. "Some owners could have cameras on their property. Some of them might even be directed toward the street."

I brightened. "You're right. Good thinking."

He took a bite of toast smothered in butter and preserves. "Were you able to show Inspector Lee the poison exhibit?"

"Yeah. It was fun to take her around. She was really impressed."

He nodded. "It's an interesting exhibit."

"She thought so." But my happy face turned glum. "Which is why she's going to shut it down."

"That doesn't seem fair."

I used a chunk of sourdough toast to emphasize my words. "That's what I told her."

"Good for you." He chuckled. "Unfortunately, though, if our killer was able to glean enough information from the exhibit to come up with a formula to kill someone, it's possible that anyone could."

"That was her point. Still, it's too bad."

We munched on toast and sipped our coffee for a few moments, then I said, "I forgot to ask how your man in Europe is doing."

"I believe I mentioned that he made it to our embassy."

"Yes. So he's okay?"

"Yes, he is. He was arrested the day before and we had to jump through dozens of hoops to appease the authorities. It was masterful negotiations by the ambassador that finally got him released."

"Your guy must've been scared to death."

"What the other side pulled was unnecessary and dangerous." Derek scowled. "We used to have a good relationship with this country but a few years ago the people elected a fascist government and those fellows love to yank the chains of the Brits and Americans."

"I just hope your guy is safe."

"We expect to have him on a plane this afternoon."

"That'll be a relief."

"Yes." Derek stood and took our dishes to the sink,

rinsed them off, and put them in the dishwasher. "What's on your agenda today?"

I checked my wristwatch. "I'll be giving my newspaper art workshop at the children's museum starting at eight thirty. They're doing the Tom Sawyer fence-painting event in the same area and it's supposed to run for at least four hours. I'd like to stay and watch some of it, but I'll have to leave at some point to do my bookbinding workshop from twelve to four."

"You're a trooper," he said, raising his coffee cup in a toast to me. "Do you expect Tom and Joseph to be there this morning?"

"I'm sure they'll be there. They represent the festival and this is the only event going on today."

He nodded thoughtfully. "I presume Ella will attend."

"I suppose so, if she isn't too traumatized from last night."

"I may or may not show up there, depending on Inspector Lee's plans. I'll call her from my office." He slipped into his suit jacket and looked ridiculously dashing, then continued. "I'd like to hear about Tom and the car incident from her vantage point and ask her about cameras in the area. And I'll see if she wishes me to join her in questioning Ella."

"So I might just see you there?"

"It's entirely possible."

"I would love that."

"Now whether I'm there or not, several of my agents will be in attendance. So if you see anything suspicious, be sure to speak to them."

"I will." I handed his briefcase to him. "If you do come by, I'll be at the children's museum until around ten or eleven. Then I might grab something to eat in the café and I'll be in the main hall doing my book-binding workshop."

"You'll be busy," he said. "But no events tonight, right?"

"Right."

"We can have a quiet evening at home."

"Yes, please." I pressed my finger against his lips to shush him. "But don't jinx it."

He grinned. "What was I thinking?"

"I don't know." I shook my head. "But yes, a quiet evening sounds like heaven."

"Hush," he said, wrapping his arms around me. "Now who's jinxing it?"

I chuckled, slipped my arms around him, and laid my head on his chest for a minute. "Maybe we could take a walk to Pietro's for pizza and salad. Unless you have something else in mind."

"What could possibly be better than pizza and salad with you?"

"Not much." I walked with him to the door. "To-morrow is the Jumping Frog Contest and I thought I'd go. Any chance you'll be there?"

"Of course I'll be there."

"Because you love frogs or because you'll be work-ing security?"

He kissed me. "Nothing against frogs, but I'll be there in a professional capacity. And I don't mean pro-fessional frog jumper."

I gazed up at him. "Do you expect trouble?"

"We'll be ready for anything."

He hadn't exactly answered the question, I thought. Or maybe he had. The fact that there had been trouble at last night's event, plus the fact that he'd scheduled agents to be at the children's museum today, plus the fact that Derek himself planned to be at the Jumping Frog event tomorrow, equaled a great big expectation of trouble.

Once Derek left for work, I took a shower, blew my hair dry, and added a few touches of makeup. I had to laugh, knowing that Derek loved me whether my face was painted or not. And the kids in my newspaper arts workshop wouldn't care how I looked, but I would. And who knew? Perhaps a few of the parents might be interested in hiring me to do bookbinding work. This was, after all, the Covington Library and I regularly did book restoration work for them.

I stared at myself in the mirror, wondering why I was justifying my reasons for putting on makeup. Just call me shallow, but I liked to look as professional as possible, especially at the Covington. Otherwise, let's face it, I'd be wearing my Birkenstocks everywhere.

I dressed in black jeans, a forest-green sweater, and short black boots. The outfit looked semidressy, but it felt casual. And everything was machine-washable, which was all that mattered when working with children. Still, I wasn't a fool. I planned to wear a smock over everything.

When I walked into the children's museum a half hour later, I was amazed to see how many kids were running around. It was only eight o'clock in the morning, but even at this early hour, the children's museum defined the term *organized chaos*.

The room was immense with large pieces of artwork displayed in all sorts of ways. The space was more modern than that of the main hall, with lots of windows and sturdy chrome fixtures that gave it a clean, uncluttered feeling.

Ian saw me and scurried across the room. "You're here. Good."

"Of course." I scanned the room, my fear mounting. Seriously, there were kids everywhere. "I hope all these children are here for the fence painting and not for my newspaper arts workshop."

He made a nervous face. "I might've booked a few extra for your workshop."

I winced. "I only brought enough supplies for ten kids."

"Well, it's your own fault," he insisted. "You're just too popular."

I scoffed. "Nice try." But I had to laugh at his pitiful mewling expression. "Lucky for you I brought extras."

He grabbed both my arms and squeezed lightly. "You're the smartest girl in class."

"And you're the bad boy who cheats off my test papers."

He laughed. "Let's keep this clever banter going and then burst into song."

"You are twisted," I said, shaking my head.

"Well, yeah. What's your point?"

I just stared at him looking sleek and sophisticated in his five-thousand-dollar business suit and perfectly knotted Hermès tie. "You should at least pretend to be the distinguished president and curator of the most renowned library in the country."

"But I want to be the bad boy," he protested.

"You are," I whispered as a well-dressed older woman approached.

"Mr. McCullough?"

Ian winked at me and turned to the other woman. "Yes, ma'am, how may I help you?"

Ian led her away and they continued their deep discussion while I set up my large workshop table, placing a newspaper at every chair. I had brought a supply of glue sticks and scissors in case of emergency—for parents only.

"Brooklyn?"

I turned and grinned. "Hi, Joseph."

He stood a few feet away, holding a paintbrush. "Good to see you." Rather than his typical elegant dark navy pin-striped suit and a red power tie, he wore torn blue jeans and an old faded sweatshirt. I would've chalked it up to working with kids and paint, but he was supposed to be playing the pauper, after all. He could hardly dress like the wealthy businessman that he really was.

"This is a madhouse," I said, "but you look like you're having fun."

"I'm having a blast and we've hardly gotten started."

"It'll get even crazier, I think."

"That's okay." He glanced at his paintbrush. "We're using nontoxic paint and hopefully no one will try to eat it."

"That's always the hope." I leaned in close. "How is Ella today?"

His smile faded. "She's still pretty upset by what happened."

"I don't blame her, and I'm so sorry." I looked around the room. "Will she be joining you?"

"She didn't want to miss it so she'll be here in a few minutes."

"She's a trooper."

"She is. And Ingrid is coming with her."

"Oh, that's good," I said, but I was thinking, *What's so good about it? Ingrid was no help at all when some-one tossed her daughter into the drink.*

"Oh hey, there's Tom," he said, then laughed. "He's surrounded by kids. I'd better go and rescue him."

"See you later." I turned and saw Tom, who was in-deed surrounded by kids who were pestering him with questions and comments. But he was smiling and didn't look at all like he needed rescuing. In fact, he ap-peared to be having a great time.

He was wearing his signature Bermuda shorts again, this time with a beautiful cashmere sweater over a white dress shirt along with his sturdy tennis shoes and clas-sic white socks.

I had begun to figure out that he wore the Bermuda shorts every day because he walked so much and got hot after a while.

Both he and Tom were good-looking men, whether they wore Bermuda shorts or faded sweatshirts. And judging by the admiring looks they received from the moms in the room, most women would agree.

I finished prepping my worktable and checked my watch. I had fifteen minutes before the workshop started, which meant that most of the kids who'd be attending my event were already running around, play-ing with the exhibits. The giant Lego monster, the pop-up books, and of course, the fence painting. The picket

fence covered the entire floor of the wide space and
Ian's assistants had covered every inch of flooring with
drop cloths.

There were dozens of small, child-sized white buckets already filled with colored paints—all nontoxic and
washable—sitting on the wide tables at the front of the
room. They were the basic colors of red, blue, and yellow, along with green and pink and black and white
and purple. Several hundred small paintbrushes were
lined up alongside the buckets.

A disaster waiting to happen, I thought, then tried
to squelch my negativity.

The decibel levels in the room were growing by the
minute. Ear-piercing screams of delight resounded off
the walls and high ceiling and I cringed a little each
time another child joined in.

I had realized after years of workshops with little
kids that some of those kids simply liked to scream.
They got so excited about stuff that they had to let it
out in earsplitting shrieks that frayed your last pulsat-
ing nerve. You know, that sudden scream that made
you jump and jolt like you'd been zapped with a stun
gun. It made you wish you'd worn earplugs and brought
along a bottle of ibuprofen—or a bottle of Jack Daniel's. For you or for the kid, I wasn't willing to say.

Anyone who'd ever had breakfast at a pancake
restaurant would recognize that deafening sound. Obviously, pancakes were a trigger for so many things.

I knew it was wrong of me to harbor this opinion, not having had any children myself—yet. I was
eight years old when my family moved to the Sonoma
wine country commune where the "It Takes a Village"

philosophy was strong. There were dozens of kids of every age and we were all brought together every day to learn and play and grow. At eight years old I first experienced the horror of that "toddler screech." It terrorized me. My little spine snapped to attention and I thought, *Danger! Danger!*

I had scanned the area for a weapon, maybe a baseball bat, because I knew the poor screaming kid had to have been seized by evil zombie kidnappers. In reality, she had simply gotten her first look at another little girl's Barbie doll and it had driven her over the edge. In retrospect, I couldn't blame her. A Barbie doll was a shriek-worthy sight to behold.

"I think we're all here," a woman to my left said. I glanced at her and thought, *Here's a mom. Thank goodness.*

She was right, of course. I scanned the table and saw ten children sitting there with ten parents—eight moms and two dads—standing behind their chairs. I loved it when parents participated.

I still expected some latecomers to show up, so I set aside four more place settings and supplies, just in case.

"Let's get started," I said.

Ian had thoughtfully placed my worktable at the far corner of the room, as distant as possible from the fence-painting activity.

Despite my occasionally cranky attitude, I really enjoyed working with kids. It helped that most of my workshop attendees were seven to ten years old. By that age, the scream gene had been coaxed or wrestled out of them.

I pulled a colorful basket out of my tote bag and held it up for my group to see. "We're all going to make a basket today. Isn't this cute?"

There were some "Yes!" replies and plenty of enthusiastic nods.

"It's fun and easy and you're not going to need scissors, or glue, or anything else. Just a newspaper. Oh, and a paper clip."

I held up a bright red paper clip, then walked around the table and gave each child one.

"What's this for?" the boy asked.

"I'll show you how to use it when we get there."

"It's pretty," one little girl said.

I smiled at her. "I think so, too."

I looked up at the moms standing near their kids. "Your whole family might enjoy this project because you can make almost any kind of basket or box to hold all sorts of things." I handed the closest mom my newspaper basket. "Pass it around. You can see how simple it is."

"Simple for you, maybe," one of the women said.

I smiled at her. "You grown-ups can always use scissors to trim the edges and a glue stick to make the corners sturdier." I looked at the kids. "But it works fine either way. So, ready to get started?"

"Yeah!" they all shouted.

"Okay."

I explained that I had precut all the double pages so that the kids would be working with single pages only.

"The first thing we're going to do is fold each page back and forth like an accordion, lengthwise, so that you end up with one long, thick strip, about an inch wide."

I held up an example for them to follow. "See?"

"Yeah," an earnest little boy said.

"And we're going to do this for eighteen pages."

"Eighteen?" one of the mothers said. "Are you kidding?"

"No," another insisted. "I'm sorry, but that's impossible. My Madison will be drenched in tears after two."

"I won't cry," Madison protested. Her mother patted her shoulder, but didn't bother to argue.

"Same with Emily," another woman said with a laugh. "And that's when I'll have to finish the project for her."

"Please have mercy," one of the fathers said.

I laughed. "Okay, I hear you." I reached into my tote bag. "And that's why I've already folded the rest of the pages for you."

"What?"

"Oh! You're a lifesaver!"

One woman clutched her chest. "Thank you! I was mentally preparing myself for the tantrum."

"No tantrums and no tears today," I said, and added silently, *Not from my project anyway.*

I passed out the ribbons of newspaper to each child. "Now we start weaving the first twelve strips." I laid six strips vertically down on the table, and began to weave six more strips, one at a time, in and out of the vertical strips. "You start in the middle and work your way out, and each new strip should be woven in the opposite way of the previous strip."

I walked around the table, helping wherever anyone needed it. But most of the kids were picking it up pretty quickly. And the moms were, too.

"At this point," I said, "you can decide how big or

small you want your basket to be. And you can decide what shape you'd like. You can make it a square or a rectangle, whatever you want."

"Oh my God," one mother whispered. "This is so easy."

I grinned. "I told you."

"The new strip is slipping," one little girl said, her voice edging toward panicky.

"Ah. This is where the paper clip comes in handy." I walked over and picked up her paper clip. "Clip the strip you just finished weaving while you work on the next one. That will hold it in place until you move on."

"Oh," the girl said. "That works. I can do it now."

"Good!" I glanced around. "Did everyone see that?"

A few kids nodded, but several raised their hands for help. I liked this group. They were hand raisers instead of yellers. "Who needs help?"

"I do," a little boy at the end of the table said.

I went around to help, and continued to give aid where I could, tweaking a strip where it needed it, adjusting the woven piece where necessary.

When everyone had their first twelve strips woven together, I said, "Now make sure all the strips are even, like this. And then we're going to start to make the sides of the basket using the remaining six strips."

As always, I was thankful for the moms, who jumped in to help their kids with the tricky spots. I explained to them that once they got home, they might want to use paper clips or scotch tape to secure the woven pieces and stiffen the sides and edges so that the basket stood erect. But for now, the kids were all enjoying the project and were only occasionally distracted by the fence-painting activity.

It sounded like Joseph was having a blast, making the occasional announcement about the children's progress and reading short quotes from *Tom Sawyer* about the so-called joy of hard work.

"Here's how the fence-painting scene evolved," Joseph said from his spot at the front of the room. "One of Tom's friends commented about his work and Tom asked him, 'What work?' Implying that Tom was enjoying the work, right?"

"Yeah, pretty tricky," one of the fathers said.

"Very tricky," Joseph agreed. "And it worked. Tom's friend Ben said, 'Hey, let me paint a little.' He even gave Tom his apple in exchange for letting him do the work."

There were smiles and chuckles among the adults in the room.

"And the rest of his friends were eventually reeled in as well," Joseph said.

"So now you've got our kids painting your fence," someone shouted.

Joseph spread his hands out and laughed. "That's how you do it."

The sudden sound of a toddler's screech stopped all activity. Nobody spoke; the earth halted on its axis. Or maybe it just felt that way, as though an air raid siren suddenly blasted the air. Everyone in the vicinity seemed affected, so clearly I wasn't the only one who freaked out when a sound hit red on the decibel scale. I took a slow breath in and out. In this child-rich environment I should've been prepared for that nails-on-the-blackboard scream, but every so often one kid's pitch soared above the normal level and took me—and everyone else—by surprise.

And then people started to laugh. I turned and watched as an adorable four-year-old girl screamed with delight, bouncing around and showing off her own little bucket of bright pink paint. Her mom came running at the sound of her daughter's high-pitched scream, probably thinking the child had been bitten by a deadly snake, or worse. But the little one was giggling, and when she saw her mom, she screamed again and excitedly flung the paintbrush every which way, drenching her mother in pink paint from her hair down to her shoes.

"Holy moly," I said, and froze again at the look of pure astonishment on the mom's face. Would she start yelling at the little one? Grab her arm and drag her out of the room?

It could've gone either way, but instead, the mom took a good long look at her little darling, then performed a perfect three-point fashion model twist-turn and said, "Pink is my color, don't you think?"

"It is now," one of the assistants said with a rueful laugh.

I noticed that Tom, Joseph, and Ashley had wisely slipped into thin white painting coveralls and booties and were helping the rest of the kids slap paint onto the fence. The two men seemed to be having a great time helping the kids splash all sorts of different colors onto the thick wooden pickets of the fence that meandered around the wide space.

Then I realized that Ashley wasn't helping any of the kids. Instead, she sat on the floor in front of her very own wooden picket and was painting it very carefully in vivid rainbow stripes.

So she was that kid, I thought, and could totally relate. I wondered if she came from a big family. But no matter where she came from or how well I could relate to someone wanting to forge their own trail, I still had to wonder if she could have been the one who pushed Ella Cabot off the riverboat last night. But to be honest, I just didn't think she would've been able to lift the taller woman up and over the railing, but stranger things had happened.

As my little students continued to work on their newspaper baskets, I took a look around the room. The face-painting artist had set up her equipment in the other corner opposite me. She already had a line of kids waiting to be adorned with a butterfly or a Spider-Man mask or whatever they wanted to be.

Floating high above the artist's head was the colorful oversized kite I had created from the pretty paper I had made with my own hands.

This looks like fun."

I turned. "Hey, Tom."

He'd put on white coveralls over his new clothes and it was a good thing, because they were splashed from top to bottom with color.

"You look like you're having fun, too." I laughed. "They didn't miss much. You've got green streaks on your face and pink and yellow spots in your hair."

"And it'll all wash off."

"Thank goodness."

"I've never had so much fun in my life," he said, laughing as a little girl holding a blue paintbrush chased a boy who'd just stolen her bucket. "Do they do this kind of stuff all the time?"

"All the time. This is the children's museum so they're always coming up with fun things for kids."

He walked around my worktable. "And you've got this going on, too. This is a really smart project. Did Ashley come up with this?"

"No. This is something I've done before. It's easy and fun for the kids, and they each end up with their own basket."

"But the newspaper. That's the key. Ashley should jump on this for the *Clarion*."

"Oh yeah," I said. "And if nothing else, it's a great way to recycle."

He nodded thoughtfully. "Sure is." He stared up at the kite and I was about to boast that I had made it when I noticed Ella Cabot standing nearby at the entryway of the museum, talking to Ian. Joseph had confirmed that she would be here, despite her traumatic fall into the Bay last night. And frankly, she looked as beautiful as ever so I hoped she wasn't suffering any distressing aftereffects. I was glad that she was able to show up and support Joseph.

Tom watched one of my kids as she struggled to weave the newspaper strip. When she looked up, he said, "You're doing a great job."

I tried to smile but I was still taken aback by Ella's appearance.

That's when Tom noticed her. And I saw his smile fade.

"She intimidates me, too," I said.

Tom looked at me and shrugged. "She doesn't intimidate me, Brooklyn. I just don't dig her vibe."

What's her vibe? I wondered. But I knew what he meant. She had a natural haughtiness that seemed to be aimed at everyone, no matter their social status.

"That kid with the yellow paint is about to drench Joseph so I'd better get back in there."

"You're welcome to stay here out of the target zone."

"And miss all the fun?" He laughed. "See you later."

I watched him jog over to Joseph, where he was immediately sprayed with yellow paint for his trouble.

It made me laugh. Tom was a really good guy and I hoped he would be happy in his life. I suddenly pictured him at Dharma, working in the vineyards. He would fit right in up there.

I tucked that little vision into my memory banks and glanced over to see if Ella was still there. Sure enough, she and Ian had their heads together. She covered her mouth to speak to him so I couldn't read her lips. Not that I was a lip reader, but her covert movement told me that she didn't want anyone to hear—or see—what she was saying.

Was she telling Ian what had really happened last night on the riverboat? She flung her arms out and shook her head dramatically, so I thought she might be reenacting the moment.

As I watched, Ella happened to look across the room and our gazes met. I waved at her and she faltered, then smiled. I decided to make nice and quickly walked over to where they were standing.

She reached for my hand. "Brooklyn, it's good to see you."

"Hi, Ella," I said. "I wanted to make sure you were doing all right after your ordeal last night."

"Thank you." Her voice was subdued, but still had

a musical lilt to it. "It was awful, but I am doing fine. Except . . ." Her eyes clouded and she shivered and rubbed her arms to ward off a chill. "I had a terrible nightmare last night. I couldn't get out of the water. I'm not sure I want to go to sleep tonight."

"I'm so sorry."

She touched my hand. "I appreciate your concern."

I turned to check on my young workshop attendees. "I'd better get back to my kids," I said. "But if there's anything Derek and I can do to help, please don't hesitate to ask."

She hugged me. "That is very sweet of you. Thank you."

I hurried back to my worktable, but made a quick mental note to find Ian after the workshop. Obviously it wasn't the right time to ask her if she'd recognized her attacker, but maybe she had told Ian something.

The fact that it was none of my business wasn't important right now.

An hour later, I was packing up my tote bag and waving goodbye to the last of my workshop students. Everyone was thrilled with their baskets and with the idea that they could do this at home anytime they wanted to. I had showed them how to weave in different trimmings and ribbons to bring more color and polish to the baskets. The mothers were doubly pleased that their kids had discovered an art project that they could easily accomplish on their own.

I was distracted by some raucous laughter at the entryway and I glanced over and saw a baby stroller that held the cutest little six-month-old boy. Clutching the handles of the stroller was a lovely blond woman wearing a tie-dyed vest over a peasant blouse and a pair of blue jeans embroidered with flowers. Her hair was pulled back in a sleek ponytail and I had to blink a few times to make sure it wasn't a mirage.

Nope, this was the real deal. The ponytail clinched it.

"Mother?"

Chapter 16

Apparently there is nothing that cannot happen.
—*Autobiography of Mark Twain*

Apparently I'd shouted the word because people were turning around and giving me looks. Jeez. *Chill out, people*, I thought. It wasn't like I was screaming like a freaked-out two-year-old.

I ignored them all and hurried across the room to wrap my mother up in a tight hug.

"Hi, sweetie," she said with an enthusiastic pat on my back.

"Mom, what are you doing here?"

A woman behind me spoke. "What Brooklyn meant to say was, 'Oh, Mom, I'm so happy to see you.'"

"She forgets her words sometimes," Mom explained.

I whipped around and saw my oldest best friend Robin, smirking at me.

"Get over here," she said, and pulled me close for a breath-stealing hug.

"I'm so happy to see you," I murmured.

It always pleased me that Robin and my mother

had a close relationship, mainly because Robin's own mother had never taken the time to get to know her daughter.

I gazed at my friend. "I miss you so much."

"That wouldn't happen if you'd visit more often."

I had to laugh. "We'll be there this weekend."

"Promise?" she said.

"Absolutely. Now let me say hello to my favorite nephew."

She beamed with pleasure. "He's been waiting to say hello to his favorite auntie."

I turned and noticed that Ian had beat me to it. He was already kneeling next to the stroller making kitchy-koo noises at little Jamie, who giggled with delight.

Ian looked up and caught my mother's gaze. "He's a gorgeous kid, isn't he?"

"The prettiest baby of them all," she said. "Don't tell the others."

I laughed. "You say that about all your grandkids."

"Because they are all perfectly beautiful."

"Yes." I nodded. "They are."

Ian stood and brushed off his trousers. "Your turn, Auntie."

I bent over and gazed at Jamie's expressive face and couldn't help smiling. "Hello, little one."

His face crinkled in a huge grin and I laughed. "You are a sweetheart." I rubbed my knuckles along his soft little jawline, then stood and looked from Mom to Robin. "Seriously, I'm so happy to see you. But what are you doing here?"

"We came to see you, goofball," Robin said. "I wanted to make sure you got a chance to see Jamie before he goes off to college."

"He's only six months old," I pointed out. "And I was just in Dharma last month."

"But in baby time, that's like ten years ago. He misses you."

I laughed. "You're really full of it, but I love you anyway."

Ian checked his watch. "You ladies should get going if you want to beat the crowd. Your brunch reservation at the Rose Room is in Brooklyn's name."

"You did that?" I kissed his cheek. "Thank you."

"Thanks, sweetie," Mom said, patting his other cheek. "Can you join us?"

"I'd love to but I've got an appointment with a donor in ten minutes."

"All right," Mom said. "But we'll see you in Dharma next weekend for the big you-know-what, right?"

I looked at the two of them. What in the world was the big *you-know-what*? I would have to corner Mom at lunch and pry it out of her.

"We'll absolutely be there." Ian gave her another kiss on the cheek. "I wouldn't miss it and neither would Jake."

"Wonderful." She turned to me. "Ready to go?"

"Yes, but I've got a workshop starting at noon."

"It's only ten thirty," Robin said. "You'll make it back in time."

"And just in case, I'll tell your audience to enjoy the latest exhibits until you get there," said Ian.

"Oh, thank you!" I gave him a hug. "You're the best."

"Yes," he said with a short bow. "Yes, I am."

The Rose Room tea shop was situated at the lower edge of the Covington's rose garden, adjacent to the

Shakespeare garden. It was a small, lovely, Victorian-styled building that housed both the tea room and the gift shop. It was one of the most popular spots on the Covington grounds and always filled up quickly.

We were seated at a booth for four, right next to the big picture window showing off a view that included the Bay in the foreground and the rugged Marin County coastline beyond. Mom and I sat facing Robin, who needed the extra space for all that paraphernalia that came along with the baby.

"What a lovely day," Mom said with a happy sigh. "This view is perfect."

"It never gets old," Robin said. She leaned over and unstrapped Jamie's stroller seat, then lifted the baby into her arms.

Behind us, the hostess busily seated two more parties for lunch.

"There was certainly a lot going on in the children's museum this morning," Mom said.

I explained the different workshops and fun stuff that Ian had arranged, all in support of the Mark Twain Festival and, specifically, the Tom Sawyer fence-painting event.

"But all those children racing around, carrying buckets of paint." She shook her head. "I wondered what Ian was thinking."

"It gave me chills," Robin confessed, and ran her hand over her baby's soft curls.

"It was fun," I said with a laugh, then relented. "Easy for me to say now. While it was happening, I was terrified that I'd get pelted."

I told them about the little girl with the pink paint

bucket and the mother who took it much better than I would have.

Mom chuckled. "Now that's a good sport."

"They offered coveralls or smocks to anyone who wanted them, but not everyone took advantage of it."

At the table directly behind us, I heard the waitress say, "It's good to see you today, Mrs. Cabot."

Mrs. Cabot? My ears perked up.

"Hello, Carmen."

"Will you be having your usual today?"

"Yes, I will. Thank you, Carmen."

"I'll bring your pot of Earl Grey first thing," the waitress said. "And your Royal Chicken Platter will be out directly."

"That sounds lovely."

Even if the waitress hadn't addressed her by name, I would've recognized that breathy, baby-soft voice tinged with Swedish sultriness.

It was Ella Cabot and she was sitting directly behind me. I was certain she was alone, but she might've been expecting someone to join her shortly. Her mother Ingrid? Her husband Joseph? Someone else?

I heard the waitress's footsteps as she padded across the room and disappeared into the kitchen.

The tea room was getting close to capacity with the brunch and lunch crowd. Distracted for a moment, I gazed at the variety of faces of the visitors who entered the room.

And slowly my brain began to register exactly what I had just heard Ella Cabot say.

She probably hadn't noticed that I was seated behind her, close enough to hear everything she said. Namely, that she was such a regular visitor to the Covington Library that the tea room waitress not only recognized her, but knew every detail of Ella's standard lunch order without being reminded.

Either Carmen was the world's best waitress, or Ella Cabot came here a lot more often than she had indicated on the night we took our little tour.

I tried to remember the words she'd said when she asked to see some of my own works on display.

"I would love to see what you've done, but I'm not familiar with the library and don't know my way around. Would you mind giving me a short tour?"

Why would she pretend that she didn't know her way around the library? She came here all the time! So what was that all about?

I remembered feeling sorry for her. I'd thought her main reason for asking me to show her around was so she could get away from her cranky mother for a while. And I still couldn't blame her for that. Ingrid had been a royal pain that night, giving Ella grief for not showing enough concern that her husband—her very wealthy, very attractive husband—was, according to Ingrid, openly flirting with Ashley Sharp, the beautiful young woman he worked with.

He wasn't, of course, because Joseph never would've done that. But that didn't keep Ingrid from insinuating that he was.

I waved those thoughts of Ingrid away because they didn't matter at the moment. What mattered were the words that Ella said to me that evening. I wanted to remember the moment correctly. Was it my imagination that she had pretended to be ignorant of the Covington exhibits? No. It wasn't. And it wasn't a coincidence and I hadn't misunderstood what she'd said.

She had lied to me. It was as simple as that.

But still, when I pictured the person who would plot out the murder of Hobson the butler, I envisioned someone with the intellectual capacity to turn what she'd read in the Poisoned Papers exhibit into reality. It would entail some knowledge of chemistry as well as some fast footwork to arrange the precise delivery of the envelope containing the poisoned documents.

I didn't think those qualities described Ella, but what did I know?

And again I had to ask whether the envelope was meant to be opened by Hobson or passed on to Joseph and Tom. Was that orchestrated as well, or did it just wind up happening that way?

And again, did I really believe that Ella was able to plot and plan and arrange a murder so cleverly and precisely?

Had her plot succeeded? Had she honestly intended for Hobson to open the envelope and die from the poisoned powder?

Or had Hobson been a mistake? Was someone else the target?

Who else could've plotted this ugly murder? Someone who was capable of working through each part of a bigger picture: working out the formula; whipping up the deadly mixture; scheduling the delivery; determining who would receive it.

Could Ella have actually carried it out? Was she really clever enough to bring about the demise of a person who had ceased to be of any use to her?

So who had ceased to be of use to her? Joseph? Hobson? Tom? I could argue that any of them might fall into that category, but only because I had heard Ella's conversation with her mother and she seemed pretty capable of disregarding any of those men.

But if not Ella, then who? Someone truly cold-blooded, I thought, feeling a sudden chill. Was it her clever and calculating mother Ingrid? Or someone altogether different? Could Joseph have carried it out?

And what about Ashley? I had no doubt that she would gladly shove Ella off the riverboat's railing and into the Bay. And she was certainly clever enough to arrange all the details involved in pulling off the murder of Hobson. But why would she kill the butler? What was her motive?

If Joseph had been the actual target, why would Ashley want to kill him? I'd seen the way she looked at him. Maybe she had meant for the poison to go to Tom. But again, why?

I thought of another peripheral character in this ugly drama. Leland Bingham. He had a motive for getting rid of Hobson because he would be the obvious choice to take over the head butler position. But Leland didn't seem to have the intestinal fortitude to make it all happen.

"Earth to Brooklyn."

I blinked and looked up to find Mom and Robin staring at me. I winced. "Sorry."

"Where did you go?"

I had to think fast. "I was just thinking about the next step in my bookbinding workshop."

"You've been so busy," Mom said, giving my arm a

comforting squeeze. "But you'll be able to relax this weekend."

Robin glanced around. "I've always loved this room. It's so quaint and peaceful."

"I haven't been here in years," Mom said. "But I enjoy it, too. I love the little touches of Victorian architecture, so different from the library itself. The widow's walk around the roof and the gingerbread bits on the porch. It's so sweet."

Robin smiled dreamily. "Brooklyn used to take me when I lived in the city."

"We had some fun times," I said.

Robin had moved out to Dharma four years ago after a man was killed in her Noe Valley flat. Once that occurred, she didn't feel safe going back home. Happily, my brother Austin had quickly realized that he was in love with her and immediately moved her into his home high up in the hills above the Dharma Winery. They were married a few years later and my best friend became my sister.

And now she was a mother, a fact that blew my mind whenever I thought about it.

Carmen the waitress stopped by our table and set down three elegant teacups. "What type of tea would you prefer?"

I looked at Mom. "Earl Grey? English Breakfast?"

"English Breakfast, I think."

"That's my favorite," Robin said.

I nodded at Carmen.

She wrote it down. "I'll bring that right out."

"Thank you."

She scurried away.

"Is he really standing up?" I asked, watching Jamie bounce.

"Yes, if I hold on to him," Robin said with a grin. "He won't stand on his own for another few months yet."

"And before you know it, he'll be walking," I said.

"And then he'll be off to college," she said. "So you'd better start visiting more often."

I laughed. "I told you we're coming this weekend."

"I think you should come every weekend."

"Oh, wouldn't that be wonderful?" Mom enthused.

"I happen to agree," I said. "Especially now that our house is finished."

"And it's so beautiful," Mom said.

"It really is," Robin said. "You guys did a great job there."

I smiled in complete agreement. "It was nice to be able to have all that time to work out exactly what we both wanted." Our charming Craftsman-style home halfway up Red Mountain Road was small enough to feel cozy and big enough to allow extra friends to visit. The view of the hills and vineyards of the Sonoma wine country was incomparable.

"Time can be such a luxury," Mom murmured.

Time, I thought, and decided that after lunch, I would take the time to track down Ian and find out everything he knew about Ella Cabot.

But for now, I needed to concentrate on something besides murder. Luckily, Carmen arrived with a large teapot.

"Would you like me to pour?" she asked.

"That would be best," Mom said.

As she poured the tea, little Jamie stood on Robin's lap and bounced up and down.

When Carmen was finished pouring, she smiled at Jamie. "Hello, little man."

Jamie's way of saying hello to Carmen was to bounce even more energetically.

Carmen was charmed by him. She took our orders and walked away chuckling.

"Does Austin have a good time with Jamie?" I asked.

"He's the best dad in the world," Robin said, gazing down at her baby boy with love. "And Jamie is so in love with his daddy. Sometimes I'll walk in and catch Austin stretched out on the living room carpet with the baby asleep on his chest." She patted her heart. "It fills me with so much happiness, I can't even describe it."

"You deserve all that happiness and more," I said with sincerity.

Mom reached over and squeezed Robin's hand. "You certainly do, sweetie."

Robin was in danger of bursting into tears, and if she did, I would join her since no one cried alone when I was around. For my own sake, I wanted to change the subject, but Mom got there first.

"We heard about the murder," she said.

I cringed. I was afraid of that. "It was . . . unfortunate," I managed.

"I should think so," Mom said. "I know how these things affect you. How are your chakras?"

I felt my eyes widen in alarm. "Just fine, thanks."

Her eyes narrowed in on me. "Oh, sweetie. I can tell you're troubled. You could use a Panchakarma cleanse."

Oh my God. A Panchakarma cleanse was all about bringing one's system back into balance by collecting the toxins in one's body. The process could go on for

weeks. Different clinics recommended different proce-
dures, but Mom always like to start it off by sipping
ghee—clarified butter—mixed with various medicinal
herbs. After three days, one's system could no longer
absorb the ghee and she moved on to therapeutic
vomiting.

There were several more steps in the process, but it
was better to leave it there for now.

"No, Mom. But thanks."

She brightened. "I've added a little cannabis to the
program."

"That's a big plus, but still. No thanks." Like my
dad, my mom was a Grateful Dead fan from way back.
I had a feeling cannabis had always been part of the
program.

"It's legal now, you know."

"I've heard that, but I'm going to pass."

I could hear Robin trying to stifle her laughter. She
knew how I felt about my mother's constant experimen-
tation with new age practices. Mom had astral-traveled
with her spirit guide, Ramlar X. She made regular pil-
grimages to the Laughing Goat Sweat Lodge. And she
was a big fan of drum circles. But then, who wasn't?

If I wasn't vigilant, she'd whip out some crystals and
lay down a protection spell on me right here in the tea
room. She was never very subtle about these things.

She was still watching me way too closely. "Let me
run a protection spell on you."

I blinked. What did I tell you? "That's not necessary, Mom."

"Then just a little extra bump up." She reached over,
pressed her fingers against my forehead, and chanted,
"Om shanti, shanti, shanti." She whispered some words

that I couldn't understand and a few seconds later, she beamed at me. "There. All is good."

I had to smile. "Thanks, Mom."

The phrase *Om shanti, shanti, shanti* was essentially a wish for peace times three. Peace in body, peace in speech, and peace in mind. And who didn't need a little peace in their life?

Mom patted my hand. "Being here reminds me of your wedding day."

Derek and I had been married in the Covington Library's beautiful rose garden.

Robin grinned at me. "All that's missing are a couple of killers."

"Oh, weren't they awful?" Mom said. "A couple of nasty bad men."

"They were memorable anyway," Robin said.

"Despite that little hiccup," I said, "it was a beautiful day. The best day of my life."

They both smiled and Robin added, "It really was a fabulous wedding. And as far as those, um, nasty bad men are concerned, that was amazing. Your mom kicked ass."

It was true. My mother and Derek's mother Meg had brought down the nasty bad guys using nothing but a hair dryer and a shower brush. It was epic.

We sipped our tea and I finally asked a question that had been on my mind for a little while. "Mom, did any of your kids ever screech like the Bride of Frankenstein sometimes? You know the kind of scream that brings goose bumps to your skin and rips your eardrums?"

Robin nodded. "There's a toddler at my Baby and Me class who bursts into that scream every so often. Freaks me out."

"Yes!" I was glad to know I wasn't the only one. "So, what's up with that?"

"Some children are overly excitable," Mom said. "I had one of them."

"You had a kid that screamed like that?" Robin asked.

"Yes."

I looked at her, frowning. "It had to be London."

My youngest sister was adorable but also the most uptight of all of us, until recently. "Which one of us did that, Mom?"

"You, sweetie."

"Me? No way!"

"Yes, you. You were always so excited about everything. You went crazy over the smallest thing. I swear I could feel myself losing a year of my life every time you belted one out."

I was shocked to my core. "I don't believe it."

Robin laughed out loud. "No wonder the sound bugs you so much. You're having flashbacks."

"Very funny." I scowled at her. "Does Jamie do that?"

"No. First of all, he's too young for those kinds of reactions, but second, he's pretty mellow. I doubt he'll be a screamer."

"Like me," I muttered.

Well, that was embarrassing. Time to change the subject quickly. "Can I hold Jamie for a few minutes?"

Robin smiled indulgently as she stood and handed the baby to me. "He's been wondering when you would ask."

I chuckled. "Sorry, I've been a little distracted by everything that's going on."

We ate chicken finger sandwiches and salad and

finished it all off with scones with jam and clotted cream, plus cookies and more tea.

When Carmen brought the check, I took it. "Thanks, Carmen. By the way, was that Ella Cabot sitting behind me?"

"Yes, ma'am," she said.

"She's lovely, isn't she?"

"Oh yes, ma'am," Carmen said. "She comes in here all the time and she always has a book with her."

I was not expecting that comment. A book? Seriously? Ella?

I smiled. "If she loves to read, she's come to the right place."

"Oh, she loves it here. And she's so thoughtful. Lately she always brings me a postcard from one of the exhibits she enjoyed."

"Did she give you one from the Poisoned Papers exhibit?"

Carmen nodded happily. "That's one of my favorites."

I handed her my credit card. "Thank you again."

I couldn't wait to talk to Ian.

I pushed the baby stroller and walked with Mom and Robin out to their car. After promising again that I would see them this weekend, we all waved goodbye. Then I hurried back into the library and dashed upstairs to find Ian.

"Hey, girl." He took a quick look at his watch. "You ready to get started on your workshop?"

"Yes, but I have a quick question first."

"I've got to meet someone downstairs so walk and talk with me. What's up?"

"Let's keep this confidential, okay?"

He gave me a sideways glance. "Sure."

"Does Ella Cabot come here often?"

"Oh yeah. Lately she's here a lot."

"When did that start?"

He blew out a breath. "I'd say she started showing up about two months ago and she's here at least a few times a week." He held up his hand. "Although recently I haven't seen her as much. Guess she got busy."

"But she was here today."

Ian opened the stairwell door and we started down the stairs. "Sure, because Joseph was here."

"What does she do here?"

"I usually see her in the late morning. She spends a lot of time checking out the exhibits. I swear she must've memorized them by now. And then she always goes to lunch."

"I didn't know she was such a patron of the library."

"Well, Joseph is often here as well. I thought she started coming as a way of supporting his interests."

"What does he usually do when he's here?"

"Same thing. Check out the exhibits. Make notes."

"Make notes?"

He shrugged. "Yeah. He's always watching and study-ing and finding new ways to do things. He's pretty in-novative, always looking for new angles, new stories." Ian looked at me with intensity.

I frowned. "What?"

"You're up to something," he said.

I shook my head. "Nope."

"Liar." He raised an eyebrow. "It's something about Ella."

"No," I said. "I just asked because I was curious, that's all."

We stopped on the landing and he studied me for another moment. "Does this have anything to do with their butler's murder?"

I winced. "I . . . no. I mean, hmm." I took a moment to look around, catch my breath, and try to think. Even standing inside the stairwell, I could appreciate the beauty of the Covington Library. The elegant wainscoting along the walls, the thick crown molding, the art deco lighting fixtures that illuminated the space, the wide marble stairs with brass handrails, were architectural achievements on their own.

The large side window revealed a view of the city all the way to the Sutro Tower. Finally I gazed up at Ian. "I'll have to get back to you on that."

He gently grabbed my upper arm. "Brooklyn, someone killed that butler. And if they know you're poking around, they'll come after you, too. Please be careful."

I patted his hand. "I'm always careful."

"No, you're not. But you're brave and I admire you." He sighed. "Just, watch out for those two."

He could've been talking about several different people, but I had a feeling I knew. "Which two are you talking about?"

"Oh, come on, Brooklyn. You know who I'm talking about." We reached the first floor and he opened the door that led into the lobby. He gave me a hug and whispered in my ear, "The bombshells."

Chapter 17

You never see a frog so modest and straightfor'ard as he was, for all he was so gifted. And when it come to fair-and-square jumping on a dead level, he could get over more ground at one straddle than any animal of his breed you ever see.

—Mark Twain, "The Celebrated Jumping Frog of
Calaveras County"

As soon as Derek arrived home that evening, we grabbed our jackets and took a leisurely walk up to Pietro's Pizza.

"It's getting warmer," I said, gazing up at the dark blue sky. The sun had just set, but the sky was already darkening.

"Do you think so?" He stuck his hands deeper in the pockets of his down jacket.

"No, that was a joke," I said, laughing as I pulled my coat tighter around me. Summers in San Francisco were notoriously chilly, but I still loved everything about the city.

As we crossed the street, Derek pulled my arm through his and we cuddled up close. "Tell me about your day, love."

"There's so much to tell," I said. "Where shall I start?"

"Start at the beginning," he suggested. "How was your workshop? Did you see Joseph? Did Ella make an appearance?"

"My workshop was really fun. It's always nice to have the parents participate and they were out in force. Naturally, though, we were in the same main room with Joseph's fence-painting event and that made everything wild and crazy. Every kid had their own bucket of paint and I don't think anyone walked out of there unscathed."

He shook his head. "It sounds chaotic."

"It was. But it was a lot of fun, too."

"And did you see Ella and her mother?"

"Ella was there, but I didn't see Ingrid." I frowned. "Probably just as well. She can be so grouchy."

"That's one word for it," he murmured.

"I talked to Joseph briefly. I asked how Ella was doing and he said she was still pretty upset about what happened. Then a while later I saw Ella. She said she had nightmares last night."

"Perfectly natural." Derek nodded slowly. "And I'm sorry to hear it."

"Me, too." I squeezed in a little closer to him. "But the good news is that my mother and Robin showed up. And they brought the baby."

"Did they?"

"Yes. It was great to see them." We stopped at the next block to wait for the green light and a gust of wind hit us from the cross street. Derek tightened his hold on my arm.

Despite the chill, the streets were full of people out walking because, after all, it was almost summer. The shops and cafés we passed were all open for business and it was nice to see that they were busy. Our neighborhood had become a local destination spot, thanks to the popular Courtyard shops across the street.

"They're adamant that we should visit Dharma this weekend."

He smiled. "Then we shall."

"Apparently Ian and Jake are also going to be there."

"Are they?" he said. "Then perhaps we should have a get-together at our place."

"That would be fun." I glanced up at him. "It'll probably end up being a lot of people."

"That's fine. We can grill something. Ribs, perhaps. Or chicken." He frowned. "Or fish."

"We can figure it out. And I can cut up some veggies to grill. And make some garlic toast."

"Yes, all of that is easy enough."

"I'll start texting people when we get home."

"And I'll see if any of my family are in town."

"Oh, I hope so." Ever since Derek's parents had become so close to mine, they had bought their own home in Dharma. Now Derek's brothers and their families were visiting a lot more often.

"So tell me more about your time with Robin and your mother. And the baby."

The light turned green and we crossed the street.

"Ian gave me some time off so I took them to lunch at the Rose Room. But something really weird happened while we were there."

"Do share," he said, and I could actually feel the tension building in the muscles of his arms.

He was right to tense up, I thought, because what I

told him was almost unbelievable. After listening to my story about Carmen the waitress and about the way Ella ordered her lunch as "the usual," he finally said, "So Ella Cabot is much more familiar with the Covington than she let on."

"Exactly," I said, grateful that Derek caught on without my having to go into too much explanation. "She lied to me the other night when I gave her my little tour of the Covington. She told me she didn't know her way around and that she rarely came here and she didn't know anything and would I help her and show her the way." I gritted my teeth. "Such a liar! She was just trying to get away from her mother, who was being a total cow."

"Yes, I recall her mother being quite a cow."

I had to laugh when Derek said things like that. "I suppose I should be more understanding. My point is that she's a liar."

"I'm getting your point, and I agree. She is."

I stared up at Derek. "You agree."

"Of course."

We reached Pietro's Pizza and stood outside for another few minutes to finish our conversation.

I told Derek what Carmen said about the postcard Ella gave her. "I like collecting postcards from museums, too. But for the most part I only buy photos of my favorite exhibits. So the fact that Ella bought a postcard featuring the Poisoned Papers is telling. Don't you think?"

"Yes, I do." His teeth were clenched and I knew he had grown angrier as I related the story.

"So here's what I'm thinking," I said.

"Let me brace myself," he teased, and I could see his jaw relax minutely.

I laughed. "It's no big deal. But I think you should call Joseph and wangle an invitation to his place."

"Just to say hello?" he asked.

"Not exactly. We'll go to his place, and while you're talking to him, I'll search for evidence."

His smile was deceptive. "First of all, I should remind you that Joseph is not living at his home. He's camped out at the Covington."

"Oh, rats. I forgot."

"But second of all, what evidence would you be searching for?"

I gripped his jacket. "Think about it, Derek. Maybe she held on to the information from the delivery service. You know, the one that delivered the deadly manila envelope? We might find an invoice for the items she had to buy in order to make up the poison, along with the parchment paper and that manila envelope. It is possible she didn't throw everything away."

He gazed fondly at me while he smoothed my hair back from my face. "And if she catches you in her room?"

I smiled. "I'll just tell her I got lost looking for the bathroom."

"Ah, yes," he said sardonically. "And while looking for the bathroom, you happened to end up in her room, going through her stack of bills."

I almost laughed, but this was getting serious. "Seriously, what's she going to do? Point a gun at me?"

"Please don't even mention that possibility, because it could very well happen," he said. "I'm not ready to admit that Ella pulled off this murder, but if she did, she'll be trying her best not to get caught. And she could very well have a gun."

"You can be such a killjoy," I muttered.

He chuckled. "Darling, this is why we're friends with Inspector Lee. We'll call and give her the details and ask her to get a search warrant."

"But—"

"Look at it this way. Maybe the thought of Ella doesn't put the fear of God in you. But how will you feel if Inspector Lee finds out what you did?"

"I wouldn't feel anything because I would be dead."

"Exactly."

I huffed and puffed, then admitted defeat. "Okay, killjoy. We'll call Inspector Lee."

We walked back home carrying our pizza and salad, and talked about the incident on the riverboat.

"Nobody saw anyone push her into the water," I said.

"You believe she jumped in."

"I do. I can't believe anyone would do that, but at this point, she needs to make herself look like the victim instead of a suspect. And she'll do whatever it takes to achieve that."

"If nothing else, she does seem to have a lot of chutzpah," Derek said.

I smiled briefly at his use of that word. "Did you talk to Tom after he got out of the water?"

"I listened as Inspector Lee questioned him. He didn't see the person who pushed her into the water. He simply saw her fall in and reacted accordingly."

"Like the hero that he is," I murmured, then groused, "Nobody saw who pushed her because she did it herself."

"She's obviously a lot smarter than anyone gives her credit for," Derek said.

I shrugged. "It's because everyone sees how beautiful she is and they don't look any deeper. Which isn't fair," I insisted.

"No, it's not." But then he grinned. "I'm willing to give her all the credit she deserves if she really did manage to pull off this rather diabolical murder in plain sight."

"It's weird," I said. "But when I was eavesdropping on her and her mother the other day, I remember thinking it was odd how her own mother called her silly."

Derek thought about it for a moment. "Do you think she was pulling the wool over her own mother's eyes?"

"I don't think she's silly at all, but she seems pretty capable of putting on an act."

His eyes narrowed. "Yes."

We walked in silence for half a block, then I said, "Her mother was really broken up over Hobson's death. Ella wasn't. In fact, she called him a bastard and Ingrid slapped her."

"You didn't tell me that," Derek said.

"Sorry. There was so much to remember, I must've left out some details."

"So Ella called him a bastard," Derek repeated, "and Ingrid slapped her as a way of protesting her comment."

"Exactly." We walked to the corner.

"It gives even more credence to the possibility that Ella is our killer."

I thought about it, and a picture of Ingrid ridiculing Ella popped into my head. "Maybe Ella killed him precisely to piss off her mother."

He frowned. "Not that we needed another motive, but it's quite possible that she felt she had to get rid of Hobson so he could never reveal his role in manipulating Joseph to marry her."

"Oh my God, yes! What would people think if they knew that the butler had coerced him into marrying her?" The light turned green and we walked across the street. "You know, that possibility takes this whole scenario right into the psychopathic realm."

We reached our building and walked into the lobby.

"Whatever the realm," Derek finally said, "Ella is looking more and more suspicious by the minute."

As we stepped inside the old elevator, I grabbed his arm. "We really have to search her room."

He actually laughed at me.

"What's so funny?"

"I love you," he said gently. "And that's why we're going to call Inspector Lee. She'll get a search warrant and that'll take care of it."

"Darn," I muttered. "I was really looking forward to searching that room."

We watched a favorite cop show while we ate. I had just taken the dishes into the kitchen when the doorbell rang. Since we live in a security building, I knew it had to be one of our neighbors.

"I'll get it," Derek said.

"I'll clean up." I was loading the dishwasher when I heard voices.

"Brooklyn, I have cupcakes."

Ah, the four most wonderful words in the English language. My spirits lifted and I felt lighter than air. A good thing because I was about to scarf down a fabulous cupcake made by our dear friend Alex Monroe.

"I'm in here, Alex," I cried out from the kitchen.

Seconds later, Alex appeared at the island and set down a cupcake carrier. "I could only bring you six. The rest went to an investor meeting at work."

I pouted. "Only six?"

Gabriel popped into the kitchen. "It's soooo unfair."

"It really is," I said, and grabbed him in a quick hug.

"But you'll survive, won't you?" Alex asked.

"I hope so," I said dramatically.

"Here's why you'll be okay." Gabriel held up a small bag.

"What's that?" I asked.

"I decided to try my hand at making doughnuts," Alex said with a shy smile. "I'd like to hear your opinions."

"Are you kidding?" I rounded the kitchen counter and got up close to Gabriel. "Are you going to open that bag?"

"Maybe. Eventually."

"Do it now," I said, "or suffer the consequences."

He grinned. "She's serious."

"Yes, she is," Derek said. "If I were you, I would open the bag."

Gabriel was laughing as he unfurled the bag and held it out for both of us to look inside.

I gasped at the sight of the fluffy glazed beauties. "Oh, they're so pretty."

Derek gazed at Alex reverently. "You're unbelievable."

"I kept it simple for my first try," she explained. "Just plain glazed doughnuts."

I had to back away from the bag to get my brain to start working. "But they're so big and thick and the glaze shimmers in the light."

"You guys are so easy," Alex scoffed.

"Yes, we are," I admitted, then looked at Derek. "Dessert?"

"We'll split one," he decided. "They're quite big."

Gabriel handed him the bag. "Enjoy."

"Would you like one?" Derek said.

Gabriel patted his rock-hard stomach. "I've had one. They're deadly."

I took the bag and pulled out one doughnut. After cutting it in half, I placed each half on a plate. Then I had to lick my fingers because of all the sticky, gooey, wonderful glaze.

We all sat at the dining room table and Derek and I ate the heavenly doughnut. Derek cleaned up the plates and then called out from the kitchen. "If either of you aren't too busy tomorrow, would you like to join us at the Jumping Frog Contest in Golden Gate Park?"

Gabriel and Alex exchanged a look, then Gabriel's eyes narrowed on Derek. "You're expecting trouble."

"It's the last event of the festival," Derek explained, "and so far there's been some sort of trouble every day."

I couldn't recall anything too awful happening today at the children's museum, unless you counted the fact that Ella Cabot had revealed herself to be a liar.

So yes, bad things had happened every day.

Alex frowned. "I can't make it. It's the second day of this marathon investors meeting. How about you, babe?"

"I'll be there," Gabriel said easily. "Should I be packing heat?"

Alex elbowed him. "Nobody talks like that."

"That was for Brooklyn," he said with a wink in my direction. "She digs that kind of lingo."

By eight o'clock Tuesday morning, the weather was already warm and sunny.

"A perfect day to watch frogs jump," Derek said as he read the paper, drank his coffee, and ate his half doughnut. After last night we had wised up and we were using knives and forks this morning to eat these wonderfully sticky treats.

"Alex is a force of nature," I said after finishing my half doughnut.

"She's lovely, but dangerous to our health."

"Yeah, but I can't quit her."

"Absolutely not," he said. "We'll simply have to learn to live with the consequences."

I touched his hand. "We're doing okay so far, aren't we?"

He smiled at me. "Yes, we are."

All through breakfast we had successfully avoided the subject of Ella Cabot and the fact that we both thought she was guilty of murder. Finally, though, Derek spoke up. "Darling, I really don't want us to be the ones who point the finger at Ella."

"What do you mean?"

"It would hurt Joseph a lot if he found out that we were the ones who called the police to arrest his wife."

It didn't take me long to consider. Derek was right. "If it makes you feel any better, we don't have any actual proof that she's guilty. Especially since you won't let me search her room."

He chuckled. "I intend to keep you as far away from her room as possible."

"I understand. And I agree, Joseph would never forgive us." I sighed. "So I guess you're right about calling Inspector Lee in to do the dirty work."

"I'll call her after the Jumping Frog event."

"Okay. But I still believe she's guilty."

"And while I believe a few others could've done it, I agree that she has some very strong motives for killing the butler." Derek took a big sip of coffee. "But let's allow Joseph to get through the festival first."

"We're going to have to watch her very carefully. I'm afraid that she could target someone else in the meantime."

"I agree. That's why I asked Gabriel to join us."

"You're really smart."

He chuckled. "And you're beautiful."

"Together we're perfect."

He laughed and took the last bite of doughnut.

A minute later I had to ask. "Is it dumb that we're going to waste half a day watching a frog jump across a finish line?"

Derek reached over and patted my hand. "Yes."

"I was afraid of that."

"We've bought into the entire festival project, darling, and we've got to see it through to the end. No matter how silly it sounds."

"And it does sound pretty silly."

He smiled. "It does. But we're doing it for Joseph."

"And Tom," I added.

"Yes." He nodded thoughtfully. "Tom has shown himself to be quite a good man."

"He saved Ella's life. Even if it does turn out that she jumped in on purpose, he's still a hero in my book."

"In my book as well."

"And you should've seen him with the little kids at the museum. He was really good with them. Especially the crying ones."

"He has a deep well of knowledge and a lot of warmth that I frankly didn't expect to see."

"And he's a reader, remember?" I said. "He reads a book a day, so he's got to be a pretty smart guy. And his buddy Wyatt is very loyal to him." I shook my head. "I'm making him sound like a saint."

"Or a prince," Derek said.

I blinked at the word. "Wow. So who's the prince and who's the pauper?"

"Good question," Derek said. "Frankly, both men are quite decent."

"I agree." I took my last sip of coffee. "Do you think they're related?"

"Honestly, yes."

I took a deep breath. "I agree."

"So let's make sure they both stay safe."

When we arrived at the picnic area adjacent to Stow Lake in the middle of Golden Gate Park, I couldn't believe my eyes. "There's got to be a thousand people here."

Derek continued driving until he reached the de Young Museum. He took the ramp down to the underground parking lot.

"I don't think you can park here unless you're going to the museum."

A guard signaled us to stop. Derek promptly pulled out his ID and the man waved him on.

"Seriously?"

He smiled and drove forward into a spot and turned

off the engine. "According to Joseph, he paid the museum a big pile of money to rent twenty parking spaces."

"And we get one of them?"

"Yes. Aren't we lucky?"

"I'll say. But I'm still feeling guilty, so maybe on the
way we can go into the de Young and spend a bunch of
money."

"All for a good cause?"

"Yes, because I'm feeling unworthy of this parking
place."

"You'll snap out of it."

"I suppose."

We walked up the ramp and into the park. It was a
lovely morning for a stroll so we enjoyed it until we got
close enough to hear the crowd. "I'm amazed at the
amount of people who showed up for this crazy event
on a weekday."

"You knew this was always going to be the big draw."

"Actually, I didn't think about it. But I should've
known."

The area around the actual competition was roped
off and from there we spotted Joseph and Ashley.
They had commandeered several picnic tables and
benches for their supplies and on one table sat at least
ten fish tanks. I stared at one tank and finally picked
out several frogs.

"Wow, these are the frogs." I grinned. "How exciting is that?"

Derek didn't answer, but the look he gave me said,
I'm worried about you.

I laughed. "Frogs are fun."

"That's the right attitude," Ashley said as she approached the picnic table.

I glanced back at Derek and realized that he had quickly slipped into security agent mode. He was speaking with two men and a woman and they all looked deadly serious. That was a good thing, I thought. They would keep us all safe. Especially Joseph and Tom.

And thinking of Tom, I glanced around looking for him, but didn't see him anywhere. I wasn't worried. He and his buddy Wyatt would show up any minute.

I was just beginning to wonder how we'd find Gabriel when the man himself walked up and grinned at me.

"Hey, babe."

"Hi, Gabriel. I'm glad you found us."

"I'm good at picking you out of a crowd."

"Silly," I murmured.

"Never." He winked at me, then said, "I'd better report to the chief. See you, kiddo."

He walked over to talk to Derek and I realized I'd ignored Ashley. She was filling out a notebook and didn't seem to notice.

"How are you, Ashley?" I asked.

"I'm on top of the world," she said, then shook her head. "My mother always says that. It's such a goofy old saying."

"But it makes sense," I said. "It's a beautiful day."

"Yeah, but I'm a little antsy," she said. "Everything's done so there's nothing to do but wait."

"Everything's all set up?" I asked.

"Yes. We're ready to go. We've set up a perimeter border around the competition area. And we've run chalk lines to indicate ten lanes." She glanced up at me. "Ten lanes for ten frogs."

"So nobody's bringing their own frogs," I said.

She laughed. "No way. We figured that out early on. We've brought in the frogs and people can bet on the outcome. It'll be fun for everyone and that's what counts. We've even got scorecards we'll hand out."

"Are you excited to see the end of the festival?" I asked.

"I suppose I should be, but I'm really not," she admitted. "I've had the best time of my life this week. And I feel so much closer to Joseph now. We just click on so many levels. It's a dream come true for me to be able to work with someone like him."

"He's a great guy," I said.

She sighed. "He really is."

"Have you been able to spend much time with Tom?"

"A little bit. He seems like a great guy and I wish I could hang out with him a little more. But when there isn't an event, I'm usually back at my office working on some other aspect of the festival. It's so huge and complicated, I've got to keep my eyes and ears open and stay close to my computer at all times."

"You must be exhausted," I said. "You'll need a vacation after this."

She laughed. "But that's the thing about me. I don't feel exhausted at all. I feel energized. I could do this for another month and still feel fantastic."

"You're a true extrovert," I said with a laugh.

"Oh, for sure," she agreed. "I'm that Energizer Bunny that lives for the crowds and the stress and the excitement."

I shook my head in amazement. "You're awesome."

She beamed at me. But as I watched, her expression faltered and her eyes clouded. "I'd better get moving. Talk to you later, Brooklyn."

"Sure." I turned quickly to see what she had been looking at. I thought I would see Ella and Ingrid moving through the crowd like two gorgeous jungle cats, but I didn't see anyone. I couldn't pretend to read her mind, but maybe it was simply the idea of Ella that brought a frown to Ashley's normally buoyant expression.

Had she been foolish enough to have fallen in love with her boss? It sure looked and sounded that way. And that was a great big danger sign for Joseph.

And it brought me right back to the other night on the riverboat. That was when I had suddenly started to wonder how willing Ashley was to destroy her rival in the fight to win Joseph's heart. But as quickly as the thought arrived, I brushed it away for all the reasons Derek and I had already talked about. First of all, she was barely five feet tall while Ella was close to six feet tall. And second, I just didn't think Ashley had it in her to kill someone, even if she were in love with the woman's husband. There were other reasons, but I left it there as Joseph walked to the podium.

"Welcome to this, our final event of the festival," Joseph announced. He stood on a two-foot-high riser so the impressive crowd could see him. "I want to thank everyone here today, and everyone across the city, for their interest, their participation, and their wonderful appreciation and support of our first annual Mark Twain Festival."

Joseph had to pause for the crowd to whistle and clap at his words. I took the opportunity to glance around the crowd to try and find Tom. I hadn't seen him anywhere and I wondered if he'd brushed off his driver in favor of walking to the park.

"My wife Sandra was the person who first introduced me to Mark Twain." Joseph stopped to take a breath, obviously moved by his words. "As a scholar, Sandra had studied Twain's works and she developed a particular love for *The Prince and the Pauper.* She passed her love of that book on to me, and so this festival is dedicated with love to the memory of my wife Sandra."

The crowd cheered and applauded, and I took another opportunity to search around for Ella and Ingrid. Joseph was taking quite a chance, dedicating the festival to his dead wife and possibly incurring the wrath of his new wife and mother-in-law. I wondered if, after losing Hobson, Joseph didn't care anymore.

"Because of this festival," he continued, "I was greatly honored to meet a man who personifies the meaning of the word *prince.* His name is Tom Cantwell, and he is, as they say, a prince among men. A kind, gentle, and humble man, concerned about people and content with whatever life hands him. I've known him for barely a week and he already feels like my brother—even though I don't have a brother."

The audience laughed and cheered, drowning out Joseph's words for a long moment.

"Tom," Joseph said. "You will always have a place in my home. You may not be my brother, but you will always be my friend. Thank you."

I glanced around again, searching for Tom. But he was nowhere to be seen and I was starting to get nervous.

Monsieur Grenouille was the grand prize winner of the Jumping Frog Contest. He conquered every category, jumping the highest at four feet three inches; the longest at five feet two inches; and the most continuous, never stopping until he was first to jump over the finish line and promptly disappear into a large patch of mossy ferns growing at the base of a nearby tree.

He was a true champion among frogs and Joseph sang his praises as he announced Monsieur Grenouille as the winner and declared the amount of money the little frog had raised for the cause.

"Twelve thousand three hundred dollars," Joseph said, and the crowd went crazy. "Monsieur Grenouille faced some stiff opposition," Joseph continued, "but he showed them all today. The great Monsieur is a California tree frog with a lovely grayish-green cast to his skin, and though his name is French for Mr. Frog, he is strictly a California dude."

Joseph went on to name the order of runners-up and thanked the crowd for being there and for contributing so much hard-earned money to the cause. "We truly appreciate it," he said. "And now, this is the official end of our first annual Mark Twain Festival. I want to thank everyone in the city for their support. We received thousands of photos from people who thought they spotted me out there in the wild. Everyone who sent in a photo will receive a special gift card for participating."

He continued for another minute and finally wrapped it up by saying, "I hope you'll all take a walk down this pathway to see the latest addition to this beautiful park, namely the stunning sculpture of Mark Twain that was commissioned to celebrate the first annual Mark Twain Festival. May there be many more!"

His words were drowned out by the huge applause of the appreciative crowd. When he stepped down from the riser, he looked exhausted.

I turned to Derek. "He looks sick. He should go home."

"I'll talk to him. Make sure he does."

"Good."

I lost sight of Derek as the crowd surged toward the outer limits of the park. I finally found him standing with Joseph in an isolated area behind the tree line. They were deep in conversation and it looked serious.

"What's wrong?" I asked, knowing it might be none of my business. But if something was wrong with Derek, it was totally my business. "Are you all right?"

"I'm fine, darling. But Tom is nowhere to be found."

I stared at Joseph. "I've been worried about the same thing. Do you want me to call the police?"

"No!" Joseph said immediately, shocking me enough that I took a step backward.

He reached for my arm. "I'm sorry to bark at you, but I'm very worried about Tom, especially after Hobson's murder."

That's why we should call the police, I thought, but didn't say it out loud.

"Did you call your house?" I asked.

"Of course."

I winced. "I'm sorry. Of course you're doing everything you can. I'll just shut up."

"No, please. I appreciate you trying to help."

I glanced from him to Derek. "Why not call the police?"

"Joseph doesn't want the police involved."

"Ah." I pursed my lips, trying not to judge. "Okay."

"Sorry, again." Joseph shoved his hair back from his face, clearly anxious. "I just know it would bother Tom if the police showed up. And frankly, I really don't want to make a federal case out of it. Tom could walk up any second and everything would be fine."

Ashley ran over just then and stopped in front of Joseph. "The wrangler's got his frogs all gathered up and he's taking off. I thought I'd leave for the office if you don't need me here."

"You've got a frog wrangler?" I asked.

Joseph looked appalled. "Well, of course we do. You think I'm going to wander through the forest gathering frogs when I can pay someone else to do it for me?"

Derek laughed. "Yes, and you'd have a good time doing it."

Joseph thought for a moment, then grinned. "Damned if I wouldn't." He turned to Ashley and gave her a hug. "You can take off, kiddo. Thanks for everything."

"You bet." Her wave goodbye included all of us. "See y'all later." Then she stopped abruptly. "Brooklyn, can I talk to you for a second?"

I gave Derek a quick glance. I still wasn't sure if I trusted her, but since I was in plain sight of Derek and Joseph and Gabriel and a dozen other people, I nodded. "Sure."

"Let's move away from the crowd." She led the way over toward the tree line, then stopped and stared at me.

I followed her. "What's up?"

"I hope you don't think this is odd, but I'd really like to feature you and your bookbinding on my YouTube show."

I gave her a doubtful look. "My work is slow and

kind of low-key. Not exactly a stimulating hour of television."

"Oh, come on," she said. "You don't seem that shy."

"I'm not, but the work itself is pretty quiet."

"If we have a conversation while you're doing the work, people will love it."

She was starting to bounce on her feet. I'd noticed her doing it before whenever she got really excited. "And we can advertise something. A product."

"Why would we do that?"

"I like to push good products that relate to the conversation I'm having." She shrugged. "It's an influencer thing."

I thought for a few seconds. "I have to eat chocolate while I'm working. Does that help?"

She laughed. "Oh God, that's perfect. We can approach one of the chocolate makers in town. Maybe even Ghirardelli."

"My latest favorite is Guittard chocolate," I admitted. "The name sounds French, but it's actually a local Bay Area company. Their products are gluten-free, which is something I've started looking out for because I have a little niece who's got celiac disease."

"Oh my God, that's so cool," she said, her feet bouncing, then stopping abruptly. "I mean, not the disease, but . . . you know . . ."

I laughed. "I know what you mean." And I was more convinced than ever that this woman had nothing to do with anyone's murder.

"Anyway, we can talk about that," she said. "And . . . well, we can talk about books, too. And your work. And we can rave about the Covington." She waved her hands in the air. "Whatever we come up with, *my* people will love it. Please say yes."

How could I refuse her? Her enthusiasm was infectious and it made me see why she had so many YouTube followers. "Yes. It sounds like fun."

"Fantastic! I'll call you!"

She ran off toward a skinny young man who was pushing a dolly stacked with terrariums. She said something that made him laugh and then I watched the two of them walk away.

Ashley was frenetic but she was also charming and clearly very smart. And clearly not guilty of anything but enthusiasm. It would be fun to do a show with her, but I wouldn't hold my breath waiting for her to call me.

I strolled back to Derek.

"Everything all right?" he asked.

"Everything's great. I'll tell you about it later."

"Good."

I watched Ashley and the frog wrangler walking in the distance. "I've never seen a frog wrangler before."

"Nor have I," Derek admitted.

"I wonder if he lives with a bunch of frogs all the time or if he goes out and catches them to order."

At that moment Gabriel walked up. "What's the sitch?"

Derek introduced him to Joseph, then said, "We're missing Tom, the man who won the look-alike contest."

Gabriel nodded. "Ah."

"You gave him a phone to use, right?" I asked. "Can we call that number?"

Joseph gave me a blank look.

"Sorry," I said quickly. "My mind jumps from here to there sometimes, especially when there might be trouble."

He shot Derek a look. "You're a lucky man."

"Yes, I am," Derek said.

Gabriel grinned. "I've got to agree."

I looked from one man to the other. "Okay, you guys. I got a little distracted by the frog wrangler, but now I'm just trying to greenlight some ideas here. We have to find Tom."

"Yes, we do." Joseph patted my shoulder. "And I like the way you jump right in and offer possibilities. It's nice to see."

I was taken aback. "Thank you."

"You remind me a lot of my wife Sandra," he said softly. "She was smart and clever, like you. A real idea person, if you know what I mean, always offering solutions to any problem. Instead of, you know, just whining about every little thing."

"I'm perfectly capable of whining, too," I said, smiling. But I noted that Joseph always called Sandra his *wife*. Not his "first" wife or his "late" wife. Just his *wife*. It was a very good thing that Ella wasn't nearby to hear him. *Talk about a whiner*, I thought. And it would've been even worse if Ingrid had been here. She would've had a cow.

Joseph laughed. "I seriously doubt that you whine, ever."

"She really doesn't," Derek said.

That was a lie, but I wasn't going to protest. I simply smiled and slipped my arm through his.

At that moment, Joseph's cell phone rang. "This

could be him." He stared at the screen, then answered. "Tom. Where the hell are you?"

He listened for a moment, then said, "I'll be right there."

He stared at the phone for another moment, then looked at me. "You can call your police now."

"That was Tom?" Derek said.

"Yeah. He's at the hospital."

"I was wondering why he wasn't here," I said. "Is he hurt?"

"No." Joseph looked from me to Derek to Gabriel and shook his head. "But his friend Wyatt is. He got hit by a car, badly."

I gasped. "Oh no. Not again."

"Again?" Joseph said.

I looked at Derek.

"I didn't tell him," he admitted. "Didn't want to alarm him."

"Tell me now. Alarm me," Joseph insisted.

"Sorry, mate," Derek said. "It was the day Hobson was killed. I thought you had enough on your plate."

He sighed. "Yeah, maybe I did."

"Tom and his friends walked up the hill to the Covington," I said. "A car jumped the curb and almost hit them. Wyatt shoved Tom out of the way that time, too."

"Wyatt deserves a medal," Joseph said. "He's a real hero. And a good friend."

"He really is," I agreed.

He rubbed his eyes. "But today Wyatt wasn't so lucky. He managed to save Tom, only to be hit himself." He blew out a breath. "Tom said he was hit with such force, he flew into the air and crashed into the street hard.

God." He covered his eyes and shook his head. "He's in the ICU at UCSF. I've got to go there. Tom can barely talk about it. He needs my support."

"You're not going by yourself," I said.

"I'll go with you," Derek said. "Ten of my men can stay here to watch the crowd."

"I'm going, too," I said.

"Yes, Brooklyn. You should come, too. Tom likes you."

"There you are!" a high-pitched voice cried. "I got so lost!"

We all looked around and saw Ella stepping gingerly across the grass wearing a fuzzy pink sweater, tight skirt, and four-inch heels. "I'm going to need a new pair of shoes after today."

"Where's your mother?" Joseph asked.

I honestly got the feeling that he didn't know quite what to say to his wife and that rather lame comment was the best he could come up with.

"She dropped me off and went to park the car." Ella bit one of her fingernails nervously. "It's impossible to get anywhere around here." She took a light swipe at Joseph. "Why did you even pick this spot? If I ruin these shoes, I'll be—"

A loud bang shattered the air and people began to scream and run.

"Get down!" Derek grabbed me, threw me on the ground, and wrapped his arms around me.

"That was a gunshot," I said to Derek.

"Yes, it was."

"Damn straight," Gabriel said. He was very close by.

"Sounded like a shotgun," Joseph shouted.

"And we're sitting ducks out here in the open."
Derek pointed. "We've got to get over to the tree line."

"Let's go," Joseph said.

But before any of us could take one step forward,
Ella began to scream.

Chapter 18

What a delightful thing a coincidence is! There isn't anybody to whom that mysterious conjunction which we call a coincidence is a matter barren of interest.
—Mark Twain, "The Ashcroft-Lyon Manuscript"

Ella screamed so loudly, I thought she must've injured herself. Had she twisted her ankle in those ridiculous shoes? Or maybe it was just her feelings that were hurt because we hadn't acknowledged and bowed down in her presence.

And that was just plain catty of me.

But frankly, once I'd heard that gunshot, I completely forgot that she was even there. I probably wasn't the only one. But looking at Ella, I cringed because I could tell that she knew it, especially since Joseph had been about to start running for the tree line without her.

"Okay, baby. Okay." Joseph quickly picked her up in his arms. Then he hustled back to the shelter of the tree line, where the rest of us were crouched down, waiting for whatever came next.

Gabriel was already scanning the area with a small pair of high-powered binoculars.

"See anything?" Derek asked.

"Nothing." He sounded disgusted.

Derek pressed his earpiece closer to hear what some-one was saying. "My agents are scattered across the park, combing the area for any sign of the shooter."

"Good," Gabriel said. "But I doubt they'll find any-one. The shooter has already packed his gun away and escaped."

Ella was still crying and I could see once again that Joseph had the patience of Job.

"Sweetheart," he whispered. "I know you're fright-ened, but you're safe now. Shh."

She hiccupped and tried to speak, but the tears over-whelmed her again.

"Come on now," he said. "Slow down, baby. Take a few deep breaths."

She did as he requested. Her breath was still waver-ing in and out, but finally she spoke in a whisper-soft stutter. "I-I th-think I've b-been shot."

Thirty minutes later, Derek and I stood in the waiting room of the UCSF emergency center, awaiting news of Ella's condition as well as Wyatt's. Gabriel had stayed behind at the park to help Derek's agents track down the shooter's lair.

Joseph had called ahead, and as soon as he and Ella arrived, she was rushed into one of the triage rooms and had just been seen by the top ER doctor.

"The bullet grazed her foot," Joseph reported, his expressive face revealing his guilt and misery. "There was a lot of blood and it was very painful."

I touched his arm. "This is not your fault."

"She's being well taken care of," Derek said. "The doctors here are the best in the city."

"I'm a jerk," he said, raking his fingers through his hair. "She was whining so I just ignored her."

"You're not a jerk," I insisted. "We were all wrapped up in the moment, but as soon as you realized she needed you, you stepped up. You took care of her. Don't beat yourself up."

He shook his head, clearly not assuaged. "I'm going to go check on her."

"Good idea," Derek said, patting him on the back as he followed him out of the room. Derek returned shortly.

"What did you ask him?"

He looked at me. "How do you know I asked him anything?"

"Because . . . I'm psychic?"

"Ah. I knew that."

I chuckled. "See? You're psychic, too. Anyway, I could tell you wanted to ask him something, so what is it?"

He shook his head in mock disgust. "I really must work on my inscrutability."

"No, you mustn't." I rubbed his back. "You're just as big a puzzle as ever. But I know you. So tell me."

"I simply asked him which foot was injured."

"Oh. That was smart!" I clapped my hands. "So you'd know which direction the bullet came from."

"Well now, who's the smart one?" His kiss was fast and hard and unexpected. Then he reached for his phone to call one of the agents who had remained in Golden Gate Park helping Gabriel search for signs of the shooter.

Derek asked him to also search the area where we had all been standing just before we rushed to the tree line. "You know the spot where Ella was standing. You should find the bullet itself somewhere in the dirt or grass."

He listened for a moment. "Yes. That's fine. Call me back." Derek ended the call.

I was still recovering from that kiss when Inspector Lee walked in. She checked out the other visitors in the room, then signaled Derek and me to follow her. She led us to a small office down the hall that might've been used for private talks between a doctor and a patient's family.

"How's Wyatt?" I asked.

"Still unconscious," she said gruffly. "How's Mrs. Cabot doing?"

"The bullet grazed her left foot," Derek said. "There was a good bit of blood but no real damage was done. I believe she was more frightened than anything else."

"I'll go check on her in a minute." She looked at Derek. "But her left foot, you say. So you know the direction the bullet came from."

"Yes. I've got Gabriel and several agents searching for the spot where the gunman took his shot."

Or *her* shot, I thought, but didn't say aloud. After all, there was Ingrid and Ashley to consider. I wondered if either of the two women knew how to handle a shotgun.

I couldn't imagine Ingrid shooting her own daughter, but Ashley was another story altogether.

But wait, I'd already dismissed Ashley as a possible suspect. And even if I hadn't, there was no way she could've been chatting and laughing with the frog wrangler one minute and then running into the brush and shooting off a shotgun the next minute. It hadn't been more than a couple of minutes after the two of them walked off together that Ella appeared. A minute later, the gunshot rang out.

No, Ashley couldn't have done it.

I liked Ashley, but I still scowled because my suspect list was shrinking by the minute.

Derek was still talking. "I've got others looking in the park for the bullet itself. Gabriel is supervising."

"Then it should be easy enough to find," Inspector Lee remarked.

"Gabriel will find it."

The inspector nodded absently, her thoughts going off in a different direction.

Derek's phone rang. "Hello."

He listened for a few seconds, then said, "Thanks," and ended the call.

"Speak of the devil," he said. "That was Gabriel. There's absolutely no sign of a bullet anywhere in the area where we were standing when the gunshot went off."

"But . . . that's impossible," I said.

"The woman was hit in the foot," he said. "A bullet hitting that close to the ground couldn't have bounced away."

"Could it have ricocheted off in another direction?" But I already knew the answer. It wouldn't have ricocheted off the grass, or off Ella's foot. It would've landed in the dirt and stayed there.

"No," Inspector Lee said gruffly. "And if Gabriel was conducting the search, I'm confident he knew where to look. If he couldn't find it . . ."

"Then there's no bullet out there." Derek finished the thought.

"Weird," I muttered. My mind was a muddle. I offered to get coffee and left the small office for a few minutes. I needed a break and a chance to think about everything that had happened today and every other day this week.

As I paid the cafeteria cashier, I thought about Wyatt. I wondered how Tom was holding up with his best friend lying in a hospital bed, unconscious. He probably had some broken bones along with everything else. Was Tom blaming himself? Did he happen to see the driver?

I headed back to our small office, balancing the three coffee cups. We'd spent enough time worrying about Ella, I thought. She would be fine. Right now, we needed to check up on Tom.

I handed out the coffees, then asked, "When did the attack on Wyatt occur?"

Inspector Lee seemed surprised by the question and she frowned. "Early this morning. About six thirty a.m. Why?"

"It was light outside, if that's what you're wondering," Derek said.

I shook my head. "No, I was just thinking that they were probably taken to the hospital first thing this morning and the last thing on Tom's mind would be to call and let someone know what had happened."

And I had to wonder if Tom might've been the next victim if he had actually shown up to the Jumping Frog event. But I wasn't about to say anything to Inspector Lee because she already thought I spent too much time considering things like victims and suspects and motives and such.

She was still staring at me, so I added, "Just a random thought. Don't mind me."

"Sometimes your random thoughts score big time," she said. "Keep 'em coming."

I was surprised and absurdly pleased. "I will."

Derek slung his arm around my shoulders and squeezed lightly just as Inspector Lee's phone rang. She spoke briefly and ended the call.

"Wyatt is awake."

We huddled in the visitor's room just outside the intensive care unit. Inspector Lee would be allowed to talk to Wyatt as soon as the nurse gave the okay. I would be happy just to see Tom and make sure he was all right.

Derek's phone rang and he answered, spoke to the caller for less than a minute, and ended the call. "The doctor is bandaging Ella's foot and Joseph will be taking her home within the hour. I told him we'd try to stop by later."

"Good," I said, then added, "Did Ingrid ever show up?"

"Apparently she couldn't find parking so she just drove home, figuring Ella could get a ride with Joseph."

Feel the mother love, I thought, but said nothing.

Derek turned to Inspector Lee. "Did you discover any CCTV coverage of Wyatt's attack?"

"Yes," she said, her tone victorious. "There have been so many distractions that I forgot to mention it. But yeah, the attack took place right on Clement Street, a few blocks from the Cabot home. There's that stretch of shops and restaurants near Twenty-Third Street."

"Yes, I know the area," Derek said.

"Me, too," I added.

"I've got footage from three different locations that show the attack itself. The car is a fancy imported sports car. Not sure of the make and model. In one of the shots, I can almost make out the driver's face, despite the tinted window." She glanced from Derek to me. "You two might be able to help since you know some of the players."

"I'll help in any way I can," I said.

"Thanks," she said.

"Did you find anything usable from the first attack the other day?" Derek asked.

She held out her hand and wiggled it back and forth, indicating the results weren't so great. "We found one camera from one residence that shows the street at the time of the attempted hit-and-run. But it's positioned up on the roof and we can't see the attack itself."

Derek thought about it. "I'd like to take a look at it anyway."

"I'll set it up."

While Inspector Lee questioned Wyatt, Tom walked into the visitor's room. His clothes were rumpled and his hair was mussed. He looked completely wiped out.

"You should sit down," Derek said.

"Yeah, I should." He plopped down in one of the chairs and laid his head back.

"How's Wyatt doing?" I asked.

"He woke up. He recognized me. They say that's a good sign."

"Sounds like a very good sign," Derek said. "Were you able to talk to him at all?"

"Just a few words here and there. Nothing substantive." He sighed loudly. "He remembers getting hit. Remembers flying through the air. Doesn't remember hitting the ground. But I do." He leaned his elbows on his knees and covered his face with his hands. "Jesus."

"You didn't see the driver?" Derek asked.

"No. I was clueless. Stupid. Wyatt pays a lot more attention to stuff like that than I do." He sat back in the chair. "Guess I'd better start paying attention."

"Did he push you out of the way this time?" I asked.

"Yeah." He nodded absently. "Damn it. It's like he pushed me away and then took my place. I owe him my life." He shrugged. "For what that's worth."

"To Wyatt, your life is worth everything," I said.

Tom chuckled without humor. "Same goes. I don't know what I'd do without him. I don't want to find out." He stared hard at Derek and then at me. "Promise me you'll find out who did this."

"We will," Derek said.

I reached out and squeezed his arm. "We promise."

Inspector Lee couldn't set up the CCTV videos until later that evening at her office in the Hall of Justice over on Bryant Street. Luckily for us, it was only a few blocks away from our place, so once we'd finished viewing, we could go right home.

Famous last words.

We walked into a dark room and saw a guy sitting at a utility table that was covered in electronic equipment, including the computer he was currently typing on. On the wall was a large monitor that would show the footage from the two scenes.

Inspector Lee said, "This is Dale. We'll be able to see everything on this monitor here."

Derek shook his hand. "Hello, Dale. I'm Derek Stone. Thanks for helping us out."

"No problem, man."

"Hi, Dale," I said. "I'm Brooklyn."

"Good to meetcha," he said. "Have a seat."

I sat down next to him. Derek and the inspector stood behind us.

"Can we see the earlier video first, Dale?" the inspector asked.

"Sure."

She looked at me. "I explained to Derek earlier that we won't be able to see any of the action. But you wanted to view this."

"That's right," Derek said. "I appreciate it."

"Okay. So here we go."

Dale pressed a few buttons and the street scene appeared on the large monitor. I rolled my chair back a little so I could see the screen better.

Dale let the picture roll for another two minutes, but we didn't see anything except for all the cars parked vertically on the opposite side of the street in front of a huge mansion that sat behind a very fancy set of iron gates and a thick brick wall.

Dale whistled.

"What is it?" Inspector Lee asked.

"Sorry." He chuckled. "Just noticed that car."

"Yes," Derek said. "Impressive."

"Too bad we've only got black and white," Dale said, "because that's a Lamborghini and I'm betting it's yellow."

"It's a classic," Derek murmured. "Perhaps it belongs to someone in that mansion."

"That incredibly large mansion," I emphasized. "And there's a driveway, so the owners probably park somewhere on the property."

"So one of their wealthy, Lamborghini-driving friends must be visiting," Inspector Lee said dryly.

Dale snorted a laugh. "Must be nice."

Derek touched Dale's shoulder. "Why do you think the car is yellow?"

Dale sat back in his chair. "I watch a lot of CCTV videos every day. Everything's in black and white. So I've developed my own little test where I guess the colors. I'm usually right. You know, someone's clothing, hair color, that sort of thing. And cars. They're my thing, you know? Especially the ones that're out of my price range." He grinned. "Like a Lamborghini."

"I'll admit I see more yellow Lamborghinis than any other color."

"It's a popular color because it's so bright. I mean, if you're gonna drive a Lamborghini, you want to be seen."

Derek's lips twisted into a wry smile. "Good point."

"But that's just my opinion." His smile disappeared. "When I'm viewing a video, I stick with the facts. By knowing how to differentiate between the different shades of whites and grays and blacks, I'm aiding the investigation."

"Dale is a vital part of the team," Inspector Lee said. "Okay. I think we're ready to see the more recent attack, Dale. Let's start with Video A."

"You got it." It only took Dale a few keystrokes and

we were staring at a liquor store on Clement Street. It was trash day so the big barrels were out in front of each shop along the street. Tom and Wyatt and two other men stood in the street, picking through the barrels and tossing empty bottles and cans into a large trash bag.

I watched Tom laughing at something Wyatt said. They seemed to be enjoying themselves. There was very little traffic on the street. It didn't seem like a dangerous scene at all.

But without warning, a car came out of nowhere. Wyatt gave Tom a hard shove and the car slammed into Wyatt, sideswiping the dumpster and speeding off down Clement.

"Oh God." I had to look away.

"Good Lord," Derek said. "That's horrific."

Inspector Lee blew out a breath. "Yeah. And as you saw, it's the same dark blue Porsche that Wyatt described from the first attack."

"Brutal, man," Dale said, shaking his head.

I wasn't sure I could watch it from the other two angles.

But I did. I sucked it up and watched it from those other two angles.

Poor Wyatt was lucky to be alive and all I could do was pray that his injuries would heal.

Derek wanted to see the original Pacific Avenue video again. We sat through that rather static video, then watched all three of the Clement Street videos again.

"Do you see what I see?" Derek said.

Inspector Lee gave a light snort. "No."

"I'll point it out to you. Dale, can you play the Pacific Avenue video again?"

"Here comes," Dale said.

Derek moved closer to the monitor. On the Pacific Avenue video, he pointed to the car parked vertically in front of the massive home.

"There's my Lamborghini," Dale crooned.

"Now kindly play the Clement Street Video C, please."

We had to watch the brutal attack all over again.

"Can you freeze it about four seconds from the end?" Derek asked.

"Will do." Dale ran it back, then froze the picture.

We all stared at the screen. Then Dale laughed. "Oh man! It's that same Lamborghini. Cool."

"Are you kidding me?" Inspector Lee said. She moved in closer to the screen. "How did you catch that? It's halfway down the street. Can it possibly be the same car?"

"It could be a coincidence," Derek said with a deceptively casual shrug.

"Fat chance of that," I said, knowing what Derek thought of coincidences.

"Coincidence is bull." He looked at me. "Who do we know who drives a yellow Lamborghini?"

"But that's not even the car that hit Wyatt," the inspector said, sounding frustrated.

"No," Derek replied. "It's the car that *watched* while Wyatt got hit."

We all contemplated that creepy thought for a long moment.

Inspector Lee finally broke the silence. "We've got one more thing for you to see. Dale, can you pull up that close-up you isolated for me earlier?"

"Got it right here." He tapped a key on his computer. "Let me know when you're ready."

She touched my shoulder. "If you can stand to look at this again, I'd love to have you try and figure out who's driving the car."

I took a deep breath and let it out. "Let's give it a shot."

She continued. "The camera angle that caught this shot is from the store across and down one. So you get a side angle of the driver's window, and when the light hits it, you can see an outline of the driver."

"Did you get any kind of description?" Derek asked.

"I'm going to wait on that. I'd like you both to just look at it and come to your own conclusions."

"Okay." I took a deep breath and exhaled slowly. "I'm ready."

Dale had captured less than two seconds of video, but in slow motion it became more like eight seconds. Then he'd blown up the picture enough for me to get an idea of who might've been driving the car. He played it for me three times.

I shook my head and glanced at Derek. "It looks like someone I might've seen before, but I couldn't tell you who it is."

"Break down the elements for me," Inspector Lee suggested.

"Um, okay." I stared at the frozen image on the monitor. "Male. Short, light-colored hair. Not blond, exactly. Sandy-colored maybe? Youngish. Maybe thirties? Preppy, sort of. Not too big or tall."

"Does that describe anyone you've seen around lately?"

I thought about the first night at the Covington Library. Thought of all the faces I'd seen. Then I played back the scenes from the night of Joseph's party. There were so many people I didn't know. I thought of yesterday at the children's museum and today at the park. I shook my head. Nothing was coming to me.

"Give me another minute," I said.

"Take all the time you need," she said.

A blue Porsche and a yellow Lamborghini. Why would a hit-and-run driver risk damaging an expensive car like that Porsche?

Because that was what was available? Or because they stole it from somewhere? It didn't make any sense.

But in the back of my mind, I knew I'd seen those cars before. So I closed my eyes, steadied my breath, and pictured the two cars. A yellow Lamborghini. Very flashy. Someone wanted to be seen.

And I remembered seeing it at Joseph's house. The night of the party.

I looked at Derek. "The night of the party, we watched all those cars pull up, let people out, and then one of the valet guys would drive them away. Remember?"

"Yes, at Joseph's house," he said. "You were impressed by them. I must admit I wasn't really paying attention."

"There was a yellow Lamborghini. I didn't know it was a Lamborghini, to be honest. It was just one of those ridiculously flashy cars that rich people drive."

"I don't remember seeing it," Derek admitted.

"You ran back to the car," I said. "While I was waiting for you, I watched more cars drive up."

He studied my expression. "You saw the car. Did you see the driver?"

"I'm racking my brain. I might need a little time to let it percolate."

"We could ask Joseph," he suggested.

"Oh yes! He would know if one of his friends drives a car like that."

"And perhaps he knows the driver of the blue Porsche."

I looked at my watch. Barely nine o'clock. "Is it too late to stop by now?"

Derek checked his watch, too, then said, "Does it matter?"

I had to laugh. "No."

"Hold on, you two," Inspector Lee demanded. "You're not going to walk into that house and face a possible killer all by yourselves."

"Joseph isn't a killer," I said. "We're just going to ask him about the Lamborghini."

"I'll be the one to question Mr. Cabot and everyone else in the household," she said sternly. Then she added, "However, I would appreciate you coming along to soften the blow."

In the background, I heard Dale laugh. He was obviously familiar with Inspector Lee's gruff exterior.

Finally, I said, "Okay, we'll do it for you."

Derek grabbed my hand. "Then let's be off."

Chapter 19

When we remember we are all mad, the mysteries of life disappear and life stands explained.

—Mark Twain's Notebook, 1898

As we walked toward the big beautiful terra-cotta mansion, I looked at Derek. "You know how I love to worry over murder suspects, right?"

"Oh, I do," he said with a laugh.

"Well, I've been trying to come up with suspects other than Ella for the past two days and I was hoping Ashley might be the one. But she's not working for me."

"No," he said. "She's not our killer. She had no reason to kill Hobson."

"If he was even the intended victim," I said. "We never quite figured that out."

"And why would she want to kill Joseph? She appears to be infatuated with him. And she also had no reason to kill Tom."

"Plus, she was still walking and talking with the frog wrangler when that gun went off."

"She's not our killer," he said again.

"Sadly, no. Besides, I like her and I hope we'll work together someday soon."

"Then she obviously can't be a murderer."

"Right. And all along I've suspected Ella because she comes across as such a ninny and a liar. But she couldn't have shot herself in the foot."

"No, she couldn't," he murmured. "Ninny or not."

"And there's her mother," I said. "We didn't see her in the park at all, so maybe she was hiding in the bushes with a shotgun." I shook my head. "But I can't picture it, can you?"

"Whether I can picture it or not, I still believe that anyone can be driven to kill under the right circumstances."

"Yes. And remember that fight she had with Hobson? She was so angry. We still don't know what that fight was about."

"No, we don't. But the argument sounded quite personal, don't you think?"

"Yes. I assume it had something to do with Joseph. But still, hiding in the bushes with a shotgun? And then taking a shot at your own daughter?"

"That part is hard to believe," Derek said.

"But who else is there?" I asked.

We had reached the front door and I stopped to stare at the heavy mahogany carvings.

"Are you ready for this?" he asked.

"Shouldn't we wait for Inspector Lee? Did you see her car out front?"

"I believe she was right behind us."

I heard footsteps approach and I smiled at Derek. "Nice timing."

"Let's go," she said, and knocked on the door.

After a brief wait, the door swung open and Leland Bingham stepped forward. "Good evening. May I help you?"

Inspector Lee had interviewed him before, but she still held out her identification. "We're here to speak to Mr. Cabot."

"Oh. Well." He fumbled nervously with his collar. "Good heavens."

"Let them in, Leland," Ella said from somewhere behind him.

"Yes, of course." He cleared his throat. "Please come in, Inspector. Commander Stone. Ma'am."

I figured I was *ma'am* since he didn't seem to have a clue who I was. But I was glad at least that he referred to Derek as Commander.

As we walked into the foyer, I saw Ella standing near the kitchen doorway with her foot wrapped in a bandage.

"Hello," she said to the three of us. "This is a surprise. Is something wrong?"

"Sorry to trouble you so late in the evening," Inspector Lee said, "but I need to have a word with Mr. Cabot."

"Is he home?" Derek asked.

"Of course, Derek," she said, giving him her most brilliant smile. And was she batting her eyelashes? At Derek?

And just like that, she instantly returned to the top of my suspect list.

"Why don't you all have a seat in the living room?" she suggested. "I'll go get Joseph."

"Madame, no," Leland protested. "I'll fetch him. You should rest your foot."

"Aren't you sweet?" she said, and limped courageously into the living room, where she sat in an elegantly brocaded chair facing the coffee table.

Derek and I sat on the sofa facing the foyer. Inspector Lee chose the chair opposite Ella's.

A minute later, Joseph walked across the foyer and stepped into the living room. And frowned. "Derek? What's going on?"

"Hello, Joseph," he said. "Apologies for intruding on your evening. Is there somewhere we can speak privately? It'll only take a moment."

I was watching Ella as Derek spoke. Her expression was serene, but her hand was fisted against her leg. Was she nervous? Angry? Afraid?

She gazed at Joseph through narrowed eyes and I wondered what she was thinking. It was not the gaze of a loving wife. She was appraising him, speculating what he might say to the cop.

Of course, that was all conjecture on my part. I wanted her to be guilty—and not just because she'd batted her eyelashes at Derek. I knew in my gut that she was the one who had studied the formulas in the Poisoned Papers exhibit and re-created them for her own sinister use. She was the one responsible for the death of Hobson the butler.

Ella's gaze drifted over to Leland, who stood watch under the archway of the foyer. Again, she was assessing the situation. What might the under-butler have to say for himself?

I studied Leland Bingham a little more carefully than I had before, and remembered the first time I'd seen him just last week. He had been standing in a doorway, chewing on one of his nails. Fair-haired, mid-thirties. Nice-looking, thin. He was dressed very much like Hobson. It was during the fight between Hobson and Ingrid and I thought, at the moment, that he looked as if he wanted to disappear.

"Oh."

Derek looked at me. "What is it, darling?"

I glanced over at Inspector Lee, then back at Derek. "It's the under-butler."

Because he knew me so well, he was instantly aware of what I was referring to. He looked at Leland, then back at me. "Ah, yes. You described him well."

"What are you talking about?" Joseph asked.

"Inspector," Derek said, standing. "I believe you'll want to question Mr. Bingham regarding the hit-and-run attack on Tom's friend Wyatt."

"What?" Joseph shouted.

Leland's eyes widened and he looked around for the best way to escape. Before he could make it out of the foyer, Derek had grabbed the back of his vest and pulled him all the way into the living room.

"You can't be serious," Joseph said.

"He's just a junior butler," Ella protested. "Why are you hurting him?"

"Who put you up to it?" Derek demanded.

"I-I don't know what you're talking about," the under-butler said. He wouldn't say anything else, but I knew Inspector Lee would get it out of him. The guy was just no good at lying.

"Derek!" Joseph shouted. "Damn it, tell me what's going on."

"Joseph," I said quickly since Derek was currently

wrestling Leland into another living room chair. "Do you own a midnight-blue Porsche Carrera?"

He frowned. "Not exactly."

"What about a yellow Lamborghini?" I asked.

Ella gasped, then coughed to cover it up.

"Ella drives a Lamborghini," Joseph said. When Ella reached up to hold his hand, he took hers. "Now what's this all about?"

"Tell me about the blue Porsche," Inspector Lee said.

"I'm selling it," he said, facing the inspector. "It's on consignment at the Exotic Motor Cars showroom over on Geary."

"And you know it's still there?"

"Of course," he said, then frowned. "Well, I assume it's there. I'd have to double-check with the dealer. And Leland would know. He services all of our automobiles."

"That's convenient," I muttered.

"I'm sorry, Mr. Cabot," Inspector Lee said. "But I'm afraid your Porsche was involved in a felony hit-and-run last night."

Joseph turned. "Felony hit-and . . ." He looked at Derek. "Wyatt?"

"Yes. I'm sorry."

He stared down at Leland. "Did you know about this?"

"N-no, sir."

Inspector Lee stood and stared down at Leland, too. She obviously recognized a weak link when she saw one. "Tell us who put you up to this and maybe you won't spend the rest of your life in jail."

His eyes grew even wider, but he wouldn't say a word.

Inspector Lee nodded. "Okay then." She walked over to the front door. "Come on in, guys."

Two uniformed police officers walked into the house. Inspector Lee pointed to Leland. "Leland Bingham, you're under arrest for the hit-and-run attack on Wyatt Forester. Take him in, guys. Read him his rights and then book him."

"Yes, ma'am," the first officer said.

There was a gasp from the stairway and we all looked up to see Edith the housemaid staring wide-eyed at the scene. Seconds later she turned and dashed up the stairs.

I looked at Inspector Lee. "She probably had nothing to do with this, but she hated Hobson and I think she has a crush on Leland. We all know that people do strange things for love."

"You can say that again." She signaled one of the officers to follow Edith and bring her downstairs for questioning.

Within a minute, the police had taken Leland away and Inspector Lee closed the door.

"Okay, then," Inspector Lee said easily. "Who wants to go next?"

"This is outrageous," Ella protested loudly.

The rest of us ignored her as Joseph flopped down into the chair that Leland had vacated.

"I'm so sorry." He kept shaking his head in disbelief. "I didn't know."

"I know that," Derek murmured.

Joseph looked up at him. "But why didn't I know? It was happening in my own house."

"You were busy taking care of everyone," I said. "Going to work every day, creating a good life for your wife and everyone else."

"But . . . oh God. How in the world did Leland have the wherewithal to do this?"

"He's a young man who follows orders," I said quietly. "Someone told him to do it."

"But who?" Joseph looked so miserable, I thought he might start to cry.

I touched his shoulder. "I'm sorry."

"You're sorry for him?" Ella said, sounding incredulous. "What about me? I'm in charge of running this house and I've lost my butler and now my under-butler. And my foot! Hello? What am I supposed to do?"

Joseph stared at his wife for a long moment, then gazed at me. "Why did you ask me about the yellow Lamborghini?"

"Joseph!" Ella cried. "That's not important right now!"

But he continued to stare at me. "Tell me."

"There was a yellow Lamborghini parked at each location of the hit-and-run attacks on Tom and Wyatt."

"That's a little flimsy," Ella said, dismissing the claim.

Inspector Lee ignored her. "Someone in a yellow Lamborghini wanted to make sure that Tom was hurt or killed. Unfortunately in each case, Tom's best friend Wyatt heroically pushed Tom out of the way. The second time it happened, Wyatt was hit instead of Tom. He's still in intensive care, but he's expected to recover."

Joseph turned to Ella. "Why were you so concerned

about the hit-and-run? Why were you there? What did you hope to accomplish?"

"Who says I was there?" she groused. "You don't have any proof I was there."

I laughed. "There's videotaped proof that your car was parked nearby. You showed up to make sure that Leland got the job done, didn't you?"

"Shut up!" she cried, and then began speaking rapidly in Swedish and I was pretty sure the words weren't complimentary.

Joseph shook his head. "Why were you trying to hurt Tom? He never hurt anybody. We didn't even know him a week ago."

"Don't you get it? He's probably your brother or some other close relation. And knowing you, you'd hand him a few million dollars or move him into the house to live with us because that's just the kind of thing you would do."

"I don't have a brother," he said, "but I'll admit there's a family resemblance. My doctor has scheduled a DNA test for both of us next week so we'll know for certain whether there's a connection." He paused, stared at her intently, then added, "And it's funny you should mention it, but yeah, I plan to invite him to move in. We've got more than enough room here for him to stay as long as he wants to. And as you say, it's just the kind of thing I do."

"You're insufferable," she said through gritted teeth.

"Oh, sweetheart, you have no idea."

"You make it sound like a threat." She pouted. "Why are you being so mean?"

He shook his head, not quite believing her act.

"Because I'm wondering if you're responsible for trying to kill an innocent man."

She pushed herself up from the overstuffed chair and stood. "How stupid can you get? You move him into your house and he'll take you for every cent you've got. And you'll just hand it over with a smile."

"Isn't that what you're trying to do? Take me for every cent?" He stood as well, and began to pace from the foyer to the coffee table. "Hobson warned me that you and your mother were plotting to gain control of my money."

"That's ridiculous!" Ella said.

"I thought so, too," he said, his voice flat now. He glanced at Derek. "That's why Hobson and I argued that night. Hobson wanted to stay with me during the festival, even if it meant bunking in a shabby SRO. I thought he was nuts."

"He wanted to protect you," Derek said. "He was afraid of what might happen."

"Yes. If I were all alone out there in the city, anything could happen. I could be shot, or knifed. Or hit by a car." He glared at Ella.

"He was out of his mind," Ella said flippantly. "He didn't care about you. He and my mother had it all planned out. They wanted you to marry me as soon as your first wife died."

Joseph nodded. "Well, they got that much right. But you know, divorce is pretty easy to come by these days."

"Divorce?" she shouted the word. "You dare and I'll arrange it so that I get all of your money."

"You signed a prenuptial agreement, sweetheart."

"It'll be null and void if you're dead," she said through clenched teeth.

Joseph laughed heartily. He looked at Derek and me and grinned. "Can you feel the love?"

All I could feel were shivers of fear. This woman was borderline psycho and wasn't about to give up her husband's fortune without a fight.

He stared at his wife. "You know, the night Hobson and I argued, I was on your side. I fought him because he was saying such awful things, claiming that he and your mother had rushed me into marriage in order to get ahold of my money."

"Don't be silly," she said, fluffing her hair back. "You married me because I'm hot."

"You were," he admitted dismissively. "But after a couple of months of marriage, the heat is gone."

"You pig!"

Joseph waved her away. He was running out of steam. He sat back down, exhausted. "Hobson told me that at first he went along with Ingrid because, after my wife died, he was worried about me and thought I'd be happier if I were married. But recently he realized that you two women were only out for my money. He called you both grifters. And I defended you. What a fool I've been."

Joseph looked deflated now, but I wasn't ready to quit the fight. "What was that little stunt you pulled in the park?" I asked. "There was no bullet. Did you deliberately cut your own foot? Is that how badly you crave attention? Oh, wait. You were trying to throw us off the scent, weren't you?"

"Shut up," she shouted. "Who do you think you are?"

"Who shot off the gun?" I asked. "Was that Leland?"

She stomped her good foot. "I told you to shut up."

I shook my head. "You're pathetic. You faked a gunshot wound and you tried to pass yourself as completely ignorant of the Covington Library layout and the exhibits. I know you spent a lot time there, especially in the Poisoned Papers exhibit. You even bought a postcard of the exhibit and gave it to your lovely waitress, Carmen."

Her gasp was full-throated. "No."

"Yeah," I said. "She told me all about you. So what do you think will happen if the police search your room? Do you think you got rid of all the evidence of the poison? There are so many ingredients involved. Are you sure you cleaned up everything? Maybe there's some of that golden powder residue, or the adhesive mixture. Or maybe you've got a receipt for the delivery service. You probably ran a few versions of that fake return address label you used for the Covington Library."

"Shut up!" she cried. "You're just a nosy bitch who spends all her time working on books. I mean, how boring can you get?"

"Now, that was harsh," I said. "But I have another question for you. Were you really trying to kill Hobson? What if Joseph had opened that envelope? He would be dead."

She smiled. "Oh, boo hoo. Then I would have all of his money."

I studied her. "I don't think you were ready to kill your handsome wealthy husband yet. But Hobson had definitely worn out his welcome with you. I think you were actually targeting him."

She huffed dramatically. "You don't know anything."

Inspector Lee finally moved forward. "Mrs. Cabot, I'm taking you in for questioning in the poisoning death of Hobson." She frowned at Joseph. "Was that his first name or his last name?"

"His name was John Hobson," Joseph said stoically.

"Right. I knew that." She pulled a pair of handcuffs from her belt, then grabbed Ella's left hand and turned her around.

"Stop that!" a voice shouted from the stairway. Footsteps pounded across the foyer and Ingrid appeared under the archway, holding a shotgun.

"Oh, brother," I muttered. These women were horrible.

"I suppose you're the one who shot the gun in the park," I said.

"Isn't that my shotgun?" Joseph said. "It's supposed to be in the gun locker. How did you get hold of it?"

"Oh, please," she said. "I know every secret in this house, including all of yours, Joseph."

"Oh. Well, I don't suppose they'll be secret much longer."

"I know plenty of your father's secrets as well. Hobson kept nothing from me."

"That sounds positively sordid," he said drolly. "Were you sleeping with him?"

"I did what I had to do," she said lightly.

"Were you sleeping with my father?"

She gave him a coy smile. "Your father had a healthy appetite for pleasure."

"Ewww," I said.

"Oh, grow up," she snarled.

Inspector Lee shot me a glance and I clammed up quickly.

Ingrid turned back to Joseph. "You were a twin, you know."

"What?" Ella cried. "Mother, why didn't you tell me?"

"Because I couldn't trust you to keep your mouth shut."

Ella pouted. "That's not fair!"

"Be quiet, dear," Ingrid cooed. "The grown-ups are talking."

From where I stood, I could see Joseph's jaw drop, but he just said, "Do go on."

"The boy was a sickly baby, always in and out of the hospital with heart problems. Your father had little patience for that, and finally hired a woman to take him and raise him as her own."

"That's downright medieval," Joseph said lightly. But he had to be seething inside.

"But that allowed you to gain everything," she said. "So that can't be all bad."

But it was, I thought. And Joseph's expression said the same thing. His father sounded like an awful man.

"My father was a son of a bitch," Joseph said, confirming what I had just thought. "I spent half my life trying to undo all the damage he caused."

"You don't know the half of it," Ingrid said. "The man was quite happy to deal in blood diamonds and of course he enslaved his workers in his uranium mines in South America."

With each offense she named, Joseph grew paler.

"He found it humorous to hear about all your good works. Were you trying to blot out his legacy? Trying to make up for his misdeeds? He had many good laughs over your bleeding heart tendencies."

"That's enough," Joseph said.

"Really? But I haven't even gotten to his war correspondence with Mengele, the so-called angel of death. As you must know, he sympathized with the Nazi cause."

"Enough!" Joseph said, turning to face Derek. "I have my own horror stories. Did you know that when my wife was diagnosed with cancer, my father told me I should divorce her before I got saddled with all her medical bills?"

"Nice guy," I murmured.

Ella suddenly screamed, "I hate it when you talk about your first wife! Mother, just shoot them."

"Don't shriek, sweetkins," Ingrid said.

"But I'm tired of all of them." Ella pointed at Inspector Lee. "She was going to arrest me!"

Ingrid sighed. "I'll shoot them if I must, but it will cause us more problems than we already have."

The woman had a healthy amount of self-esteem, if nothing else.

"There's no way out of this, Ms. Norden," Inspector Lee said. "I need you to surrender your weapon. I don't want anyone else to get hurt."

"What about my daughter?" Ingrid said.

Inspector Lee gave a slight shrug. "Your daughter's case is more complicated."

"No, it's not. She's innocent. Now, she and I are going to walk out of here and you won't be able to stop us."

She was obviously used to getting her own way around here, but that had to end now.

"Your daughter killed Hobson," I declared. "He was your 'protector' and she killed him. Why would you want to help her escape?"

"Brooklyn, no," Inspector Lee whispered, but it was too late.

"Blood is thicker than water," Ingrid explained, then pointed her shotgun in my direction.

I couldn't breathe.

Suddenly the front door opened and two more officers walked in. Startled, Ingrid started to swing the gun around and Derek took advantage of the distraction. He grabbed the gun from her hands and tossed it onto the carpet. Then he spun her around and pulled both of her hands behind her back.

"Let me go!" Ingrid cried.

Ella was ready to make her move and instantly headed for the shotgun. Without a second thought, I stuck out my foot and tripped her. She fell like a tree and I jumped on top of her.

She screamed even louder than her mother.

"Good job, guys," Inspector Lee said to the officers at the front door, then grinned at me. "You, too."

"Thanks." I was still sitting on Ella's back, despite her attempts to buck me off. A few seconds later, Joseph patted my shoulder. "Thanks, Brooklyn. I'll take over here."

I barely heard him. I was frozen in place, not at all willing to let Ella loose. She was a cold-blooded killer and her mother wasn't any better. The two of them deserved to rot in jail.

Joseph touched my arm. "Brooklyn. It's all right."

I exhaled. "Yes. Okay."

I stepped off Ella and Joseph yanked her to her feet. "I'll have the divorce papers delivered to your jail cell tomorrow."

Ella screamed.

"Oh, shut up," I muttered. I couldn't believe I had once thought she was a nice person. Was I naïve? I wasn't sure, but I could really kick myself sometimes.

Within seconds, Ingrid and Ella were both hand-cuffed and tucked into the back of a patrol car. We could hear them bickering all the way across the front terrace and through the gate.

"Wow. They were not going to go quietly," I said.

Joseph shook his head. "No. Never." He looked at Derek and me. "Thank you. You both saved my life, in more ways than one."

"I'm sorry," I said, and gave him a hug.

"Don't be," he said. "I should've paid more attention to what was going on around me." He sighed. "But ever since my wife died, I've allowed parts of my life to drift along aimlessly. I guess that made me a good target for grifters. I swear to you, here and now, those days are over."

"Glad to hear it."

Derek patted his back. "Will you be all right tonight?"

"Yeah. Thanks for asking."

That's when I realized that Joseph was truly alone. I felt so sorry for him, but he was probably better off alone than the alternative. "We'll check on you tomorrow and then stop by the hospital to see how Wyatt and Tom are doing."

"You'll probably find me there," he said. "I want to spend some time getting to know my brother."

Epilogue

I finished gilding the cover of *The Prince and the Pauper* without the benefit of an audience. Ian didn't care; he was thrilled with the beautiful work I'd done and promptly displayed it with other Mark Twain works as part of the permanent collection.

Happy with his praise and finished with that task, I was able to take off for the weekend guilt-free. We drove to Dharma as promised and arrived at our beautiful new home Friday evening. We sat outside on our deck in our new Adirondack chairs, staring out at the terraced hills covered in grapevines. The sun was just setting behind the farthest hill and Derek had opened a wonderful bottle of cabernet sauvignon to accompany the gooey Brie and rustic crackers we'd brought with us.

Three days ago we had been face-to-face with a

crazed, shotgun-toting Swedish mother and her even more crazed, delusional daughter. It was hard to believe that the two of them had managed to brainwash the under-butler and the housemaid to behave badly on their behalf. From where we sat now, it all seemed like a bad dream.

We went to bed early, slept wonderfully well in our new bed, and arose to make coffee and toast, which we enjoyed out on the deck.

I smiled at Derek. "I have a feeling that when we come up here, we'll be spending most of our time right in this spot."

Derek held my hand. "I can't imagine anything better."

Saturday afternoon our friends and family showed up with enough food and drinks to provide sustenance for the whole town. And I was pretty sure the whole town had shown up here for our little party.

When Ian and Jake walked into the yard, I looked at Derek. "What is going on?"

Mom grabbed both men's arms and faced the crowd. "Everybody here knows Ian and his husband Jake. Well, this week they officially became fathers to a darling set of twins, Priscilla and Nathan."

I gasped. "Are you kidding? Oh my God, I'm so happy for you!" Then I burst into tears and grabbed them both in a three-way bear hug.

After a long moment, I glanced around and saw that all my sisters had tears in their eyes. Like me, they couldn't allow anyone to cry alone.

"You guys, I just saw you a few days ago. How did you keep this quiet?"

"We knew you wouldn't be able to keep it a secret," Ian said. "Your mother was the only one who knew."

"My mother." I stared at Mom through narrowed eyes. "Did you work some kind of spell?"

She laughed. "Oh, sweetie. It doesn't work like that."

Ian and Jake moved through the crowd, sharing photographs of their darling tiny babies, who were still in the hospital and would hopefully come home next week. I could hardly catch my breath from that announcement when I saw Tom and Joseph walk onto the patio.

"Tom?" I stared at Joseph. "Joseph? What are you two doing here?"

"Derek suggested that we might enjoy a day or two away from the city, so I drove Tom out here and . . . well, here we are."

"I'm going back first thing in the morning," Tom said. "I want to check on Wyatt."

"How is he doing?" I asked as Derek walked over and slipped his arm around my waist.

"A lot better," Tom said. He glanced around at the surrounding hills covered in lush grapevines. "I wish he could've come out here with me. He grew up surrounded by apple orchards so I think he would dig this."

"Bring him back," I said. "We would love to have you both visit."

"You've got yourself a deal," he said.

"Everything is changing," I said to Derek a few minutes later when we were standing alone.

"Mostly for the better," Derek said.

"Yes. Much better." I glanced across the deck at Joseph. "I hope he knows he's better off."

"It might take a while, but he's strong. He'll get through this."

I nodded.

My sister China approached us. "Have I told you how much I love your house?" she said. "It's so clean."

I had to laugh. "We don't live here, that's why."

"That was really smart," she said, swilling a fruit-jar-sized glass of lager.

"Do you want another beer?" I asked.

"No. I-I can't. I mean, thanks, but I'm full."

"Wait. What did all that mean?"

"Oh, damn it. I mean, darn it. I'm not supposed to swear around Hannah."

"Hannah's in the bedroom playing Barbie dolls with the other girls. What's going on?"

She let out a heavy sigh. "I'm pregnant."

"What? Are you kidding?" I grabbed her glass. "You should be drinking water."

"It's okay. It's nonalcoholic."

"But . . . well. What's going on around here? There are babies springing up all over!"

She laughed.

I waved my hands. "What am I thinking? Come here." I grabbed her in a big hug. "Congratulations, sweetie!"

"Thanks, Brooklyn. Don't say anything, okay? I haven't told Mom or anyone else."

"You know that's a big mistake, right?"

"Yeah, yeah. She probably knows already. She checks her scrying mirror daily."

It was my turn to laugh. "Of course she knows. But

why aren't you telling everyone you're pregnant? It's wonderful news."

"Here's the thing," China said. "Robin just had little Jamie six months ago. She should be basking in the joy of everyone lauding her and bringing her presents and rubbing her feet. And now Ian and Jake have just told everyone about their darling little twins. If I announce that I'm pregnant, I'll steal their thunder."

"That's a load of nonsense."

"And Mom will go crazy."

"Everyone will, in a good way, including Jake and Ian. And especially Robin."

"I'm not so sure."

"Robin loves you," I said. "And she'll be extra thrilled to know that Jamie will have a little playmate in nine months."

"Five months, but who's counting?"

"What are you two talking about?" Robin asked, coming up behind me. "You both look very serious."

I stared at China and she stared back. Then she rolled her eyes. "Go ahead and tell her. You won't be able to keep it secret for another minute."

"Let's get Mom over here," I said.

"You guys," Robin said. "What's up?"

China dragged Mom over to our little group and said to me, "Okay, go ahead and tell her."

"Wait. I'm not the one who's going to tell them. You are."

China whined. "No, you tell them."

"Snap out of it," I said, "and spill."

Mom and Robin looked at each other, then turned and looked at China and said, "You're pregnant."

I finally learned what being "gobsmacked" looked like, because China looked that way.

"Oh, sweetie," Mom whispered, wrapping China in her arms. "Did you really think you could keep it a secret?" She and China gently rocked back and forth.

I glanced at Robin and saw that her eyes were damp. "I'm so happy. Jamie will have a little friend and cousin to play with."

Needless to say, our impromptu housewarming turned into a celebration of a new baby on the way and new baby twins to meet soon. And if one more person looked at me slyly and said, "You're next," I was going to have to sell my beautiful house and slink back to the city, never to return again.

Despite that, the party was wonderful and I was thrilled for my sister. And Mom. And Robin. And Ian and Jake. My extended family continued to grow.

Derek and I had a wonderful time and the weekend ended much too soon. We drove back to town early Monday morning, and as we drove through Berkeley on our way to the Bay Bridge, Derek's phone rang.

"Hello." He didn't say anything for a full minute, then he said, "That's very good news." Another minute passed and he said into the phone, "But you already knew that."

He ended the call and smiled at me. "That was Joseph."

"I had a feeling," I said. "What's up?"

"First of all, Wyatt is doing much better. He still has a long road ahead before he's fully recovered. But there shouldn't be any lasting damage."

"That's a miracle."

"Joseph has invited Wyatt to move into the house,

too, but Wyatt won't do that unless he can do some work in exchange for the room and board."

"That's reasonable."

"It turns out that he used to be a landscape architect. He had an accident and got hooked on the pain pills, but now he's clean and sober. So is Tom, by the way."

"So he'll be able to work on that beautiful property."

"Yes. Isn't that nice how things turn out?"

"It really is. I'm happy for them. And I was thinking, we should have them up to Dharma again soon. Wyatt might be interested in working in the vineyards. Or not. But from what Tom said, they will definitely enjoy it."

"We can ask them next time we see them. And there's one more thing."

"Is this the thing where you said that Joseph already knew?"

He laughed. "That's the one. They ran a quick DNA test over the weekend. Joseph and Tom are brothers."

"Aww." I reached over and gave him a quick kiss, then felt my eyes welling up. "And the happy news keeps on coming."

ACKNOWLEDGMENTS

I am the luckiest writer in the world to work with Executive Editor Michelle Vega, who is brilliant, insightful, and kind. Thank you for always coming up with the perfect solution!

Many thanks, as well, to Jenn Snyder and the stellar team at Berkley, including Elisha Katz, Dache' Rogers, Yazmine Hassan, and my fantastic cover artist, Daniel Craig. You all rock! Thanks for making my books shine so brightly.

I count my lucky stars daily that I have superagent Christina Hogrebe and the Jane Rotrosen Agency on my side.

I wouldn't make it through a day or a book without my awesome plot pals, Jenn McKinlay and Paige Shelton. And I wouldn't be anywhere without my superstar assistant, Jenel Looney, watching my back.

Many thanks and big hugs and kisses to my fellow bubble dwellers, Don, Jane, Jim, Tim, and Pam. And virtual kisses to Dan, Debby, Campbell, Casey, and Callan. I love you all!

Finally, thank you to my wonderful readers. I'm so grateful for you! And muchas gracias to the delightfully clever and inventive readers and reviewers of Bookstagram who are so supportive and fun to hang out with.

Keep reading for an excerpt from
Kate Carlisle's next Bibliophile Mystery

The Twelve Books
of Christmas

I stared out the wide kitchen window as a black stretch limousine pulled to a stop in front of our new second home in Dharma. Less than two minutes later, another limo arrived, and I had to take a few bracing breaths. "Have we done the right thing?"

My darkly handsome husband, Derek, quirked an eyebrow. "Regrets already, darling?"

"God, yes." I tried to laugh, but the sound bordered on hysterical. "We couldn't settle for a cozy dinner for four, could we? No way. We had to invite thirty-four people for dinner on Christmas Eve. Thirty-four people! Or is it thirty-five?" Did it really matter? Either way, we were about to be besieged in our brand-new house. By family and friends, but still. "Are we crazy?"

"Of course not," he said, his distinguished British accent lending extra credibility to the statement. "It's a perfectly respectable thing to invite favorite friends and family members over for Christmas Eve dinner."

"Is it?" I wondered. "We're likely to cause a frenzy."

He laughed. "Would that be so bad?"

I gaped at him.

"Maybe they won't all show up," he said, but he was still laughing.

"Oh, please," I said. "You know they'll all be here."

He gently rubbed my shoulders. "All the people we love best."

His kind words calmed me down a smidge, as they usually did. It would all work out and we would have a good time. After all, this was the reason we'd built our second home in Dharma, the small town in the Sonoma wine country where I'd grown up. We wanted to be close to family, so now we were about to welcome my parents, two brothers, three sisters, various spouses, and lots of children to spend Christmas Eve with us. Derek's parents were coming, too, along with several of his brothers, their wives, and more children. We were also expecting our good friends Gabriel and Alex, along with my parents' guru Robson Benedict, and his aunt Trudy. It was going to be an interesting evening.

"It'll be lovely," Derek insisted.

"It'll be chaos."

He chuckled and rubbed his hands up and down my arms. "As it should be, darling. After all, it's Christmas."

I tried to remember to breathe. "Christmas. Right." I watched another limo drive up and park. It sounded extravagant, but we had gone ahead and ordered a number of limousines so our friends wouldn't have to drive through the hills after a long night of good food and lots of wine. It just made sense.

Derek kissed me, then slowly let me go and gazed out the window. "Look on the bright side. At least you don't have to cook."

"Good point." I was the absolute worst cook in the world, and everybody knew it. Happily, the entire evening was being catered by my sister Savannah's fabulous restaurant in downtown Dharma. Most of her staff had been here all day, prepping and cooking a huge feast, using our brand-new clean garage as their backstage area. Across the living and dining rooms, tables had been beautifully set for dinner. Tasting stations had been arranged outside on the terrace, where Savannah's staff would serve cocktails, wine, and a number of yummy hors d'oeuvres and munchies before the dinner began.

The entire house looked festive and smelled wonderful. Our Christmas tree was magical with flickering fairy lights and at least a hundred handmade ornaments covering its boughs. I had to admit I'd gotten carried away with crafting dozens of tiny three-dimensional books—with tiny first-chapter pages included!—that we would be giving to our guests as Christmas ornament takeaways. As a bookbinder specializing in rare book restoration, I considered it my duty to always give books as gifts, and I tried to be creative about it.

Scattered under the tree and spreading nearly halfway across the living room were oodles of beautifully wrapped gifts. Most were for the children, and yes, we had gone overboard, but why not? This was our first time hosting Christmas Eve, and we wanted it to be special.

When the front doorbell finally rang, I took a few more seconds to silently freak out, then rested my head on Derek's strong shoulder. Smiling bravely, I said, "I'll get it."

He reached for my hand. "We'll go together."

Ready to find
your next great read?

Let us help.

Visit prh.com/nextread

Penguin
Random
House